✔ KT-495-002

Clare Mackintosh spent twelve years in the police force, including time on CID, and as a public order commander. She left the police in 2011 to work as a freelance journalist and social media consultant and is the founder of the Chipping Norton Literary Festival. She now writes full time and lives in the Cotswolds with her husband and their three children. Her second novel *I See You* was published in July 2016.

Clare's debut novel, *I Let You Go*, is a *Sunday Times* Bestseller and is the fastest selling title by a new crime writer in 2015. It has been selected for both the Richard and Judy Book Club, and was the winning title of the readers' vote for the summer 2015 selection, and ITV's Loose Women's 'Loose Books'. *I Let You Go* also won the Theakston Old Peculier Crime Novel of the Year in 2016.

For more information visit Clare's website

www.claremackintosh.com or find her at
www.facebook.com/ClareMackWrites or on Twitter
@ClareMackint0sh #ILetYouGo #ISeeYou

Praise for *I Let You Go*

'A terrific, compelling read with an astonishing twist that floored me. I loved it and did not want it to end'
Peter James

'A hugely assured and gripping debut and a twist that made me green with envy'
Mark Billingham

'Clare Mackintosh's inside knowledge of police work illuminates this gripping – and moving – psychological thriller. I couldn't put it down'
Lucie Whitehouse

'Extraordinarily atmospheric, Mackintosh's emotional debut doesn't miss a beat'
Alex Marwood

'Absorbing, authentic and deeply unsettling: a stellar
achievement, and so deliciously clever'
Elizabeth Haynes

'A superb debut, Clare Mackintosh writes eloquently about
grief, guilt and fear and delivers some shocking twists'
Cath Staincliffe

'Such an accomplished debut – tautly plotted, emotionally
engaging and with twists I genuinely didn't see coming'
Veronica Henry

'A storming psychological thriller that has everything: breath-
taking twists, great pace and pitch-perfect characterisation. *I
Let You Go* will squeeze your heart and punch you
in the gut. What a debut!'
Mark Edwards

'With its authentic voices, switchback twists and delicate
character studies, this is a rewarding read from a writer with a
real understanding of what makes a gripping crime novel'
Sarah Hilary

'A heart-wrenchingly emotional psychological thriller with
stunning twists and turns. Deft and seamless, it pulls you in
from page one and doesn't let you go'
Julie Cohen

'From the chilling and tragic opening, to the very last page, I
literally couldn't read fast enough'
Samantha Hayes

'Page-turning, utterly convincing, unputdownable. The twists
kept me guessing until the riveting, satisfying conclusion'
Julia Crouch

'A clever, compelling and deftly plotted book packed full of
tension, superb characterisation and tight
storytelling. I loved it'
Amanda Jennings

I
LET
YOU
GO

Clare Mackintosh

sphere

SPHERE

First published in Great Britain in 2014 by Sphere
This paperback edition published in 2015 by Sphere

19 20

A CIP catalogue record for this book
is available from the British Library.

ISBN 978-0-7515-5415-1

Typeset in Sabon by Palimpsest Book Production Limited,
Falkirk, Stirlingshire
Printed and bound in Great Britain by
Clays Ltd, St Ives plc

Papers used by Sphere are from well-managed forests
and other responsible sources.

MIX
Paper from
responsible sources
FSC
www.fsc.org   FSC® C104740

Sphere
An imprint of
Little, Brown Book Group
Carmelite House
50 Victoria Embankment
London EC4Y 0DZ

An Hachette UK Company
www.hachette.co.uk

www.littlebrown.co.uk

For Alex.

Prologue

The wind flicks wet hair across her face, and she screws up her eyes against the rain. Weather like this makes everyone hurry; scurrying past on slippery pavements with chins buried into collars. Passing cars send spray over their shoes; the noise from the traffic making it impossible for her to hear more than a few words of the chattering update that began the moment the school gates opened. The words burst from him without a break, mixed up and back to front in the excitement of this new world into which he is growing. She makes out something about a best friend; a project on space; a new teacher, and she looks down and smiles at his excitement, ignoring the cold that weaves its way through her scarf. The boy grins back and tips up his head to taste the rain; wet eyelashes forming dark clumps around his eyes.

'And I can write my name, Mummy!'

'You clever boy,' she says, stopping to kiss him fiercely on his damp forehead. 'Will you show me when we get home?'

They walk as quickly as five-year-old legs will allow, her free hand holding his bag, which bangs against her knees.

Nearly home.

Headlights glint on wet tarmac, the dazzle blinding them every few seconds. Waiting for a break in the traffic they duck across the busy road, and she tightens her grip on the small hand inside the soft woollen glove, so he has to run to keep up. Sodden leaves cling to the railings, their bright colours darkening to a dull brown.

They reach the quiet street where home lies just around the corner, its seductive warmth a welcome thought. Secure in the environs of her own neighbourhood she lets go of his hand to push away the strands of wet hair from her eyes, laughing at the cascade of droplets it causes.

'There,' she says, as they make the final turn. 'I left the light on for us.'

Across the street, a red-brick house. Two bedrooms, the tiniest kitchen, and a garden crammed with pots she always means to fill with flowers. Just the two of them.

'I'll race you, Mummy . . .'

He never stops moving; full of energy from the second he wakes until the moment his head hits the pillow. Always jumping, always running.

'Come on!'

It happens in a heartbeat; the feeling of space by her side as he runs towards home, seeking out the warmth of the hall, with its porch-light glow. Milk; biscuit; twenty minutes of television; fish-fingers for tea. The routine they have fallen into so quickly, barely halfway through that first term at school.

The car comes from nowhere. The squeal of wet brakes, the thud of a five-year-old boy hitting the windscreen and the spin of his body before it slams on to the road. Running after him, in front of the still-moving car. Slipping and falling heavily on to outstretched hands, the impact taking her breath away.

It's over in a heartbeat.

She crouches beside him, searching frantically for a pulse. Watches her breath form a solitary white cloud in the air. Sees the dark shadow form beneath his head and hears her own wail as though it comes from someone else. She looks up at the blurred windscreen, its wipers sending arcs of water into the darkening night, and she screams at the unseen driver to help her.

Leaning forward to warm the boy with her body, she holds her coat open over them both, its hem drinking surface water from the road. And as she kisses him and begs him to wake, the pool of yellow light that envelops them shrinks to a narrow beam; the car backs up the street. Engine whining in admonishment, the car makes two, three, four attempts to turn in the narrow street, scraping in its haste against one of the huge sycamore sentries lining the road.

And then it is dark.

PART ONE

1

Detective Inspector Ray Stevens stood next to the window and contemplated his office chair, on which an arm had been broken for at least a year. Until now he had simply taken the pragmatic approach of not leaning on the left side, but while he was at lunch someone had scrawled 'defective' in black marker pen across the back of it. Ray wondered if Business Support's newfound enthusiasm for equipment audits would extend to a replacement, or whether he was destined to run Bristol CID from a chair that cast serious doubts over his credibility.

Leaning forward to find a marker pen in his chaotic top drawer, Ray crouched down and changed the label to 'detective'. The door to his office opened and he hastily stood up, replacing the lid on the pen.

'Ah, Kate, I was just . . .' He stopped, recognising the look on her face almost before he saw the Command and Control printout in her hand. 'What have you got?'

'A hit-and-run in Fishponds, guv. Five-year-old boy killed.'

Ray stretched out a hand for the piece of paper and scanned it, while Kate stood awkwardly in the doorway. Fresh from shift, she had only been on CID for a couple of months and was still finding her feet. She was good though: better than she knew.

'No registration number?'

'Not as far as we know. Shift have got the scene contained and the skipper's taking a statement from the child's mother as we speak. She's badly in shock, as you can imagine.'

'Are you all right to stay late?' Ray asked, but Kate was nodding before he'd even finished the question. They exchanged half-smiles in mutual acknowledgement of the adrenalin rush it always felt so wrong to enjoy when something so horrific had happened.

'Right then, let's go.'

They nodded a greeting to the throng of smokers clustered under cover by the back door.

'All right, Stumpy?' Ray said. 'I'm taking Kate out to the Fishponds hit-and-run. Can you get on to Area Intelligence and see if anything's come in yet?'

'Will do.' The older man took a final drag of his roll-up. Detective Sergeant Jake Owen had been called Stumpy for so much of his career that it was always a surprise to hear his full name read out in court. A man of few words, Stumpy had more war stories than he chose to share, and was without a shadow of a doubt Ray's best DS. The two men had been on shift together for several years, and with a strength that belied his small stature, Stumpy was a handy crewmate to have on your side.

In addition to Kate, Stumpy's team included the steady Malcolm Johnson and young Dave Hillsdon, an enthusiastic but maverick DC, whose determined efforts to secure convictions sailed a little too close to the wind for Ray's liking. Together they made a good team, and Kate was learning fast from them. She had a fiery passion that made Ray nostalgic for his days as a hungry DC, before seventeen years of bureaucracy had ground him down.

Kate drove the unmarked Corsa through mounting rush-hour traffic to Fishponds. She was an impatient driver; tutting when a red light held them back, and craning her neck to see past a hold-up. She was perpetually in motion: tapping fingers on the steering wheel, screwing up her nose, shifting in her seat. As the traffic started moving again, she leaned forward as though the action would propel them along faster.

'Missing blues and twos?' Ray said.

Kate grinned. 'Maybe a bit.' There was eye-liner smudged around her eyes, but otherwise her face was clean of make-up. Dark brown curls fell messily about her face, despite the tortoise-shell clip presumably intended to hold them back.

Ray fished for his mobile to make the necessary calls, confirming that the Collision Investigation Unit was en route, the duty superintendent had been informed, and that someone had called out the Ops wagon – a lumbering vehicle stuffed to the gunnels with tenting, emergency lights and hot drinks. Everything had been done. In all honesty, he thought, it always had been, but as duty DI the buck stopped with him. There was usually a bit of hackle-rising from shift when CID turned up and started going over old ground, but that was just the way it had to be. They'd all been through it; even Ray, who had spent as little time in uniform as possible before moving on.

He spoke to Control Room to let them know they were five minutes away, but didn't call home. Ray had taken to phoning Mags instead on the rare occasion when he was going to be on time, which seemed a much more practical approach to the long hours the job demanded of him.

As they rounded the corner Kate slowed the car to a crawl. Half a dozen police cars were strewn haphazardly down the street; lights throwing a blue glow across the scene every other second. Floodlights were mounted on metal tripods, their strong beams picking out the fine mist of rain, which had thankfully abated in the last hour.

Kate had stopped on their way out of the station to grab a coat and exchange her heels for wellies. 'Practicality before style,' she had laughed, throwing the shoes into her locker and pulling on the boots. Ray rarely gave much thought to either principle, but he wished now he'd at least brought a coat.

They parked the car a hundred metres away from a large white tent, erected in an attempt to protect from the rain whatever evidence might have been left. One side of the tent was open, and inside they could see a Crime Scene Investigator on her hands and knees, swabbing at something unseen. Further up the street a second paper-suited figure was examining one of the huge trees that lined the road.

As Ray and Kate drew near to the scene they were stopped by a young PC, his fluorescent jacket zipped so high Ray could barely make out a face between the peak of his hat and his collar.

'Evening, sir. Do you need to see the scene? I'll have to sign you in.'

'No thank you,' said Ray. 'Can you tell me where your sergeant is?'

'He's at the mother's house,' the PC said. He pointed down the street to a row of small terraced houses, before retreating into his collar. 'Number four,' came the muffled afterthought.

'God, that's a miserable job,' said Ray, as he and Kate walked away. 'I remember doing a twelve-hour scene watch in the pouring rain when I was a probationer, then getting told off by the DCI for not smiling when he turned up at eight o'clock the next morning.'

Kate laughed. 'Is that why you specialised?'

'Not entirely,' Ray said, 'but it was certainly part of the appeal. No, it was mainly because I was sick of passing all the big jobs over to the specialists and never seeing anything through to the end. How about you?'

'Sort of similar.'

They reached the row of houses the PC had pointed towards. Kate carried on talking as they looked for number four.

'I like dealing with the more serious jobs. But mainly it's because I get bored easily. I like complicated investigations that make my head hurt to figure them out. Cryptic crosswords rather than simple ones. Does that make sense?'

'Perfect sense,' said Ray. 'Although I've always been useless at cryptic crosswords.'

'There's a knack,' said Kate, 'I'll teach you sometime. Here we are, number four.'

The front door was smartly painted and slightly ajar. Ray pushed it open and called inside. 'CID. All right if we come in?'

'In the sitting room,' came the response.

They wiped their feet and walked up the narrow hallway, pushing past an over-loaded coat rack, beneath which sat a pair of child's red wellies, neatly placed beside an adult pair.

The child's mother was sitting on a small sofa, her eyes fixed on the blue drawstring school bag clutched on her lap.

'I'm Detective Inspector Ray Stevens. I'm so sorry to hear about your son.'

She looked up at him, twisting the drawstring so tightly around her hands the cord gouged red grooves in her skin. 'Jacob,' she said, dry-eyed. 'His name is Jacob.'

Perched on a kitchen chair next to the sofa, a uniformed sergeant was balancing paperwork on his lap. Ray had seen him around the nick but didn't know his name. He glanced at his badge.

'Brian, would you mind taking Kate into the kitchen and filling her in on what you've got so far? I'd like to ask the witness a few questions, if that's okay? It won't take long. Perhaps you could make her a cup of tea at the same time.'

From the reaction on Brian's face, it was clear this was the last thing he wanted to do, but he stood up and left the room with Kate, no doubt to moan to her about CID pulling rank. Ray didn't dwell on it.

'I'm sorry to ask you even more questions, but it's vital we get as much information as we can, as early as possible.'

Jacob's mother nodded, but didn't look up.

'I understand you couldn't see the car's number plate?'

'It happened so quickly,' she said, the words triggering a release of emotion. 'He was talking about school, and then . . . I only let go for a second.' She pulled the drawstring cord tighter round her hand, and Ray watched the colour drain from her fingers. 'It was so fast. The car came so fast.'

She answered his questions quietly, giving no sign of the frustration she must surely be feeling. Ray hated causing such intrusion, but he had no choice.

'What did the driver look like?'

'I couldn't see inside,' she said.

'Were there passengers?'

'I couldn't see inside the car,' she repeated, her voice dull and wooden.

'Right,' said Ray. Where on earth were they going to start?

She looked at him. 'Will you find him? The man who killed Jacob. Will you find him?' Her voice cracked and the words fell apart, morphing into a low moan. She bent forward, hugging the school bag into her stomach, and Ray felt a tightening in his chest. He took a deep breath, forcing the feeling away.

'We'll do everything we can,' he said, despising himself for the cliché.

Kate came back from the kitchen with Brian behind her, carrying a mug of tea. 'All right if I finish this statement now, guv?' he asked.

Stop upsetting my witness, you mean, Ray thought. 'Yes, thank you – sorry for interrupting. Got everything we need, Kate?'

Kate nodded. She looked pale, and he wondered if Brian had said something to upset her. In a year or so he would know her as well as he knew the rest of the team, but he hadn't quite sussed her out yet. She was outspoken, he knew that much, not too nervous to put her point across at team meetings, and she learned fast.

They left the house and walked in silence back to the car.

'Are you okay?' he asked, although it was clear she wasn't. Her jaw was rigid; the colour had completely drained from her face.

'Fine,' Kate said, but her voice was thick and Ray realised she was trying not to cry.

'Hey,' he said, reaching out and putting an awkward arm round her shoulder, 'is it the job?' Over the years Ray had built a defensive mechanism against the fall-out of cases like this one. Most police officers had one – it's why you had to turn a blind eye to some of the jokes bandied about the canteen – but perhaps Kate was different.

She nodded and took a deep, juddering breath. 'I'm sorry, I'm not normally like this, I promise. I've done dozens of death knocks, but . . . God, he was five years old! Apparently Jacob's father never wanted anything to do with him, so it's always been the two of them. I can't imagine what she's going through.' Her voice cracked, and Ray felt the tightness in his chest return. His coping mechanism relied on focusing on the investigation – on the hard evidence before them – and not dwelling too deeply on the emotions of the people involved. If he thought too long about how it must feel to watch your child die in your arms, he would be no use to anyone, not least to Jacob and his mother. Ray's thoughts flicked involuntarily to his own children, and he had an irrational desire to call home and check they were both safe.

'Sorry.' Kate swallowed and gave an embarrassed smile. 'I promise I won't always be like this.'

'Hey, it's okay,' Ray said. 'We've all been there.'

She raised an eyebrow. 'Even you? I didn't have you down as the sensitive type, boss.'

'I have my moments.' Ray squeezed her shoulder before taking his arm away. He didn't think he'd ever actually shed tears at a job, but he'd come pretty close. 'You going to be okay?'

'I'll be fine. Thank you.'

As they pulled away, Kate looked back at the scene, where the CSIs were still hard at work. 'What sort of bastard kills a five-year-old boy, then drives off?'

Ray didn't hesitate. 'That's exactly what we're going to find out.'

2

I don't want a cup of tea, but I take it anyway. Cradling the mug in both hands I press my face into the steam until it scalds me. Pain pricks my skin, deadening my cheeks and stinging my eyes. I fight the instinct to pull away; I need the numbness to blur the scenes that won't leave my head.

'Shall I get you something to eat?'

He towers over me and I know I should look up, but I can't bear to. How can he offer me food and drink as though nothing has happened? A wave of nausea wells up inside me and I swallow the acrid taste back down. He blames me for it. He hasn't said so, but he doesn't have to, it's there in his eyes. And he's right – it was my fault. We should have gone home a different way; I shouldn't have talked; I should have stopped him . . .

'No, thank you,' I say quietly, 'I'm not hungry.'

The accident plays on a loop in my head. I want to press pause but the film is relentless: his body slamming onto the bonnet time after time after time. I raise the mug to my face again, but the tea has cooled and the warmth on my skin isn't enough to hurt. I can't feel the tears forming, but fat droplets burst as they hit my knees. I watch them soak into my jeans, and scratch my nail across a smear of clay on my thigh.

I look around the room at the home I have spent so many years creating. The curtains, bought to match the cushions; the artwork, some of my own, some I found in galleries and loved too much to leave behind. I thought I was making a home, but I was only ever building a house.

My hand hurts. I can feel my pulse beating rapid and light in my wrist. I'm glad of the pain. I wish it were more. I wish it had been me the car hit.

He's talking again. *Police are out everywhere looking for the car . . . the papers will appeal for witnesses . . . it will be on the news . . .*

The room spins and I fix my gaze on the coffee table, nodding when it seems appropriate. He strides two paces to the window, then back again. I wish he would sit down – he's making me nervous. My hands are shaking and I put down my untouched tea before I drop it, but I clatter the china against the glass tabletop. He shoots me a look of frustration.

'Sorry,' I say. There's a metallic taste in my mouth, and I realise I've bitten through the inside of my lip. I swallow the blood, not wanting to draw attention to myself by asking for a tissue.

Everything has changed. The instant the car slid across the wet tarmac, my whole life changed. I can see everything clearly, as though I am standing on the sidelines. I can't go on like this.

When I wake, for a second I'm not sure what this feeling is. Everything is the same, and yet everything has changed. Then, before I have even opened my eyes, there is a rush of noise in my head, like an underground train. And there it is: playing out in Technicolor scenes I can't pause or mute. I press the heels of my palms into my temples as though I can make the images subside through brute force alone, but still they come, thick and fast, as if without them I might forget.

On my bedside cabinet is the brass alarm clock Eve gave me when I went to university – 'Because you'll never get to lectures, otherwise' – and I'm shocked to see it's ten-thirty already. The pain in my hand has been overshadowed by a headache that blinds me if I move my head too fast, and as I peel myself from the bed every muscle aches.

12

I pull on yesterday's clothes and go into the garden without stopping to make a coffee, even though my mouth is so dry it's an effort to swallow. I can't find my shoes, and the frost stings my feet as I make my way across the grass. The garden isn't large, but winter is on its way, and by the time I reach the other side I can't feel my toes.

The garden studio has been my sanctuary for the last five years. Little more than a shed to the casual observer, it is where I come to think, to work, and to escape. The wooden floor is stained from the lumps of clay that drop from my wheel, firmly placed in the centre of the room, where I can move around it and stand back to view my work with a critical eye. Three sides of the shed are lined with shelves on which I place my sculptures, in an ordered chaos only I could understand. Works in progress, here; fired but not painted, here; waiting to go to customers, here. Hundreds of separate pieces, yet if I shut my eyes, I can still feel the shape of each one beneath my fingers, the wetness of the clay on my palms.

I take the key from its hiding place under the window ledge and open the door. It's worse than I thought. The floor lies unseen beneath a carpet of broken clay; rounded halves of pots ending abruptly in angry jagged peaks. The wooden shelves are all empty, my desk swept clear of work, and the tiny figurines on the window ledge are unrecognisable, crushed into shards that glisten in the sunlight.

By the door lies a small statuette of a woman. I made her last year, as part of a series of figures I produced for a shop in Clifton. I had wanted to produce something real, something as far from perfection as it was possible to get, and yet for it still to be beautiful. I made ten women, each with their own distinctive curves, their own bumps and scars and imperfections. I based them on my mother; my sister; girls I taught at pottery class; women I saw walking in the park. This one is me. Loosely, and not so anyone would recognise, but nevertheless me. Chest a little too flat; hips a little too narrow; feet a little too big. A tangle of hair twisted into a knot at the base of the neck. I bend down and pick her up. I had thought her intact, but as I touch her the clay moves beneath my hands, and I'm left with two broken pieces. I look at them, then I hurl them with all my strength towards the wall, where they shatter into tiny pieces that shower down on to my desk.

I take a deep breath and let it slowly out.

I'm not sure how many days have passed since the accident, or how I have moved through the week when I feel as though I'm dragging my legs through treacle. I don't know what it is that makes me decide today is the day. But it is. I take only what will fit into my holdall, knowing that if I don't go right now, I might not be able to leave at all. I walk haphazardly about the house, trying to imagine never being here again. The thought is both terrifying and liberating. Can I do this? Is it possible to simply walk away from one life and start another? I have to try: it is my only chance of getting through this in one piece.

My laptop is in the kitchen. It holds photos; addresses; important information I might one day need and hadn't thought to save elsewhere. I don't have time to think about doing this now, and although it's heavy and awkward I add it to my bag. I don't have much room left, but I can't leave without one final piece of my past. I discard a jumper and a fistful of T-shirts, making room instead for the wooden box in which my memories are hidden, crammed one on top of another beneath the cedar lid. I don't look inside – I don't need to. The assortment of teenage diaries, erratically kept and with regretted pages torn from their bindings; an elastic band full of concert tickets; my graduation certificate; clippings from my first exhibition. And the photos of the son I loved with an intensity that seemed impossible. Precious photographs. So few for someone so loved. Such a small impact on the world, yet the very centre of my own.

Unable to resist, I open the box and pick up the uppermost photo: a Polaroid taken by a soft-spoken midwife on the day he was born. He is a tiny scrap of pink, barely visible beneath the white hospital blanket. In the photo my arms are fixed in the awkward pose of the new mother, drowning in love and exhaustion. It had all been so rushed, so frightening, so unlike the books I had devoured during my pregnancy, but the love I had to offer never faltered. Suddenly unable to breathe, I place the photo back and push the box into my holdall.

Jacob's death is front-page news. It screams at me from the garage forecourt I pass, from the corner shop, and from the bus-stop queue where I stand as though I am no different to anyone else. As though I am not running away.

Everyone is talking about the accident. How could it have happened? Who could have done it? Each bus stop brings fresh news, and the snatches of gossip float back across our heads, impossible for me to avoid.

It was a black car.

It was a red car.

The police are close to an arrest.

The police have no leads.

A woman sits next to me. She opens her newspaper and suddenly it feels as though someone is pressing on my chest. Jacob's face stares at me; bruised eyes rebuking me for not protecting him, for letting him die. I force myself to look at him, and a hard knot tightens in my throat. My vision blurs and I can't read the words, but I don't need to – I've seen a version of this article in every paper I've passed today. The quotes from devastated teachers; the notes on flowers by the side of the road; the inquest – opened and then adjourned. A second photo shows a wreath of yellow chrysanthemums on an impossibly tiny coffin. The woman tuts and starts talking: half to herself, I think, but perhaps she feels I will have a view.

15

'Terrible, isn't it? And just before Christmas, too.'

I say nothing.

'Driving off like that without stopping.' She tuts again. 'Mind you,' she continues, 'five years old. What kind of mother allows a child that age to cross a road on his own?'

I can't help it – I let out a sob. Without my realising, hot tears stream down my cheeks and into the tissue pushed gently into my hand.

'Poor lamb,' the woman says, as though soothing a small child. It's not clear if she means me, or Jacob. 'You can't imagine, can you?'

But I can, and I want to tell her that, whatever she is imagining, it is a thousand times worse. She finds me another tissue, crumpled but clean, and turns the page of her newspaper to read about the Clifton Christmas lights switch-on.

I never thought I would run away. I never thought I would need to.

3

Ray made his way up to the third floor, where the frantic pace of twenty-four-seven policing gave way to the quiet carpeted offices of the nine-to-fivers and reactive CID. He liked it here best in the evening, when he could work through the ever-present stack of files on his desk without interruption. He walked through the open-plan area to where the DI's office had been created from a partitioned corner of the room.

'How did the briefing go?'

The voice made him jump. He turned to see Kate sitting at her desk. 'Party Four's my old shift, you know. I hope they at least pretended to be interested.' She yawned.

'It was fine,' Ray said. 'They're a good bunch, and if nothing else it keeps it fresh in their minds.' Ray had managed to keep details of the hit-and-run on the briefing sheet for a week, but it had inevitably been pushed off as other jobs came in. He was trying his best to get round all the shifts and remind them he still needed their help. He tapped his watch. 'What are you doing here at this hour?'

'I'm trawling through the responses to the media appeals,' she said, flicking her thumb across the edge of a pile of computer printouts. 'Not that it's doing much good.'

'Nothing worth following up?'

'Zilch,' Kate said. 'A few sightings of cars driving badly, the odd sanctimonious judgement on parental supervision, and the usual line-up of crackpots and crazies, including some bloke

17

predicting the Second Coming.' She sighed. 'We badly need a break – something to go on.'

'I realise it's frustrating,' Ray said, 'but hang on in there, it'll happen. It always does.'

Kate groaned and pushed her chair away from the mound of paper. 'I don't think I'm blessed with patience.'

'I know the feeling.' Ray sat on the edge of her desk. 'This is the dull bit of investigating – the bit they don't show on TV.' He grinned at her doleful expression. 'But the pay-off is worth it. Just think: in amongst all those pieces of paper could be the key to solving this case.'

Kate eyed her desk dubiously and Ray laughed.

'Come on, I'll make us a cup of tea and give you a hand.'

They sifted through each printed sheet, but didn't find the nugget of information Ray had hoped for.

'Ah well, at least that's another thing ticked off the list,' he said. 'Thanks for staying late to go through them all.'

'Do you think we'll find the driver?'

Ray nodded firmly. 'We have to believe we will, otherwise how can anyone have confidence in us? I've dealt with hundreds of jobs: I haven't solved them all – not by any means – but I've always been convinced the answer lies just around the corner.'

'Stumpy said you've requested a *Crimewatch* appeal?'

'Yes. Standard practice with a hit-and-run – especially when there's a kid involved. It'll mean a lot more of this, I'm afraid.' He gestured to the pile of paper, now fit for nothing but the shredder.

'That's okay,' Kate said. 'I could do with the overtime. I bought my first place last year and it's a bit of a stretch, to be honest.'

'Do you live on your own?' He wondered if he was allowed to ask that sort of thing nowadays. In the time he'd been a copper, political correctness had reached a point where anything remotely personal had to be skirted around. In a few years' time people wouldn't be able to talk at all.

'Mostly,' Kate said. 'I bought the place on my own, but my boyfriend stays over quite a lot. Best of both worlds, I reckon.'

Ray picked up the empty mugs. 'Right, well you'd better head off home,' he said. 'Your chap will be wondering where you are.'

'It's okay, he's a chef,' Kate said, but she stood up too. 'He works worse shifts than I do. How about you? Doesn't your wife despair of the hours you do?'

'She's used to it,' Ray said, raising his voice to continue the conversation as he went to get his jacket from his office. 'She was a police officer too – we joined together.'

The police training centre in Ryton-on-Dunsmore had few redeeming features, but the cheap bar had definitely been one of them. During a particularly painful karaoke evening Ray had seen Mags sitting with her classmates. She was laughing, her head thrown back at something a friend was saying. When he saw her stand up to get a round in, he downed his almost-full pint so he could join her at the bar, only to stand there tongue-tied. Fortunately Mags was less reticent, and they were inseparable for the remainder of their sixteen-week course. Ray suppressed a grin as he remembered creeping from the female accommodation block to his own room at six in the morning.

'How long have you been married?' Kate said.

'Fifteen years. We got hitched once we were through our probation.'

'But she's not in the job any more?'

'Mags took a career break when Tom was born, and never went back after our youngest arrived,' Ray said. 'Lucy's nine now, and Tom's settling into his first year at secondary school, so Mags is starting to think about returning to work. She wants to retrain as a teacher.'

'Why did she stop work for so long?' There was genuine curiosity in Kate's eyes and Ray remembered Mags being similarly incredulous, in the days when they were both young in service. Mags' sergeant had left to have children and Mags had told Ray she didn't see the point of a career if you were only going to give it all up.

'She wanted to be home for the kids,' Ray said. He felt a stab of guilt. Had Mags wanted that? Or had she simply felt it was the right thing to do? Childcare was so expensive that Mags stopping work had seemed an obvious decision, and he knew she wanted to be there for the school runs, and for sports days and harvest festivals. But Mags was just as bright and as capable as he was – more so, if he was honest.

'I guess when you marry into the job you have to accept the crappy conditions with it.' Kate switched off the desk lamp and they dropped into darkness for a second, before Ray walked into the corridor and triggered the automatic light there.

'Occupational hazard,' Ray agreed. 'How long have you been with your chap?' They walked down towards the yard where their cars were parked.

'Only about six months,' Kate said. 'That's pretty good going for me, though – I normally dump them after a few weeks. My mother tells me I'm too fussy.'

'What's wrong with them?'

'Oh, all sorts,' she said cheerfully. 'Too keen, not keen enough; no sense of humour, total buffoon . . .'

'Tough critic,' said Ray.

'Maybe.' Kate wrinkled her nose. 'But it's important, isn't it – finding The One? I was thirty last month, I'm running out of time.' She didn't look thirty, but then Ray had never been a great judge of age. He still looked in the mirror and saw the man he'd been in his twenties, even though the lines on his face told a different tale.

Ray reached into his pocket for his keys. 'Well, don't be in too much of a hurry to settle down. It's not all roses round the door, you know.'

'Thanks for the advice, Dad . . .'

'Hey, I'm not that old!'

Kate laughed. 'Thanks for your help tonight. See you in the morning.'

Ray chuckled to himself as he eased his car out from behind a marked Omega. *Dad*, indeed. The cheek of her.

When he arrived home Mags was in the sitting room with the television on. She wore pyjama bottoms and one of his old sweatshirts, and her legs were curled up beneath her like a child. A newsreader was recapping on the events of the hit-and-run for the benefit of any local resident who had somehow missed the extensive coverage of the past week. Mags looked up at Ray and shook her head. 'I can't stop watching it. That poor boy.'

He sat down next to her and reached for the remote to mute the sound. The screen switched to old footage of the scene, and Ray saw the back of his own head as he and Kate walked from their car. 'I know,' he said, putting an arm round his wife. 'But we'll get them.'

The camera changed again, filling the screen with Ray's face as he delivered a piece to camera, the interviewer out of shot.

'Do you think you will? Have you got any leads?'

'Not really.' Ray sighed. 'No one saw it happen – or if they did, they're not saying anything – so we're relying on forensics and intelligence.'

'Could the driver have somehow not realised what they'd done?' Mags sat up and turned so she was facing him. She pushed her hair impatiently behind her ear. Mags had worn her hair the same way since Ray had known her: long and straight, with no fringe. It was as dark as Ray's, but unlike his it showed no sign of grey. Ray had tried to grow a beard shortly after Lucy had been born, but had stopped after three days when it was clear there was more salt than pepper. Now he stayed clean-shaven, and tried to ignore the sprinkling of white at his temples that Mags told him was 'distinguished'.

'Not a chance,' Ray said. 'He went straight on to the bonnet.'

Mags didn't flinch. The emotion on her face he had seen when he came home had been replaced by a look of concentration he remembered so well from their days on shift together.

'Besides,' Ray continued, 'the car stopped, then backed up and turned round. The driver might not have known Jacob had died, but they couldn't have missed the fact they'd hit him.'

'Have you got someone on to the hospitals?' Mags said. 'It's possible the driver sustained an injury too, and—'

Ray smiled. 'We're on it, I promise.' He stood up. 'Look, don't take this the wrong way, but it's been a long day and I just want to have a beer, watch a bit of TV and go to bed.'

'Sure,' Mags said tightly. 'You know – old habits, and all that.'

'I know, and I promise you we'll get the driver.' He kissed her on the forehead. 'We always do.' Ray realised he had given Mags the very same promise he refused to give Jacob's mother because he couldn't possibly guarantee it. *We'll do our best,* he had told her. He only hoped their best was good enough.

He walked into the kitchen to find a drink. It was the involvement of a child that would have upset Mags. Perhaps telling her the details of the crash hadn't been such a good idea – after all, he was finding it hard enough to keep a lid on his own emotions, so it was understandable Mags would feel the same way. He would make an extra effort to keep things to himself.

Ray took his beer back into the sitting room and settled down next to her to watch the television, flicking away from the news on to one of the reality TV shows he knew she liked.

Arriving in his office with a clutch of files scooped up from the post-room, Ray dumped the paperwork on top of his already laden desk, causing the entire pile to slide to the floor.

'Bugger,' he said, eyeing his desk dispassionately. The cleaner had been in, emptying the bin and making a vague attempt to dust around the mess, leaving a skirt of fluff around his in-tray. Two mugs of cold coffee flanked his keyboard and several Post-it notes stuck to his computer screen bore phone messages of varying degrees of importance. Ray plucked them off and attached them to the outside of his diary, where there was already a neon-pink Post-it reminding him to do his team's appraisals. As if they didn't all have enough to do. Ray fought an ongoing battle with himself about the bureaucracy of his day-to-day job. He couldn't quite bring himself to rail against it – not when the next rank was so tantalisingly within his grasp – but neither would he ever embrace it. An hour spent discussing his personal development was an hour wasted, as far as he was concerned, especially when there was a child's death to investigate.

As he waited for the computer to boot up, he tipped his chair on to its back legs and looked at the photo of Jacob pinned to the opposite wall. He had always kept out a photo of whoever was central to the investigation, ever since he started on CID, when his DS had reminded him gruffly that fingering a collar was all well and good, but Ray should never forget 'what we're doing this shit for'. The photos used to be on his desk, until Mags had come to the office one day, years ago. She'd brought him something – he couldn't remember what now; a forgotten file, maybe, or a packed lunch. He remembered feeling annoyed by the interruption when she called from the front desk to surprise him, and the annoyance turning to guilt when he realised she'd gone out of her way to see him. They had stopped en route to Ray's office so Mags could say hello to her old guv'nor, now a superintendent.

'Bet it feels odd, being here,' Ray had said, when they reached his office.

Mags had laughed. 'It's like I never left. You can take the girl out of the police, but you'll never take the police out of the girl.' Her face was animated as she walked about the office, her fingers trailing lightly over his desk.

'Who's the other woman?' she had teased him, picking up the loose photograph propped up against the framed picture of her and the kids.

'A victim,' Ray had replied, taking the photo gently from Mags and replacing it on his desk. 'She was stabbed seventeen times by her boyfriend because she was late getting the tea on.'

If Mags was shocked, she didn't show it. 'You don't keep it in the file?'

'I like to have it where I can see it,' Ray said. 'Where I can't forget what I'm doing, why I'm working these hours, who it's all for.' She had nodded at that. She understood him better than he realised, sometimes.

'But not next to our photograph. Please, Ray.' She had reached out a hand to take the photo again, looking around the office for somewhere more suitable. Her eyes settled on the redundant corkboard at the back of the room and, taking a drawing pin from the pot on his desk, she had fixed the picture of the smiling dead woman decisively in the middle of the board.

And there it stayed.

The smiling woman's boyfriend had long since been charged with murder, and a steady succession of victims had taken her place. The old man beaten black and blue by teenage muggers; the four women sexually assaulted by a taxi driver; and now Jacob, beaming in his school uniform. All of them relying on Ray. He scanned the notes he had made in his daybook the night before, preparing for this morning's briefing. They didn't have a lot to go on. As his computer beeped to tell him it had finally booted up, Ray mentally shook himself. They might not have a long list of leads, but there was still work to be done.

Shortly before ten o'clock, Stumpy and his team trooped through the door into Ray's office. Stumpy and Dave Hillsdon took up residence in two of the low chairs grouped around the coffee table, while the others stood at the back of the room, or leaned against the wall. The third chair had been left empty in an unspoken nod to chivalry, and Ray was amused to see that Kate ignored the offering and joined Malcolm Johnson to stand at the back. Their numbers had been temporarily boosted by two officers on loan from shift, looking uncomfortable in hastily borrowed suits, and PC Phil Crocker from the Collision Investigation Unit.

'Good morning, everyone,' Ray said. 'I won't keep you long. I'd like to introduce Brian Walton from Party One, and Pat Bryce from Party Three. It's good to have you lads, and there's plenty to do, so just muck in.' Brian and Pat nodded in acknowledgement. 'Okay,' Ray continued. 'The purpose of this briefing is to revisit what we know about the Fishponds hit-and-run, and where we go next. As you can imagine, the chief is all over this one like a rash.' He looked at his notes, although he knew the contents by heart. 'At 1628 on Monday, 26 November 999 operators picked up a call from a woman living in Enfield Avenue. She had heard a loud bang, and then a scream. By the time she got outside, it was all over, and Jacob's mother was crouching over him in the road. The ambulance response time was six minutes, and Jacob was pronounced dead at the scene.'

Ray paused for a moment, to let the gravity of the investigation sink in. He glanced at Kate, but her expression was neutral, and he didn't know if he was relieved or saddened that she had managed to build her defences so successfully. She wasn't the only one apparently devoid of emotion. A stranger scanning the room might assume the police couldn't care less about the death of this little boy, when Ray knew it had touched them all. He continued with the briefing.

'Jacob turned five last month, soon after starting school at St Mary's, in Beckett Street. On the day of the hit-and-run,

Jacob had been at an after-school club, while his mum was working. Her statement says they were walking home, and chatting about the day, when she let go of Jacob's hand and he ran across the road towards their house. From what she's said it's something he's done before – he didn't have good road sense and his mum always made sure she held on to him when they were near a road.' Except this one time, he added silently. One tiny lapse of concentration, and she wouldn't ever be able to forgive herself for it. Ray shuddered involuntarily.

'What did she see of the car?' Brian Walton asked.

'Not a lot. She claims that, far from braking, the car was speeding up when it hit Jacob, and that she narrowly avoided being hit as well; in fact she fell and hurt herself. The attending officers noticed she had injuries, but she refused treatment. Phil, can you talk us through the scene?'

The only uniformed officer in the room, Phil Crocker was a collision investigator, and with years of experience on the Roads Policing department he was Ray's go-to man for all traffic matters.

'There's not much to say.' Phil shrugged. 'The wet weather means no tyre marks, so I can't give you an estimate on speed, or tell you if the vehicle was braking prior to impact. We seized a piece of plastic casing about twenty metres from the point of collision, and the vehicle examiner has confirmed it's from the fog light of a Volvo.'

'That sounds encouraging,' Ray said.

'I've given the details to Stumpy,' Phil said. 'Other than that, I'm afraid I've got nothing.'

'Thanks, Phil.' Ray picked up his notes again. 'Jacob's post-mortem report shows he died from blunt force trauma. He had multiple fractures and a ruptured spleen.' Ray had attended the autopsy himself, less because of the need for evidential continuity, and more because he couldn't bear to think of Jacob alone in the cold mortuary. He had looked without seeing, keeping his eyes away from Jacob's face, and focusing on the evidence the Home Office pathologist had issued in staccato sound bites. They were both glad when it was over.

'Judging from the point of impact, we're looking at a small vehicle, so we can rule out people-carriers or four-by-fours. The pathologist recovered fragments of glass from Jacob's body, but I understand there's nothing to tie it to a particular vehicle – isn't that right, Phil?' Ray glanced at the collision investigator, who nodded.

'The glass itself isn't vehicle-specific,' Phil said. 'If we had an offender they might have matching particles in their clothing – it's almost impossible to get rid of. But we didn't find any glass at the scene, which suggests the windscreen cracked on impact, but didn't shatter. Find me the car, and we'll match it to the pieces on the victim, but without that . . .'

'But it does at least help to confirm what damage might be on the car,' Ray said, trying to put a positive spin on the few lines of enquiry they did actually have. 'Stumpy, why don't you run through what's been done so far?'

The DS looked at the wall of Ray's office, where the investigation played out in a series of maps, charts and flipchart sheets, each with a list of actions. 'House-to-house was done on the night, and again the following day by shift. Several people heard what they've described as a "loud bang", followed by a scream, but no one saw the car. We've had PCSOs out on the school run talking to parents, and we've letter-dropped in the streets either side of Enfield Avenue, appealing for witnesses. The roadside signs are still out, and Kate's following up on the few calls we've had as a result of those.'

'Anything useful?'

Stumpy shook his head. 'It's not looking good, boss.'

Ray ignored his pessimism. 'When does the *Crimewatch* appeal go out?'

'Tomorrow night. We've got a reconstruction of the accident, and they've put together some whizzy slides with what the car

27

might look like, then they'll run the studio piece the DCI did with their presenter.'

'I'll need someone to stay late to pick up any strong leads as soon as it airs, please,' Ray said to the group. 'The rest we can get to in slow-time.' There was a pause and he looked around expectantly. 'Someone's got to do it . . .'

'I don't mind.' Kate waved a hand in the air and Ray gave her an appreciative glance.

'What about the fog light Phil mentioned?' Ray said.

'Volvo have given us the part number, and we've got a list of all the garages who have been sent one in the last ten days. I've tasked Malcolm with contacting them all – starting with the local ones – and getting the index numbers of cars they've been fitted to since the collision.'

'Okay,' Ray said. 'Let's keep that in mind when we're making enquiries but remember it's just one piece of evidence – we can't be absolutely certain it's a Volvo we're looking for. Who's leading on CCTV?'

'We are, boss.' Brian Walton raised his hand. 'We've seized everything we could get our hands on: all the council CCTV, and anything from the businesses and petrol stations in the area. We've gone for just the half-hour before the collision and the half-hour afterwards, but even so there are several hundred hours to get through.'

Ray winced at the thought of his overtime budget. 'Let me see the list of cameras,' he said. 'We won't be able to watch all of it, so I'd like your thoughts on what to prioritise.'

Brian nodded.

'Plenty to be getting on with, then,' Ray said. He gave a confident smile, despite his misgivings. They were a fortnight on from the 'golden hour' immediately following a crime, when chances of detection were highest, and although the team was working flat out, they were no further forward. He paused, before breaking the bad news. 'You won't be surprised to hear that all leave has been cancelled until further notice. I'm sorry, and I'll do what I can to make sure you all get some time with your families over Christmas.'

There was a murmur of dissent as everyone filed out of the office, but no one complained, and Ray knew they wouldn't. Although no one voiced it, they were all thinking of what Christmas would be like for Jacob's mother this year.

4

My determination falters almost as soon as we leave Bristol. I hadn't considered where I might go. I head blindly west, thinking perhaps I might go to Devon, or to Cornwall. I think wistfully of childhood holidays; building sandcastles on the beach with Eve, sticky with ice lollies and sun cream. The memory draws me towards the sea; calls me away from the tree-lined avenues of Bristol, away from the traffic. I feel an almost physical fear of these cars that can't wait to overtake as the bus pulls into the station. I wander aimlessly for a while, then hand over ten pounds to a man in a kiosk by the Greyhound coaches who doesn't care where I'm going any more than I do.

We cross the Severn Bridge, and I look down at the swirling mass of bilge-grey water that is the Bristol Channel. The coach is quietly anonymous, and here no one is reading the *Bristol Post*. No one is talking about Jacob. I lean back into my seat. I'm exhausted but I don't dare close my eyes. When I sleep I'm assaulted by the sights and sounds of the accident; by the knowledge that had I been just a few minutes earlier, it would never have happened.

The Greyhound coach is going to Swansea, and I steal a glance around to see the company I'm keeping. They are students, in the main, plugged into music and engrossed in magazines. A woman my age is reading through papers and making neat notes in the margins. It seems ludicrous that I've never been to Wales, but now I'm glad I have no connection here. It is the perfect place for a new beginning.

I'm the last to get off, and I wait at the bus station until the coach has left, the adrenalin of my departure a distant memory. Now that I've made it as far as Swansea, I have no idea where to go. A man is slumped on the pavement; he looks up and mumbles something incoherent, and I back away. I can't stay here, and I don't know where I'm going, so I start walking. I play a game with myself: I'll take the next left, no matter where it goes; the second right; straight ahead at the first crossroads. I don't read the road signs, taking instead the smallest road offered at each junction, the least-travelled option. I feel light-headed – almost hysterical. What am I doing? Where am I going? I wonder if this is what it's like to lose one's mind, and then I realise I don't care. It doesn't matter any more.

I walk for miles, leaving Swansea far behind. I hug the hedgerow when cars pass, which they do with decreasing frequency now that the evening is drawing in. My holdall is slung on to my back, like a rucksack, and the straps carve grooves into my shoulders, but my pace is steady and I don't stop. All I can hear is my breathing, and I begin to feel calmer. I don't let myself think about what has happened, or where I'm going, I just walk. I pull my phone from my pocket and, without looking to see how many missed calls it shows, I drop it into the ditch beside me, where it splashes into the pooled water. It is the last piece connecting me to my past, and almost immediately I feel freer.

My feet start to ache and I know that, if I were to stop, and lie down here by the side of the road, I would never get up. I slow down, and as I do so, I hear a car behind me. I step on to the grass verge and turn away from the road as it passes, but instead of disappearing round the corner, it slows to a halt about five metres in front of me. There is a faint hiss from the brakes, and a smell of exhaust. Blood pounds in my ears, and without thinking I turn and run, my bag banging against my spine. I run clumsily, my blistered feet rubbing against my boots, and sweat trickles down my back and between my breasts. I can't hear the car, and when I look over my shoulder, the movement almost unbalancing me, it has gone.

I stand foolishly in the empty road. I'm so tired, and so hungry I can't think straight. I wonder even if there was a car at all, or whether I have projected on to this silent road the sound of rubber on tarmac because it is all I hear in my head.

Darkness descends. I know I'm near the coast now: I can taste salt on my lips, and hear the sound of the waves hitting the shore. The sign reads 'Penfach' and it's so quiet I feel as though I'm trespassing as I walk through the village, glancing up at the drawn curtains keeping out the chill of the winter evening. The light from the moon is flat and white, making everything seem two-dimensional and stretching my shadow out in front of me until I'm walking far taller than I feel. I walk through the town until I can look down on to the bay, where cliffs encircle a stretch of sand as though protecting it. I pick my way down a winding path, but the shadows are deceptive and I feel the panic of empty space before my foot slides on the shale and I cry out. Unbalanced by my makeshift rucksack, I lose my balance, and bump, roll and slide my way down the rest of the path. Damp sand crunches beneath me, and I take a breath, waiting for something to hurt. But I am fine. I wonder briefly if I have become immune to physical pain: if the human body is not designed to handle both physical and emotional hurt. My hand still throbs, but at a distance, as though it belongs to someone else.

I have a sudden urge to feel something. Anything. I take off my shoes in spite of the cold and feel the grains of sand pressing against the soles of my feet. The sky is inky blue and free of clouds, and the moon sits full and heavy above the sea, its twin reflected in shimmering slices below. Not home. That is the most important thing. It doesn't feel like home. I wrap myself in my coat and sit on my bag, my back pressed into the hard rock, to wait.

When morning comes, I realise I must have slept; snatches of exhaustion broken by the crash of waves as they move up the shore. I stretch painful, frozen limbs and stand to watch the vivid orange blush spread across the skyline. Despite the light there's no warmth in the sun, and I'm shivering. This has not been a well-thought-out plan.

The narrow path is easier to negotiate in daylight, and I see now that the cliffs are not – as I had thought – deserted. A low building sits half a mile away, squat and utilitarian, next to neat rows of static caravans. It's as good a place to start as any other.

'Good morning,' I say, and my voice sounds small and high in the relative warmth of the caravan park shop. 'I'm looking for somewhere to stay.'

'Here on holiday, are you?' The woman's ample bosom is resting on a copy of *Take a Break* magazine. 'Funny time of year for it.' A smile takes the sting out of her words, and I try to smile back, but my face doesn't respond.

'I'm hoping to move here,' I manage. I realise I must look wild: unwashed and unkempt. My teeth are chattering and I begin to shake violently, the cold seeming to reach deep into my bones.

'Ah, well then,' the woman says cheerily, seemingly unperturbed by my appearance, 'you'll be looking for somewhere to rent, then? Only we're closed till the end of the season, see? Just the shop open till March. So it's Iestyn Jones you want – him with the cottage along the way. I'll ring him, shall I? How about a nice cup of tea first? It's bitter out, and you look half-frozen.'

She shepherds me on to a stool behind the counter, and disappears into the next room, continuing a stream of chatter above the sound of a boiling kettle.

'I'm Bethan Morgan,' she says. 'I run this place – that's Penfach Caravan Park – and my husband Glynn keeps the farm going.' She pops her head round the door and smiles at me. 'Well, that's the idea, anyway, although farming's no easy business nowadays, I can tell you. Oh! I was going to ring Iestyn, wasn't I?'

Bethan doesn't pause for an answer, vanishing for a few minutes while I chew at my bottom lip. I try to think of responses to the questions she will ask, once we're sitting here with our mugs of tea, and the balloon in my chest grows bigger and tighter.

But when Bethan returns, she doesn't ask me anything. Not when did I arrive, or what made me choose Penfach, or even where have I come from. She simply passes me a chipped mug full of sweet tea, then wedges herself into her own chair. She wears so many different clothes it's impossible to see what shape she is, but the arms of her chair dig into soft flesh in a way that can't possibly be comfortable. She is in her forties, I guess, with a smooth, round face which makes her look younger, and long dark hair tied back in a ponytail. She wears lace-up boots beneath a long black skirt and several T-shirts, over which she has pulled an ankle-length cardigan that trails on the dusty floor as she sits. Behind her, a burnt-out incense stick has left a line of ash on the windowsill, and a lingering smell of sweet spice in the air. There is tinsel taped to the old-fashioned till on the counter.

'Iestyn's on his way up,' she says. She has placed a third mug of tea on the counter next to her, so I assume Iestyn – whoever he is – is only a few minutes away.

'Who is Iestyn?' I ask. I wonder if I've made a mistake, coming here where everybody knows everybody. I should have headed for a city, somewhere more anonymous.

'He owns a farm down the road,' Bethan says. 'It's the other side of Penfach, but he's got goats up on the hillside here, and along the coastal path.' She waves an arm in the direction of the sea. 'We'll be neighbours, you and I, if you take his place – but it's no palace.' Bethan laughs, and I can't help but smile. Her straight-forwardness reminds me of Eve, although I suspect my neat, slim sister would be horrified by the comparison.

'I don't need much,' I tell her.

'He's not one for small talk, Iestyn,' Bethan tells me, as though I might find this disappointing, 'but he's a nice enough man. He keeps his sheep up here next to ours,' she gestures vaguely inland, 'and like the rest of us he needs a few more strings to his bow. What do they call it? Diversification?' Bethan gives a derisive snort. 'Anyway, Iestyn has a holiday house in the village, and Blaen Cedi: a cottage up the way.'

'And that's the one you think I'll want to take?

'If you do, you'll be the first in a while.' The man's voice makes me start, and I turn round to see a slightly built figure standing in the doorway.

'It's not that bad!' chides Bethan. 'Now drink your tea and then take the lady up to see it.'

Iestyn has a face so brown and lined that his eyes almost disappear into it. His clothes are hidden beneath dark-blue overalls, dusty and with finger wipes of grease across each thigh. He slurps his tea through a white moustache yellowed with nicotine, and eyes me appraisingly. 'Blaen Cedi is too far from the road for most people,' he says, in a thick accent I struggle to decipher. 'They don't want to carry their bags that far, see?'

'Can I look at it?' I stand up, wanting this unwanted, abandoned cottage to be the answer.

Iestyn continues drinking, swilling each mouthful around his teeth before swallowing it. Finally he lets out a satisfied sigh and walks out of the room. I look at Bethan.

'What did I say? A man of few words.' She laughs. 'Go on with you – he won't wait.'

'Thank you for the tea.'

'My pleasure. You come and see me, once you're settled in down the road.'

I make the promise automatically, although I know I won't keep it, and hurry outside, where I find Iestyn sitting astride a quad bike, filthy with encrusted mud.

I take a step back. He surely doesn't expect me to get on behind him? A man I've known for less than five minutes?

'Only way of getting around,' he shouts over the engine noise.

My head is reeling. I try to balance my practical need to see this house with the primitive fear that is rooting my feet to the ground.

'On you get, then, if you're coming.'

I make my feet move forward and sit gingerly behind him astride the bike. There's no handle in front of me and I can't bring myself to put my arms around Iestyn, so I hang on to my seat as he turns the throttle and the bike shoots off across the bumpy coastal path. The bay stretches out alongside us, the tide now fully in and crashing against the cliffs, but as we draw level with the path running up from the beach, Iestyn turns the quad bike away from the sea. He shouts something over his shoulder and gestures for me to look inland. We bounce over uneven terrain and I search for what I hope will be my new home.

Bethan described it as a cottage, but Blaen Cedi is little more than a shepherd's hut. Once painted white, the render has long since abandoned its battle with the elements, leaving the house a dirty grey. The large wooden door looks out of proportion with the two tiny windows that peer out from beneath the eaves, and a skylight tells me there must be a second floor, although there hardly seems room for it. I can see why Iestyn has struggled to market it as a holiday let. The most creative of property agents would have a hard time playing down the damp inching up the walls outside, or the slipped slate tiles on the roof.

While Iestyn unlocks the door, I stand with my back to the cottage and look towards the coast. I had thought I might see the caravan park from here, but the path has dropped down from the coast, leaving us in a shallow dip that hides the horizon from us. Neither can I see the bay, although I can hear the sea crashing against the rocks, three beats between each wave. Gulls wheel overhead, their cries like kittens, mewling in the fading light, and I shiver involuntarily, wanting suddenly to be inside.

The ground floor is barely twelve feet long; an uneven wooden table separating the living space from where the galley kitchen squats beneath a great oak beam.

Upstairs, the space is split between the bedroom and a tiny bathroom with a half-sized tub. The mirror is spotted with age; the mottled crazing distorting my face. I have the pale complexion common to redheads, but the poor lighting makes my skin seem even more translucent, starkly white against the dark-red hair that falls past my shoulders. I go back downstairs, to find Iestyn stacking wood next to the fire. He finishes the pile and crosses the room to stand against the range.

'She's a bit temperamental, so she is,' he says. He pulls open the warming drawer with a bang that makes me jump.

'Can I take the cottage?' I say. 'Please?' There is a note of desperation in my voice, and I wonder what he must make of me.

Iestyn eyes me suspiciously. 'You can pay, can you?'

'Yes,' I say firmly, although I have no idea how long my savings will last, or what I will do when they run out.

He is unconvinced. 'Do you have a job?'

I think of my studio with its carpet of clay. The pain in my hand is no longer as intense, but I have so little sensation in my fingers I'm frightened I won't be able to work. If I am no longer a sculptor, what am I?

'I'm an artist,' I say eventually.

Iestyn grunts as though that explains everything.

We settle on a rent which, though ridiculously low, will soon race through the money I have been putting aside. But the tiny stone cottage is mine for the next few months, and I breathe a sigh of relief that I have found somewhere.

Iestyn scrawls a mobile number on the back of a receipt he pulls from his pocket. 'Drop this month's rent into Bethan's, if you like.' He nods to me and strides out to the quad bike, starting it up with a roar.

I watch him leave, then I lock the door and drag across the stubborn bolt. Despite the winter sun, I run upstairs to draw the bedroom curtains, shutting the bathroom window, which has been left ajar. Downstairs, the drapes stick on the metal curtain pole as if unused to being closed, and I tug at them, releasing a cloud of dust from their folds. The windows rattle in the wind and the curtains do little to stop the icy chill that creeps around the loose-fitting frames.

I sit on the sofa and listen to the sound of my own breathing. I can't hear the sea, but the plaintive call of a lone gull sounds like a baby crying, and I put my hands over my ears.

Exhaustion overtakes me and I curl up in a ball, wrapping my arms around my knees, and pressing my face against the rough denim of my jeans. Although I know it's coming, the wave of emotion engulfs me, bursting from me with such force I can barely breathe. The grief I feel is so physical it seems impossible that I am still living; that my heart continues to beat when it has been wrenched apart. I want to fix an image of him in my head, but all I can see when I close my eyes is his body, still and lifeless in my arms. I let him go, and I will never forgive myself for that.

5

'Have you got time for a chat about the hit-and-run, boss?' Stumpy stuck his head round Ray's door, Kate hovering behind him.

Ray looked up. Over the last three months the investigation had gradually been scaled back, making way for other, more pressing jobs. Ray still went over the actions a couple of times a week with Stumpy and his team, but the calls had dried up, and there had been no fresh intelligence in weeks.

'Sure.'

They came in and sat down. 'We can't get hold of Jacob's mother,' Stumpy said, getting straight to the point.

'What do you mean?'

'Just that. Her phone's dead and the house is empty. She's disappeared.'

Ray looked at Stumpy and then at Kate, who was looking uncomfortable. 'Please tell me that's a joke.'

'If it is, we don't know what the punchline is,' Kate said.

'She's our only witness!' Ray exploded. 'Not to mention the victim's mother! How on earth could you lose her?'

Kate flushed, and he forced himself to calm down.

'Tell me exactly what happened.'

Kate looked at Stumpy, who nodded for her to explain. 'After the press conference we didn't have much to do with her,' she said. 'We had her statement and she'd been debriefed, so we left her in the hands of the Family Liaison Officer.'

'Who was the FLO?' Ray asked.

'PC Diana Heath,' Kate said, after a pause, 'from Roads Policing.'

Ray made a note in his blue daybook and waited for Kate to continue.

'Diana went round the other day to see how Jacob's mum was doing, only to find the house empty. She'd cleared off.'

'What do the neighbours say?'

'Not a lot,' said Kate. 'She didn't know any of them well enough to leave a forwarding address, and no one saw her go. It's like she's vanished into thin air.'

She glanced at Stumpy, and Ray narrowed his eyes. 'What aren't you telling me?'

There was a pause before Stumpy spoke.

'Apparently there was a bit of backlash on a local web-forum – someone stirring up trouble, suggesting she was an unfit mother, that sort of thing.'

'Anything libellous?'

'Potentially. It's all been deleted now, but I've asked ICT to try and retrieve the cached files. That's not all, though, boss. By all accounts, when she was interviewed by uniform immediately after the accident, they might have pushed a bit too hard. Been a bit insensitive. It seems Jacob's mum thought we held her responsible, and consequently decided we wouldn't be making much effort to find the driver.'

'Oh God,' Ray groaned. He wondered if it was too much to hope for that the chief might not have picked up on any of this. 'Did she give any indication at the time she wasn't happy with police action?'

'This is the first we've heard of it from the FLO,' Stumpy said.

'Speak to the school,' Ray said. 'Someone must have stayed in contact with her. And ask at the GP surgeries. There can't be more than two or three in her local area, and with a child, she's bound to have been registered at one of them. If we can find out which one, they might have sent her records on to her new surgery.'

'Will do, boss.'

'And for God's sake, don't let the *Post* know we've lost her.' He gave a wry smile. 'Suzy French will have a field day.'

No one laughed.

'The loss of key witnesses aside,' Ray said, 'is there anything else I need to know?'

'I've drawn a blank with cross-border enquiries,' Kate said. 'There were a couple of stolen cars that came on to our patch, but they're all accounted for. I've eliminated the list of vehicles that triggered speed cameras that night, and I've been to every garage and body shop in Bristol. No one remembers anything suspicious – at least, not that they'll tell me.'

'How are Brian and Pat getting on with the CCTV?'

'Getting square eyes,' Stumpy said. 'They've been through the police and council footage, and now they're working on the petrol stations. They've picked up what they think is the same car on three different cameras, coming from the Enfield Avenue direction just a few minutes after the hit-and-run. It makes a couple of dangerous attempts to overtake, then it goes out of shot and we haven't managed to pick it up again. They're trying to work out what make it is, although there's nothing to say it's involved at all.'

'Great, thanks for the update.' Ray looked at his watch to hide his disappointment at the lack of progress. 'Why don't you two head off to the pub? I've got to call the superintendent, but I'll be with you in half an hour or so.'

'You're on,' said Stumpy, who never had to be persuaded into a pint. 'Kate?'

'Why not?' she said. 'As long as you're buying.'

It was closer to an hour before Ray got to the Nag's Head, and the others were already on their second round. Ray envied them their ability to switch off: his conversation with the super-intendent had left an uncomfortable knot in his stomach. The senior officer had been nice enough, but the writing on the wall was clear: this investigation was coming to an end. The pub was warm and quiet, and Ray wished he could put work to one side for an hour and talk about football, or the weather, or anything else that didn't involve a five-year-old child and a missing car.

'Trust you to arrive just after I've been to the bar,' Stumpy grumbled.

'You don't mean to say you got your wallet out?' Ray said. He winked at Kate. 'Wonders will never cease.' He ordered a pint of bitter and returned, throwing three packets of crisps on to the table.

'How did it go with the superintendent?' Kate asked.

He couldn't ignore her, and he certainly couldn't lie. Ray took a gulp of his pint to buy some time. Kate watched him, eager to hear if they'd been given more resources, or a bigger budget. He hated to disappoint her, but she had to know some-time. 'Pretty shit, to be honest. Brian and Pat have been taken back to shift.'

'What? Why?' Kate put down her drink with such force that wine sloshed up the inside of the glass.

'We were lucky to have them for as long as we did,' Ray said, 'and they've done a great job with the CCTV. But shift can't carry on back-filling their absence, and the harsh truth is that we can't justify spending any more money on this investi-gation. I'm sorry.' He added the apology as if he were person-ally responsible for the decision, but it didn't make any difference to Kate's reaction.

'We can't just give up on it!' She picked up a beer mat and began digging pieces out of the edges.

Ray sighed. It was so hard, that balance between the cost of an investigation and the cost of a life – the cost of a child's life. How could you put a value on that?

'We're not giving up,' he said, 'you're still working your way through those fog lights, aren't you?'

Kate nodded. 'There were seventy-three fitted as replacement parts in the week following the hit-and-run,' she said. 'The insurance jobs have all been genuine cases, so far, and I'm tracing the registered keepers for all the ones who paid privately.'

'You see? Who knows what that will turn up. All we're doing is scaling things back a bit.' He looked at Stumpy for moral support, but didn't find it.

'The bosses are only interested in quick results, Kate,' Stumpy said. 'If we can't solve a job in a couple of weeks – a couple of days, ideally – it drops off the list of priorities and something else takes its place.'

'I know how it works,' Kate said, 'but it doesn't make it right, does it?' She pushed the tiny scraps of beer mat into a mound in the centre of the table. Ray noticed her fingernails were unpainted, and bitten angrily to the quick. 'I have this feeling the last bit of the puzzle is just around the corner, you know?'

'I do,' said Ray, 'and maybe you're right. But in the meantime, expect to be working on the hit-and-run in between other jobs. The honeymoon period is over.'

'I was thinking I might make some enquiries at the Royal Infirmary,' Kate said. 'It's possible the driver sustained injuries during the collision: whiplash, something like that. We sent a patrol car to A&E on the night, but we should follow up with more specific slow-time enquiries, in case they didn't seek treatment straight away.'

'That's good thinking,' Ray said. The suggestion stirred something at the back of his mind, but he couldn't place it. 'Don't forget to check Southmead and the Frenchay, as well.' His phone, face down on the table in front of him, vibrated with an incoming text message, and Ray picked it up to read it. 'Shit.'

The others looked up at him, Kate in surprise and Stumpy with a grin.

'What have you forgotten to do?' he said.

Ray grimaced but didn't explain. He drained his pint and pulled a tenner out of his pocket, handing it to Stumpy. 'Get a drink for the pair of you – I need to get home.'

Mags was loading the dishwasher when he walked in, dropping the plates into the rack with such force Ray winced. Her hair was tied back in a loose plait, and she wore tracksuit bottoms and an old T-shirt of his. He wondered when she had stopped caring about what she wore, and straight away hated himself for the thought. He was hardly one to talk.

'I'm so sorry,' he said. 'I completely forgot.'

Mags opened a bottle of red wine. She had only got out one glass, Ray noticed, but he decided it would be unwise to mention it.

'It's very rare,' she said, 'that I ask you to be somewhere at a particular time. I know that sometimes the job has to come first. I get that. I really do. But this appointment has been in the diary for two weeks. Two weeks! And you promised, Ray.'

Her voice wobbled, and Ray put a tentative arm around her. 'I am sorry, Mags. Was it awful?'

'It was okay.' She shrugged off Ray's arm and sat at the kitchen table, taking a deep slug of wine. 'I mean, they didn't say anything dreadful, only that Tom doesn't seem to have settled into school as well as the other kids and they're a bit worried about him.'

'So what are the teachers doing about it?' Ray fetched a wine glass from the cupboard, filled it, and joined Mags at the table. 'Presumably they've spoken to him?'

'Apparently Tom says everything's fine.' Mags shrugged. 'Mrs Hickson has tried everything she can to motivate him and get him to be more engaged in class, but he won't say a word. She said she had wondered if he was simply one of the quiet ones.'

Ray snorted. 'Quiet? Tom?'

'Well, exactly.' Mags looked at Ray. 'I really could have done with you there, you know.'

'It totally slipped my mind. I'm so sorry, Mags. It was another full-on day, and then I popped to the pub for a quick pint.'

'With Stumpy?'

Ray nodded. Mags had a soft spot for Stumpy, who was Tom's godfather, and indulged his and Ray's after-work pints with the tolerance of a wife who recognises a husband's need for 'man time'. He didn't mention Kate, and he wasn't entirely sure why.

Mags sighed. 'What are we going to do?'

'He'll be fine. Look, it's a new school, and it's a huge deal for kids, moving up to secondary school. He's been a big fish in a small pond for a long time, and now he's swimming with the sharks. I'll speak to him.'

'Don't give him one of your lectures—'

'I'm not going to give him a lecture!'

'—it'll only make things worse.'

Ray bit his tongue. He and Mags were a good team, but they had very different approaches when it came to parenting. Mags was much softer with the kids; more inclined to molly-coddle them instead of letting them stand on their own two feet.

'I won't give him a lecture,' he promised.

'The school has suggested we see how things go for the next couple of months, and have another chat to them a few weeks after half term.' Mags looked pointedly at Ray.

'Name the date,' he said. 'I'll be there.'

6

Headlights glint on wet tarmac, the dazzle blinding them every few seconds. People scurry past on slippery pavements; passing cars sending spray over their shoes. Piles of leaves lie in sodden heaps against railings, their bright colours darkening to dull brown.

An empty road.

Jacob running.

The squeal of wet brakes, the thud as he hits the car and the spin of his body before it slams on to the road. A blurred windscreen. Blood pooling beneath Jacob's head. A single cloud of white breath.

The scream cuts through my sleep, jolting me awake. The sun isn't up yet, but the light in the bedroom is on: I can't bear to feel the darkness around me. Heart pounding, I concentrate on slowing my breathing.

In and out.

In and out.

The silence is oppressive rather than calming, and my fingernails carve crescents into my palms as I wait for the panic to subside. My dreams are becoming more intense, more vivid. I *see* him. I hear the sickening crack of his head on the tarmac . . .

The nightmares didn't start straight away, but now they're here, they won't stop. I lie in bed each night, fighting sleep and playing out scenarios in my head like those children's books where the reader chooses the ending. I squeeze my eyes tightly shut and walk through my alternative ending: the one where we set off five minutes earlier, or five minutes later. The one where Jacob lives, and is even now asleep in his bed, dark eyelashes resting upon rounded cheeks. But nothing changes. Each night I will myself to wake earlier, as though by disturbing the nightmare I can somehow reverse reality. But it seems a pattern has been set, and for weeks now I have woken several times a night to the thud of a small body on the bumper, and to my own fruitless scream as he rolls off and slams on to the wet road.

I have become a hermit, cloistered within the stone walls of this cottage, venturing no further than the village shop to buy milk, and living off little more than toast and coffee. Three times I've decided to visit Bethan at the caravan park; three times I've changed my mind. I wish I could make myself go. It's been a very long time since I had a friend, and just as long since I have needed one.

I make a fist with my left hand, then unfurl my fingers, stiff from a night's sleep. The pain rarely troubles me now, but I have no sensation in my palm, and two of my fingers have stayed numb. I squeeze my hand to chase away the pins and needles. I should have gone to the hospital, of course, but it seemed so insignificant in comparison to what had happened to Jacob; the pain so justly deserved. So instead I bandaged the injury as best I could, gritting my teeth as each day I pulled away the dressing from the damaged skin. Gradually it healed: the life line on my palm hidden forever beneath a layer of scars.

I swing my legs out from under the pile of blankets on my bed. There is no heating upstairs, and the walls glisten with condensation. I swiftly pull on tracksuit bottoms and a dark-green sweatshirt, leaving my hair tucked into the collar, and pad downstairs. The cold floor tiles make me gasp and I slide my feet into trainers, before pulling back the bolt to unlock the front door. I have always been an early riser; up with the sun to work in my studio. I feel lost without my work, as though I am flailing around looking for a new identity.

In the summer there will be tourists, I suppose. Not at this hour, and perhaps not as far inland as my cottage, but on the beach, certainly. But for now it is mine, and the solitude is comforting. A dull winter sun pushes its way over the clifftop, and there is an icy glint on the puddles punctuating the coastal path that runs around the bay. I begin to run, my breath leaving bursts of mist in my wake. I never jogged in Bristol, but here I make myself go on for miles.

I settle into a rhythm that echoes my heart, and run steadily towards the sea. My shoes make a noise as they hit the stony floor, but my daily runs have made me sure-footed. The path leading down on to the beach is so familiar now I could walk it blindfold, and I jump the last few feet on to the damp sand. Hugging the cliff, I jog slowly around the bay, until the line of rocks pushes me towards the sea.

The tide is as far out as it can go, a line of driftwood and tattered rubbish left on the sand like a dirty ring around a bathtub. Turning away from the cliff, I up my pace and sprint through the shallows, wet sand sucking at my feet. My head bent low against the biting wind, I fight the tide and run full-pelt along the shore until my lungs burn and I can hear the blood whistling in my ears. As I draw near to the end of the sands, the opposing cliff looms up above me, but instead of checking my pace, I speed up. The wind whips my hair across my face and I shake my head to clear it. I run faster, and the split-second before I smash into the waiting cliff, I stretch my arms in front of me and slam my hands against the cold rock. Alive. Awake. Safe from nightmares.

As the adrenalin leaves me I start to shake, and I walk back the way I came. The wet sand has swallowed my footprints, leaving no trace of my sprint between the cliffs. There is a piece of driftwood by my feet and I pick it up and idly drag a channel around me, but the beach closes around the wood before I have even lifted it from the ground. Frustrated, I walk a few paces inland, where the sand is drying, and trace another circle with the stick. It's better. I have a sudden urge to write my name in the sand, like a toddler on holiday, and I smile at my childishness. The driftwood is unwieldy and slippery but I finish the letters and stand back to admire my handiwork. It seems strange to see my name so bold and unashamed. I've been invisible for so long, and what am I now? A sculptor who doesn't sculpt. A mother without a child. The letters are not invisible. They are shouting: large enough to be seen from the clifftops. I feel a shiver of fear and excitement. I'm taking a risk, but it feels good.

At the top of the cliff an ineffective fence reminds walkers not to stray too close to the crumbling rock edge. I ignore the sign and step over the wire to stand inches away from the drop. The expanse of sand is slowly turning from grey to gold as the sun climbs higher, and my name dances across the middle of the beach, daring me to catch it before it disappears.

I'll take a picture of it before the tide comes in and swallows it up, I decide, so I can capture the moment I felt brave. I run back to the cottage for my camera. My steps feel lighter now and I realise it's because I'm running towards something, and not away from it.

That first photograph is nothing special. The framing is all wrong, the letters too far from the shore. I run back down to the beach, covering the smooth stretch of sand with names from my past, before letting them sink back into the wet sand. Others I write further up the beach; characters from books I read as a child, or names I love simply for the sweep of the letters they contain. Then I bring out my camera, crouching low to the sand as I play with the angles, layering my words first with the surf, then with rocks, then with a rich slash of blue sky. Finally,

I climb the steep path to the top of the cliff to take my final shots, balancing precariously on the edge, turning my back on the clutch of fear it gives me. The beach is covered with writing of all sizes, like the scribbled ramblings of a madman, but I can already see the incoming tide licking at the letters, swirling the sand as it inches up the beach. By this evening, when the tide retreats once more, the beach will be clean, and I can start again.

I have no sense of what time it is now, but the sun is high, and I must have a hundred photos on my camera. Wet sand clings to my clothes and when I touch my hair it's stiff with salt. I don't have any gloves, and my fingers are painfully cold. I will go home and have a hot bath, then load the photos on to my laptop and see if I've taken anything passable. I feel a surge of energy; it's the first time since the accident that my day has had purpose.

I head towards the cottage, but when I reach the fork in the path I hesitate. I picture Bethan at the caravan park shop, and the way she reminded me of my sister. I feel an ache of homesickness and before I can change my mind I take the path leading to the caravan park. What reason can I give for visiting the shop? I don't have any money with me, so I can't pretend I've come for milk or bread. I might ask a question, I suppose, but I struggle to think of something plausible. Whatever I come up with, Bethan will know it is an excuse. She'll think I'm pathetic.

My resolve fades before I've walked a hundred yards, and when I reach the car park I stop. I look across to the shop and see a shape in the window – I can't tell if it's Bethan and I don't wait to find out. I turn and run back to the cottage.

I reach Blaen Cedi and pull the key from my pocket, but when I put my hand on the door it moves a little, and I realise it isn't locked. The door is old and the mechanism unreliable: Iestyn showed me how to pull the door just so, and turn the key at such an angle it clicks home, but at times I've spent ten minutes or more trying. He left me his number, but he doesn't know I threw away my mobile phone. There's a phone line to the cottage, but no telephone installed, so I will have to walk to Penfach and find a telephone box to see if he'll come and fix it.

I have only been inside for a few minutes, when there is a knock at the door.

'Jenna? It's Bethan.'

I contemplate staying where I am, but my curiosity gets the better of me, and I feel a leap of excitement as I open the door. For all that I sought an escape, I'm lonely here in Penfach.

'I brought you a pie.' Bethan holds up a tea-towel-covered dish and comes in without waiting for an invitation. She puts it down in the kitchen next to the range.

'Thank you.' I search for small talk, but Bethan just smiles. She takes off her heavy woollen coat and the action galvanises me. 'Would you like tea?'

'If you're making,' she says. 'I thought I'd come by and see how you're doing. I did wonder if you might have popped in to see me before now, but I know what it's like when you're settling into a new place.' She looks around the cottage and stops talking, taking in the sparse sitting room, no different from when Iestyn first brought me here.

'I don't have much,' I say, embarrassed.

'None of us does, round here,' Bethan says cheerfully. 'As long as you're warm and comfortable, that's the main thing.'

I move around the kitchen as she talks, making the tea, grateful for something to do with my hands, and we sit at the pine table with our mugs.

'How are you finding Blaen Cedi?'

'It's perfect,' I say. 'Exactly what I needed.'

'Tiny and cold, you mean?' Bethan says, with a ripple of laughter that slops tea over the rim of her mug. She gives an ineffective rub at her trousers and the liquid sinks into a dark patch on her thigh.

'I don't need much room, and the fire keeps me warm enough.' I smile. 'Really, I like it.'

'So what's your story, Jenna? How did you come to be in Penfach?'

'It's beautiful here,' I say simply, wrapping my hands around my mug and looking down into it, to avoid meeting Bethan's sharp eyes. She doesn't push me.

'That's true enough. There are worse places to live, although it's bleak at this time of year.'

'When do you start letting the caravans?'

'We open at Easter,' Bethan says, 'then it's all systems go for the summer months – you won't recognise the place – and we finally wind down after the October half-term. Let me know if you've got family visiting and need a 'van – you'll never squeeze guests in here.'

'That's kind of you, but I'm not expecting anyone to visit.'

'You don't have any family?' Bethan looks directly at me, and I find myself unable to drop my gaze.

'I have a sister,' I admit, 'but we don't speak any more.'

'What happened?'

'Oh, the usual sibling tensions,' I say lightly. Even now, I can see Eve's angry face as she implored me to listen to her. I was too proud, I can see that now; too blinded by love. Perhaps if I had listened to Eve, things would have been different.

'Thank you for the pie,' I say. 'It's very kind of you.'

'Nonsense,' Bethan says, unperturbed by the change in subject. She puts on her coat and wraps a scarf several times round her neck. 'What are neighbours for? Now, you'll be dropping in for tea at the caravan park before too long.'

It's not a question, but I nod. She fixes me with rich brown eyes and I suddenly feel like a child again.

'I will,' I say. 'I promise.' And I mean it.

When Bethan has gone I take the memory stick from my camera and load the photos on to my laptop. Most are no use, but there are a few that capture perfectly the writing in the sand, against a backdrop of fierce winter sea. I put the kettle on the range to make more tea, but I lose track of time, and it's half an hour later when I realise it still hasn't boiled. I put out a hand only to discover the range is stone cold. It's gone out again. I was so engrossed in editing photos that I didn't notice the temperature falling, but now my teeth start to chatter and I can't make them stop. I look at Bethan's chicken pie and feel my stomach growl with hunger. The last time this happened it took me two days to relight it, and my heart sinks at the thought of a repeat performance.

I shake myself. When did I become so pathetic? When did I lose the ability to make decisions; to solve problems? I'm better than this.

'Right,' I say out loud, my voice sounding strange in the empty kitchen. 'Let's sort this out.'

The sun is rising over Penfach before I am warm again. My knees are stiff after hours spent crouching on the kitchen floor, and I have smears of grease in my hair. But I have a sense of achievement I haven't felt in a long time, as I place Bethan's pie in the range to warm through. I don't care that it's closer to breakfast than supper, or that my hunger pangs have been and gone. I set the table for dinner, and I relish every single bite.

7

'Come on!' Ray bellowed up the stairs to Tom and Lucy, looking at his watch for the fifth time in as many minutes. 'We're going to be late!'

As if Monday mornings weren't stressful enough, Mags had spent the night at her sister's and wasn't due back until lunchtime, so Ray had been flying solo for twenty-four hours. He had – rather unwisely, he now saw – allowed the children to stay up late to watch a film the previous night, and had had to prise even the ever-chirpy Lucy out of bed at seven-thirty. Now it was eight-thirty-five and they were going to have to get a shift on. Ray had been summoned to the chief constable's office at nine-thirty, and at this rate he was still going to be standing at the foot of the stairs shouting at his children.

'Get a move on!' Ray marched out to the car and started the engine, leaving the front door swinging open. Lucy came racing through it, unbrushed hair flying about her face, and slid into the front seat beside her dad. Her navy school skirt was crumpled, and one knee-length sock was already round her ankle. A full minute later Tom sauntered out to the car, his shirt untucked and flapping in the breeze. He had his tie in his hand and showed no sign of putting it on. He was going through a growth spurt and carried his new-found height awkwardly, his head permanently bowed and his shoulders stooped.

Ray opened his window. 'Door, Tom!'

'Huh?' Tom looked at Ray.

'The front door?' Ray clenched his fists. How Mags did this

every day without losing her temper, he would never know. The list of things he had to do loomed large in his mind, and he could have done without the school run today of all days.

'Oh.' Tom meandered back to the house and pulled the front door closed with a bang. He got into the back seat. 'How come Lucy's in the front?'

'It's my turn.'

'It isn't.'

'It is.'

'Enough!' Ray roared.

Nobody spoke, and by the time they had driven the five minutes to Lucy's primary school, Ray's blood pressure had subsided. He parked his Mondeo on yellow zig-zags and marched Lucy round to her classroom, kissing her on the forehead and legging it back just in time to find a woman noting down his registration number.

'Oh, it's you!' she said, when he skidded to a halt by the car. She wagged her finger. 'I would have thought you would have known better, Inspector.'

'Sorry,' Ray said. 'Urgent job. You know how it is.'

He left her tapping her pencil on her notepad. Bloody PTA mafia, he thought. Too much time on their hands, that was the trouble.

'So,' Ray started, glancing over to the passenger seat. Tom had slid into the front as soon as Lucy had got out, but he was staring resolutely out of the window. 'How's school?'

'Fine.'

Tom's teacher said that while things hadn't got worse, they certainly hadn't got better. He and Mags had gone to the school and heard a report of a boy who had no friends, didn't do more than the bare minimum in lessons, and never put himself forward.

'Mrs Hickson said there's a football club starting after school on Wednesdays. Do you fancy it?'

'Not really.'

'I used to be quite the player in my day – maybe some of it

has rubbed off on you, eh?' Even without looking at Tom, Ray knew the boy was rolling his eyes, and he winced at how much like his own father he was sounding.

Tom pushed his headphones into his ears.

Ray sighed. Puberty had turned his son into a grunting, uncommunicative teenager, and he was dreading the day the same thing happened to his daughter. You weren't supposed to have favourites, but he had a soft spot for Lucy, who at nine would still seek him out for a cuddle and insist on a bedtime story. Even before adolescent angst had hit, Tom and Ray had locked horns. Too similar, Mags said, although Ray couldn't see it.

'You can drop me here,' Tom said, unbuckling his seat belt while the car was still moving.

'But we're two streets away from the school.'

'Dad, it's fine. I'll walk.' He reached for the door handle and for a moment Ray thought he was going to open the door and simply hurl himself out.

'All right, I get it!' Ray pulled over to the side of the road, ignoring the road markings for the second time that morning. 'You know you're going to miss registration, don't you?'

'Laters.'

And with that, Tom was gone, slamming the car door and slipping between the traffic to cross the road. What on earth had happened to his kind, funny son? Was this terseness a rite of passage for a teenage boy – or something more? Ray shook his head. You'd think having kids would be a walk in the park compared to a complex crime investigation, but he'd take a suspect interview over a chat with Tom any day. And get more of a conversation, he thought wryly. Thank God Mags would be picking the kids up from school.

By the time Ray reached headquarters he had put Tom to the back of his mind. It didn't take a genius to work out why the chief constable wanted to see him. The hit-and-run was almost six months old and the investigation had all but ground to a halt. Ray sat on a chair outside the oak-panelled office, and the chief's PA gave him a sympathetic smile.

'She's just finishing up a call,' she said. 'It won't be much longer.'

Chief Constable Olivia Rippon was a brilliant but terrifying woman. Rising rapidly through the ranks, she had been Avon and Somerset's chief officer for seven years. At one stage tipped to be the next Met Commissioner, Olivia had 'for personal reasons' chosen to stay in her home force, where she took pleasure in reducing senior officers to gibbering wrecks at monthly performance meetings. She was one of those women who were born to wear uniform, her dark brown hair pulled into a severe bun, and solid legs hidden beneath thick black tights.

Ray rubbed his palms on his trouser legs to make sure they were perfectly dry. He had heard a rumour that the chief had once blocked a promising officer's promotion to chief inspector because the poor man's sweaty palms didn't 'inspire confidence'. Ray had no idea if it was true, but he wasn't going to take any chances. They could get by on his inspector salary, but things were a bit tight. Mags was still on about becoming a teacher, but Ray had done the sums, and if he could manage another couple of promotions, they'd have the extra money they needed without her having to work. Ray thought about the morning's chaos and decided Mags already did more than enough – she shouldn't have to get a job just so they could afford a few luxuries.

'You can go in now,' the PA said.

Ray took a deep breath and pushed open the door. 'Good morning, ma'am.'

There was silence as the chief made copious notes on a pad in her trademark illegible handwriting. Ray loitered by the door and pretended to admire the numerous certificates and photographs that littered the walls. The navy blue carpet was thicker and plusher than in the rest of the building, and an enormous conference table dominated one half of the room. At the far end, Olivia Rippon sat at a big curved desk. Finally, she stopped writing and looked up.

'I want you to close the Fishponds hit-and-run case.'

It was clear he wasn't going to be offered a seat, so Ray picked the chair closest to Olivia, and sat down regardless. She raised an eyebrow, but said nothing.

'I think that if we just had a little more time—'

'You've had time,' Olivia said. 'Five and a half months, to be exact. It's an embarrassment, Ray. Every time the *Post* prints another of your so-called updates, it simply serves as a reminder of a case the police have failed to solve. Councillor Lewis rang me last night: he wants it buried, and so do I.'

Ray felt the anger building inside him. 'Isn't Lewis the one who opposed the residents' bid for the limit on the estates to be dropped to twenty miles per hour?'

There was a beat, and Olivia regarded him coolly.

'Close it, Ray.'

They looked at each other across the smooth walnut desk without speaking. Surprisingly, it was Olivia who gave in first, sitting back in her chair and clasping her hands in front of her.

'You are an exceptionally good detective, Ray, and your tenacity does you credit. But if you want to progress, you need to accept that policing is about politics as much as it is investigating crime.'

'I do understand that, ma'am.' Ray fought to keep the frustration out of his voice.

'Good,' Olivia said, taking the lid off her pen and reaching for the next memo in her in-tray. 'Then we're in agreement. The case will be closed today.'

For once Ray was glad of the traffic that held him up on his way back to CID. He was not looking forward to telling Kate, and he wondered why that should be his overriding thought. She was so new to CID still, he supposed: she wouldn't yet have been through the frustrations of having to file an investigation in which so much energy had been invested. Stumpy would be more resigned.

As soon as he got back to the station, he called them into his office. Kate came in first, carrying a mug of coffee she put down next to his computer, where three others sat, each half-full of cold black coffee.

'Are they from last week?'

'Yep – the cleaner refuses to wash them up any more.'

'I'm not surprised. You can do them yourself, you know.' Kate sat down, just as Stumpy came in and nodded a greeting to Ray.

'Do you remember the car Brian and Pat saw on the CCTV for the hit-and-run?' Kate said, as soon as Stumpy was sitting down. 'The one that seemed to be in a hurry to get away?'

Ray nodded.

'We can't make out what type of car it is from the footage we've got, and I'd like to take it to Wesley. If nothing else we might be able to eliminate it from our enquiries.'

Wesley Barton was an anaemic, scrawny individual who had somehow secured approval as a police CCTV expert. Working from a windowless basement in a stuffy house on Redland Road, he used a staggering array of equipment to enhance CCTV images until they were suitable to be used as evidence. Ray assumed Wesley must be clean, given his police association, but there was something seedy about the whole set-up that made him shudder.

'I'm sorry, Kate, but I can't authorise the budget for that,' Ray said. He hated the thought of telling her all her hard work was about to come to an abrupt end. Wesley was expensive, but he was good, and Ray was impressed with Kate's lateral thinking. He hated admitting it, even to himself, but he'd taken his eye off the ball in recent weeks. All this business with Tom was distracting him, and for a moment he felt a stab of resentment towards his son. It was inexcusable to let his home life affect work, particularly such a high-profile case as this one. Not that it mattered, he thought bitterly, now that the chief had issued her decree.

'It's not a huge cost,' Kate said, 'I've spoken to him, and—'

Ray cut her off. 'I can't authorise the budget on anything,' he said meaningfully. Stumpy looked at Ray. He'd been around the block enough times to know what was coming next.

'The chief has told me to close the investigation,' Ray said, keeping his eyes on Kate.

There was a brief pause.

'I hope you told her where to stick it.' Kate laughed, but no one joined in. She looked between Ray and Stumpy, and her face fell. 'Are you serious? We're just going to give up on it?'

'There's nothing to give up on,' Ray said. 'There isn't anything else we can do. You've got nowhere with tracing the fog light casing—'

'There are a dozen or more index numbers outstanding,' Kate said. 'You wouldn't believe the number of mechanics who don't keep paperwork for their jobs. That doesn't mean I won't be able to trace them, it just means I need more time.'

'It's a waste of effort,' Ray said gently. 'Sometimes you have to know when to stop.'

'We've done everything we can,' Stumpy said, 'but it's like looking for a needle in a haystack. No index number, no colour, no make or model: we need more, Kate.'

Ray was grateful for Stumpy's backing. 'And we don't have more,' he said. 'So I'm afraid we need to draw a line under this investigation for the time being. Obviously, if a genuine development comes in, we'll follow it up, but otherwise . . .' He trailed off, conscious that he was sounding like one of the chief's press releases.

'This is down to politics, isn't it?' Kate said. 'The chief says "jump" and we say "How high?"' Ray realised how personally she was taking this.

'Come on, Kate, you've been in the job long enough to know that sometimes there are difficult choices to make.' He stopped abruptly, not wanting to patronise her. 'Look, it's been nearly six months and we have nothing concrete to go on. No witnesses, no forensics, nothing. We could throw all the resources in the world at this job and we'd still have no solid leads. I'm sorry, but we've got other investigations, other victims to fight for.'

'Did you even try?' Kate said, her cheeks flushed with anger. 'Or did you just roll over?'

'Kate,' Stumpy said warningly, 'you need to calm down.'

She ignored him and stared defiantly at Ray. 'I suppose you've got your promotion to think about. It wouldn't do to pick a fight with the chief, would it?'

'That has nothing to do with it!' Ray was trying to remain calm, but the retort came out louder than he had intended. They stared at each other. From the corner of his eye he could see Stumpy looking at him expectantly. Ray should be telling Kate to get out. To remember she was a DC in a busy CID office, and that if her boss said a case was closing, then it was closing. End of. He opened his mouth but couldn't speak.

The trouble was that she was spot on. Ray didn't want to close the hit-and-run job any more than Kate did, and there was a time when he'd have stood in front of the chief and argued his case the way Kate was doing now. Maybe he'd lost his touch, or maybe Kate was right: perhaps he did have too much of an eye on the next rank.

'It's tough, when you've put a lot of work in, I know,' he said gently.

'It's not the work' – Kate pointed to the photo of Jacob on the wall – 'it's that little boy. It just seems wrong.'

Ray remembered Jacob's mother sitting on the sofa, grief etched on her face. He couldn't counter Kate's argument, and he didn't try. 'I'm really sorry.' He cleared his throat, and tried to focus on something else. 'What else has the team got on at the moment?' he asked Stumpy.

'Malcolm's in court all week on the Grayson job, and he's

got a file to get in on the GBH in Queen's Street – CPS have gone for a charge. I'm working on the intel from the Co-op robberies, and Dave's seconded to the knife crime initiative. He's at the college today doing some "community engagement".'

Stumpy uttered the term as though it were a swear word, and Ray laughed.

'Gotta move with the times, Stumpy.'

'You can talk to those kids till you're blue in the face,' Stumpy said. 'It's not going to stop them carrying a blade.'

'Well, maybe, but at least we'll have tried.' Ray scribbled a reminder to himself in his diary. 'Let me have an update before morning meeting tomorrow, will you? And I'd like your thoughts on a knife amnesty to coincide with the school holidays. Let's try and get as many off the streets as we can.'

'Will do.'

Kate was staring at the floor, picking at the skin around her fingernails. Stumpy thumped her gently on the arm, and she turned to look at him.

'Bacon sandwich?' he said quietly.

'It won't make me feel better,' Kate muttered.

'No,' Stumpy continued, 'but it might make me feel better if you don't spend all morning with a face like a bulldog chewing a wasp.'

Kate gave a half-hearted laugh. 'I'll see you up there.'

There was a pause, and Ray saw she was waiting until Stumpy had left the room. He closed the door and returned to his desk, sitting down and folding his arms in front of him. 'Are you okay?'

Kate nodded. 'I wanted to apologise, I shouldn't have spoken to you like that.'

'I've had worse,' Ray said with a grin. Kate didn't smile and he realised she wasn't in the mood for jokes. 'I know this case means a lot to you,' he said.

Kate looked again at Jacob's photo. 'I feel like I've let him down.'

Ray felt his own defences crumble. It was true, they had let Jacob down, but it wouldn't help Kate to hear that. 'You've given everything you had,' he said. 'That's all you can ever do.'

'It wasn't enough though, was it?' She turned to look at Ray and he shook his head.

'No. It wasn't enough.'

Kate left his office, closing the door behind her, and Ray thumped his desk hard. His pen rolled across the desktop and dropped on to the floor. He leaned back in his chair and laced his fingers together behind his head. His hair felt thin and he closed his eyes, feeling suddenly very old and very tired. Ray thought of the senior officers he came across on a daily basis: most older than him, but a fair few younger, hurtling through the ranks without stopping. Did he have the energy to compete with them? Did he even want to?

All those years ago, when Ray joined the job, it had seemed very simple. Lock up the bad guys and keep the good folk safe. Pick up the pieces from stabbings and assaults; rapes and criminal damages, and do his bit to make the world a better place. But was he really doing that? Stuck in his office from 8 a.m. to 8 p.m. most days, only getting out to a job when he turned a blind eye to the paperwork; forced to toe the corporate line even when it went against everything he believed.

Ray looked at Jacob's file; stuffed with the results of wild-goose chases and fruitless enquiries. He thought of the bitterness on Kate's face, and her disappointment that he hadn't fought harder against the chief's decision, and he hated the fact that she thought less of him as a result. But the chief's words were still ringing in his ears, and Ray knew better than to go against direct orders, no matter how strongly Kate felt about it. He picked up Jacob's file and placed it firmly in the bottom drawer of his desk.

8

The sky has been threatening rain since I came down on to the beach at dawn, and I pull up my hood against the first drops. I've already taken the shots I wanted, and the beach is filled with words. I've become adept at keeping the sand around my letters smooth and untouched, and more skilled at handling my camera. I studied photography as part of my art degree, but sculpture was always my great passion. Now I'm enjoying getting to know the camera again, playing with the settings in different lights, and carrying it everywhere with me so it becomes as much a part of me as the lumps of clay I used to work with. And although my hand still throbs after a day holding it, I have enough movement left to take pictures. I've taken to coming down here every morning, while the sand is damp enough to be malleable, but I often return in the afternoon when the sun is at its highest. I'm learning the times of the tides and for the first time since the accident I'm starting to think about the future; looking forward to the summer, to seeing the sun on the beach. The caravan park is open for the tourist season now, and Penfach is full of people. I find it funny how 'local' I have become already: grumbling about the onslaught of tourists; possessive about my quiet beach.

The sand becomes pockmarked from the rain, and the swollen tide begins to sweep away the shapes I have made in the wet sand at the bottom of the beach, undoing the triumphs as well as the mistakes. It has become routine to begin each day by writing my own name close to the shore, and I shiver to see it sucked into the sea. Even though photographs of my morning's work are safely inside my camera, I'm not used to this lack of permanence. There is no lump of clay I can return to again and again, perfecting its shape, revealing its true form. By necessity I have to work quickly, and I find the process both exhilarating and exhausting.

The rain is insistent, working its way inside my coat and the tops of my boots. When I turn to leave the beach, I see a man walking towards me, a large dog loping along beside him. I hold my breath. He's still some distance from me, and I can't tell if he's deliberately approaching me, or simply heading towards the sea. There is a metallic taste in my mouth and I lick my lips, searching for moisture but finding only salt. I've seen this man and his dog before: I watched from the clifftop yesterday morning until they left, and the beach was empty again. Despite the acres of open space, I feel trapped, and I begin walking along the water's edge, as though I'd always intended to wander this way.

'Morning!' He alters his path slightly until he is walking parallel to me.

I can't speak.

'Lovely day for a walk,' he says, tipping his head up to the sky. He's in his fifties, I think: grey hair under a waxed hat, a closely trimmed beard covering almost half of his face.

I let out a slow breath. 'I must get back,' I say vaguely. 'I have to . . .'

'Enjoy your day.' The man gives a tiny nod of his head and calls for his dog, and I turn inland and jog towards the cliff. Halfway across the beach I turn and check behind me, but the man is still down by the water's edge, throwing a stick into the sea for his dog. My heartbeat slowly returns to normal, and now I just feel absurd.

By the time I've climbed to the top of the cliff I'm soaked through. I decide to visit Bethan, walking quickly to the caravan park before I can change my mind.

Bethan greets me with a broad smile.

'I'll put the kettle on.'

She busies herself at the back of the shop, keeping up a cheery monologue about the weather forecast, the threatened closure of bus routes and Iestyn's broken fence, which resulted in seventy goats escaping overnight.

'Alwen Rees wasn't best pleased, I can tell you!'

I laugh – less at the tale itself and more at Bethan's telling of it, which is accompanied by the flamboyant hand gestures of a born performer. I wander around the shop while she finishes the tea. The floor is concrete, and the walls whitewashed, with shelves that cover two sides of the room. The first time I came here they were empty: now they're packed with cereal, tins, fresh fruit and veg, ready for holiday-makers. A large chiller cabinet houses a few cartons of milk and other fresh produce. I pick up some cheese.

'That's Iestyn's goat cheese,' Bethan says. 'You're as well to get some while you can – it flies out of the door when we're busy. Now, come and sit down by the heater and tell me how you're getting on up there.' A black-and-white kitten mews by her ankles and she picks it up and drapes it across her shoulder. 'You don't want a kitten for company, do you? I've three of these little ones to give away – our mouser had a litter a few weeks back. Heaven knows who the dad is.'

'No, thank you.' The kitten is absurdly sweet: a ball of fur with a twitching tail like a metronome. The sight of it causes a forgotten memory to surge to the surface, and I shrink back into my chair.

'Not a cat person?'

'I couldn't take care of one,' I say. 'I can't even keep a spider plant alive. Everything I look after dies.'

Bethan laughs, although I wasn't making a joke. She draws up a second chair, and puts down a mug of tea on the counter next to me.

'Been taking some snaps, have you?' Bethan indicates the camera around my neck.

'Just a few photos of the bay.'

'Can I see?'

I hesitate, but unhook the strap over my head and turn on the camera, showing Bethan how to flick between images on the screen.

'These are beautiful!'

'Thank you.' I feel myself blushing. I've never been good at receiving praise. As a child my teachers would commend my artwork, and display it in reception where visitors sat, but it wasn't until I was twelve that I began to realise I had a talent, albeit raw and unshaped. The school held an exhibition – a local show for parents and residents – and my parents came to see it together, which was a rarity, even then. My father stood in silence in front of the section where my paintings were displayed, along with a statue of a bird I had made from twisted metal. I held my breath for the longest time, and found myself crossing my fingers in the folds of my skirt.

'Incredible,' he said. He looked at me as though he were seeing me for the first time. 'You're incredible, Jenna.'

I could have burst with pride, and I slipped my hand in his and took him to Mrs Beeching, who talked about art colleges and bursaries and mentoring. And I just sat and gazed at my father, who thought I was incredible.

I'm glad that he isn't here any more. I would hate to see disappointment in his eyes.

Bethan is still looking at the landscapes I have taken of the bay. 'I mean it, Jenna, they're lovely photographs. Are you going to sell them?'

I almost laugh, but she isn't smiling and I realise it is a serious suggestion.

I wonder if it might be possible. Perhaps not these – I'm still practising, still getting the lighting right – but if I work on them . . . 'Maybe,' I say, surprising myself.

Bethan scrolls through the remaining photographs, laughing when she comes across her own name written in the sand.

'It's me!'

I flush. 'I was trying something out.'

'I love it – can I buy it?' Bethan holds up the camera and admires the photograph again.

'Don't be silly,' I say. 'I'll get it printed for you. It's the least I can do: you've been so kind.'

'The Post Office in the village has one of those machines where you can print them yourself,' Bethan says. 'I'd love this one, with my name, and this one here – where the tide is out.' She has chosen one of my favourites: I took it in the evening, as the sun was sinking beneath the horizon. The sea is almost flat, a shimmering mirror of pink and orange, and the surrounding cliffs nothing more than smooth silhouettes on either side.

'I'll get them done this afternoon.'

'Thank you,' Bethan says. She puts the camera firmly on the side and turns to face me, her no-nonsense look already familiar to me. 'Now, let me do something for you.'

'There's no need,' I begin, 'you've already—'

Bethan waves away my protestations. 'I've been having a sort-out, and there are a few things I need to get rid of.' She gestures to two black sacks sitting neatly by the door. 'Nothing exciting: cushions and throws from when we redid the static caravans, and some clothes that will never fit me again even if I gave up chocolate for the rest of my life. Not fancy stuff – there's not much call for ball gowns in Penfach – but some jumpers and jeans and a couple of dresses I should never have bought.'

'Bethan, you can't give me your clothes!'

'Why on earth not?'

'Because . . .'

She looks me straight in the eye and I trail off. She's so

68

matter-of-fact I can't feel embarrassed, and I can't keep wearing the same things day in, day out.

'Look, it's only stuff I'll end up taking to the charity shop. Have a sift through and take what you can use. It's common sense, isn't it?'

I leave the caravan park laden with warm clothes and a bag of what Bethan calls 'home comforts'. Back in the cottage I spread them all out on the floor like Christmas presents. The jeans are a little too big, but will be fine with a belt, and I almost weep at the softness of the thick fleece jumper she has put by for me. The cottage is freezing and I'm permanently cold. The few clothes I brought with me from Bristol – I realise I have stopped calling it 'home' – are worn and stiff from salt, and from washing by hand in the bathtub.

It's Bethan's 'home comforts' I am most excited by. I drape the battered sofa with an enormous patchwork bedspread in bright reds and greens, and immediately the room feels warmer and more welcoming. On the mantel is a collection of stones I gathered from the beach, polished smooth by the sea: I add to these a vase from Bethan's thrift-shop bag, and decide to collect some willow stems for it this afternoon. The promised cushions go on the floor, next to the fire, where I habitually sit to read or to edit my photographs. At the bottom of the bag I find two towels, a bathmat and another throw.

I don't believe for a second that Bethan was throwing all these things out, but I know her well enough not to query it.

There's a knock on the door and I stop what I'm doing. Bethan told me that Iestyn would be coming by today, but I wait for a moment, just in case.

'You in there, then?'

I pull back the bolt to open the door. Iestyn acknowledges me with his habitual gruffness, and I welcome him warmly. What I had at first taken for dismissal, even rudeness, I have come to realise is simply the hallmark of a man who keeps himself to himself, worrying more about the welfare of his goats than the sensibilities of his kinfolk.

'I brought you some logs,' he says, indicating the firewood stacked haphazardly in the trailer attached to his quad bike. 'Can't have you running out. I'll bring them in for you.'

'Can I make you a cup of tea?'

'Two sugars,' Iestyn shouts over his shoulder, as he strides back to the trailer. He begins piling logs into a bucket, and I put the kettle on.

'What do I owe you for the logs?' I ask, when we are sitting at the kitchen table drinking tea.

Iestyn shakes his head. 'It's odds and ends left over from a load I had. It's not good enough to sell.'

The wood he has stacked neatly by the fire will last for a month at least. I suspect Bethan's hand again, but I'm in no position to refuse such a generous gift. I must think of a way to repay him, and Bethan too.

Iestyn shrugs off my thanks. 'I wouldn't have recognised the place,' he says, looking around at the colourful throw and the collections of shells and reclaimed treasures. 'How's the range been? Not played you up too much?' He indicates the ancient Aga. 'They can be tricky buggers.'

'It's been fine, thank you.' I suppress a smile. I've become an old hand now; coaxing the range into life again within minutes. It's a small success, but I store it away with the others, stacking them up as though they might one day cancel out the failures.

'Well, I must be going,' Iestyn says. 'The family's coming this weekend and you'd think they were royalty, the amount Glynis has been flapping. I told her, they don't care if the house is clean or there are flowers in the dining room, but she wants everything right for them.' He rolls his eyes in apparent exasperation, but his tone is soft as he speaks about his wife.

'Is it your children visiting?' I ask him.

70

'Both daughters,' he says, 'with their husbands and the little ones. It'll be a squeeze, but nobody minds when it's family, do they?' He bids me goodbye and I watch his quad bike bounce across the uneven ground.

I shut the door and stand there, looking at the cottage. The sitting room, which just a moment ago seemed so cosy and welcoming, now feels empty. I imagine a child – my child – playing on the rug in front of the fire. I think of Eve, and the niece and nephew growing up without me in their lives. I may have lost my son, but I still have a family, no matter what happened between us.

I got on well with Eve when we were children, despite the four-year age gap between us. I looked up to Eve, and in turn she cared for me, seeming never to resent her baby sister tagging along. We were quite different; me with my unruly auburn mop, and Eve with poker-straight mouse-brown hair. We both did well at school, but Eve was more diligent than me, burying her head in a textbook long after I had flung my own across the room. Instead I spent hours in the art studio at school, or on the floor of the garage – the only part of our home where my mother allowed me to pull out my clay and paints. My fastidious sister would turn her nose up at such pursuits, squealing as she ran away from my outstretched arms, splattered with wet clay. 'Lady Eve', I called her one day, and the name stuck, long after we had grown up and built our own families. Eve secretly enjoyed the moniker, I always thought, as over the years I watched her take compliments for a wonderful dinner party, or beautiful gift-wrapping.

We weren't as close after Dad left. I could never forgive our mother for driving him away, and didn't understand how Eve could do so. Nevertheless I miss my sister desperately, now more than ever. Five years of someone's life is too much to lose over a throwaway comment.

I look on my laptop and find the photos Bethan has asked for. I add three more that I want to put on the wall of the cottage in frames I'll make from driftwood. They are all of the bay: all taken from exactly the same point, but each quite different. The bright blue water of the first picture, sunlight sparkling across the bay, gives way to the flat grey of the second photo, the sun barely visible in the sky. The third picture is my favourite: taken when the winds were so high it was all I could do to keep my balance on the clifftop, and even the gulls had given up their perpetual sweep of the skies. The photo shows black clouds streaking downwards as the sea hurls its waves in their faces. The bay was so alive that day, I had felt my heartbeat pulse through me as I worked.

I add one more photo to my memory stick: a photo taken that first day I wrote in the sand, when I filled the beach with names from my past.

Lady Eve.

I can't risk my sister knowing where I am, but I can tell her that I'm safe. And that I'm sorry.

9

'I'm going to Harry's for lunch, boss, do you want anything?'

Kate appeared in the doorway to Ray's office. She wore tailored grey trousers and a close-fitting sweater, over which she had put on a light jacket, in preparation for heading out.

Ray got to his feet and plucked his jacket from the back of the chair. 'I'll come with you – I could do with some fresh air.' He usually ate in the canteen, or at his desk, but lunch with Kate was a more appealing prospect. Besides, the sun was finally shining, and he hadn't looked up from his desk since he got in at eight that morning. He deserved a break.

Harry's was busy, as always, with a queue that snaked along the counter and on to the pavement. It was popular with officers not only because of its proximity to the station, but because the sandwiches were sensibly priced, and quickly put together. There was nothing more frustrating for a hungry response cop than picking up an immediate before the lunch order turned up.

They shuffled forward in the queue. 'I can bring yours back to the office if you're in a hurry,' she said, but Ray shook his head.

'I'm in no rush,' he told her. 'I'm going through the plans for Operation Break and I could do with some time out. Let's eat in.'

'Good idea. Break is the laundering job, right?' Kate spoke quietly, mindful of the people around them, and Ray nodded.

'That's right. I can take you through the file, if you like, so you get a feel for how it's come together.'

'Great, thanks.'

They ordered their sandwiches and found a couple of high stools in the window, one eye on Harry, who within minutes was waving their brown paper bags in the air. A pair of uniformed officers walked past the window and Ray raised his hand in greeting.

'More fuel for the "CID don't do any work" argument,' he said to Kate with a laugh.

'They don't know the half of it,' Kate said, picking tomato out of her sandwich and eating it separately. 'I've never worked as hard as I did on the Jacob Jordan case. And all for nothing.'

Ray couldn't miss the bitterness in her voice. 'It wasn't for nothing, you know that. One day someone will talk about what they did, and word will spread, and we'll have them.'

'That's not good policing, though.'

'What do you mean?' Ray wasn't sure if he was amused or insulted by her directness.

Kate put down her sandwich. 'It's reactive, not proactive. We shouldn't be sitting back, waiting for intelligence to come to us: we should be out there looking for it.'

It was like listening to an echo of himself in his early days as a DC. Or perhaps Mags, although he didn't remember Mags being quite so assertive as Kate. She was eating her sandwich again now, but even that was done with a degree of determination. Ray hid a smile. She said exactly what came into her head, without any censorship or concern about whether it was her place to say it. She would ruffle a few feathers at the station, but Ray had no issue with plain-speaking. In fact he found it quite refreshing.

'It really got to you, didn't it?' Ray said.

She nodded. 'I hate the fact that the driver's still out there, thinking he's got away with it. And I hate that Jacob's mum left Bristol thinking we didn't care enough to find out who did it.' She opened her mouth to carry on, then looked away as though she had thought better of it.

'What?'

Her cheeks coloured slightly, but she raised her chin defiantly. 'I haven't stopped working on it.'

Over the years, Ray had on several occasions uncovered festering paperwork that had been ignored by officers either too busy or too lazy to action it. But doing *too* much work? That was a new one.

'It's been in my own time – and nothing that would get you in trouble with the chief, I promise. I've been reviewing the CCTV footage, and checking through the *Crimewatch* appeal calls to see if we missed anything.'

Ray thought of Kate sitting at home, case papers spread out on the floor, hours of grainy CCTV on the screen in front of her. 'And you did that because you think we can find the driver?'

'I did it because I don't want to give up.'

Ray smiled.

'Are you going to tell me to stop?' Kate bit her lip.

That was precisely what he had been about to say. But she was so keen, so single-minded. Besides, even if she never got any further with the investigation, what harm could it do? It was the sort of thing he might once have done himself.

'No,' he said. 'I'm not going to tell you to stop. Mainly because I'm not entirely convinced it would make a difference if I did.'

They both laughed.

'But I want you to keep me up to speed with what you're doing, and be sensible about how many hours you do. And this doesn't take priority over live jobs. Deal?'

Kate eyed him appraisingly. 'Deal. Thanks, Ray.'

He screwed up their paper bags into a ball. 'Come on, we'd better head back. I'll show you the Op Break file, then I need to get off home, else I'll be in trouble. Again.' He rolled his eyes in a mock grimace.

'I thought Mags didn't mind you working late?' Kate said, as they made their way back to the station.

'I don't think we're getting on too well lately,' he said, feeling instantly disloyal. He rarely spoke about his personal life to people at work, except to Stumpy, who had known Mags for almost as long as Ray had. But he was hardly shouting his mouth off: it was only Kate.

'You don't *think* so?' she laughed. 'Don't you know?'

Ray gave a wry smile. 'I don't feel I know anything at the moment. It's nothing I can put my finger on, just . . . oh, you know. We're having problems with our eldest, Tom. He's not settling in well at school, and he's become really moody and insular.'

'How old is he?'

'Twelve.'

'Sounds like normal behaviour for that age,' Kate said. 'My mum tells me I was an absolute horror.'

'Ha – I can believe that,' Ray said. Kate aimed a punch at him and he laughed. 'I know what you mean, but honestly, it's really unusual behaviour for Tom and it happened almost overnight.'

'Do you think he's being bullied?'

'It has crossed my mind. I don't like to ask too much in case he thinks I'm hassling him. Mags is better at that sort of stuff, but even she can't get anything out of him.' He sighed. 'Kids – who'd have 'em?'

'Not me,' Kate said, as they reached the station. She swiped her access fob to open the side door. 'Not for ages, anyway. There's far too much fun to be had first.' She laughed, and Ray felt a flash of envy for her uncomplicated life.

They walked up the stairs. When they got to the second-floor landing, where the CID office was, Ray paused with his hand on the door. 'About the Jordan job . . .'

'It's between you and me. I know.'

She grinned, and Ray gave an inward sigh of relief. If the chief knew he still had resources – even unpaid ones – on a job she had expressly ordered closed, she would waste no time in letting him know what she thought. He'd be back in uniform before she'd put the phone down.

Back in his office, he began working through the plans for Operation Break. The chief had asked him to take the lead on an investigation into alleged money-laundering. Two nightclubs in the city centre were being used as a front for a variety of illicit activities, and there was a wealth of intelligence to wade through. With both nightclub owners prominent figures in the business community, Ray knew the chief was testing him, and he intended to rise to the challenge.

He spent the rest of the afternoon going through Team Three's cases. The DS, Kelly Proctor, was off on maternity leave, and Ray had asked the most experienced DC on that team to act up. Sean was doing a good job, but Ray wanted to make sure nothing slipped through the net while Kelly was away.

It wouldn't be long before Kate could be put forward for some acting duties, he thought. She was so bright, she could teach some of his more experienced detectives a thing or two, and she'd enjoy the challenge. He remembered the flash of defiance as she told him what she'd been doing on the hit-and-run: there was no denying she was dedicated.

He wondered what was driving her. Was it simply that she didn't want to be beaten by a case, or could she really see a positive result from it? Had he been too quick to agree with the chief that they should close the file? He thought for a moment, drumming his fingers on his desk. He was technically off duty now, and he had promised Mags he wouldn't be late, but he could spare half an hour and still be home at a decent time. Before he could change his mind, he opened the bottom drawer of his desk and pulled out Jacob's case file.

It was well over an hour later before he noticed the time.

10

'Ah, I thought it was you!' Bethan catches up with me on the path to Penfach, out of breath and her coat flapping behind her. 'I'm popping to the Post Office. It's a good thing I bumped into you – I've got a bit of news.'

'What is it?' I wait for Bethan to get her breath back.

'We had the sales rep in yesterday from one of the greetings cards companies,' she says. 'I showed him your photographs and he thinks they'd make great postcards.'

'Really?'

Bethan laughs. 'Yes, really. He'd like you to get some samples printed up and he'll pick them up when he's next round our way.'

I can't stop the grin forming on my face. 'That's amazing news, thank you.'

'And I'll definitely stock them in the shop for you. In fact, if you can knock up a website and get a few photos online, I'll send out the details to our mailing list. There are bound to be people who want a beautiful picture of somewhere they've been on holiday.'

'I will,' I tell her. I don't have the faintest idea how to set up a website.

'You could write messages as well as names, couldn't you? "Good luck", "Congratulations" – that sort of thing.'

'Yes, I could.' I imagine a whole series of my cards slotted into a display rack, recognisable from the sloping 'J' I would use as a logo. No name, just an initial. They could have been taken by anyone. I have to do something to start bringing in some money. My outgoings are low – I eat next to nothing – but it won't be long before my savings run out, and I don't have any other source of income. Besides, I miss working. The voice in my head laughs at me, and I force myself to block it out. Why shouldn't I set up another business? Why shouldn't people buy my photographs, like they used to buy my sculptures?

'I'll do it,' I say.

'Well then, that's sorted,' Bethan says, pleased. 'Now, where are you off to today?'

We have arrived in Penfach without my realising. 'I thought I might explore the coast a bit more,' I say. 'Take some photos of different beaches.'

'You won't find a prettier one than Penfach,' Bethan says. She checks her watch. 'But there's a bus leaves in ten minutes for Port Ellis – that's as good a place as any to start.'

When the bus arrives I climb on gratefully. It is empty, and I sit far enough back from the driver to avoid conversation. The bus picks its way inland through narrow roads, and I watch the sea retreat, then search for its reappearance as we approach our destination.

The quiet road where the bus stops is sandwiched between stone walls that seem to run the length of Port Ellis, and there is no pavement, so I walk on the road towards what I hope is the centre of the village. I will explore inland, then head for the coast.

The bag is half-hidden in the hedge; black plastic tied in a knot and slung into the shallow ditch by the side of the road. I almost miss it entirely, dismissing it as rubbish, discarded by holiday-makers.

But then it moves, just slightly.

So slightly I almost think I am imagining it, that it must be the wind rustling the plastic. I lean into the hedge and reach for the bag, feeling as I do the unmistakable sensation of something alive inside.

I drop to my knees and rip open the bin bag. A fetid stench of fear and excrement hits me and I retch, forcing down nausea at the sight of the two animals inside. One puppy lies still, the skin on its back clawed raw by the frantic, wriggling dog beside it, its crying barely audible. I let out a sob and pick up the live puppy, cradling it inside my coat. I get clumsily to my feet and look around, calling to a man crossing the road a hundred metres further on.

'Help! Please help!'

The man turns and ambles towards me, seemingly unmoved by my panic. He's old, and his back curves forward, pushing his chin on to his chest.

'Is there a vet here?' I ask, as soon as he is close enough.

The man looks at the puppy, quiet and still now in my coat, and peers into the black bag on the floor. He makes a clicking sound, shaking his head slowly.

'Alun Mathews' son,' he says. He jerks his head, presumably indicating where the son is to be found, and picks up the black sack, with its gruesome contents. I follow him, feeling the warmth from the puppy spreading through my chest.

The surgery is a small white building at the end of a lane, with a sign above the door that reads 'Port Ellis Veterinary Surgery'. Inside the tiny waiting room a woman sits on a plastic chair, a cat basket on her lap. The room smells of disinfectant and dog.

The receptionist looks up from her computer. 'Hello, Mr Thomas, what can we do for you?'

My companion nods a greeting and hefts the black sack on the counter. 'This one's found a couple of pups dumped in the hedge,' he says. 'Bloody shame.' He leans towards me and pats me carefully on the arm. 'They'll see you right,' he says, and leaves the surgery, making the bell above the door jingle enthusiastically.

'Thanks for bringing them in.'

The receptionist wears a badge on her bright blue tunic, with the name 'Megan' embossed in black.

'Lots of people wouldn't, you know.'

Keys swing from a lanyard studded with brightly coloured animal badges and charity tie pins, like the sort worn by nurses on a children's ward. She opens the bag and blanches momentarily, before discreetly disappearing from view with it.

Seconds later a door into the waiting room opens, and Megan smiles at me. 'Do you want to bring this little one through? Patrick will see you straight away.'

'Thank you.' I follow Megan into an oddly shaped room with cupboards shoe-horned into the corners. At the far end is a kitchen counter and a small stainless steel sink, at which a man is washing his hands with lurid green soap that foams up his forearms.

'Hello, I'm Patrick. The vet,' he adds, then laughs. 'But you probably guessed that.' He is a tall man – taller than me, which is unusual – with dirty blond hair in no discernible style. Under his blue scrubs he wears jeans and a checked shirt rolled up at the sleeves, and a smile that shows even white teeth. I guess him to be in his mid-thirties, perhaps a little older.

'My name's Jenna.' I open my coat to take out the black-and-white puppy, who has fallen asleep and is making quiet snuffling noises, apparently unaffected by the traumatic demise of his brother.

'And who do we have here?' says the vet, taking the puppy gently from me. The action wakes up the dog, who flinches, cowering away from him. Patrick hands him back to me. 'Would you hold him on the table for me?' he says. 'I don't want to unsettle him even more. If it was a man who put the dogs in the bag, you might find it takes a while for him to trust them

81

again.' He runs his hands over the puppy, and I crouch down and whisper soothing chatter into his ear, not caring what Patrick thinks of my nonsense.

'What sort of dog is he?' I ask.

'A bitza.'

'A Bitza?' I stand up, keeping a careful hand on the puppy, who has relaxed now under Patrick's gentle examination.

Patrick grins. 'You know: bitza this, bitza that. Mostly spaniel, I'd say, judging from these ears, but heaven knows what the rest is. Collie, maybe, or even a bit of terrier. They wouldn't have been dumped if they'd been pure-breds, that's for sure.' He picks up the puppy and hands him to me to cuddle.

'How awful,' I say, breathing in the warmth of the little dog. He pushes his nose into my neck. 'Who would do something like that?'

'We'll let the police know, but the chances of them finding out anything are pretty slim. They're a silent lot, the folk round here.'

'What will happen to this one?' I ask.

Patrick shoves his hands deep into the pockets of his scrubs, and leans against the sink.

'Are you able to keep him?'

He has tiny white lines at the corners of his eyes, as though he's been squinting into the sun. He must spend a lot of time outdoors.

'Given the way he was found, it's not likely anyone will come forward to claim him,' Patrick says, 'and we're struggling for space in the kennels. It would be a great help if you could give him a home. He's a nice dog, by the looks of things.'

'Oh goodness, I couldn't look after a dog!' I exclaim. I can't shake the feeling that this has only happened because I came to Port Ellis today.

'Why not?'

I hesitate. How can I explain that bad things happen around

me? I would love to have something to look after again, but at the same time it terrifies me. What if I couldn't look after him? What if he got sick?

'I don't even know if my landlord would let me,' I say, finally.

'Where are you living? Are you in Port Ellis?'

I shake my head. 'I'm over in Penfach. In a cottage not far from the caravan park.'

There is a flash of recognition in Patrick's eyes. 'Are you renting Iestyn's place?'

I nod. It no longer surprises me to discover that everyone knows Iestyn.

'You leave him to me,' Patrick says. 'Iestyn Jones was at school with my dad, and I've got enough dirt on him to let you keep a herd of elephants, if you wanted them.'

I smile. It's hard not to.

'I think I'd draw the line at elephants.' I say, and immediately feel myself redden.

'Spaniels are great with kids,' he says. 'Do you have any?'

The pause seems to go on for ever.

'No,' I say eventually. 'I don't have any children.'

The dog wriggles free from my hand and begins licking my chin furiously. I feel his heart beating against mine.

'Okay,' I say. 'I'll take him.'

11

Ray eased himself out of bed, trying not to disturb Mags. He had promised her a work-free weekend, but if he got up now he could have an hour's worth of emails done before she surfaced, and get a head-start on the Operation Break file. They would execute two simultaneous warrants on the clubs, and if their sources were to be believed, would find large quantities of cocaine in both, as well as documentation that would show the flow of money in and out of the supposedly legitimate businesses.

He pulled on his trousers and went in search of coffee. As the kettle was boiling he heard footsteps padding into the kitchen behind him, and he turned.

'Daddy!' Lucy flung her arms around his waist. 'I didn't know you were awake!'

'How long have you been up?' he said, unpeeling her arms and bending down to give her a kiss. 'Sorry I didn't see you before you went to bed yesterday. How was school?'

'Okay, I guess. How was work?'

'Okay, I guess.'

They grinned at each other.

'Can I watch telly?' Lucy held her breath and looked up at him with beseeching eyes. Mags had strict rules about television in the morning, but it was the weekend, and it would leave Ray free to work for a while.

'Oh, go on, then.'

She scuttled into the sitting room before Ray could change

his mind, and he heard the pop of the television warming up, before the high-pitched tones of some cartoon or other. Ray sat at the kitchen table and switched on his BlackBerry.

By eight o'clock he had dealt with most of his emails, and he was making himself a second cup of coffee when Lucy came into the kitchen to complain that she was starving and where was breakfast?

'Is Tom still asleep?' Ray asked.

'Yes. Lazybones.'

'I am not lazy!' came an indignant voice from up the stairs.

'You are!' shouted Lucy.

Footsteps stomped across the landing and Tom hurtled down the stairs, his face screwed up and cross beneath messy hair. An angry outbreak of spots ran across his forehead. 'I am NOT!' he shouted, shoving his sister with an outstretched hand.

'Ow!' screamed Lucy, tears springing instantly to her eyes. Her bottom lip wobbled.

'That wasn't hard!'

'Yes it was!'

Ray groaned and wondered if all siblings fought as much as these two. Just as he was about to forcibly separate his children, Mags came downstairs.

'Eight o'clock is hardly lazy, Lucy,' she said mildly. 'Tom, don't hit your sister.' She picked up Ray's coffee. 'Is that for me?'

'Yes.' Ray put the kettle on again. He looked at the kids, who were now sitting at the table planning what they were going to do over the summer holidays, their quarrel forgotten – for the time being, at any rate. Mags always managed to defuse rows in a way he had never mastered. 'How do you do that?'

'It's called parenting,' Mags said, 'You should try it sometime.'

Ray didn't bite. Lately all they seemed to be doing was sniping at each other, and he wasn't in the mood for another debate about full-time working versus full-time parenting.

Mags moved around the kitchen, putting breakfast things out on the table; deftly making toast and pouring juice between sips of coffee. 'What time did you get in last night? I didn't hear you come home.' She slipped an apron on over her pyjamas and began scrambling eggs. The apron was one Ray had given her for Christmas years ago. He had meant it as a joke – like those awful husbands who buy their wives saucepans or ironing boards – but Mags had worn it ever since. It had a picture of a 1950s housewife on it, and the slogan read, 'I love cooking with wine – sometimes I even put some in the food.' Ray remembered coming home from work and slipping his arms around his wife as she stood at the stove, feeling the apron crease beneath his hands. He hadn't done that for a while.

'About one, I think,' Ray said. There had been an armed robbery at a petrol station on the outskirts of Bristol. Uniform had managed to bring in all four men involved within a few hours of the incident, and Ray had stayed in the office more as a gesture of solidarity to his team than out of any real necessity.

The coffee was too hot to drink but he took a sip anyway, and burned his tongue. His BlackBerry buzzed and he glanced at the screen. Stumpy had emailed to say that the four offenders had been charged and put before Saturday-morning court, where the magistrates had remanded them. Ray tapped out a quick email to the superintendent.

'Ray!' Mags said. 'No work! You promised.'

'Sorry, I was catching up on last night's job.'

'It's only two days, Ray – they'll have to manage without you.' She put a pan of eggs on the table and sat down.

'Careful,' she said to Lucy, 'it's hot.' She looked up at Ray. 'Do you want some breakfast?'

'No thanks, I'll grab something later. I'm going to have a shower.' He leaned against the doorframe for a moment, watching the three of them eat.

'We need to leave the gate open for the window-cleaner on

Monday,' Mags said, 'so can you remember to unlock it when you take the bins out tomorrow night? Oh, and I went round to see next door about the trees, and they're going to get them cut back in the next couple of weeks, although I'll believe that when I see it.'

Ray wondered if the *Post* would run a story on last night's job. They were quick enough to pick up on the ones the police didn't solve, after all.

'That sounds great,' he said.

Mags put down her fork and looked at him.

'What?' Ray said. He went upstairs to shower, pulling out his BlackBerry to drop a line to the on-call press officer. It would be a shame not to capitalise on a job well done.

'Thank you for today,' Mags said. They were sitting on the sofa, but neither of them had so far bothered to turn on the television.

'What for?'

'For putting work aside for once.' Mags tipped her head back and closed her eyes. The lines at the corners of her eyes relaxed and she looked instantly younger: Ray realised how often she seemed to be frowning, nowadays, and he wondered if he did the same.

Mags had the sort of smile Ray's mother used to call 'generous'. 'That just means I've got a big mouth,' Mags laughed, the first time she heard it.

Ray's own mouth twitched at the memory. Maybe she did smile a little less nowadays, but she was still the same Mags she'd been all those years ago. She frequently moaned about the weight she had put on since the kids were born, but Ray rather liked the way she was now; her stomach round and soft, her breasts low and full. His compliments fell on deaf ears, and he had long since given up on them.

'It was great,' Ray said. 'We should do it more often.' They had spent the day at home, pottering about and playing cricket in the garden, making the most of the sunshine. Ray had got out the old Swingball set from the shed, and both kids had messed around with it for the rest of the afternoon, despite Tom saying loudly how 'lame' it was.

'It was nice to see Tom laughing,' Mags said.

'He's not done a lot of that lately, has he?'

'I'm worried about him.'

'Do you want to speak to the school again?'

'I don't think there's any point,' Mags said. 'It's nearly the end of the school year. I'm hoping a change of teacher will make a difference, plus he won't be one of the youngest any more – maybe that'll give him a bit of confidence.'

Ray was trying to sympathise with his son, who had drifted through the last term at school with the same lack of enthusiasm that had concerned his teacher at the start of the year.

'I just wish he'd talk to us,' Mags said.

'He swears blind nothing's wrong,' Ray said. 'He's a typical adolescent boy, that's all, but he's going to have to snap out of it, because if he still has the same attitude to school when he gets to GCSE year, he's buggered.'

'You two seemed to get on better today,' Mags said.

It was true, they had survived the whole day without arguing. Ray had bitten his tongue at Tom's occasional back-chat, and Tom had cut down on the eye-rolling. It had been a good day.

'And it wasn't that bad, switching off the BlackBerry, was it?' Mags said. 'No palpitations? Cold sweats? DTs?'

'Ha ha. No, it wasn't that bad.' He hadn't switched it off, of course, and it had vibrated constantly in his pocket throughout the day. Eventually he had retired to the loo to sift through his emails and make sure he wasn't missing anything urgent. He had replied to one from the chief about Op Break, and glanced at a message from Kate about the hit-and-run, that he was itching to go and read properly. What Mags didn't understand was that ignoring the BlackBerry for a weekend would leave him with so much to do on Monday that he would spend the rest of the week catching up with it, unable to deal with anything else that came in.

He stood up. 'I'm going to go into the study and do an hour or so now, though.'

'What? Ray, you said no work!'

Ray was confused. 'But the kids are in bed.'

'Yes, but I'm—' Mags stopped and gave a tiny shake of her head, as though she had something in her ear.

'What?'

'Nothing. It's fine. Do what you have to do.'

'I'll be down in an hour, I promise.'

It was closer to two hours later when Mags pushed open the door to the study. 'I thought you might like a cup of tea.'

'Thank you.' Ray stretched, groaning as he felt something click in his back.

Mags put the mug down on his desk and peered over Ray's shoulder at the thick sheaf of papers he was reading. 'Is this the nightclub job?' She scanned the uppermost sheet. 'Jacob Jordan? Wasn't that the boy who was killed in the hit-and-run last year?'

'That's the one.'

Mags looked puzzled. 'I thought that had been filed.'

'It has.'

Mags sat on the arm of the easy chair they kept in the study because it clashed with the sitting-room carpet. It didn't really fit in Ray's office, but it was the most comfortable armchair he had ever sat in, and he refused to part with it. 'So why is CID still working on it?'

Ray sighed. 'They're not,' he said. 'The case is closed, but I never filed the paperwork. We're just taking a look through with a fresh pair of eyes, to see if we missed anything.'

'*We?*'

Ray paused. 'The team.' He didn't know why he didn't mention Kate, but it would be strange to make a point of it now. Better to keep her out of it, in case the chief did ever get wind of it. No need for Kate's copybook to be blotted so early in her career.

'Oh, Ray,' Mags's voice was soft, 'haven't you got enough on your plate with live jobs, without doing cold case reviews?'

'This one's still warm,' Ray said. 'And I can't help feeling we were pulled off it too soon. If we could take another pass at it, we might find something.'

There was a pause before Mags spoke. 'It's not like Annabelle, you know.'

Ray tightened his grip on the handle of his mug.

'Don't.'

'You can't torture yourself like this over every job you don't solve.' Mags leaned forward and squeezed his knee. 'You'll drive yourself mad.'

Ray took a sip of tea. Annabelle Snowden had been the first job he had dealt with when he took over as DI. She had gone missing after school and her mum and dad had been frantic. At least, they had seemed frantic. Two weeks later, Ray had charged her father with murder, after Annabelle's body was found hidden in the divan base of a bed at his flat; she had been kept alive there for more than a week.

'I knew there was something odd about Terry Snowden,' he said, finally looking at Mags. 'I should have fought harder to have him arrested as soon as she went missing.'

'There was no evidence,' said Mags. 'Copper's instinct is all very well, but you can't run an investigation on hunches.' Gently, she closed Jacob's file. 'Different job,' she said. 'Different people.'

'Still a child,' Ray said.

Mags took his hands. 'But he's already dead, Ray. You can work all the hours God sends and you won't change that. Let it go.'

Ray didn't answer. He turned back to his desk and opened up the file again, hardly noticing as Mags left the room and went to bed. When he logged into his email there was a new message from Kate, sent a couple of minutes previously. He typed a quick reply.

You still up?

The response came seconds later.

Checking to see if Jacob's mum is on Facebook. And watching an eBay bid. You?
Looking through the reports of burned-out vehicles in neighbouring forces. Here for a while.
Great, you can keep me awake!

Ray imagined Kate curled up on the sofa, her laptop to one side and a pile of snacks to the other.
Ben and Jerry's? he typed.

How did you know?!

Ray grinned. He dragged the email window to a corner of the screen where he could keep an eye on new messages, and began reading through the faxed hospital reports.

Didn't you promise Mags you'd take the weekend off?
I AM taking the weekend off! I'm just doing a bit of work now that the kids are asleep. Someone's got to keep you company . . .
I'm honoured. What better way to spend a Saturday night?

Ray laughed. Any joy on Facebook? he typed.

A couple of possibles, but they don't have profile pics. Hang on, phone's ringing. Back in a mo.

Reluctantly, Ray closed down his email and turned his attention to the pile of hospital records. It had been months since Jacob died, and there was a nagging voice in Ray's head that told him all this extra work was a fruitless exercise. The piece of Volvo fog light had turned out to belong to a housewife who had skidded on ice and hit one of the trees lining the road. All those hours of work for nothing, and still they carried on. Ray was playing with fire, going against the chief's wishes, not to mention letting Kate do the same. But he was in too deep now – he couldn't stop even if he wanted to.

12

It'll be warmer later in the day, but for now the air is still cool, and I pull my shoulders up to my ears.

'It's chilly today,' I say out loud.

I've started talking to myself, like the old woman who used to walk along the Clifton Suspension Bridge, laden down with carrier bags stuffed with newspapers. I wonder if she's still there; if she still crosses the bridge every morning, and crosses back again each night. When you leave a place it's easy to imagine life going on there the same way as before, even though nothing really stays the same for long. My life in Bristol could have belonged to someone else.

I shake the thought away and pull on my boots, wrapping a scarf around my neck. I have my daily battle with the lock, which grips on to the key and refuses to let it turn. Eventually I manage to secure the door, and I drop the key into my pocket. Beau trots at my heels. He follows me like a shadow, unwilling to let me out of his sight. When he first came home he cried all night, asking to come and sleep on my bed with me. I hated myself for it, but I held a pillow over my ears and ignored his cries, knowing that if I let myself get close to him, I would regret it. Several days went by before he stopped crying, and even now he sleeps at the bottom of the stairs, awake as soon as he hears the creak of the bedroom floorboards.

I check I have today's list of orders – I can remember them all, but it wouldn't do to make a mistake. Bethan continues to promote my pictures to her holiday-makers, and although I can hardly believe it, I am busy. Not in the same way as before, with exhibitions and commissions, but nevertheless busy. I have twice restocked the caravan shop with postcards and a trickle of orders has come through my home-made website. It's far from the smart web-presence I used to have, but every time I look at it I feel a flash of pride that I made it myself, without help. It is a small thing, but I am slowly beginning to think that perhaps I am not as useless as I once believed.

I haven't put my name on the website: just a gallery of photos, a rather clumsy and basic ordering system, and the name of my new business: 'Written in the Sand'. Bethan helped me choose it, over a bottle of wine in the cottage one evening, when she talked about my business with such enthusiasm I couldn't help but go along with it. 'What do you think?' she kept asking. I hadn't been asked for my opinion for a very long time.

August is the busiest month for the caravan park and although I still see Bethan at least once a week, I miss the quiet of the winter, when we would talk for an hour or more, feet pressed against the oil-filled radiator in the corner of the shop. The beaches are busy too, and I have to get up soon after sunrise to ensure a smooth stretch of sand for my photos.

A gull calls out to us and Beau races across the sand, barking as the bird taunts him from the safety of the sky. I kick through the debris on the beach and pick up a long stick. The tide is on its way out, but the sand is warm, and it is already drying. I will write today's messages close to the sea. I pull a piece of paper from my pocket and remind myself of the first order. 'Julia,' I say. 'Well, that's straightforward enough.' Beau looks at me enquiringly. He thinks I am talking to him. Perhaps I am, although I mustn't let myself become reliant on him. I see him as I imagine Iestyn sees his sheep dogs: tools of the trade; there to perform a function. Beau is my guard dog. I haven't needed protection yet, but I might.

I lean forward and draw a large J, standing back to check

the size, before writing the rest of the name. Happy with it, I discard the stick and take up my camera. The sun has risen properly now, and the low light casts a pink glow across the sand. I take a dozen shots, crouching down to look through my viewfinder, until the writing is iced with the sea's white froth.

For the next order I look for a clean stretch of beach. I work quickly, gathering armfuls of sticks from the piles thrown up by the sea. When the last piece of driftwood is in place I cast a critical eye over my creation. Strands of still-glistening seaweed soften the edges of the sticks and pebbles I have used to frame the message. The driftwood heart is six feet across: large enough to house the swirling script in which I have written 'Forgive me, Alice'. As I reach over to move a piece of wood, Beau hurtles out of the sea, barking excitedly.

'Steady!' I call. I put a protective arm over the camera slung across my body, in case he should jump up at me. But the dog ignores me, racing past in a spray of wet sand, to the other side of the beach, where he bounds around a man walking across the sand. At first I think it's the dog-walker who spoke to me once before, but then he pushes his hands into the pockets of his waxed jacket and I take a sharp intake of breath because the movement is familiar to me. How can that be? I know no one here, save Bethan and Iestyn, yet this man, who must be barely a hundred metres away now, is walking purposefully towards me. I can see his face. I know him, yet I don't know him, and my inability to place him makes me vulnerable. I feel a bubble of panic rising in my throat and I call to Beau.

'It's Jenna, isn't it?'

I want to run, but my feet are rooted to the spot. I'm mentally scrolling through everyone I knew in Bristol. I know I've met him somewhere before.

'Sorry, I didn't mean to scare you,' the man says, and I realise I'm shaking. He seems genuinely regretful, and he smiles broadly as if to make amends. 'Patrick Mathews. The vet at Port Ellis,' he adds. And at once I remember him, and the way he pushed his hands into the pockets of his blue scrubs.

'I'm so sorry,' I say, finally finding my voice, which feels small and unsure. 'I didn't recognise you.' I glance up to the empty coastal path. Soon people will begin arriving for a day at the beach: insured against all weather conditions with windbreaks, sunscreen and umbrellas. For once I'm glad it's high season and Penfach is full of people: Patrick's smile is warm, but I've been taken in by a warm smile once before.

He reaches down to rub Beau's ears.

'Looks like you've done a good job with this chap. What did you call him?'

'His name's Beau.' I can't help myself: I take two hardly noticeable steps backwards, and immediately feel the knot in my throat soften. I make myself drop my hands down to my sides, but straight away I find they have risen and have found each other at my waist.

Patrick kneels down and fusses Beau, who rolls on to his back to have his tummy scratched, delighted by the unaccustomed affection.

'He doesn't seem nervous at all.'

I'm reassured by Beau's relaxed manner. Don't they say dogs are good judges of character?

'No, he's doing well,' I say.

'He certainly is.' Patrick stands up and brushes the sand off his knees, and I hold my ground.

'No problems with Iestyn, I take it?' Patrick grins.

'None at all,' I tell him. 'In fact, he seems to think a dog is an essential part of any household.'

'I'm inclined to agree with him. I'd have one myself, only I work such long hours it wouldn't be fair. Still, I get to meet enough animals during the day, so I shouldn't complain.'

He seems very at home here by the sea, his boots engrained

with sand and the creases of his coat scored with salt. He nods towards the heart in the sand.

'Who's Alice, and why do you want her forgiveness?'

'Oh, it's not mine.' He must think me extraordinary, drawing pictures in the sand. 'At least, the sentiment isn't. I'm taking a photo of it for someone.'

Patrick looks confused.

'It's what I do,' I say. 'I'm a photographer.' I hold up my camera as though he might not otherwise believe me. 'People send me messages they want written in the sand and I come down here, write them and then send them the photograph.' I stop, but he seems genuinely interested.

'What sort of messages?'

'Mostly they're love letters – or marriage proposals – but I get all sorts. This one's an apology, obviously, and sometimes people ask me to write famous quotations, or lyrics from favourite songs. It's different every time.' I stop, blushing furiously.

'And you make a living doing that? What an amazing job!' I search his voice for sarcasm, but find none, and I let myself feel a little proud. It *is* an amazing job, and I created it from nothing.

'I sell other photos too,' I say, 'mostly of the bay. It's so beautiful, lots of people want a piece of it.'

'Isn't it? I love it here.'

We stand in silence for a few seconds, watching the waves build up and then break apart as they run up the sand. I begin to feel fidgety, and I try think of something else to say.

What brings you on to the beach?' I ask. 'Not many people venture down here at this time of day unless they've got a dog to walk.'

'I had to release a bird,' Patrick explains. 'A woman brought in a gannet with a broken wing and he's been staying at the surgery while he recovered. He's been with us for a few weeks and I brought him to the clifftop today to let him go. We try to release them in the same place they were found, to give them every chance of survival. When I saw your message on the beach I couldn't resist coming down and finding out who you were writing to. It was only when I got down here that I realised we'd already met.'

'Did the gannet fly okay?'

Patrick nods. 'He'll be fine. It happens fairly often. You're not local, are you? I remember you saying you'd not long arrived in Penfach when you brought Beau in. Where did you live before?'

Before I can think of an answer, a phone rings, its tinny tune sounding out of place out here on the beach. Inwardly I sigh with relief, although I have a well-worn story now, trotted out for Iestyn and Bethan, and the occasional walker who heads my way in search of conversation. I am an artist by trade, but I injured my hand in an accident and cannot work, so have taken up photography. It's not so far from the truth, after all. I haven't been asked about children, and I wonder if I carry the answer so visibly about me.

'Sorry,' says Patrick. He searches in his pockets and brings out a small pager, buried in a handful of pony nuts and bits of straw, that drop on to the sand. 'I have to have it on its loudest setting otherwise I don't hear it.' He glances at the screen. 'I must dash, I'm afraid. I volunteer at the lifeboat station at Port Ellis. I'm on call a couple of times a month, and it looks like we're needed now.' He pushes the phone back into his pocket. 'It was lovely seeing you again, Jenna. Really lovely.'

Raising an arm to bid me farewell, he runs across the beach and up the sandy path, and is gone before I can agree with him.

Back at the cottage, Beau flops into his basket, exhausted. I load the morning's images on to the computer while I wait for the kettle to boil. They are better than I expected, given the interruption: the letters stand out against the drying sand, and my driftwood heart makes the perfect frame. I leave the best image on the screen to look at again later, and take my coffee upstairs. I will regret this, I know, but I can't help myself.

Sitting on the floor, I put my mug down on the bare floorboards and reach under the bed for the box I haven't touched since arriving in Penfach. I pull it towards me and sit cross-legged to open the lid, breathing in memories along with the dust. It starts to hurt almost immediately, and I know I should close the box without delving further. But like an addict seeking a fix, I am resolute.

I take out the small photo album lying on top of a sheaf of legal documents. One by one, I stroke my fingers across snapshots of a time so removed it is like looking through a stranger's photographs. There I am standing in the garden; there again in the kitchen, cooking. And there I am pregnant, proudly showing off my bump and grinning at the camera. The knot in my throat tightens and I feel the familiar prickle at the back of my eyes. I blink them away. I was so happy, that summer, certain that this new life was going to change everything, and we would be able to start again. I thought it would be a new beginning for us. I stroke the photograph, tracing the outline of my bump and imagining where his head would have been; his curled limbs; his barely formed toes.

Gently, as though it might disturb my unborn child, I close the photo album and place it back in the box. I should go downstairs now, while I am still in control. But it is like worrying at a sore tooth or picking at a scab. I feel around until my fingers touch the soft fabric of the rabbit I slept with every night when I was pregnant, so that I could give it to my son and it would smell of me. Now I hold it to my face and inhale, desperate for a trace of him. I let out a stifled wail and Beau pads quietly upstairs and into my bedroom.

'Downstairs, Beau,' I tell him.

The dog ignores me.

'Get out!' I scream at him, a madwoman clutching a baby's toy. I scream and I can't stop, even though it's not Beau I'm seeing, but the man who took my baby from me; the man who ended my life when he ended my son's. 'Get out! Get out! Get out!'

Beau drops to the floor, his body tensed and his ears flattened against his head. But he doesn't give up. Slowly, inch by inch, he moves towards me, never taking his eyes off me.

The fight leaves me as fast as it arrived.

Beau stops next to me, still crouched close to the floorboards, and rests his head on my lap. He closes his eyes and I feel the weight and the warmth of him through my jeans. Unbidden, my hand reaches out to stroke him, and my tears begin to fall.

13

Ray had put together his team for Operation Break. He had given Kate the role of exhibits officer, which was a big ask for someone who had only been on the team for eighteen months, but he was certain she could handle it.

'Of course I can!' she said, when he mentioned his concerns. 'And I can always come to you if I have any issues, can't I?'

'Any time,' Ray said. 'Drink after work?'

'Just try stopping me.'

They had taken to meeting two or three times a week after work to go over the hit-and-run. As the outstanding enquiries petered out, they spent less time talking about the case, and more time talking about their lives outside of work. Ray had been surprised to discover that Kate was as passionate a Bristol City supporter as he was himself, and they had spent many a pleasant evening mourning their recent relegation. For the first time in years he felt as though he wasn't only a husband, or a father, or even a police officer. He was Ray.

Ray had been careful not to work on the hit-and-run during his normal working hours. He was directly contravening the chief's order, but as long as he wasn't doing it on job time, he reasoned she couldn't have an issue with it. And if they came up with a strong lead that resulted in an arrest – well, she'd be singing a different tune then.

The need to conceal their work from the rest of the CID team meant Ray and Kate had taken to meeting in a pub further away than the usual police haunts. The Horse and Jockey was quiet, with high-backed booths where they could spread out paperwork without fear of being overlooked, and the landlord never glanced up from his crossword. It was an enjoyable way to round off the day and de-stress before going home, and Ray found himself watching the clock until it was time to leave the office.

Typically, a phone call at five delayed him, and by the time he reached the pub, Kate was halfway through her drink. The unspoken arrangement was that whoever got there first got in the drinks, and his pint of Pride was waiting on the table.

'What kept you?' Kate asked, pushing it towards him. 'Anything interesting?'

Ray took a gulp of his pint. 'Some intelligence that might end up coming our way,' he said. 'There's a drug dealer on the Creston estate using six or seven smaller pushers to do his dirty work – it's looking like it'll shape up into a nice little job.' A particularly vocal Labour MP had taken to using the drug problem as a basis to pontificate as publicly as possible about the threat to society posed by 'lawless estates', and Ray knew that the chief was keen that they be seen to be taking a proactive stance. Ray was hopeful that if Operation Break went well, he might be sufficiently in the chief's good books to lead on this one, too.

'The Domestic Abuse team has had contact with Dominica Letts,' he told Kate, 'the girlfriend of one of the dealers, and they're trying to convince her to press charges against him. Obviously we don't want to spook him by bringing the police in for that when we're trying to put together a job, but at the same time we've got a duty of care to his girlfriend.'

'Is she in danger?'

Ray paused before answering. 'I don't know. DA have graded her high risk, but she's adamant she won't give evidence against him and at the moment she isn't cooperating with the unit at all.'

'How long before we can move?'

'It could be weeks,' Ray said. 'Too long. We'll need to look at getting her into a refuge – assuming she'll go – and holding the assault allegations until we get him in for the drugs job.'

'Hobson's choice,' Kate said thoughtfully. 'What's more important: drug-dealing or domestic violence?'

'It's not as simple as that though, is it? What about the violence caused by drug abuse? The robberies committed by addicts looking for their next fix? The effects of dealing might not be as immediate as a punch to the face, but they're far-reaching and just as painful.' Ray realised he was speaking louder than normal, and he stopped abruptly.

Kate put a calming hand over his. 'Hey, I'm playing devil's advocate. It's not an easy decision.'

Ray gave a sheepish grin. 'Sorry, I'd forgotten how wound up I can get about this sort of thing.' In fact, it had been a while since he had thought about it at all. He had been in the job for so many years, his reasons for doing it had become buried beneath paperwork and personnel issues. It was good to be reminded of what really mattered.

His eyes met Kate's for a moment, and Ray felt the heat of her skin against his. A second later she pulled her hand away, laughing awkwardly.

'One for the road?' Ray said. By the time he returned to the table, the moment had passed, and he wondered if he had imagined it. He put down the drinks and tore open a packet of crisps so it lay flat between them.

'I've got nothing new on the Jacob job,' he said.

'Me neither,' Kate sighed. 'We're going to have to give up, aren't we?'

He nodded. 'It looks that way. I'm sorry.'

'Thank you for letting me carry on for as long as you did.'

'You were right not to give up,' Ray said, 'and I'm glad we kept working on it.'

'Even though we're not any further forward?'

'Yes, because now it feels right to stop, doesn't it? We've done everything we possibly could have done.'

Kate nodded slowly. 'It does feel different, yes.' She looked at Ray appraisingly.

'What?'

'I guess you're not the chief's yes-man, after all.' She grinned, and Ray laughed. He was glad to have gone up in her estimation.

They ate the crisps in companionable silence, and Ray checked his phone in case Mags had sent a text message.

'How are things at home?'

'Same old,' Ray said, tucking his phone back in his pocket. 'Tom still grunts his way through meal-times, and Mags and I still argue about what we should do about it.' He gave a short laugh, but Kate didn't join in.

'When are you next seeing his teacher?'

'We were at the school again yesterday,' Ray said grimly. 'Barely six weeks into the new school year and it seems Tom's been skipping lessons.' He drummed his fingers on the desk. 'I don't understand that kid. He was fine over the summer, but as soon as he went back it was the same old Tom: uncommunicative, surly, uncooperative.'

'Do you still think he's being bullied?'

'The school says not, but then they would, wouldn't they?' Ray didn't hold a particularly high opinion of Tom's head teacher, who had been quick to place the blame on Mags and Ray for not presenting a 'united front' at parents' evenings. Mags had threatened to come to Ray's office and forcibly drag him to the next meeting, and Ray had been so worried he would forget that he had worked from home all day, so he could drive to the appointment with Mags. Not that it had made a blind bit of difference.

'Tom's teacher says he's a bad influence on the rest of the

class,' Ray said. 'Apparently he's "subversive".' He gave a derisive snort. 'At his age!' It's bloody ridiculous. If they can't deal with uncooperative kids they shouldn't have gone into teaching. Tom's not subversive, he's just bloody-minded.'

'I wonder where he gets that from,' Kate said, suppressing a smile.

'Watch it, DC Evans! Or do you want to end up back in uniform?' He grinned.

Kate's laugh turned into a yawn. 'Sorry, I'm knackered. I think I'm going to call it a night. My car's in the garage, so I need to check what time the buses run.'

'I'll give you a lift.'

'Are you sure? It's not exactly on your way.'

'It's no trouble. Come on – you can show me what the posh end of town's like.'

Kate's apartment was in a smart block of flats in the centre of Clifton, where prices were, in Ray's view, vastly inflated.

'My parents helped me out with a deposit,' Kate explained. 'I'd never have afforded it otherwise. Plus it's tiny; technically two bedrooms, but only if you don't actually want to put a bed in the second one.'

'Surely you'd have got far more for your money if you'd bought elsewhere?'

'Probably, but Clifton has everything!' Kate waved an arm expansively. 'I mean, where else can you get falafel at three in the morning?'

As the only thing Ray ever wanted at three in the morning was a pee, he failed to see the attraction.

Kate unclipped her seat belt and stopped, her hand on the door handle. 'Do you want to come up and see the flat?' Her tone was casual, but the air was suddenly thick with anticipation, and at that instant Ray knew he was crossing a line he had been refusing to acknowledge for months.

'I'd like that,' he said.

Kate's apartment was on the top floor, with a swanky lift that arrived in seconds. When the doors opened they were on a small carpeted landing with a cream-painted front door immediately opposite them. Ray followed Kate out of the lift, and they stood in silence as the doors slid shut. She was looking directly at him, her chin lifted a little, and a strand of hair falling across her forehead. Ray suddenly found he was in no hurry to leave.

'This is me,' Kate said, without taking her eyes off him.

He nodded, reaching out to tuck the errant strand of hair behind her ear. Then, before he could question what was happening, he was kissing her.

14

Beau pushes his nose into the crook of my leg and I reach down to fuss his ears. I haven't been able to prevent myself from loving him, and so he sleeps on my bed as he has wanted to do from the start. When the nightmares come, and I wake screaming, he's there to lick my hand and reassure me. Gradually, without my noticing, my grief has changed shape; from a raw, jagged pain, that won't be silenced, to a dull, rounded ache I'm able to lock away at the back of my mind. If it is left there, quiet and undisturbed, I find I'm able to pretend that everything is quite all right. That I never had another life.

'Come on, then.' I reach out to switch off the bedside light, which can't compete with the sunlight streaming through the window. I know the seasons of the bay now, and there is a pleasing satisfaction in having seen almost a full year here. The bay is never the same from one day to the next. Changing tides, unpredictable weather, even the rubbish thrown up on the beach alters it hourly. Today the sea is swollen from a night's rain, the sand grey and waterlogged beneath heavy clouds. There are no tents at the caravan park now, only Bethan's static caravans and a handful of motorhomes owned by holiday-makers taking advantage of the late-season discounts. Before too long the park will close, and the bay will be mine again.

Beau races ahead and runs down on to the beach. The tide is in and he dives into the sea, barking at the cold waves. I laugh out loud. He is more spaniel than collie now, with the slightly-too-long legs of a teenager, and so much energy I wonder if he could ever run it off.

I scan the clifftop, but it's empty, and I allow myself a twinge of disappointment before I shake it off. It's ridiculous to hope to see Patrick, when we've met here on the beach just that one time, but I can't stop the thought forming.

I find a stretch of sand on which to write. I suspect things will slow down over the winter, but for the time being the business is doing well. I get a jolt of pleasure every time an order arrives, and I enjoy guessing the stories behind the messages. Most of my customers have some connection to the sea, and many email after they've received their order, to tell me how much they loved the picture; how they spent their childhood on the beach, or saved for family holidays by the coast. Sometimes they ask me which beach it is, but I never reply.

As I'm about to start work, Beau barks, and I look up to see a man walking towards us. My breath catches, but he raises a hand in greeting and I realise it's him. It's Patrick. I can't hide my smile, and although my heart is racing, it isn't through fear.

'I hoped I might find you here,' he says, before he has even reached me. 'How do you fancy an apprentice?' He isn't wearing boots today, and his corduroy trousers are laced with wet sand. The collar on his waxed jacket is turned up on one side and I resist the temptation to reach up and smooth it back down.

'Good morning,' I say. 'An apprentice?'

He makes a sweeping gesture with his left arm, encompassing most of the beach. 'I thought I could help you work.'

I'm not sure if he's making fun of me. I don't say anything.

Patrick takes the stick from my hand and stands expectantly, poised over the empty patch of sand. I'm suddenly flustered. 'It's harder than it looks, you know,' I say, adopting a serious tone to cover my awkwardness. 'I can't have any footprints in the shot, and we have to work quickly, otherwise the tide will come in too close.'

108

I can't recall anyone ever wanting to share this part of my life: art was always something to be shut away in another room, something for me to do on my own, as though it didn't belong in the real world.

'Got it.' He has an air of concentration on his face I find touching. It is, after all, just a message in the sand.

I read the order aloud. 'Nice and simple: "Thank you, David".'

'Aha – thank you for *what*, exactly, I wonder?' says Patrick, leaning over the sand to write the first word. 'Thank you for feeding the cat? Thank you for saving my life? Thank you for agreeing to marry me even after I had that fling with the postman?'

The corners of my mouth twitch. 'Thank you for teaching me flamenco dancing,' I proffer, pretending to be serious.

'Thank you for the selection of fine Cuban cigars.'

'Thank you for extending my overdraft.'

'Thank you for . . .' Patrick reaches his arm out to complete the final word and loses his balance, toppling forward and only managing to stay upright by planting a foot firmly in the middle of the writing. 'Oh, bugger.' He steps back to eye the ruined message and looks apologetically at me.

I burst out laughing. 'I did say it was harder than it looked.'

He passes me back the stick. 'I bow to your superior artistic skills. Even without the footprint, my effort isn't terribly impressive. The letters are all different sizes.'

'It was a valiant attempt,' I tell him. I look around for Beau, calling him away from a crab he is intent on playing with.

'How's this?' Patrick says. I look at the message he has written in the sand, expecting a second attempt at the 'thank you'.

Drink?

'Better,' I say, 'although that's not one of—' I break off, feeling foolish. 'Oh, I see.'

'At the Cross Oak? This evening?' Patrick falters a little, and I realise he's nervous too. It gives me confidence.

I hesitate, but only for a second, ignoring the thumping in my chest. 'I'd like that.'

I regret my impetuousness for the rest of the day, and by the evening I am so anxious I am shaking. I count the ways in which this could go wrong, and replay everything Patrick has ever said to me, looking for warning signs. Is he as straightforward as he appears? Is anyone? I think about walking into Penfach to phone the vet's surgery and cancel, but I know I won't have the nerve. I take a bath to kill some time, running the water so hot it turns my skin pink, then I sit on my bed and wonder what I should wear. It's ten years since I last went on a date, and I am frightened of breaking the rules. Bethan has continued to clear out her wardrobe of clothes she can no longer fit into. Most are too big for me, but I try on a skirt in deep purple and although I have to tie it at the waist with a scarf I don't think it looks too bad. I walk around the room, enjoying the unfamiliar sensation of my legs touching as I walk; the swing of the fabric about my thighs. I feel a glimmer of the girl I used to be, but when I look in the mirror I realise the hem is above my knee, and my legs stretch boldly out beneath. I take it off and throw it into a ball at the back of the wardrobe, reaching instead for the jeans I've only just taken off. I find a clean top and brush my hair. I look exactly as I did an hour ago. Exactly as I always do. I think of the girl who would spend hours getting ready to go out: music playing, make-up scattered about the bathroom, the air thick with perfume. I had no idea, back then, what real life was like.

I walk to the caravan park, where I have arranged to meet Patrick. At the last minute I decided to bring Beau with me, and his presence gives me back a little of the bravado I felt on the beach this morning. When I reach the caravan park Patrick is standing by the open door to the shop, Bethan leaning in the doorway talking to him. They are laughing about something, and I can't help but wonder if it's me.

Bethan sees me, and Patrick turns and smiles as I approach. I think at first he's going to kiss me on the cheek, but he simply touches me gently on the arm as he says hello. I wonder if I look as terrified as I feel.

'Be good, you two!' Bethan says with a grin.

Patrick laughs and we walk towards the village. He finds conversation easy, and although I'm certain he exaggerates the antics of some of his patients, I'm grateful for his storytelling, and I find myself relaxing a little as we arrive in the village.

The landlord of the Cross Oak is Dave Bishop, a Yorkshireman who arrived in Penfach only a few years before me. Dave and his wife Emma are firmly rooted in the community now, and – like the rest of Penfach – know everyone's name and everyone's business. I've never been inside the pub, but I have said hello to Dave when I've come by with Beau on my way to the little Post Office shop.

Any hope I might have had of a quiet drink evaporates the moment we step through the door.

'Patrick! Your round, isn't it?'

'I need to get you out to look at Rosie again, she's still not right.'

'How's your old man? Not missing the Welsh weather too much?'

The onslaught of conversation, coupled with the enclosed space of the bar, makes me anxious. I close my hand around Beau's lead and feel the leather slip against my damp palm. Patrick has a few words for everyone but doesn't stop to chat. He places a hand on my back and steers me gently through the throng of people to stand at the bar. I feel the heat of his hand on the small of my back and am both relieved and disappointed when he takes it away and folds his arms on the bar. 'What would you like?'

I wish he had ordered first. I long for a cold bottled lager, and I scan the pub to see if any of the women are drinking beer.

Dave coughs politely. 'A gin and tonic,' I say, flustered. I have never drunk gin. This inability to make decisions isn't new, but I can't remember when it started.

Patrick orders a bottle of Becks and I watch the condensation form on the outside of the glass.

'So you'll be the photographer staying at Blaen Cedi? We wondered where you'd been hiding.'

The man talking to me is around the same age as Iestyn, with a tweed cap on his head and whiskery sideburns.

'This is Jenna,' Patrick says. 'She's been building up a business, so she hasn't had much time for sinking pints with you old lags.'

The man laughs, and I flush, grateful for Patrick's easy explanation for my seclusion. We choose a table in the corner, and although I'm conscious of the eyes upon us, and the gossip that is no doubt now rife, after a while the group of men turn back to their pints.

I'm careful not to talk too much, and fortunately Patrick is full of tales and interesting snippets of local history.

'It's a lovely place to live,' I say.

He stretches long legs out in front of him. 'It is that. Not that I felt that way when I was growing up here. Kids don't appreciate beautiful countryside, or a sense of community, do they? I used to nag my parents endlessly to move us to Swansea – I became convinced it would transform my life, and I'd suddenly become really popular, with an amazing social life and a string of girlfriends.' He grins. 'But they wouldn't entertain the idea of a move, and I went to the local comprehensive.'

'Did you always want to be a vet?'

'Ever since I was a toddler. Apparently I used to line up all my stuffed toys in the hall and make my mother bring them

into the kitchen one at a time so I could operate on them.'
When he talks, his whole face is animated; the corners of his
eyes crinkling a split second before his smile breaks. 'I scraped
through with the A-levels I needed and went to Leeds University
to do Veterinary Science, where I finally got the social life I'd
been desperate for.'

'And the string of girlfriends?' I say. Patrick grins.

'Maybe one or two. But after all that time desperately trying
to escape Wales, I missed it terribly. When I graduated I found
a job near Leeds, but when a partnership became available at
the surgery in Port Ellis I jumped at the chance. Mum and Dad
were getting on a bit by then, and I couldn't wait to be back
by the sea.'

'So your parents lived in Port Ellis?' I'm always curious about
people who have close relationships with their parents. I'm not
envious, I simply can't imagine it. Perhaps if my father had
stayed, things might have been different.

'Mum was born here. Dad moved here with his family when
he was a teenager and married Mum when they were both
nineteen.'

'Was your dad a vet, too?' I'm asking too many questions,
but I'm scared that, if I stop, I'll be the one expected to give
answers. Patrick doesn't seem to mind, filling me in on a family
history that puts a nostalgic smile on his face.

'An engineer. He's retired now, but he worked for a gas
company in Swansea all his life. It's because of him I'm a
volunteer lifeboatman, though. Dad did it for years. He used
to dash off halfway through Sunday lunch, and Mum would
make us all say a prayer that everyone would be brought safely
to shore. I used to think he was an actual super-hero.' He took
a swig of his pint. 'That was back in the days of the old lifeboat
station at Penfach – before they built the new one in Port Ellis.'

'Are you called out often?'

'It depends. More in the summer, when the caravan parks

are full. It doesn't matter how many signs there are, telling people the cliffs are dangerous, or not to swim at high tide – they don't take any notice.' He looks suddenly serious. 'You must be careful swimming in the bay – the undercurrent is fierce.'

'I'm not a strong swimmer,' I tell him. 'I haven't been in over my knees yet.'

'Don't,' Patrick says. There is an intensity in his eyes that scares me, and I shift uncomfortably in my seat. Patrick drops his gaze and takes a long swallow of his pint. 'The tide,' he says softly, 'it catches people out.'

I nod, and promise I won't swim.

'It sounds strange, but the safest swimming is further out.' Patrick's eyes light up. 'In the summer it's great to take a boat out beyond the bay, and dive straight into the deep water. I'll take you sometime, if you like.'

It's a casual offer, but I shiver. The thought of being alone with Patrick – with anyone – in the middle of the ocean is utterly terrifying.

'The water's not as cold as you think,' Patrick says, misunderstanding my discomfort. He stops talking, and there is an awkward silence.

I lean down and stroke Beau, who is asleep under the table, and try to think of something to say. 'Do your parents still live here?' I finally manage. Was I always this dull? I try to think back to university, when I was the life and soul of a party; friends throwing their heads back in laughter at something I said. Now simply making conversation is an effort.

'They moved to Spain a couple of years ago, lucky buggers. Mum has arthritis and I think the warm weather helps her joints – that's her excuse, anyway. How about you? Are your parents still around?'

'Not exactly.'

Patrick looks curious and I realise I should have simply said 'no'. I take a deep breath. 'I never really got on with my mum,' I tell him. 'She threw my dad out when I was fifteen and I haven't seen him since – I never forgave her for it.'

'She must have had her reasons.' He makes a question of it, but I'm nevertheless defensive.

'My father was an amazing man,' I say. 'She didn't deserve him.'

'So you don't see your mother, either?'

'I did, for years, but we had a falling-out after I . . .' I stop myself. 'We had a falling-out. A couple of years ago my sister wrote to tell me she had died.' I see sympathy in Patrick's eyes, but I shrug it off. What a mess I make of everything. I don't fit into the neat mould Patrick will be used to: he must wish he hadn't asked me for a drink. This evening is only going to get more awkward for both of us. We have run out of small talk and I can't think of anything else to say. I'm frightened of the questions I can see brimming in Patrick's mind: why I came to Penfach; what made me leave Bristol; why I'm here on my own. He will ask out of politeness, not realising that he doesn't want to know the truth. Not realising I can't tell him the truth.

'I should be getting back,' I say.

'Now?' He must be relieved, although he doesn't show it. 'It's still early – we could have another drink, or something to eat.'

'No, really, I had better go. Thank you for the drink.' I stand up before he feels the need to suggest we see each other again, but he pushes his chair back at the same time.

'I'll walk you home.'

I hear warning bells in my head. Why would he want to come with me? It's warm in the pub, and his friends are here; he has half a pint untouched in his glass. My head pounds. I think of how isolated the cottage is; how no one would hear if he refused to leave. Patrick might seem kind and honest now, but I know how quickly things can change.

115

'No. Thank you.'

I push through the group of locals, not caring what they think of me. I manage not to run until I have left the pub and turned the corner, but then I tear along the road to the caravan park and on to the coastal path that will take me home. Beau chases at my feet, surprised by the sudden change in pace. The freezing air hurts my lungs, but I don't stop until I reach the cottage, where I once again battle to turn the key in the lock. Eventually I get inside, and I slam the bolt home and lean against the door.

My heart is thumping and I'm struggling to catch my breath. I'm not even sure now that it's Patrick I'm frightened of; he's become mixed up in my head with the panic that grips me every day. I don't trust my instincts any more – they've been wrong so many times before – and so the safest thing to do is to stay well away.

15

Ray turned over and buried his face into the pillow to escape the morning light filtering through the slatted blinds. For a moment he couldn't pinpoint the feeling that weighed heavy inside him, then he recognised it. Guilt. What had he been thinking? He had never felt tempted to cheat on Mags – not once in fifteen years of marriage. He replayed the events of the previous evening in his head. Had he taken advantage of Kate? Before he could intercept it, the idea that she might put in a complaint came into his head, and he instantly despised himself for the thought. She wasn't like that. But nevertheless the worry almost pushed aside the guilt.

The measured breathing next to him told Ray he was the only one awake, and he eased himself out of bed, glancing at the sleeping mound next to him, the duvet pulled up around her head. If Mags were to find out . . . it didn't bear thinking about.

As he stood up, the duvet stirred, and Ray froze. Cowardly though it was, he had been hoping to sneak out without having to make conversation. He would have to face her at some point, but he needed a few hours to get his head round what had happened.

'What time is it?' Mags mumbled.

'Just gone six,' Ray whispered. 'I'm going into work early. Catch up with some paperwork.'

She grunted and went back to sleep, and Ray let out a silent breath of relief. He showered as quickly as he could, and was in the office a little over half an hour later, shutting the door and ploughing through paperwork as though he could eradicate what had happened. Fortunately Kate was out on enquiries, and at lunchtime Ray risked a quick trip to the canteen with Stumpy. They found a free table and Ray carried over two plates of what was billed as lasagne but bore very little resemblance to it. Moira, the station dinner lady, had lovingly chalked an Italian flag next to the dish of the day, and had beamed at them as they placed their order, so Ray manfully worked his way through an enormous portion, trying to ignore the persistent feeling of nausea that had plagued him since he got up. Moira was large and of indeterminate age, perennially cheerful despite a skin complaint that caused silvery flakes to fly off her arms when she took off her cardigan.

'You all right, Ray? Something on your mind?' Stumpy scraped up the remains of his lunch with his fork. Blessed with an iron stomach, Stumpy seemed not only to tolerate Moira's food, but to positively relish it.

'I'm fine,' Ray said, relieved when Stumpy didn't persist. He looked up to see Kate coming into the canteen, and wished he had eaten faster. Stumpy stood up, the metal legs of his chair scraping against the floor. 'I'll see you in the office, boss.'

Unable to think of a plausible reason to either call Stumpy back, or abandon his lunch before Kate sat down, Ray forced a smile. 'Hi, Kate.' He felt a hot flush spreading over his face. His mouth was bone-dry and he swallowed hard.

'Hey.' She sat down and unwrapped her sandwiches, seemingly unaware of his discomfort.

Her face was inscrutable, and the feeling of nausea increased. He pushed his food to one side, deciding Moira's wrath was the lesser of two evils, and looked around to check that no one was listening.

'About last night . . .' he began, feeling like an awkward teen.

Kate jumped in. 'I'm so sorry. I don't know what came over me – are you all right?'

Ray let out a breath. 'More or less. You?'

Kate nodded. 'Bit embarrassed, to be honest.'

'You've got nothing to be embarrassed about,' Ray said. 'I should never—'

'It should never have happened,' Kate said. 'But it was just a kiss.' She grinned at Ray, then took a bite of her sandwich, talking through a mouthful of cheese and pickle. 'A nice kiss, but just a kiss.'

Ray let out a slow breath. It was going to be all right. It was an awful thing to have happened, and if Mags were to ever find out it would be devastating, but it was all okay. They were both grown-ups and they could chalk it up to experience and carry on as if nothing had happened. For the first time in twelve hours, Ray let himself remember how good it had felt, kissing someone so full of energy, so alive. He felt the heat rising up to his face again, and he coughed, pushing the thought away.

'As long as you're okay,' he said.

'Ray, it's fine. Really. I'm not going to file a complaint against you, if that's what you're worried about.'

Ray reddened. 'God no! That hadn't crossed my mind. It's just that, you know, I'm married, and—'

'And I'm seeing someone,' Kate said, bluntly. 'And we both know the score. So it's forgotten, okay?'

'Okay.'

'Now,' Kate said, suddenly business-like, 'the reason I came to find you was to ask what you thought about doing an anniversary appeal for the Jacob Jordan job.'

'Has it been a year already?'

'Next month. We're unlikely to get a huge response, but if someone's talked we might get some intel at least, and there's always the possibility that someone's finally ready to clear their conscience. Someone has to know who was driving that car.'

Kate's eyes were bright, and she had the determined look on her face he knew so well.

'Let's do it,' he said. He imagined the chief's response to the proposal, and knew it wouldn't bode well for his career path. But an anniversary appeal was a good idea. It was something they did from time to time on unsolved cases, if only to reassure families the police hadn't given up completely – even if the case was no longer being actively investigated. It was worth a shot.

'Great. I've got some paperwork to finish off from this morning's job, but shall we get together this afternoon and plan the appeal?' She gave Moira a cheery wave as she left the canteen.

Ray wished he had Kate's ability to put the events of the previous night behind him. He was finding it hard to look at her without remembering her arms locked around his neck. He hid his leftover lasagne under a paper napkin and stacked his plate on the rack by the door. 'Top job, Moira,' he said as he passed the serving hatch.

'Greek day tomorrow!' she called after him.

Ray made a mental note to bring in sandwiches.

He was on the phone when Kate opened the door to his office without knocking. Realising Ray was busy, she mouthed apologetically and began to back out, but he gestured to her to sit down. She closed the door carefully and settled in one of the low chairs to wait for him to finish. He saw her glance at the photo of Mags and the children on his desk, and felt a fresh wave of remorse, struggling to keep his mind on his conversation with the chief constable.

'Is it really necessary, Ray?' Olivia was saying. 'The chances of someone coming forward are slim, and my concern is that it will simply draw attention to the fact that we didn't lock anyone up for the child's death.'

His name is Jacob, Ray told her silently, echoing the words

120

the boy's mother had spoken, almost a year ago. He wondered if his boss was really as uncaring as she appeared.

'And as there's no one baying for justice, it seems unnecessary to stir the whole thing up again. I would have thought you had enough on your plate, what with the chief inspector boards coming up.'

The implication was obvious.

'I had been thinking of asking you to take on the Creston estate drugs issue,' the chief said, 'but if you'd rather focus on an old job . . .' Operation Break had been a success, and this wasn't the first time in the last few weeks that the chief had dangled the carrot of an even bigger job in front of him. He wavered for a moment, then caught Kate's eye. She was watching him intently. Working with Kate had reminded him why he joined the police all those years ago. He had found his old passion for the job, and from now on he was going to do what was right, not what suited the bosses.

'I can do both,' he said firmly. 'I'm going to run the appeal. I think it's the right decision.'

There was a pause before Olivia spoke. 'One article in the *Post*, Ray, and some roadside appeal banners. Nothing more – and it's all taken down within a week.' She ended the call.

Kate waited for him to speak, anxiously tapping her pen against the arm of her chair.

'We're on,' Ray said.

Kate's face split into an enormous grin. 'Well done. Is she furious?'

'She'll get over it,' Ray said. 'She just wants to make it known that she doesn't approve, so she can be self-righteous when it backfires and public confidence takes a nose-dive again.'

'That's a bit cynical!'

'That's senior management for you.'

'And you still want to get promoted?' Kate's eyes twinkled, and Ray laughed.

'I can't stay here for ever,' he said.

'Why not?'

Ray thought how good it would be to be able to ignore the politics of promotion, and simply focus on his job – a job he loved. 'Because I have two kids to put through university,' he said finally. 'Anyway, I'll be different, I won't forget what it's like on the ground.'

'I'll remind you of that when you're chief constable,' said Kate, 'and you're telling me I can't run an anniversary appeal.'

Ray grinned. 'I've spoken to the *Post* already: Suzy French is happy for us to piggy-back on to their anniversary feature with a call for witnesses and information leading to . . . et cetera. They'll do the background stuff on Jacob, but I'd like you to call Suzy with the appeal details and phone number, and an official police quote about how we're keen to speak to people in confidence.'

'No problem. What are we going to do about his mother?'

Ray shrugged. 'Run the appeal without her, I suppose. Talk to the head teacher at Jacob's school, ask her whether she'd be happy to speak to the paper. It would be good to get an angle they've not had before, if that's possible. Maybe they've got a piece of artwork he did at school? A painting or something. We'll wait and see if the appeal turns up anything before we start looking for the mother – she seems to have disappeared off the face of the earth.'

Ray was furious with the Family Liaison Officer for not keeping better tabs on Jacob's mother. Not that he was surprised the woman had gone. In his experience, most people had one of two reactions when they lost someone: either they vowed never to move house, keeping rooms exactly the way they'd been left, like some sort of shrine; or they made a clean break, unable to bear the thought of living every day as though nothing had changed, when in fact their whole world had shifted.

After Kate had left his office, he contemplated Jacob's photo, which was still pinned to the corkboard on the wall. The edges had curled a little, and Ray pulled it carefully off the board and smoothed it out. He propped Jacob's photo against the framed picture of Mags and the kids, where he could see it more easily.

The anniversary appeal was a last-ditch effort, and one unlikely to succeed, but at least it was something. And if it didn't work, then he would send the papers for filing, and move on.

16

I sit at the kitchen table in front of my laptop, my knees drawn up underneath the big cable-knit sweater I used to wear in my studio in the winter months. I'm right next to the range, but I'm shaking, and I pull my sleeves down over my hands. It's not even lunchtime, but I have poured myself a large glass of red wine. I type into the search engine then pause. So many months since I tortured myself by looking. It won't help – it never does – but how can I not think about him, today of all days?

I take a sip of wine and click return.

In seconds the screen is flooded with news reports on the accident; message boards and tributes to Jacob. The colour of the text on the links shows I've visited each site before.

But today, exactly a year after my world collapsed, there is a new article in the online edition of the *Bristol Post*.

I let out a strangled sob, my fists screwed so tightly the knuckles turn white. After devouring the brief article, I return to the start to read it again. There have been no developments: no police leads, no information about the car, just a reminder that the driver is wanted by police for causing death by dangerous driving. The term sickens me, and I shut down the internet, but even the background photo of the bay doesn't calm me. I haven't been down to the shore since my date with Patrick. I have orders I need to fulfil, but I'm so ashamed of how I behaved I can't bear the thought of bumping into him on the beach. When I woke the day after our date, it seemed ridiculous that I should have felt frightened, and I had almost enough courage to call him and apologise. But as time went by I lost my nerve, and now it's been nearly a fortnight and he has made no attempt to contact me. I feel suddenly sick. I tip my wine down the sink and decide to take Beau for a walk along the coastal path.

We walk for what feels like miles, rounding the headland approaching Port Ellis. Beneath us is a grey building I realise must be the lifeboat station, and I stand for a while and imagine the lives saved by the volunteers who man it. I can't help but think of Patrick as I march onwards along the path that leads to Port Ellis. I don't have a plan, I simply continue walking until I reach the village, and make my way to the vet's surgery. It's only when I am opening the door, and the little bell rings above my head, that I wonder what on earth I am going to say.

'How can I help you?' It's the same receptionist, although I wouldn't have remembered her, were it not for her coloured badges.

'Would it be possible to see Patrick for a moment?' It occurs to me that I should come up with a reason, but she doesn't ask me for one.

'I'll be right back.'

I stand awkwardly in the waiting room, where a woman is sitting with a small child and something in a wicker basket. Beau strains at his lead and I pull him away.

A few minutes later I hear footsteps and Patrick appears. He wears brown corduroy trousers and a checked shirt, and his hair is messy, as if he has been running his fingers through it.

'Is something the matter with Beau?' He is polite, but he doesn't smile, and I lose a little of my resolve.

'No. I wondered if I could speak with you. Just for a moment.'

He hesitates, and I'm certain he is going to say no. My cheeks burn and I am acutely conscious of the receptionist watching us.

'Come through.'

I follow him into the room where he first examined Beau, and he leans against the sink. He says nothing – he's not going to make this easy for me.

'I wanted to . . . I wanted to apologise.' I feel a pricking sensation at the back of my eyes and I will myself not to cry.

Patrick gives a wry smile. 'I've been given the elbow before, but not usually with quite such speed.' His eyes are softer now, and I risk a small smile.

'I'm so sorry.'

'Did I do something wrong? Was it something I said?'

'No. Not in the slightest. You were . . .' I struggle to find the right word, and give up. 'It's my fault, I'm not very good at this sort of thing.'

There is a pause, and Patrick grins at me. 'Maybe you need practice.'

I can't help but laugh. 'Maybe.'

'Look, I've got another two patients to see, then I'm done for the day. How about I cook you supper? I've got a stew bubbling in the slow cooker as we speak, and there's more than enough for two. I'll even throw in a portion for Beau.'

If I say no now, I won't see him again.

'I'd like that.'

Patrick looks at his watch. 'Meet me back here in an hour – will you be all right till then?'

'I'll be fine. I wanted to take some pictures of the village, anyway.'

'Great, then I'll see you shortly.' His smile is broader now, and reaches his eyes, which crinkle at the corners. He shows me out and I catch the eye of the receptionist.

'All sorted?'

I wonder what she thinks I wanted to see Patrick for, and then I decide I don't care. I have been brave: I may have run away, but I came back, and tonight I will be having dinner with a man who likes me enough not to be put off by my nervousness.

The frequency with which I check my watch doesn't make the hour go any faster, and Beau and I complete several circuits of the village before it is time to return to the surgery. I don't want to go inside, and I'm relieved when Patrick comes out, pulling on a waxed jacket and smiling broadly. He fusses Beau's ears, then we walk to a small terraced house in the next street from the surgery. He ushers us into the sitting room, where Beau immediately flops down in front of the fireplace.

'Glass of wine?'

'Please.' I sit down, but I'm nervous and stand up again almost at once. The room is small but welcoming, with a rug covering most of the floor. An armchair sits either side of the hearth and I wonder which is his – nothing indicates that either is more used than the other. The small television seems incidental to the room, but two enormous bookcases fill the alcoves next to the armchairs. I tilt my head to read the spines.

'I've got far too many books,' Patrick says, coming back with two glasses of red wine. I take one, grateful for something to do with my hands. 'I should get rid of some of them really, but I end up hanging on to them.'

'I love reading,' I say, 'although I've hardly picked up a book since I moved here.'

Patrick sits down in one of the armchairs. I take his cue and sit in the other, fiddling with the stem of my glass.

'How long have you been a photographer?'

'I'm not, really,' I say, surprising myself with my honesty. 'I'm a sculptor.' I think of my garden studio: the smashed clay, the splinters from the finished sculptures ready for delivery. 'At least, I was.'

'You don't sculpt any more?'

'I can't.' I hesitate, then open the fingers on my left hand,

127

where scarred skin runs angrily across my palm and wrist. 'I had an accident. I can use my hand again now, but I can't feel anything in my fingertips.'

Patrick lets out a low whistle. 'You poor thing. How did it happen?'

I have a sudden flashback to that night, a year ago, and I push it back down inside me. 'It looks worse than it is,' I say. 'I should have been more careful.' I can't look at Patrick, but he deftly changes the subject.

'Are you hungry?'

'Starving.' My stomach is growling at the delicious smell coming from the kitchen. I follow him through to a surprisingly large room, with a pine dresser that runs the length of one wall. 'It was my grandmother's,' he says, switching off the slow cooker. 'My parents had it after she died, but they moved abroad a couple of years ago and I inherited it. Enormous, isn't it? There's all manner of things stuffed in there. Whatever you do, don't open the doors.'

I watch Patrick as he carefully spoons casserole on to two plates, wiping away a splatter of gravy with the corner of a tea-towel, and leaving an even bigger smear behind.

He carries the hot plates across to the table and sets one in front of me. 'It's pretty much the only thing I know how to make,' he says apologetically. 'I hope it's okay.' He spoons some into a metal dish and, on cue, Beau trots into the kitchen, waiting patiently for Patrick to put the bowl on the floor for him.

'Not just yet, chap,' Patrick says. He picks up a fork and turns the meat over in the bowl to cool it down.

I look down to hide my smile. You can tell a lot about someone by the way they treat animals, and I can't help but warm towards Patrick. 'It looks delicious,' I say. 'Thank you.' I can't remember the last time someone looked after me like this. It was always me doing the cooking, the tidying, the home-making. So many years spent trying to build a happy family, only to have it come crashing down around me.

'My mum's recipe,' Patrick says. 'She tries to add to my repertoire every time she comes over – I think she imagines I live on pizza and chips when she's not here, like Dad does.'

I laugh.

'They'll have been together forty years, this autumn,' he says. 'I can't imagine that, can you?'

I can't. 'Have you ever been married?' I ask.

Patrick's eyes darken. 'No. I thought I might marry, once, but it didn't work out that way.'

There is a brief pause, and I think I see relief on his face when it is clear I'm not going to ask why.

'How about you?'

I take a deep breath. 'I was married for a while. We wanted different things, in the end.' I smile at the understatement.

'You're very isolated at Blaen Cedi,' Patrick says. 'Doesn't it bother you?'

'I like it. It's a beautiful place to live, and I have Beau for company.'

'You don't get lonely, without any other houses nearby?'

I think of my broken nights, when I wake up screaming with no one to comfort me. 'I see Bethan most days,' I say.

'She's a good friend to have. I've known her for years.'

I wonder how close Patrick and Bethan have been. He begins telling me a story about the time they borrowed a boat from Patrick's father without asking, and rowed out into the bay.

'We were spotted within minutes, and I could see Dad standing on the shore with his arms folded, next to Bethan's dad. We knew we'd be in terrible trouble, so we stayed in the boat, and they stayed on the beach, for what seemed like hours.'

'What happened?'

Patrick laughed. 'We gave in, of course. We rowed back and faced the music. Bethan was a good few years older than me so she got most of the blame, but I was grounded for a fort-night.'

I smile as he shakes his head in mock sorrow at the punish-ment. I can imagine him as a boy, his hair as dishevelled as it is now, and his head full of mischief.

My empty plate is replaced with a bowl filled with apple crumble and custard. The smell of hot cinnamon makes my mouth water. I spoon the custard away from the buttery crumble topping and eat that, toying with the food so as not to appear rude.

'Don't you like it?'

'It's lovely,' I say. 'I just don't really eat puddings.' A dieting habit is hard to break.

'You're missing out.' Patrick finishes his in a few mouthfuls. 'I didn't make it – one of the girls at work brought it in for me.'

'Sorry.'

'Really, it's fine. I'll let it cool down a bit, then Beau can polish it off.'

The dog's ears prick up at the sound of his name.

'He's such a lovely dog,' Patrick says, 'and a lucky one.'

I nod my agreement, although I know now that I need Beau as much as he needs me. I'm the lucky one. Patrick has one elbow on the table and his chin is resting in his cupped palm as he strokes Beau. Relaxed and contented: a man without secrets or pain.

He looks up and catches me watching him. Feeling awkward, I look away and notice another set of shelves in the corner of the kitchen. 'More books?'

'I can't help myself,' Patrick says with a grin. 'That one's mostly cookbooks Mum's given me over the years, although there are some crime novels there too. I'll read anything with a decent plot.'

He begins clearing the table, and I sit back in my chair and watch him.

130

Shall I tell you a story, Patrick?

A story about Jacob, and the accident. About running away because I couldn't see any other way of surviving except starting over; and about screaming every night because I can never be free from what happened.

Shall I tell you that story?

I see him listening, his eyes growing wider as I tell him about the screech of brakes; the crack of Jacob's head on the windscreen. I want him to reach for me across the table, but I can't make him take my hand, even in my imagination. I want him to say he understands; that it wasn't my fault; that it could have happened to anyone. But he shakes his head; gets up from the table; pushes me away. He is disgusted. Revolted.

I could never tell him.

'Are you okay?' Patrick is looking at me strangely, and for a second it feels as though he can read my thoughts.

'It was a lovely meal,' I say. I have two choices: either I walk away from Patrick, or I hide the truth from him. I hate lying to him, but I can't bear to let him go. I look at the clock on the wall. 'I shall have to go,' I say.

'Not another Cinderella flit?'

'Not this time.' I redden, but Patrick is smiling. 'The last bus to Penfach is at nine o'clock.'

'You don't have a car?'

'I don't like to drive.'

'I'll take you back. I've only had a small glass of wine – it's no trouble.'

'Really, I'd rather make my own way home.'

I think I detect a note of exasperation in Patrick's eyes.

'Perhaps I'll see you at the beach tomorrow morning?' I say.

He relaxes, and smiles. 'That would be great. It was really good to see you again – I'm glad you came back.'

'So am I.'

He fetches my things and we stand in the tiny hallway while

131

I do up my coat. There is barely room for me to move my elbows, and the proximity makes me clumsy. I fumble with the zip.

'Here,' he says. 'Let me.'

I watch his hand carefully fit the two parts together, and draw the zip upwards. I am rigid with anxiety, but he stops just short of my chin and wraps my scarf around my neck. 'There. Will you call me when you get home? I'll give you my number.'

His concern takes me aback. 'I would, but I don't have a phone.'

'You don't have a mobile?'

I almost laugh at his incredulity. 'No. There's a phone line to the cottage, for the internet, but I don't have a phone connected. I'll be fine, I promise.'

Patrick puts his hands on my shoulders and before I have a chance to react he leans forward and kisses me softly on the cheek. I feel his breath on my face and am suddenly unsteady.

'Thank you,' I say, and although it is not only inadequate but unoriginal, he smiles at me as if I have said something profound, and I think how easy it is to be with someone so undemanding.

I clip on Beau's lead and we say goodbye. I know that Patrick will be watching us, and when I turn at the end of the road I see him still standing in the door.

Ray's mobile rang as he was sitting down to breakfast. Lucy was working towards her cooking badge in Brownies, and taking it far more seriously than the occasion merited. The tip of her tongue protruded from the corner of her mouth, as she carefully transferred burnt bacon and rubbery egg to her parents' plates. Tom had been for a sleepover and wasn't due back until lunchtime: Ray had agreed with Mags when she remarked how nice it was that Tom was making friends, but privately he was simply enjoying the peace of a house free from slamming doors and angry shouts.

'It looks delicious, sweetheart.' Ray dug his phone out of his pocket and peered at the screen.

He looked at Mags. 'Work.' Ray wondered if it was an update on Operation Falcon – the name assigned to the Creston estate drugs job. The chief had dangled her carrot for another week before finally dropping it in Ray's lap, with the firm instruction that he focus on Falcon above any other job. She didn't mention the anniversary appeal. She didn't need to.

Mags glanced at Lucy, who was absorbed in arranging the food on the plates. 'Have breakfast first. Please.'

Reluctantly, Ray pressed the red button to reject the call and divert it to voicemail. He had no sooner loaded a fork with bacon and eggs when the house phone rang. Mags picked it up.

'Oh, hello, Kate. Is it urgent? We're in the middle of breakfast.'

Ray felt suddenly uncomfortable. He scrolled through the emails on his BlackBerry to give himself something to do, glancing quickly up at Mags, who managed to convey through rigid shoulders alone that she was not happy at the intrusion. Why was Kate phoning him at home? And on a Sunday? He strained to try and hear Kate's voice over the line, but couldn't make anything out. The familiar feeling of nausea that had plagued him in the last few days returned, and he looked at his bacon and eggs without enthusiasm.

Mags passed Ray the phone wordlessly.

'Hi, Ray,' Kate was cheerful, unaware of his internal conflict. 'What are you up to?'

'Just family stuff. What is it?' He felt Mags' eyes on him and knew he was being uncharacteristically curt.

'I'm so sorry to disturb you,' Kate said drily, 'but I didn't think you'd want to wait till tomorrow.'

'What is it?'

'A response to the hit-and-run anniversary appeal. We've got a witness.'

Ray was in his office within half an hour.

'So what have we got?'

Kate scanned the printed email that had come through from the Police Enquiry Centre.

'A guy who said he'd been cut up by a red car driving erratically about the time the accident took place,' she said. 'He meant to report it, but never did.'

Ray felt a surge of adrenalin. 'Why didn't he get in touch when the first lot of witness appeals went out?'

'He isn't local,' Kate said. 'He was up visiting his sister for her birthday – that's how he can be certain about the date – but he went back down to Bournemouth the same day and didn't hear anything about the hit-and-run. Anyway, he only put two and two together when his sister mentioned the appeal to him on the phone last night.'

'Is he credible?' Ray asked. Witnesses were an unpredictable breed. Some people had great memories for detail – others couldn't tell you what colour shirt they had on without checking first; and even then they got it wrong.

'Don't know – we've not spoken to him yet.'

'Why the hell not?'

'It's half past nine,' Kate said, defensiveness making her snap. 'We only got the information about five minutes before I rang you, and I thought you'd want to speak to him yourself.'

'Sorry.'

Kate shrugged off the apology.

'And I apologise if I sounded off when you rang. It felt a bit, you know, awkward.'

'Is everything okay?'

The question was loaded. Ray nodded.

'It's fine. I felt uncomfortable, that's all.'

They looked at each other for a moment, before Ray broke away.

'Right, well, let's get him in. I want every last detail he can give us about that car. The make, colour, index – anything at all about who was driving it. Looks like we've got another shot at this one; let's do it right this time.'

'Not a fucking clue!' Ray paced in front of the window in his office, making no attempt to mask his frustration. 'Can't tell us how old the driver was, whether they were black or white – Jesus! He doesn't even know if it was a man or a woman!' He rubbed his head vigorously, as though the stimulation might spark an idea.

'Visibility was bad,' Kate reminded him, 'and he was concentrating on keeping control of his own vehicle.'

Ray wasn't in the mood to be generous. 'The bloke shouldn't be on the road if a bit of rain's going to affect him that much.' He sat down heavily and took a slurp of coffee, wincing as he realised it was stone cold. 'One of these days, I'll actually get to drink a whole cup of coffee,' he muttered.

'A J-reg Ford,' Kate said, reading from her notes, 'with a cracked windscreen. Possibly a Fiesta or a Focus. It's something, at least.'

'Well, it's better than nothing,' Ray said. 'Let's get going. I'd like you to prioritise finding Jacob's mother. If – when – we get someone in the traps for this, I want her to see we didn't give up on her son.'

'Understood,' said Kate. 'I got on well with the head teacher at the school when I rang about the appeal. I'll call again now and do some more digging. Someone must have stayed in touch with her.'

'I'll get Malcolm to work on the car. We'll get a PNC check on all the Bristol-registered Fiestas and Focuses, and I'll stand you lunch while we go through the printout.'

Pushing aside the remains of what Moira had optimistically offered as paella, Ray rested a hand on the pile of paperwork in front of him. 'Nine hundred and forty-two.' He whistled.

'And that's just in this area,' Kate said. 'What if it was just passing through?'

'Let's see if we can narrow it down a bit.' He folded the printout and handed it to Kate. 'Check this list against the ANPR: say half an hour before the hit-and-run until half an hour after it. We'll see how many of them were on the road during that time, and start eliminating them from there.'

'We're getting close,' Kate said, her eyes shining. 'I can feel it.'

Ray grinned. 'Let's not get ahead of ourselves. What other work have you got on at the moment?'

She counted jobs off on her fingers. 'The Londis robbery, series of assaults on Asian taxi-drivers, and a possible sexual assault coming our way from shift. Oh, and I've got a two-day Diversity course next week.'

Ray snorted. 'Consider yourself off the Diversity hook,' he

said. 'And pass your other jobs to me to reallocate. I want you working full-time on the hit-and-run.'

'Officially, this time?' Kate said, raising an eyebrow.

'Totally above board,' Ray said, grinning. 'But go easy on the overtime.'

18

As the bus arrives in Port Ellis, Patrick is already waiting for me. We've met on the beach every morning for the last fortnight, and when he suggested we spend his afternoon off together, I only hesitated for a moment. I can't spend my whole life afraid.

'Where are we going?' I ask, looking around for clues. His house is in the opposite direction, and we pass the village pub without stopping.

'You'll see.'

We leave the village and follow the road that drops down towards the sea. As we walk, our hands touch and his fingers lace between mine. I feel a jolt of electricity and I let my hand relax into his.

The news that I have been spending time with Patrick has spread through Penfach at an astonishing rate. Yesterday I ran into Iestyn at the village shop.

'I hear you've been seeing Alun Mathews' boy,' he said, with a lop-sided smile. 'He's a good lad, Patrick, you could do a lot worse for yourself.' I felt myself redden.

'When will you be able to look at my front door?' I asked him, changing the subject. 'It's no better: the lock sticks so badly the key sometimes won't turn at all.'

'You don't need to be worrying about that,' Iestyn replied. 'There's no one would be stealing anything around here.'

I had to take a breath before answering, knowing he found me strange for locking the door at all. 'All the same,' I said to him, 'I'd feel better if it were fixed.'

Once again Iestyn promised to come up to the cottage to sort it out, but when I left at lunchtime there had been no sign of him, and it took me a full ten minutes to force the door shut.

The road continues to narrow, and I can see the swell of the ocean at the end of the lane. The water is grey and unforgiving, white spray bursting into the air from the wrestling waves. The gulls sweep in dizzying circles, buffeted by the winds that wrap themselves around the bay. Finally I realise where Patrick is taking me.

'The lifeboat station! Can we go in?'

'That's the idea,' he says. 'You've seen the vet's surgery; I thought you might like to see this place – I seem to spend almost as much time here.'

Port Ellis Lifeboat Station is an odd, squat building, which could be mistaken for industrial premises, were it not for the lookout tower perched on top; its four glass windows reminding me of an aircraft control tower.

We walk past a huge pair of blue sliding doors at the front of the building, and Patrick presses an entry-code into a grey box next to a smaller door to one side.

'Come on, I'll show you around.'

Inside, the station smells of sweat and the sea; of the sharp tang of salt that lingers on clothing. The boathouse is dominated by what Patrick tells me is called 'the Craft'; a bright orange rigid inflatable boat.

'We're clipped on,' he says, 'but when the weather's bad, sometimes it's all you can do to stay in the boat.'

I wander around the boathouse, taking in the notices pinned to the door, the equipment lists carefully ticked off with each daily check. On the wall is a plaque, commemorating three volunteers who lost their lives in 1916.

'Coxswain P. Grant and Crew Members Harry Ellis and Glyn Barry,' I read aloud. 'How awful.'

'They were responding to a steamship in distress off the Gower peninsula,' Patrick says, joining me and putting an arm around my shoulder. He must see my face, because he adds, 'It was very different then – they didn't have half the kit we have now.'

He takes my hand and leads me out of the boathouse into a small room where a man in a blue fleece is making coffee. His face has the leathery complexion of someone who has spent a lifetime outside.

'All right, David?' Patrick says. 'This is Jenna.'

'Showing you the ropes, is he?' David winks at me, and I smile at what is clearly a well-worn joke.

'I never gave much thought to lifeboats before,' I say. 'I just took for granted the fact they were there.'

'They won't be here for much longer if we don't keep fighting for them,' David says, stirring a heaped spoon of sugar into syrupy coffee. 'Our running costs are paid by the RNLI, not the government, so we're forever trying to raise money, not to mention looking for volunteers.'

'David is our operations manager,' says Patrick. 'He runs the station – keeps us all in check.'

David laughs. 'He's not far wrong.'

A telephone rings, the sound shrill in the empty crewroom, and David excuses himself. Seconds later he is back, unzipping his fleece and running into the boat room.

'Canoe capsized off Rhossili Bay,' he shouts to Patrick. 'Father and son missing. Helen's called Gary and Aled.'

Patrick opens a locker and pulls out a tangle of yellow rubber, a red life vest and a dark blue oilskin. 'I'm sorry, Jenna, I have to go.' He tugs the waterproofs over his jeans and sweatshirt. 'Take the keys and wait at my house. I'll be back before you know it.' He moves quickly and before I can reply he runs into the boat room, just as two men rush in through the sliding door, pulled wide open in readiness. Within minutes, the four men are dragging the craft down to the water, leaping effortlessly aboard. One of the crew – I can't tell which – pulls the cord to start the outboard motor, and the boat shoots away from the beach, bouncing over the choppy waves.

I stand there, watching the speck of orange get smaller, until it is swallowed up by grey.

'Fast, aren't they?'

I turn to see a woman leaning against the door to the crewroom. She is well into her fifties, with streaks of grey through her dark hair, and she wears a patterned blouse with an RNLI badge pinned to one side.

'I'm Helen,' she says. 'I answer the phone, show visitors around, that sort of thing. You must be Patrick's girl.'

I redden at the familiarity. 'I'm Jenna. My head's spinning: that can't have taken more than fifteen minutes from start to finish.'

'Twelve minutes, thirty-five seconds,' Helen says. She smiles at my obvious surprise. 'We have to keep a record of all shouts and our response times. All our volunteers live just a few minutes away. Gary's up the road, and Aled has the butcher's in the high street.'

'What happens to the shop when he's called out?'

'He hangs a sign in the door. The locals are used to it – he's been doing it for twenty years.'

I turn back to watch the water, empty of boats now, save for a huge vessel far out to sea. Heavy clouds have sunk so low the horizon has disappeared, the sky and the ocean a single mass of swirling grey.

'They'll be okay,' Helen says, softly. 'You never quite stop worrying, but you get used to it.'

I look at her, curious.

'David's my husband,' Helen explains. 'After he retired he was spending more time at the station than at home, so eventually I thought: if you can't beat 'em, join 'em. I hated it the first time I saw him head off on a shout. It was one thing waving him off at home, but to actually see them get in the boat . . . and when the weather's like this – well . . .' She gives a shiver. 'But they come back. They always come back.'

She puts a hand on my arm, and I am grateful for the older woman's understanding.

'It makes you realise, doesn't it?' I say. 'How much . . .' I stop, unable to admit it, even to myself.

'How much you need them to come home?' Helen says quietly.

I nod. 'Yes.'

'Do you want me to show you around the rest of the station?'

'No, thank you,' I say. 'I think I'll go back to Patrick's house and wait for him there.'

'He's a good man.'

I wonder if she's right. I wonder how she knows. I walk up the hill, turning every few paces in the hope of seeing the orange boat again. But I can't see anything, and my stomach is gripped with anxiety. Something bad is going to happen, I just know it.

It feels strange to be at Patrick's house without him, and I resist the temptation to go upstairs and look around. For want of anything to do, I tune the radio to a local station, and do the washing-up, which is piled high in the sink.

'*A man and his teenage son are missing, after their canoe capsized a mile from Rhossili Bay.*'

The radio crackles with static and I fiddle with the tuning button in an attempt to find a better signal.

'*Port Ellis lifeboat was launched after locals raised the alarm, but so far they have been unable to recover the two missing men. We'll have more on this story later.*'

The wind is battering the trees until they are almost bent double. I can't see the sea from the house, and I'm not sure if I'm glad of this fact, or if I should give in to the pull I feel to

142

walk down to the lifeboat station and watch for that tiny orange speck.

I finish the washing-up and dry my hands with a tea-towel as I walk around the kitchen. The dresser is piled high with papers and I find its haphazardness curiously comforting. I put my hand on the cupboard handle, hearing Patrick's words in my head.

Whatever you do, don't open the doors.

What's in there he doesn't want me to see? I look over my shoulder, as though he might walk in at any moment, and pull open the door decisively. Immediately something falls towards me and I gasp, putting out a hand and catching a vase before it falls on to the tiled floor and shatters. I replace it among the jumble of glassware; the air inside the dresser is perfumed with a trace of musty lavender from the stacked linen within. There is nothing sinister here: just a collection of memories.

I am about to close the door when I see the silver edge of a photo frame protruding from between a pile of tablecloths. I pull it out carefully. It's a photo of Patrick, his arm around a woman with short blonde hair and straight white teeth. They are both smiling, not at the camera, but at each other. I wonder who she is, and why Patrick has hidden the photo from me. Is this the woman he thought he was going to marry? I look at the photo, trying to find something that will tell me when it was taken. Patrick looks the same as he does now, and I wonder if this woman is in his past, or still a part of his life. Perhaps I'm not the only one keeping secrets. I replace the photo frame between the tablecloths and shut the cupboard door, leaving the contents as I found them.

I pace the kitchen, but grow tired of my restlessness, and make a cup of tea, which I sit at the table to drink.

The rain stings my face, blurring my eyes and filling my vision with shadowy shapes. I can barely hear the noise of the engine

above the wind, but still I hear the thud as he hits the bonnet,
the slam as he smashes on to the tarmac.

And then suddenly the water in my eyes isn't rain, but seawater.
And the engine isn't a car, but the chug chug chug of the life-
boat. And although the scream is my own, the face that looks
up at me – the dark pools of eyes with their clumps of wet
lashes – that face isn't Jacob's, but Patrick's.

'I'm sorry,' I say, unsure if I am speaking out loud, 'I never
meant—'

I feel a hand shake my shoulder, pulling me roughly from
sleep. Confused, I raise my head from my folded arms, the
square of wooden table still warm from my breath, and feel
the chill of the kitchen hit my face. I screw up my eyes against
the harsh electric light, pulling up my arm to cover my face.
'No!'

'Jenna, wake up. Jenna, you're dreaming.'

Slowly, I drop my arm, opening my eyes to see Patrick kneeling
in front of my chair. I open my mouth, but can't speak, hungover
from my nightmare and overwhelmed with relief that he is
there.

'What were you dreaming about?'

I drag the words together. 'I – I'm not sure. I was frightened.'

'You don't have to be frightened any more,' Patrick says, and
he smooths the damp hair from my temples and cups my face
between his hands. 'I'm here.'

His face is pale, and there is rain on his hair and clinging to
his eyelashes. His eyes, which usually seem so full of light, are
empty and dark. He looks broken, and without stopping to
think, I lean forward and kiss him on the lips. He responds
hungrily, holding my face in his hands, then he suddenly releases
me and rests his forehead against mine.

'They called off the search.'

'Called it off? You mean they're still missing?'

Patrick nods, and I see the weight of emotion fill his eyes. He sinks back on to his heels. 'We'll go out again at first light,' he says, flatly, 'but no one's pretending any more.' Then he closes his eyes and rests his head on my lap, and weeps openly for the father and teenage son who had so confidently taken out their boat despite all the warning signs.

I stroke his hair and let my own tears fall. I cry for a teenage boy alone in the sea; I cry for his mother; I cry for the dreams that haunt my nights; for Jacob; for my baby boy.

19

It is Christmas Eve when the bodies are washed up, days after Patrick and the rest of the crew have stopped searching for them. I had naively assumed they would appear together, but I should have known by now the tide is never predictable. The son came first, carried gently into Rhossili Bay by a rippling sea that seemed too mild to have inflicted the terrible injuries seen on his father, washed up a mile down the coast.

We are on the beach when Patrick gets the call, and I know from his grimly set jaw that the news is not good. He walks a little away from me, as if to shield me, and turns to stare at the sea as he listens in silence to David. After he finishes the call, he stays rooted to the spot, scanning the horizon as if searching for answers. I walk over to him and place my hand on his arm, and he jumps, as though he has forgotten I was there at all.

'I'm so sorry,' I say, hopelessly trying to find the right words.

'I was seeing a girl,' he says, still looking out to sea. 'I met her at university and we lived together in Leeds.'

I listen, unsure where this is going.

'When I came back here I brought her with me. She didn't want to come, but we didn't want to be apart, so she gave up her job and came to live in Port Ellis with me. She hated it. It was too small, too quiet, too slow for her.'

I feel a sense of discomfort, as though I am intruding. I want to tell him to stop talking, that he doesn't need to tell me this, but it's as if he can't stop.

'We had a row one day, in the middle of summer. It was the same old argument: she wanted to return to Leeds, I wanted to stay here and build up the practice. She stormed off and went down to the beach to surf, but she got caught in a riptide and never came back.'

'Oh God, Patrick.' There is a lump in my throat. 'How awful.'

He finally turns to look at me. 'Her surfboard washed up the next day, but we never found her body.'

'"We",' I say. 'You searched for her yourself?' I can't imagine how painful that must have been.

He shrugged. 'We all did. That's our job, isn't it?'

'Yes, but . . .' I trail off. Of course he searched for her – how could he not?

I put my arms around Patrick and he leans into me, his face pressed into my neck. I had imagined his life to be perfect: for there to be nothing more to him than the funny, easy-going persona he presents. But the ghosts he battles are as real as my own. For the first time I'm with someone who needs me as much as I need him.

We walk slowly to the cottage, where Patrick tells me to wait for him while he fetches something from his car.

'What is it?' I say, intrigued.

'You'll see.' The sparkle is back in his eyes now, and I marvel at his ability to cope with such sadness in his life. I wonder if it's the passing years that have given him the strength, and hope that one day I will find the same.

When Patrick returns, he has a Christmas tree slung casually across his shoulder. I feel a pang of sadness as I recall how excited I used to get about Christmas. When we were children, Eve and I would follow strict rituals of decoration: lights first, then tinsel, then the solemn placing of baubles, and finally the battered angel teetering at the top of the tree. I imagine her following those traditions with her own children.

I don't want a tree in my house. Decorations are for children;

147

for families. But Patrick insists. 'I'm not taking it away now,' he says, pulling it through the doorway and leaving a scattering of pine-needles on the floor. He sets it on its crude wooden stand and checks that it is standing upright. 'Besides, it's Christmas. You have to have a tree.'

'But I don't have anything to put on it!' I protest.

'Take a look in my bag.'

I open Patrick's navy rucksack, and see a battered shoebox, the lid held on with a thick rubber band. Lifting the lid, I find a dozen red baubles, the glass crazed with age.

'Oh,' I whisper, 'they're so beautiful.' I hold one up and it spins in dizzying circles, reflecting my face a hundred times.

'They were my grandmother's. I told you there was all sorts in that old dresser of hers.'

I hide a blush at the memory of searching through Patrick's cupboards, and at the discovery of the photograph of Patrick with the woman I now realise must be the girl who drowned.

'They're lovely. Thank you.'

We dress the tree together. Patrick has brought a string of tiny lights, and I find ribbon to weave amongst the branches. There are only twelve baubles, but the light bounces between each one like shooting stars. I breathe in the smell of pine, wanting to store for ever this snapshot of happiness.

When the tree is finished, I sit with my head on Patrick's shoulder, watching the light dance off the glass and make shapes on the wall. He traces circles on the exposed skin on my wrist, and I feel more at ease than I have felt in years. I turn to kiss him, my tongue searching out his, and when I open my eyes I see that his are open too.

'Come upstairs,' I whisper. I don't know what makes me want this now, right this moment, but I feel a physical need to be with him.

'Are you sure?' Patrick pulls back a little, and looks me straight in the eye.

I nod. I'm not sure, not really, but I want to find out. I need to know if it can be different.

He runs his hands through my hair, kissing my neck, my cheek, my lips. Standing up, he leads me gently to the stairs, his thumb still rubbing my palm as though he can't bear not to be caressing me, even for a moment. As I climb the narrow staircase, he follows behind me, hands touching lightly on my waist. I feel my heart race.

Away from the fire and the warmth of the range, the bedroom is cold, but it's anticipation, not the temperature, that makes me shiver. Patrick sits on the bed and pulls me gently down to lie beside him. He raises a hand and pushes the hair back from my face, running a finger behind my ear and down my neck. I feel a rush of nerves: I think how unexciting I am, how dull and unadventurous, and I wonder if he will still want to be with me once he realises this. But I want him so much, and this stirring of desire in my belly is so unknown to me that it is even more arousing. I move closer to Patrick: so close it is impossible to tell whose breath is whose. For a full minute we lie that way; lips grazing but not kissing, touching but not tasting. Slowly he undoes my shirt, his eyes never leaving mine.

I can't wait any longer. I reach to unbutton my jeans and push them down, kicking them off my feet with reckless haste, then clumsily undo Patrick's shirt buttons. We kiss fiercely, and abandon our clothes until he is naked and I am wearing only my knickers and a T-shirt. He takes hold of the hem of my T-shirt and I shake my head a fraction.

There is a pause. I expect him to insist, but he holds my gaze for a moment, then bends his head to kiss my breasts through the soft cotton. As he moves lower I arch back from him and give myself up to his touch.

I am drifting off in a tangle of sheets and limbs when I sense, rather than see, Patrick reaching across to turn off the bedside light.

'Leave it on,' I say, 'please,' and he doesn't question why. Instead he wraps me in his arms, dropping a kiss on my forehead.

When I wake, I realise instantly something is different, but I'm dazed from sleep and can't tell straight away what it is. It isn't the presence of someone in bed with me, although the weight next to me feels strange, but the realisation that I have actually slept. A slow smile spreads across my face. I have woken naturally. No scream has dragged me from sleep; no screech of brakes or crack of skull against glass. For the first night in more than twelve months I haven't dreamed about the accident.

I contemplate getting up and making coffee, but the warmth of the bed pulls me back under the duvet, and instead I wrap myself around Patrick's naked body. I run a hand down his side, feeling the tautness of his stomach, the strength in his thigh. I feel a stirring between my legs and am again astounded by the reaction of my own body, which aches to be touched. Patrick stirs, lifting his head a fraction and smiling at me, his eyes still closed.

'Happy Christmas.'

'Do you want a coffee?' I kiss his naked shoulder.

'Later,' he says, and he pulls me under the duvet.

We stay in bed until noon, luxuriating in each other and eating soft bread rolls with sweet, sticky blackcurrant jam. Patrick goes downstairs for more coffee and when he returns he is carrying the presents we laid carefully under the tree last night.

'A coat!' I exclaim, as I tear the paper off the squashy, badly wrapped package Patrick hands me.

'It's not very romantic,' he says, sheepishly, 'but you can't keep wearing that tatty old raincoat when you're out on the beach in all weathers – you'll freeze.'

I slip it on immediately. It is thick and warm and waterproof, with deep pockets and a hood. It is a million times better than the coat I have been wearing, which I found hanging up in the porch of the cottage when I moved in.

'I think keeping me warm and dry is an extremely romantic thing to do,' I say, kissing Patrick. 'I love it, thank you.'

'There's something in the pocket,' he says. 'Not really a present – just something I think you should have.'

I push my hand into the pockets and pull out a mobile phone.

'It's an old one I had lying around. Nothing fancy, but it works – and it'll mean you don't have to go all the way to the caravan park when you need to make a call.'

I am about to tell him that the only person I ever call is him, when I realise that perhaps that's what he meant. That he doesn't like the fact I am uncontactable. I'm not certain how I feel about this, but I thank him, and remind myself that I don't need to keep it switched on.

He hands me a second present, expertly packaged in deep purple paper and ribbon. 'I didn't wrap this one,' he confesses unnecessarily.

I carefully unfold the paper and open the slim box with the reverence I can tell it deserves. Inside is a mother-of-pearl brooch in the shape of a sea shell. It catches the light and a dozen colours dance across its surface.

'Oh, Patrick.' I am overwhelmed. 'It's beautiful.' I take it out and pin it to my new coat. I'm embarrassed to produce the pencil drawing I have done for Patrick of the beach at Port Ellis; the lifeboat – not going out, but returning safely to shore.

'You are so talented, Jenna,' he says, holding up the framed picture to admire it. 'You're wasted here in the bay. You should hold an exhibition – get your name out there.'

'I couldn't,' I say, but I don't tell him why. Instead I suggest a walk, to try out my new coat, and we take Beau down to the shore.

The bay is deserted, the tide out as far as it can go, leaving a vast stretch of pale beach. Snow-laden clouds sit heavily above the cliffs, seeming even whiter against the deep blue of the sea. The gulls wheel overhead, their plaintive cries echoing in the emptiness, and the waves break rhythmically on the sands.

'It almost seems a shame to leave footprints.' I slip my hand into Patrick's as we wander. For once, I haven't brought my camera. We walk into the sea, letting the icy foam engulf the toes of our boots.

'My mother used to swim in the sea on Christmas Day,' Patrick says. 'She'd have arguments with Dad about it. He knew how dangerous the tides could be, and he'd tell her she was being irresponsible. But she'd grab her towel and race down for a dip as soon as all the stockings had been opened. We all thought it was hilarious, of course, and we'd be cheering her on from the sidelines.'

'Crazy.' I'm mindful of the girl who drowned, and I wonder how he can bear to be near the water after such tragedy. Beau rushes at the waves, snapping his jaws at each surge of seawater.

'How about you?' Patrick says. 'Any mad family traditions?'

I think for a while, smiling as I recall the excitement I had felt as a child when the Christmas holidays arrived. 'Nothing like that,' I say eventually, 'but I used to love our family Christmases. My parents would start getting ready for Christmas in October, and the house would be full of exciting packages hidden in cupboards and under beds. After Dad left, we did the same things, but they were never quite the same.'

'Did you ever try to find him?' He squeezes my hand.

'Yes. When I was at university. I tracked him down and discovered he had a brand-new family. I wrote to him, and he wrote back saying the past was best left in the past. I was heartbroken.'

'Jenna, that's awful.'

I shrug, pretending I don't care.

'Are you close to your sister?'

152

'I was.' I pick up a stone and try to skim it across the surface of the water, but the waves are too quick. 'Eve sided with Mum after Dad left, and I was furious with Mum for throwing him out. In spite of that, we looked out for each other, but I haven't seen her in years. I sent her a card a few weeks ago. I don't know if she got it – I don't even know if she lives in the same place.'

'Did you fall out?'

I nod. 'She didn't like my husband.' It feels daring to say it out loud, and a shiver of fear runs across my shoulders.

'Did *you* like him?'

It's a strange question, and I pause to think about it. I've spent so long hating Ian; being scared of him. 'I did once,' I say finally. I remember how charming he was; how different from the college boys with their clumsy fumbles and gutter humour.

'How long have you been divorced?'

I don't correct him. 'A while.' I pick up a handful of stones and begin throwing them into the sea. A stone for every year since I felt loved. Looked after. 'Sometimes I wonder if he might come back.' I give a tiny laugh, but it sounds hollow even to me, and Patrick eyes me thoughtfully.

'And you didn't have children?'

I bend over and pretend to be searching for pebbles. 'He wasn't keen on the idea,' I say. It isn't so far from the truth, after all. Ian never wanted anything to do with his son.

Patrick puts an arm around my shoulders. 'I'm sorry, I'm asking too many questions.'

'It's okay,' I say, and I realise I mean it. I feel safe with Patrick. We walk slowly up the beach. The path is slippery with ice and I am glad of Patrick's arm around me. I've told him more than I ever intended to, but I can't tell him everything. If I do, he'll leave, and I'll have no one to stop me from falling.

20

Ray woke up feeling optimistic. He had taken Christmas off, and although he had popped into the office a couple of times, and brought work home with him, he had to admit the break had done him good. He wondered how Kate had got on with the hit-and-run investigation.

Out of their list of nine hundred or so Bristol-registered red Ford Focuses and Fiestas, just over forty had triggered the Automatic Number Plate Recognition system. The images were deleted after ninety days, but armed with a list of index numbers, Kate was tracing each registered keeper to interview them about their movements on the day of the hit-and-run. In the last four or five weeks she had made swift inroads into the list, but the results were slowing down. Cars sold without the correct paperwork; registered keepers moving with no forwarding address – it was a wonder she had eliminated as many as she had, especially given the time of year. Now that the holidays were over, it was surely time for a breakthrough.

Ray stuck his head round the door of Tom's bedroom. Only the top of Tom's head was visible from underneath a mound of duvet, and Ray closed the door again silently. His New Year optimism didn't quite extend to his son, whose behaviour had worsened to the extent that he had been issued two formal warnings by the head teacher. The next one would result in temporary exclusion, which seemed to Ray to be an absurd sanction for a child who was already skipping more classes than he attended, and clearly hated the very idea of being in school.

'Is Lucy still asleep?' Mags said, when he joined her in the kitchen.

'They both are.'

'We'll have to get them into bed early tonight,' Mags said. 'They're back to school in three days.'

'Have I got any clean shirts?' Ray said.

'You mean you didn't wash any?' Mags disappeared into the utility room and returned with a stack of ironed shirts draped over her arm. 'Good job someone did. Don't forget we've got drinks with the neighbours tonight.'

Ray groaned. 'Do we have to?'

'Yes.' Mags handed him the shirts.

'Who has the neighbours round on the day after New Year's?' Ray said. 'What a ridiculous time for a party.'

'Emma says it's because everyone's so busy over Christmas and New Year. She thinks it's a nice pick-me-up once the festivities have finished.'

'It's not,' Ray said. 'It's a bloody pain in the neck. They always are. All anyone wants to talk to me about is how they got caught doing thirty-seven in a thirty zone, nowhere near a school, and what an utter travesty of justice it is. It turns into a massive police-bashing.'

'They're only trying to make conversation, Ray,' Mags said patiently. 'They don't spend much time with you—'

'There's a very good reason for that.'

'—so all they have to talk to you about is your job. Go easy on them. If you hate it that much, change the subject. Make small talk.'

'I hate small talk.'

'Fine.' Mags banged a pan on the counter with unnecessary force. 'Then don't come, Ray. Frankly, it would be better for you not to be there than to turn up in this sort of mood.'

155

Ray wished she wouldn't speak to him as if he were one of the children. 'I didn't say I wasn't going to come, I just said it will be dull.'

Mags turned to face him, with a look that was now less impatient, and more disappointed. 'Not everything in life can be exciting, Ray.'

'Happy New Year, you two.' Ray walked into the CID office and dumped a tin of Quality Street on Stumpy's desk. 'Thought it might make up for having to work over Christmas and New Year.' The office ran on a skeletal shift on public holidays, and Stumpy had drawn the short straw.

'It'll take more than a box of chocolates to make up for a seven a.m. start on New Year's Day.'

Ray grinned. 'You're too old for late-night parties anyway, Stumpy. Mags and I were asleep long before midnight on New Year's Eve.'

'I think I'm still recovering,' Kate said, yawning.

'Good party?' Ray said.

'The bits I can remember.' She laughed, and Ray felt a pang of envy. He doubted Kate's parties involved tedious conversations about speeding tickets and littering, which was what he had to look forward to that evening.

'What's on the books for today?' he said.

'Some good news for you,' Kate said. 'We've got an index number.'

Ray broke into a grin. 'About time. How confident are you it's the right one?'

'Pretty confident. There have been no ANPR hits on it since the hit-and-run, and although the tax has lapsed, it hasn't been declared SORN, so my guess is it's been dumped or burned out. The car's registered to an address in Beaufort Crescent, about five miles from where Jacob was hit. Stumpy and I went out to see it yesterday, but it's empty. It's a rental property, so

Stumpy's trying to get hold of the Land Registry office today to see if the landlord has a forwarding address.'

'But we've got a name?' Ray said, unable to hide the surge of excitement he felt.

'We've got a name,' Kate grinned. 'No trace on PNC or voters' register, and I can't find anything online, but we'll crack it today. I've got data protection waivers in with the utility companies, so now that Christmas is over we should start getting some call-backs.'

'We've made some progress on Jacob's mother, too,' Stumpy said.

'That's great,' Ray said. 'I should take annual leave more often. Have you spoken to her?'

'There's no phone number,' Stumpy said. 'Kate finally got hold of a supply teacher at St Mary's who knew her. Apparently, after the accident, Jacob's mother felt that everyone blamed her. She was consumed with guilt and furious that the driver had been allowed to get away with it . . .'

'"Allowed to get away with it"?' Ray said. 'We sat back and did nothing, did we?'

'I'm only repeating what I've been told,' Stumpy said. 'Anyway, she severed all ties and left Bristol to make a fresh start.' He tapped the file, which seemed to have grown an extra inch since Ray last saw it. 'I'm waiting for an email from the local police, but we should have an address by the end of the day.'

'Good work. It's really important we get mum onside in case we end up in court. The last thing we want is some anti-police maverick mouthing off to the papers about how it's taken over a year to charge someone.'

Kate's phone rang.

'CID, DC Evans speaking.'

Ray was turning away in the direction of his office when Kate began gesticulating wildly at him and Stumpy.

'Amazing!' she said into the phone. 'Thank you so much.'

She scribbled furiously on an A4 pad on her desk, and was still grinning when she put down the phone a second later.

'We got the driver,' she said, waving the piece of paper triumphantly.

Stumpy broke into a rare smile.

'That was BT,' Kate said, bouncing up and down on her chair. 'They processed our data protection waiver on the ex-directory entry and they've got an address for us!'

'Where is it?'

Kate tore the front sheet from her pad and gave it to Stumpy.

'Brilliant work,' said Ray. 'Let's get moving.' He snatched two bunches of car keys from the metal cabinet on the wall and threw one at Stumpy, who caught it deftly. 'Stumpy, take the file with what we've got on Jacob's mother. Head for the local nick and tell them we couldn't wait for a call – we need that address now. Don't come back until you find her, and when you do, make sure she knows that no one's getting away with anything – we're doing everything we can to bring someone to justice for Jacob's death. Kate and I will go and nick the driver.' He paused and chucked the other set of keys at Kate. 'On second thoughts, you had better drive. I need to cancel my plans for this evening.'

'Were you going somewhere nice?' Kate said.

Ray grinned. 'Trust me, I'd rather be here.'

21

The knock at the door makes me jump. Is it that time already? I can lose hours editing photos. Beau pricks up his ears but doesn't bark, and I ruffle his head on my way to the door. I pull back the bolt.

'You must be the only person in the bay who locks their front door,' Patrick grumbles good-naturedly. He steps inside and gives me a kiss.

'City habits, I guess,' I say lightly. I slide the bolt home again, and battle to turn the key to lock the door.

'Has Iestyn still not fixed this?'

'You know what he's like,' I say. 'He keeps promising he'll sort it, but he never actually gets round to it. He said he'll come up this evening, but I'm not holding my breath. I think he finds it absurd that I want to lock it at all.'

'Well, he's got a point.' Patrick leans on the door and grips the big key, forcing it into the lock. 'I don't think there's been a burglary in Penfach since 1954.' He grins, and I ignore the jibe. Patrick doesn't know how I search the house at night when he's not with me, or the way I wake with a start at a noise outside. The nightmares might have stopped, but the fear is still here.

'Come and stand by the Aga and warm up,' I say. It is bitter outside and Patrick looks frozen.

'The weather's set to stay like this for a while.' He takes my advice and leans against the ancient range. 'Have you got enough logs? I could bring some tomorrow.'

'Iestyn's given me enough for weeks,' I tell him. 'He comes

to collect the rent on the first of the month, and he generally turns up with a load of firewood in his trailer – he won't take any money for it.'

'He's a good bloke. He and my dad go way back – they used to spend all evening in the pub, then creep home and try to pretend to my mum they weren't drunk. I can't imagine he's changed much.'

I laugh at the thought. 'I like him.' I take two beers from the fridge and hand one to Patrick. 'So what's the mystery dinner ingredient?'

He phoned this morning to say he would be bringing supper, and I'm curious to see what is in the cool-bag he has left by the front door.

'It was delivered today by a grateful client,' Patrick says. He unzips the bag and reaches inside. Like a magician producing a rabbit, he pulls out a glossy blue-black lobster, its claws waving lazily at me.

'Oh my goodness!' I am at once delighted and daunted by the proposed menu, having never attempted anything so complicated. 'Do many of your customers pay you in lobsters?'

'A surprising number,' Patrick says. 'Others pay in pheasants, or rabbits. Sometimes they'll offer up front, but often I'll turn up to work and find something on the doorstep.' He grins. 'I've learned not to ask exactly where it's come from. It's tricky to pay the tax man with pheasants, but fortunately we still have enough people with cheque books to keep the practice afloat. I couldn't turn away a sick animal just because there was no money to treat it.'

'You're an old softie,' I say, and I put my arms around him, kissing him slowly on the lips.

'Shh,' he says, as we pull apart, 'you'll ruin the macho image I've been building up. Besides, I'm not too soft to skin a fluffy rabbit or boil a lobster.' He gives the over-the-top laugh of a cartoon villain.

'Idiot,' I say, laughing at him. 'I do hope you know how to cook it, because I certainly don't.' I eye the lobster warily.

'Watch and learn, madam,' Patrick says, draping a tea-towel over his arm and bowing extravagantly. 'Dinner will be served shortly.'

I find my largest saucepan and Patrick zips the lobster safely back in the cool-bag while we wait for the Aga to boil the water. I fill the sink to wash the lettuce and we work in companionable silence, Beau occasionally weaving between our legs, reminding us gently of his presence. It's easy and non-threatening, and I smile to myself, sneaking a glance at Patrick, who is engrossed in the sauce he is making.

'Okay?' he asks, catching my eye and resting the wooden spoon against the pan. 'What are you thinking?'

'Nothing,' I say, turning back to my salad.

'Oh go on, tell me.'

'I was thinking about us.'

'Now you *have* to tell me!' Patrick says, laughing. Reaching into the sink, he wets his hand and flicks the droplets of water at me.

I scream. I can't help it. Before my head has a chance to reason with me, and tell me this is Patrick – just Patrick messing around – I spin away from him and pull my arms about my head. A visceral, instinctive reaction, that sends my pulse racing and makes my palms sweat. The air swirls around me and for a second I am transported to another time. Another place.

The silence is palpable, and I slowly straighten, standing upright, my heart banging against my ribcage. Patrick's hands are by his sides, his expression horrified. I try to speak, but my mouth is devoid of moisture and the feeling of panic in my throat has yet to subside. I look at Patrick, at the confusion and guilt on his face, and I know I will have to explain. 'I'm so sorry,' I begin. 'I . . .' I bring my hands up to my face in dismay.

Patrick steps forward. He tries to take me in his arms but I push him away, ashamed of my reaction and battling with this sudden impulse to tell him everything.

'Jenna,' he says softly, 'what happened to you?'

There's a knock at the door and we look at each other.

'I'll go,' Patrick says, but I shake my head.

'It'll be Iestyn.' I'm grateful for the diversion, and I scrub at my face with my fingers. 'I'll be back in a minute.'

As soon as I open the door, I know exactly what is happening.

All I ever wanted was an escape: to pretend to myself that the life I lived before the accident belonged to someone else, and to fool myself that I could be happy again. I've often wondered what my reaction would be when I was found. I wondered how it would feel to be brought back, and whether I would fight it.

But when the policeman says my name I simply nod.

'Yes, that's me,' I say.

He's older than me, with dark hair cropped short, and a sombre suit. He looks kind, and I wonder what sort of life he has; whether he has children, a wife.

The woman next to him steps forward. She looks younger, with dark hair that curls around her face. 'Detective Constable Kate Evans,' she says, opening a leather wallet to show a flash of metal badge. 'Bristol CID. I'm arresting you for causing death by dangerous driving, and for failing to stop at the scene of an accident. You do not have to say anything, but it may harm your defence if you do not mention, when questioned, something which you later rely on in court . . .'

I shut my eyes and exhale slowly. It's time to stop pretending.

PART TWO

22

You were sitting in a corner of the Student Union when I first saw you. You didn't notice me, not then, although I must have stood out: a solitary suit among a crowd of students. Surrounded by friends, you were laughing so hard you had to wipe your eyes. I took my coffee to the next table, where I flicked through the paper and listened to your exchanges, which flitted incomprehensibly between topics in the way women's conversations do. Eventually I put down my paper and simply watched you. I learned you were all art students, and that you were in your final year. I might have guessed that from the easy confidence with which you took over the bar, calling to friends on the other side of the room and laughing with no regard to what others might think. It was then that I found out your name: Jenna. I felt faintly disappointed when I heard it. Your luxurious hair and pale skin gave you a Pre-Raphaelite quality, and I had been imagining something a little more classic. Aurelia, perhaps, or Eleanor. You were, however, undoubtedly the most attractive of the group. The others were all too brash; too obvious. You must have been the same age as them – fifteen years younger than me, at least – but you had a maturity that showed on your face even then. You looked around the bar, as though searching for someone, and I smiled at you, but you didn't see, and I had to leave for my lecture a few minutes later.

I had agreed to deliver six of these guest lectures; part of a drive to integrate the college into the business community. They were easy enough: the students were either half asleep, or keenly attentive, leaning forward to hang on every word I uttered about entrepreneurship. Not bad for someone who never even went to college. Surprisingly for a Business Studies course, there were a number of girls in attendance, and I hadn't missed the exchange of glances between them when I walked into the lecture theatre that first day. I was a novelty, I supposed: older than the boys in halls, yet younger than their professors and resident lecturers. My suits were handmade; my shirts well-fitted, with flashes of silver at the cuffs. I had no grey in my hair – not back then – and no middle-aged spread to hide beneath my jacket.

As I spoke I would make a point of pausing mid-sentence and making eye contact with a female student – a different one each week. They would blush under my gaze, returning my smile before dropping their eyes away as I continued with the lecture. I enjoyed seeing what spurious reason they would find to hang back after class, falling over themselves in their effort to reach me before I packed up my books and left. I would sit against the edge of the table, one hand supporting my weight as I leaned forward to hear their question, watching the glimmer of hope in their eyes fade as they realised I wasn't going to ask them out. They didn't interest me. Not like you did.

The following week you were there again with your friends, and when I walked past your table you looked at me and smiled; not through politeness, but a wide smile that reached your eyes. You were wearing a bright-blue vest top under which the straps and lacy edging of a black bra could be seen, and baggy combat trousers that hung low on your hips. A tiny ripple of smooth, tanned flesh protruded between the two, and I wondered if you realised, and if so, why it didn't bother you.

The conversation moved from coursework to relationships. Boys, I suppose, although you called them men. Your friends spoke in lowered tones I had to strain to hear, and I braced myself to hear your part in this litany of one-night-stands and careless flirtations. But I had judged you correctly, and all I

166

heard from you were peals of laughter and good-humoured digs at your friends. You weren't like them.

I thought about you all that week. At lunchtime I took a walk through the college grounds, in the hope I would bump into you. I saw one of your friends – the tall one, with dyed hair – and I walked behind her for a while, but she disappeared into the library and I couldn't follow her inside to see if she was meeting you.

On the day of my fourth lecture I arrived early and was rewarded for my efforts by the sight of you sitting alone, at the same table I had seen you on the previous two occasions. You were reading a letter, and I realised you were crying. Your mascara had smudged beneath your eyes, and although you would not have believed it, you were far more beautiful that way. I carried my coffee over to your table.

'Do you mind if I sit here?'

You pushed the letter into your bag. 'Go ahead.'

'We've seen each other here before, I think,' I said, sitting opposite you.

'Have we? I'm sorry, I don't remember.'

It was irritating that you had so easily forgotten, but you were upset, and perhaps not thinking clearly.

'I'm lecturing here at the moment.' I had discovered early on that being on the teaching establishment held immediate appeal for students. Whether it was the desire for someone to 'put in a good word', or simply the contrast with the male students, barely out of their teens, I wasn't sure, but it hadn't failed yet.

'Really?' Your eyes lit up. 'What subject?'

'Business Studies.'

'Oh.' The spark disappeared, and I felt a burst of resentment that you could write off something so important so quickly. Your art was hardly going to feed and clothe a family, or regenerate a town, after all.

'So what do you do when you're not giving lectures?' you asked.

It shouldn't have mattered what you thought, but it was suddenly important to me that you were impressed. 'I own a software company,' I told you. 'We sell programs all over the world.' I didn't mention Doug, whose share was sixty per cent to my forty, and I didn't clarify that 'all over the world' currently meant Ireland. The business was growing – I wasn't telling you anything I hadn't told the bank manager on our last loan application.

'You're in your final year, right?' I changed the subject.

You nodded. 'I'm doing—'

I held up my hand. 'Don't tell me, let me guess.'

You laughed, enjoying the game, and I took my time pretending to think about it, letting my eyes run over your striped Lycra dress; the scarf tied around your hair. You were heavier back then, and the swell of your breasts stretched the fabric taut across your chest. I could see the outline of your nipples and I wondered if they would be pale or dark.

'You're doing art,' I said finally.

'Yes!' You looked amazed. 'How did you know?'

'You look like an artist,' I said, as if it were obvious.

You didn't say anything, but two spots of colour appeared high on your cheekbones, and you couldn't stop the smile spreading across your face.

'Ian Petersen.' I held out my hand to shake yours, feeling the coolness of your skin against my fingers, and keeping it there for a fraction longer than necessary.

'Jenna Gray.'

'Jenna,' I repeated. 'That's an unusual name. Is it short for something?'

'Jennifer. But I've never been called anything other than Jenna.' You gave a careless laugh. The last trace of your tears had disappeared, and with it the vulnerability I had found so compelling.

'I couldn't help but notice you were a little upset.' I indicated the letter, stuffed into your open bag. 'Have you had bad news?'

Your face darkened immediately. 'It's from my father.'

I said nothing, just tilted my head slightly to one side, and waited. Women rarely need an invitation to talk about their problems, and you were no exception.

'He left when I was fifteen, and I haven't seen him since. Last month I tracked him down and wrote to him, but he doesn't want to know. Says he has a new family and we should "leave the past in the past".' You sketched quote marks in the air and affected a sarcastic air that didn't hide your bitterness.

'That's terrible,' I said. 'I can't imagine anyone not wanting to see you.'

You softened instantly, and blushed. 'His loss,' you said, although your eyes were glistening again and you looked down at the table.

I leaned forward. 'Can I get you a coffee?'

'That would be lovely.'

When I got back to the table you had been joined by a group of friends. I recognised two of the girls, but there was a third with them, and a boy with pierced ears and long hair. They had taken all the chairs, and I had to fetch one from another table in order to sit down myself. I handed you your cup, and waited for you to explain to the others that we were mid-conversation, but you just thanked me for the coffee and introduced your friends, whose names I instantly forgot.

One of your friends asked me a question, but I couldn't take my eyes off you. You were talking earnestly with the long-haired boy about some end-of-year assignment. Your hair fell across your face and you tucked it impatiently behind your ear. You must have felt my gaze on you because you turned your head. Your smile was apologetic and I at once forgave you for the discourtesy of your friends.

My coffee grew cold. I didn't want to be the first to leave, and have them all talk about me, but there were only a few minutes before my lecture. I stood up and waited until you noticed me.

'Thanks for the coffee.'

I wanted to ask if we could see each other again, but how could I with all your friends around you?

'Next week, perhaps?' I said, as though it really didn't matter to me in the slightest. But you had turned back to your friends, and I left with the sound of your laugh ringing in my ears.

That laugh stopped me returning the following week, and when we met again a fortnight later the relief on your face showed me I had done the right thing by staying away. I didn't ask to join you that time, just carried across two coffees; yours black with one sugar.

'You remembered how I like my coffee!'

I shrugged, as if it were nothing, although I had noted it in my diary against the day we met, as I always do.

That time I took care to ask you more about yourself, and I watched you unfurl like a leaf seeking moisture. You showed me your drawings, and I flicked through pages of competent but unoriginal artwork and told you they were exceptional. When your friends arrived I was about to stand and fetch more chairs, but you told them you were busy; said you would join them later. At that moment, any concern I had about you disappeared, and I held your gaze until you broke off, flushed and smiling.

'I won't see you next week,' I said. 'Today is my last lecture.'

I was touched to see disappointment cross your face.

You opened your mouth to speak, but stopped yourself, and I waited, enjoying the anticipation. I could have asked you myself, but I preferred to hear it from you.

'Perhaps we could have a drink sometime?' you said.

I took my time answering, as though the thought had not occurred to me. 'How about dinner?' There's a new French restaurant open in town – perhaps we could try it out this weekend?'

Your undisguised delight was endearing. I thought of Marie,

and how she was so coldly indifferent to everything; so unfazed by surprises and bored by life. I had not previously thought it down to age, but when I saw your childish pleasure at the thought of dinner in a smart restaurant, I knew I had been right to look for someone younger. Someone less worldly-wise. I did not think you a complete innocent, of course, but you had at least not yet become cynical and untrusting.

I picked you up from your halls of residence, ignoring the interested glances from students walking past your door, and I was pleased to see you come out in an elegant black dress, your long legs encased in thick black tights. When I opened the car door for you, you gave a start of surprise.

'I could get used to this.'

'You look lovely, Jennifer,' I said, and you laughed.

'No one ever calls me Jennifer.'

'Do you mind?'

'No, I suppose not. It just sounds funny.'

The restaurant didn't merit the early rave reviews I had read, but you didn't seem to mind. You ordered sautéed potatoes with your chicken and I commented on your choice. 'It's rare to find a woman who doesn't care about putting on weight.' I smiled, to show you I was making light of it.

'I don't diet,' you said. 'Life's too short.' But although you ate the creamy sauce on your chicken, you left your potatoes. When the waiter offered the dessert menus I waved them away.

'Just coffee, please.' I saw your disappointment but you did not need fat-laden puddings. 'What will you do when you graduate?' I asked.

You sighed. 'I don't know. Some day I'd like to open a gallery, but for now I just need to find a job.'

'As an artist?'

'If only it were that easy! I'm a sculptor, mostly, and I'll try to sell what I make, but it'll mean getting any old job – bar

171

work, perhaps, or stacking shelves – to pay the bills. I'll probably end up moving back with Mum.'

'Do you get on with her?'

You wrinkled your nose the way a child does. 'Not really. She's very close to my sister, but we've never really seen eye to eye. It was her fault my dad left without saying goodbye.'

I poured us both another glass of wine. 'What did she do?'

'She threw him out. She told me she was sorry, but that she had a life to live too, and she couldn't live this one any longer. Then she refused to talk about it. I think it's the most selfish thing I've ever come across.'

I could see the hurt in your eyes and I reached over to rest my hand on yours.

'Will you write back to your dad?'

You shook your head violently. 'He made it quite clear in his letter I should leave him alone. I don't know what Mum did, but it was bad enough for him not to want to see us again.'

I laced my fingers through yours and stroked my thumb across the smooth skin between your thumb and forefinger. 'You can't choose your parents,' I said, 'more's the pity.'

'Are you close to yours?'

'They're dead.' I had told the lie so often I nearly believed it myself. It might even have been true – how would I have known? I'd never sent them my address when I moved down south, and I can't imagine they lost much sleep over my departure.

'I'm sorry.'

You squeezed my hand and your eyes became shiny with compassion.

I felt a stirring in my groin and I dropped my eyes to the table. 'It was a long time ago.'

'We have something in common then,' you said. You gave a brave smile which showed you thought you understood me. 'We're both missing our fathers.'

It wasn't clear if your ambiguity was intentional – you were wrong on both counts – but I let you think you had worked me out. 'Forget him, Jennifer,' I said. 'You don't deserve to be treated like that. You're better off without him.'

You nodded, but I could tell you didn't believe me. Not then, anyway.

You expected me to come home with you, but I had no wish to spend an hour in a student bedsit, drinking cheap coffee out of chipped mugs. I would have taken you back to mine, but Marie's things were still there, and I knew you would object to that. Besides, this felt different. I didn't want a one-night-stand: I wanted you.

I walked you to your door.

'Chivalry isn't dead, after all,' you joked.

I gave a little half-bow, and when you laughed I felt absurdly pleased to have made you happy.

'I don't think I've ever been taken out by a proper gentleman before.'

'Well then,' I said, and I took your hand and brought it briefly to my lips, 'we must make a habit of it.'

You flushed and bit your lip. Lifted your chin a fraction, ready for my kiss.

'Sleep well,' I said. I turned and walked back to my car, and didn't look back over my shoulder. You wanted me – that much was obvious – but you didn't yet want me enough.

23

Ray was floored by Jenna Gray's lack of emotion. There was no cry of outrage, no fierce denial or rush of remorse. He watched her face carefully as Kate carried out the arrest, but all he saw was the faintest flicker of what looked like relief. He felt oddly uneasy, as though his legs had been taken from under him. After more than a year of searching for the person who killed Jacob, Jenna Gray wasn't at all what he had expected.

She was striking, rather than pretty. Her nose was slim, but long, and her pale skin covered with freckles that joined up in places. Her green eyes slanted fractionally upwards, giving her a cat-like appearance, and dark auburn hair swung about her shoulders. She wore no make-up, and although her baggy clothes concealed her figure, narrow wrists and a slim neck indicated she was slightly built.

Jenna asked if she could have a few moments to gather her things. 'I have a friend here at the moment – I'll need to explain this to him. Could you leave us alone for a minute or two?' She spoke so quietly Ray had to lean forward to hear.

'I'm afraid not,' he said. 'We'll come through with you.'

She bit her lip and paused for an instant, then stepped back to allow Ray and Kate into the cottage. A man stood in the kitchen, a glass of wine in his hand. Any emotion that was missing from Jenna's face was writ large upon the face of the individual Ray assumed must be her boyfriend.

The place was so small it was hardly surprising he'd overheard, Ray thought, glancing around the cluttered room. A line of carefully arranged rocks was gathering dust above the fireplace, in front of which a dark crimson rug was spattered with tiny burns. A blanket covered the sofa in a kaleidoscope of colours, presumably in an attempt to brighten the place up, but the lighting was dim and the cottage's low ceilings made even Ray duck his head to avoid the beam between the sitting area and the kitchen. What a place to live. Miles from anywhere and freezing, despite the fire. He wondered why she had chosen it; whether she thought she would be better hidden here than anywhere else.

'This is Patrick Mathews,' Jenna said, as if they were standing around at a social gathering. But then she turned her back on Ray and Kate, and Ray immediately felt as though he were intruding.

'I have to go with these police officers.' Her words were clipped and flat. 'Something terrible happened last year and I have to put it right.'

'What's going on? Where are they taking you?'

Either he knew nothing about what she had done, or he was an accomplished liar, Ray thought. 'We'll be taking her to Bristol,' he said, stepping forward to hand Patrick a card, 'where she'll be interviewed.'

'Can't this be dealt with tomorrow? I could give her a lift into Swansea in the morning.'

'Mr Mathews,' Ray said, his patience wearing thin. It had taken three hours to get to Penfach and another hour to track down Blaen Cedi Cottage. 'Last November a five-year-old boy was knocked over and killed by a car that failed to stop. I'm afraid that's something that can't wait until the morning.'

'But what's that got to do with Jenna?'

There was a pause. Patrick looked first at Ray, then at Jenna. He shook his head slowly. 'No. There must be some mistake. You don't even drive.'

She held his gaze. 'There's no mistake.'

Ray felt a shiver run through him at the coldness in her voice. For the last year he had tried to imagine who could be cold-hearted enough to drive away from a dying child. Now that he was face to face with her, he was battling to remain professional. He knew it wasn't only him: his colleagues would find it equally difficult to deal with, just as they found it a challenge to be polite to sex offenders and child abusers. He glanced at Kate, and saw she felt it too. The sooner they got back to Bristol, the better.

'We need to get moving,' he said to Jenna. 'When we get to the custody suite you'll be interviewed and you'll have an opportunity to tell us what happened. Until then we can't talk about the case. Do you understand?'

'Yes.' Jenna picked up a small rucksack from where it had been slung across the back of a chair. She looked at Patrick. 'Would you be able to stay and look after Beau? I'll try to call when I know what's happening.'

He nodded, but didn't speak. Ray wondered what he was thinking. What must it be like to discover you had been lied to by someone you thought you knew?

Ray placed the handcuffs on Jenna's wrists, checking they weren't too tight, and noticing there was not even a flicker of reaction as he did so. He saw a flash of scarred tissue on her palm, but she closed her fist and it was gone.

'The car's quite some way away, I'm afraid,' he said. 'We couldn't get any closer than the caravan park.'

'No,' Jenna said. 'The road ends half a mile away.'

'Is that all?' Ray said. It had felt longer when he and Kate were inching their way along it. Ray had found a torch rattling around in the boot of the car, but the batteries were dying and he'd had to shake it every few metres to get it to work.

'Call me as soon as you can,' said Patrick, as they escorted Jenna outside. 'And get a solicitor!' he called after them, but the dark night swallowed up his words and she didn't answer him.

They made an awkward trio, stumbling along the path to the caravan park, and Ray was glad that Jenna was cooperative. She may have been slim, but she was as tall as Ray, and she clearly knew the path far better than they did. Ray was thoroughly disorientated and not even sure how close they were to the edge of the cliff. Every now and then he heard a crash of waves so loud he half expected to feel spray on his cheek. He was relieved to reach the caravan park without mishap, and he opened the back door of the unmarked Corsa for Jenna, who got in without a murmur.

He and Kate moved a few metres away from the car to talk.

'Do you think she's all there?' Kate said. 'She's hardly said two words.'

'Who knows? Maybe she's in shock.'

'I guess she thought she'd got away with it, after all this time. How can anyone be so heartless?' Kate shook her head.

'Let's hear what she's got to say, first, shall we?' Ray said. 'Before we hang her.' After the euphoria of finally identifying the driver, the arrest had felt peculiarly anticlimactic.

'You know that pretty girls can be murderers too, right?' Kate said. She was laughing at him. But before he could reply, she had swiped the car keys from his hands and was striding towards the car.

The drive back was tedious, with nose-to-tail traffic crawling along the M4. Ray and Kate talked in low voices about harmless topics: office politics; the new cars; the advert in Weekly Orders for Major Crime jobs. Ray had assumed Jenna was asleep, but she spoke as they were approaching Newport.

'How did you find me?'

'It wasn't that hard,' Kate said, when Ray didn't answer. 'You've got a broadband account in your name. We double-checked with your landlord to make sure we had the right place – he was very helpful.'

Ray looked back to see how Jenna was taking this, but she was looking out of the window at the heavy traffic. The only sign that she was anything other than perfectly relaxed was the fists bunched in her lap.

'It must have been tough for you,' Kate continued, 'living with what you'd done.'

'Kate,' Ray said warningly.

'Tougher for Jacob's mother, of course . . .'

'That's enough, Kate,' Ray said. 'Save it for interview.' He shot her a cautionary glance and she glared back defiantly. It was going to be a long night.

24

In the dark of the police car I let myself cry. Hot tears fall on to my clenched fists as the detective speaks to me, making little attempt to disguise the contempt in her voice. It's no less than I deserve, but even so it's hard to take. Not once have I forgotten Jacob's mother. Not once have I stopped thinking about her loss – a loss far greater than my own. I hate myself for what I've done.

I make myself breathe deeply and evenly, hiding my sobs; not wanting the police officers to pay me any more attention. I imagine them knocking on Iestyn's door, and my cheeks burn with shame. News that I was going out with Patrick spread so fast round the village: perhaps the gossips already have hold of this latest scandal.

Nothing could be worse than the look in Patrick's eyes when I walked back into the kitchen with the police. I read the betrayal on his face as clearly as if it had been written in letters ten-foot tall. Everything he believed of me was a lie, and a lie built to cover up an inexcusable crime. I can't blame him for the look in his eyes. I should have known better than to let myself get close to anyone – to let someone get close to me.

We're already on the outskirts of Bristol. I need to clear my thoughts. They will take me into an interview room, I imagine; suggest that I call a lawyer. The police will ask questions and I'll answer them as calmly as I can. I won't cry, or offer excuses. They will charge me, I'll go to court, and it will be over. Justice will finally be done. Is that how it works? I'm not sure. My knowledge of the police is gleaned from detective novels and newspaper articles – I hadn't ever expected to end up on this side of the fence. I see a stack of newspapers in my mind, my photo blown up to show every line on my face. The face of a killer.

A woman has been arrested in connection with the death of Jacob Jordan.

I don't know if the papers will print my name, but even if they don't, they're sure to run the story. I put my hand on my chest and feel the hammering of my heart against my palm. I'm hot and clammy, as though I'm coming down with a fever. Everything is unravelling.

The car slows and turns into the car park of an unattractive cluster of grey buildings, set apart from surrounding office blocks only by the Avon and Somerset Constabulary crest above the main entrance. The car is expertly manoeuvred into a tiny space between two marked police cars, and the female detective opens my door.

'Okay?' she asks. Her voice is softer now, as though she regrets the harsh words she threw at me earlier.

I nod, pathetically grateful.

There isn't space for the door to open fully, and it's awkward getting out with my wrists cuffed together. The resulting clumsiness leaves me feeling even more frightened and disorientated, and I wonder if that's the real purpose of handcuffs. After all, if I ran off now, where would I go? The backyard is surrounded by high walls, with electric gates blocking the exit. When I'm finally upright DC Evans takes hold of my upper arm and guides me away from the car. She doesn't grip me hard, but the act makes me claustrophobic and I have to fight the urge to shake her off. She leads me to a metal door, where the male detective presses a button and speaks into an intercom.

'DI Stevens,' he says. 'Zero nine with one female.'

The heavy door clicks open and we walk through into a large

room with dirty white walls. The door slams behind us with a noise that seems to stay in my ears for a full minute. The atmosphere is stale, in spite of a noisy air-conditioning unit fixed to the ceiling, and a rhythmic banging comes from somewhere within the warren of walls that lead away from the central area. At the edge of the room is a grey metal bench screwed to the floor, where a young man in his twenties sits, biting his nails and spitting the results on to the floor. He wears blue tracksuit bottoms with frayed hems, trainers and a filthy grey sweatshirt with an indiscernible logo. The stench of his body odour catches the back of my throat and I turn away before he can see the mixture of fear and pity in my eyes.

I'm too slow.

'Get a good look, did you, sweetheart?' The man's voice is high and nasal, like a boy's. I glance back at him but don't speak.

'Come and check out the goods, if you like!' He grabs his crotch and laughs, the burst of sound incongruous in this grey, cheerless box.

'Cut it out, Lee,' DI Stevens says, and the man smirks and slumps back against the wall, chuckling at his own wit.

DC Evans takes hold of my elbow again, her nails digging into my skin as she steers me across the room to stand in front of a high desk. Wedged behind a computer is a uniformed officer, his white shirt strained across an enormous belly. He nods at DC Evans but affords me no more than a cursory glance.

'Circumstances?'

DC Evans takes off my handcuffs and instantly it's as though I can breathe more easily. I rub the red grooves on my wrists and find perverse pleasure from the twinge of pain it gives me.

'Sarge, this is Jenna Gray. On the twenty-sixth of November 2012 Jacob Jordan was hit by a car on the Fishponds estate. The driver failed to stop. The car has been identified as a red

Ford Fiesta, index J634 OUP, registered owner Jenna Gray. Earlier today we attended Blaen Cedi, a cottage near Penfach in Wales, where at 19.33 I arrested Gray on suspicion of causing death by dangerous driving and failing to stop at the scene of a road traffic collision.'

A low whistle comes from the bench at the back of the custody suite, and DI Stevens turns to shoot Lee a look of warning. 'What's he doing there, anyway?' he asks of nobody in particular.

'Waiting for his brief. I'll get him out of the way.' Without turning round, the custody sergeant yells, 'Sally, get Roberts back in trap two, will you?' A stocky female gaoler comes out of the office behind the custody desk, a huge ring of keys clipped to her belt. She is eating something, and she brushes crumbs off her tie. The gaoler leads Lee into the bowels of the custody suite, and he flashes me a look of disgust as he rounds the corner. That's how it will be in prison, I think, when they find out I have killed a child. Disgust on the faces of other inmates; people turning away when I walk by. Then I bite my bottom lip as I realise it will be much, much worse than that. My stomach clenches with fear, and for the first time I wonder if I can get through this. I remind myself I've survived worse.

'Belt,' the custody sergeant says, holding out a clear plastic bag.

'I'm sorry?' He is speaking to me as though I know the rules, but I'm lost already.

'Your belt. Take it off. Are you wearing any jewellery?' He's getting impatient now, and I fumble with my belt, dragging it out of the loops on my jeans and dropping it into the bag.

'No, no jewellery.'

'Wedding ring?'

I shake my head, instinctively fingering the faint indentation on my fourth finger. DC Evans is going through my bag. There's nothing particularly personal in there, but still it feels like

182

watching a burglar ransack my house. A tampon rolls on to the counter.

'Will you need this?' she asks. Her tone is matter-of-fact, and neither DI Stevens nor the custody officer says anything, but I blush furiously.

'No.'

She drops it into the plastic bag, before opening my purse to take out the few cards that are there and tipping the coins on to the side. It's then that I notice the pale-blue card lying amongst the receipts and the bank cards. The room seems to fall silent and I can almost hear my heart banging against my ribs. When I glance at DC Evans I realise she has stopped writing and is looking straight at me. I don't want to look at her, but I can't drop my gaze. *Leave it,* I think, *just leave it.* Slowly and deliberately she picks up the card and looks at it. I think she is going to ask me about it, but she lists it on the form and drops it into the bag with the rest of my possessions. I breathe out slowly.

I'm trying to concentrate on what the sergeant is saying, but I'm lost in a litany of rules and rights. No, I don't want anyone told I'm here. No, I don't want a solicitor . . .

'Are you sure?' DI Stevens interrupts. 'You're entitled to free legal advice while you're here, you know.'

'I don't need a solicitor,' I say softly. 'I did it.'

There is a silence. The three police officers exchange glances.

'Sign here,' says the custody sergeant, 'and here, and here, and here.' I take the pen and scrawl my name next to thick black crosses. He looks at DI Stevens. 'Straight into interview?'

The interview room is stuffy and smells of stale tobacco, despite the 'no smoking' sticker peeling away from the wall. DI Stevens gestures to where I should sit. I try to pull my chair closer to the table, but it's bolted to the floor. On the surface of the table someone has gouged a series of swear words in biro. DI Stevens flicks a switch on a black box on the wall beside him, and a high-pitched tone sounds. He clears his throat.

'It's 22.45 on Thursday the second of January 2014 and we're in interview room three at Bristol police station. I'm Detective Inspector 431 Ray Stevens and with me is Detective Constable 3908 Kate Evans.' He looks at me. 'Could you give your name and date of birth for the tape, please?'

I swallow and try to make my mouth work. 'Jenna Alice Gray, twenty-eighth August 1976.'

I let his words wash over me; the seriousness of the allegation against me, the consequences of the hit-and-run on the family, on the community as a whole. He's not telling me anything I don't know, and he couldn't add to the weight of guilt I already feel.

Finally it's my turn.

I speak quietly, my eyes fixed on the table between us, hoping he won't interrupt me. I only want to say it once.

'It had been a long day. I had been exhibiting on the other side of Bristol and I was tired. It was raining and I couldn't see well.' I keep my voice measured and calm. I want to explain how it happened, but I don't want to come across as defensive – how could I defend what happened? I've thought so often about what I would say if it ever came to this, but now that I'm here, the words seem awkward and insincere.

'He came out of nowhere,' I say. 'One minute the road was clear, the next there he was, running across it. This little boy, in a blue woolly hat and red gloves. It was too late, too late to do anything.'

I grip the edge of the table with both hands, anchoring myself in the present as the past threatens to take over. I can hear the screech of brakes, smell the acrid stench of burning rubber on wet tarmac. When Jacob hit the windscreen, for an instant he was just inches away from me. I could have reached out and touched his face through the glass. But he twisted from me into the air and slammed on to the road. It was only then that I saw his mother, crouching over the lifeless boy, searching for a pulse. When she couldn't find one, she screamed; a primordial sound that wrenched every last gasp of air from her, and I watched, horrified, through the blurred windscreen, as a pool of blood formed beneath the boy's head, tainting the wet road until the tarmac shimmered red under the beam of the head-lights.

'Why didn't you stop? Get out? Call for help?'

I drag myself back to the interview room, staring at DI Stevens. I had almost forgotten he was there.

'I couldn't.'

25

'Of course she could have stopped!' Kate said, pacing the short distance between her desk and the window, then back again. 'She's so cold – she makes me shiver.'

'Will you sit down?' Ray drained his coffee and stifled a yawn. 'You're making me even more knackered.' It was past midnight when Ray and Kate reluctantly called a halt to the interview to allow Jenna some sleep.

Kate sat down. 'Why do you think she's rolled over so easily now, after more than a year?'

'I don't know,' said Ray, leaning back on his chair and putting his feet on Stumpy's desk. 'There's something not quite right about it.'

'Like what?'

Ray shook his head. 'Just a feeling. I'm probably tired.' The door to the CID office opened and Stumpy came in. 'You're back late. How was the big smoke?'

'Busy,' Stumpy said. 'God knows why anyone would want to live there.'

'Did you win over Jacob's mother?'

Stumpy nodded. 'She won't be starting a fan club any time soon, but she's onside. After Jacob's death she felt there was a lot of criticism levelled at her by the community. She said it had been hard enough being accepted as a foreigner, and the accident was more fuel for the fire.'

'When did she leave?' Kate asked.

'Straight after the funeral. There's a big Polish community in

London, and Anya's been staying with some cousins in a multi-occupancy house. Reading between the lines, I think there's a bit of a question mark over her eligibility to work, which didn't help matters when it came to tracing her.'

'Was she happy to talk to you?' Ray stretched out his arms in front of him and cracked his knuckles. Kate winced.

'Yes,' Stumpy said. 'In fact, I got the impression she was relieved to have someone to speak to about Jacob. You know, she hasn't told her family back home? She says she's too ashamed.'

'Ashamed? Why on earth would she be ashamed?' Ray said.

'It's a long story,' Stumpy said. 'Anya came over to the UK when she was eighteen. She's a bit cagey about how she got here, but she ended up doing cash-in-hand cleaning for the offices on the Gleethorne industrial estate. She got friendly with one of the guys working there, and next thing she knows, she's pregnant.'

'And she's no longer with the dad?' Kate guessed.

'Precisely. By all accounts, Anya's parents were horrified that she'd had a baby out of wedlock and demanded she go home to Poland where they could keep an eye on her, but Anya refused. She says she wanted to prove she could do it alone.'

'And now she blames herself.' Ray shook his head. 'Poor girl. How old is she?'

'Twenty-six. When Jacob was killed she felt it was her punishment for not listening to them.'

'That's so sad.' Kate was sitting in silence, her knees drawn up to her chest. 'But it wasn't her fault – she wasn't driving the bloody car!'

'I told her that, of course, but she's carrying around a lot of guilt over the whole thing. Anyway, I let her know we had someone in custody and were expecting a charge – that's assuming you two have done your job properly.' He glanced sidelong at Kate.

'Don't try and wind me up,' Kate said. 'It's too late and my sense of humour's gone AWOL. We did get a cough from Gray, as it happens, but it got late, so she's been bedded down till the morning.'

'Which is precisely what I'm going to do,' said Stumpy. 'If that's all right with you, boss?' He undid his tie.

'You and me both,' Ray said. 'Come on, Kate, time to call it a night. We'll give it one more shot in the morning and see if we can get Gray to tell us where the car is.'

They walked down to the back yard. Stumpy held up his hand in a salute as he drove though the big metal gates, leaving Ray and Kate standing in the near-darkness.

'Long day,' Ray said. Despite the tiredness, he suddenly didn't feel like going home.

'Yes.'

They were so close he could smell a faint trace of Kate's perfume. He felt his heart banging against his ribcage. If he kissed her now, there'd be no going back.

'Night, then,' Kate said. She didn't move.

Ray took a step away and fished his keys out of his pocket. 'Night, Kate. Sleep well.'

He let out a breath as he drove away. So close to crossing the line.

Too close.

It was two before Ray fell into bed and what seemed like a matter of seconds before his alarm sent him back to work. He had slept fitfully, unable to stop thinking about Kate, and he battled to keep her out of his head during the morning briefing.

At ten o'clock they met in the canteen. Ray wondered if Kate had spent the night thinking about him, and immediately chided himself for the thought. He was being ridiculous, and the sooner he put it behind him, the better.

'I'm too old for these late nights,' he said, as they stood in line for one of Moira's breakfast specials, commonly known as a 'clutcher', thanks to its artery-hardening properties. He half hoped Kate would contradict him, then felt instantly ridiculous for the thought.

'I'm just grateful I'm not still on shift,' she said. 'Remember the 3 a.m. slump?'

'God, do I ever? Fighting to stay awake and desperate for a car chase to get the adrenalin going. I couldn't do that again.'

They carried plates of bacon, sausage, egg, black pudding and fried bread over to a free table, where Kate flicked through a copy of the *Bristol Post* as she ate. 'The usual scintillating read,' she said. 'Council elections, school fêtes, complaints about dog shit.' She folded the paper and put it to one side, where Jacob's photograph looked up at them from the front page.

'Did you get anything more from Gray this morning?' Ray said.

'She gave the same account as yesterday,' Kate said, 'so at least she's consistent. But she wouldn't answer any questions about where the car is now, or why she didn't stop.'

'Well, fortunately our job is to find out *what* happened, not *why* it happened,' Ray reminded her. 'We've got enough to charge. Run it by the CPS and see if they'll make a decision today.'

Kate looked thoughtful.

'What is it?'

'When you said yesterday that something didn't feel right . . .' she tailed off.

'Yes?' Ray prompted.

'I feel the same.' Kate took a sip of her tea and placed it carefully on the table, staring at her mug as though she might find the solution there.

'You think she might be making it up?'

It happened occasionally – particularly with high-profile cases like this one. Someone would come forward to confess to a crime, then you'd get halfway through interview and discover they couldn't possibly have done it. They'd miss out some vital fact – something deliberately held back from the press – and their whole story would collapse.

'Not making it up, no. It's her car, after all, and her account matches Anya Jordan's almost exactly. It's just . . .' She leaned back in her chair and looked at Ray. 'You know in interview, when she described the point of impact?'

Ray nodded for her to carry on.

'She gave so much detail about what Jacob looked like. What he was wearing, the bag he was carrying . . .'

'So she's got a good memory. Something like that would be imprinted on your brain, I would have thought.' He was playing devil's advocate; predicting what the superintendent would say – what the chief would say. Inside, Ray felt the same nagging feeling that had troubled him the previous day. Jenna Gray was keeping something back.

'We know from the tyre marks that the car didn't slow down,' Kate went on, 'and Gray said herself that Jacob appeared "from nowhere".' She sketched quote marks in the air. 'So if it all happened so fast, how come she saw so much? And if it didn't happen fast, and she had plenty of time to see him and notice what he was wearing, how come she still hit him?'

Ray didn't speak for a moment. Kate's eyes were bright, despite the little sleep she must have had, and he recognised the determined look on her face. 'What are you saying?'

'I don't want to charge her yet.'

He nodded slowly. Releasing a suspect after a full admission: the chief would hit the roof.

'I want to find the car.'

'It won't make any difference,' Ray said. 'The most we'll get is Jacob's DNA on the bonnet, and Gray's prints on the wheel. It won't tell us anything we don't already know. I'm more interested in finding her mobile. She claims she threw it away when she left Bristol because she didn't want anyone to contact her – but what if she threw it away because it was evidence? I want to know who she called immediately before and after the collision.'

'So we bail her,' Kate said, fixing Ray with a questioning look.

He hesitated. Charging Jenna would be the easy route to take. Plaudits at the morning meeting; a pat on the back from the chief. But could he charge, knowing there could be more to it than met the eye? The evidence told him one thing; his instinct was telling him another.

Ray thought about Annabelle Snowden, alive in her father's flat even as he begged the police to find her kidnapper. His instincts had been right then, and he'd ignored them.

If they bailed Jenna for a few weeks they could try to form a better picture: make sure there were no stones unturned when it came time to put her before the court.

He nodded at Kate. 'Let her go.'

26

I didn't call until nearly a week after our first date, and I could hear the uncertainty in your voice when I did. You were wondering if you'd misread the signs, weren't you? If you'd said the wrong thing, or worn the wrong dress . . .

'Are you free tonight?' I said. 'I'd love to take you out again.' As I spoke I realised how much I was looking forward to seeing you. It had been surprisingly difficult, waiting a week to speak to you.

'That would have been lovely, but I already have plans.' There was regret in your voice, but I knew that tactic of old. The games women play at the start of a relationship are varied but largely transparent. You had doubtless conducted a post-mortem of our date with your friends, who would have dished out advice like washerwomen leaning on the garden fence.

Don't come across as too keen.

Play hard to get.

When he calls, pretend you're busy.

It was tiresome and childish. 'That's a shame,' I said casually. 'I've managed to get hold of a couple of tickets to see Pulp tonight and I thought you might like to come.'

You hesitated and I thought I had you, but you held fast.

'I really can't, I'm so sorry. I promised Sarah we'd have a girls' night out at the Ice Bar. She's just split up with her boyfriend, and I can't let her down too.'

It was convincing, and I wondered if you had prepared the lie in advance. I let a silence hang between us.

'I'm free tomorrow night?' you said, your upward inflection turning it into a question.

'I'm afraid I'm already doing something tomorrow. Some other time, maybe. Have fun tonight.' I hung up and sat by the phone for a while. A muscle flickered at the corner of my eye and I rubbed it irritably. I hadn't expected you to play games, and I was disappointed that you felt it necessary.

I couldn't settle for the rest of the day. I cleaned the house and swept up all Marie's things from every room and gathered them in a pile in the bedroom. There was more than I thought, but I could hardly give it back to her now. I stuffed it all in a suitcase to take to the tip.

At seven o'clock I had a beer, and then another. I sat on the sofa with my feet on the coffee table, some inane quiz show on the television, and I thought about you. I contemplated ringing your hall to leave a message, and being surprised when you were there after all. But by the time I had finished my third beer I had changed my mind.

I drove to the Ice Bar and found a space not far from the entrance. I sat in the car for a while, watching people go through the door. The girls were in the shortest of skirts, but my interest was nothing more than idle curiosity. I was thinking about you. I was unsettled by how much you occupied my thoughts, even then, and how important it suddenly seemed that I knew whether you had told me the truth. I had gone there to catch you out: to walk through the crowded bar and see no sign of you, because you were back in your room, sitting on the bed with a bottle of discount wine and a Meg Ryan movie. But I realised that wasn't what I wanted: I wanted to see you walk past me, ready for your girls' night out with your miserable, dumped friend. I wanted to be proved wrong. It was such a novel sensation I almost laughed.

I got out of the car and went into the bar. I bought some Becks and began weaving my way through the packed room.

Someone jostled against me and sloshed beer on to my shoes, but I was too intent on my search to demand an apology.

And then I saw you. You were standing at the end of the bar, waving a ten-pound note in vain at the bar staff, who were working their way through a queue four-people deep. You saw me and for a second you looked blank, as though you couldn't place me, then you smiled, although the smile was more guarded than the last time I had seen it.

'What are you doing here?' you said, when I had pushed my way through to you. 'I thought you were seeing Pulp.' You seemed a little cagey. Women say they like surprises, but the reality is they would rather know in advance, so they can prepare.

'I gave the tickets to a guy at work,' I said. 'I didn't fancy it on my own.'

You looked abashed to be the cause of my change in plans. 'But,' you said, 'how come you ended up here? Have you been before?'

'I bumped into a mate,' I said, holding up the two bottles of Becks I had had the foresight to buy. 'I went to the bar and now I can't find him anywhere. I guess he got lucky!'

You laughed. I held out one of the bottles of beer. 'Can't have it going to waste, can we?'

'I should really get back. I'm supposed to be getting a round in – that's if I ever get served. Sarah's saving a table over there.' You glanced over to the corner of the room, where the tall girl with dyed hair was sitting at a small table, talking to a guy in his mid-twenties. As we watched, he leaned forward and kissed her.

'Who's she with?' I asked.

You paused and shook your head slowly. 'I have no idea.'

'Looks like she's really cut up about the ex-boyfriend, then,' I said. You laughed.

'So . . .' I held out the beer again. You grinned and took it, clinking it against mine before taking a deep swallow and then

194

licking your bottom lip as you lowered the bottle. It was intentionally provocative and I felt myself harden. You held my gaze almost challengingly as you took another slug of beer.

'Come back to mine,' I said suddenly. Sarah had vanished, presumably with her new man. I wondered if he minded that she was so easy.

You hesitated for a second, still looking at me, then you gave a tiny shrug and slipped your hand into mine. The bar was heaving with people, and I pushed my way through, keeping tight hold of your hand so I didn't lose you. Your keenness to come with me both excited and dismayed me: I couldn't help but wonder how often you did this, and with whom.

We burst from the hot fug of the Ice Bar on to the street and you shivered as the cold hit you.

'Did you not bring a coat?'

You shook your head and I slipped off my jacket and put it round your shoulders as we walked to the car. You smiled gratefully at me and I felt a warmth of my own.

'Should you be driving?'

'I'm fine,' I said shortly. We drove in silence for a while. Your skirt had ridden up as you sat down, and I reached out my left hand and placed it just above your knee, my fingers touching the inside of your lower thigh. You moved your leg: only a fraction, but enough to shift my hand on to your kneecap instead of your thigh.

'You look sensational tonight.'

'Do you really think so? Thank you.'

I removed my hand to change gear. When I put it back on your leg, I slid my hand an inch higher, my fingers gently caressing your skin. This time you didn't move.

Back at the house you walked around the sitting room, picking things up to look at them. It was disconcerting, and I made the coffee as quickly as I could. It was a pointless ritual: neither of us wanted a drink, although you said you did. I placed them on the glass-topped table and you sat next to me on the sofa, half-facing me. I tucked your hair behind your ears, keeping my hands either side of your face for a moment, before leaning forward and kissing you. You responded instantly, your tongue exploring my mouth and your hands running over my back and shoulders. I pushed you slowly backwards, still kissing you, until you were lying underneath me. I felt your legs wrap themselves around mine: it was good to be with someone so eager, so quick to respond. Marie had been so unenthusiastic that at times it was as if she was entirely absent, her body going through the motions but her mind somewhere else.

I slid my hand up your leg and felt the soft, smooth flesh of your inner thigh. My fingertips brushed against lace, then you pulled your mouth away from mine, and wriggled up the sofa, away from my hand.

'Slow down,' you said, but your smile showed me you didn't mean it.

'I can't,' I said. 'You're so gorgeous – I can't help myself.'

A pink flush spread across your face. I rested on one arm and with the other pulled up your skirt around your waist. Slowly, I ran a finger under the elastic of your knickers.

'I don't—'

'Hush,' I said, kissing you. 'Don't spoil it. You're the most lovely thing, Jennifer. You turn me on so much.'

You kissed me back and stopped pretending. You wanted it just as much as I did.

27

The train from Bristol to Swansea takes nearly two hours, and although I'm desperate for a glimpse of the sea, I'm glad of the solitude and the time to think. I didn't sleep at all in custody, my mind racing as I waited for morning. I was frightened that if I closed my eyes the nightmares would come back. So I stayed awake, sitting on the thin plastic mattress and listening to the shouts and thumps from up and down the corridor. This morning the gaoler offered me a shower, indicating a concrete enclosure in the corner of the female wing. The tiles were wet, and a clump of hair covered the plughole like a squatting spider. I declined the offer, and the stale stench of the custody suite still clings to my clothes.

They interviewed me again, the female detective and the older man. They were frustrated by my silence, but I wouldn't be drawn on more detail.

'I killed him,' I repeated, 'isn't that enough?'

Eventually they gave up and sat me on the metal bench by the custody desk while they had whispered conversations with the sergeant.

'We're bailing you,' DI Stevens said eventually, and I looked at him blankly until he explained what it meant. I hadn't expected to be released, and I felt guilty at how relieved I was to hear that I had another few weeks of freedom.

The two women across the aisle get off at Cardiff in a flurry of shopping and nearly forgotten coats. They leave behind a copy of today's *Bristol Post*, and I reach across for it, only half wanting to read it.

It's on the front page: *Hit-and-run driver arrested.*

My breath quickens as I scan the article for my name, and I let out a small sigh of relief when I see they haven't printed it.

A woman in her thirties has been arrested in connection with the death of five-year-old Jacob Jordan, who died in November 2012 following a hit-and-run in Fishponds. The woman was released on bail, to appear at Bristol Central police station next month.

I imagine this paper in homes all over Bristol: families shaking their heads and holding their children a little closer. I read the piece again, making sure I haven't missed anything that might give away where I am living, and then I fold it carefully so the story is on the inside.

At Swansea bus station I find a bin and push the newspaper underneath the Coke cans and fast-food wrappers. The ink has come off on my hands, and I try to rub it off, but my fingers are stained black.

The bus to Penfach is late, and when I finally arrive in the village it's getting dark. The Post Office store is still open, and I pick up a basket to collect a few groceries. The shop has two counters, at opposite ends, both staffed by Nerys Maddock, helped after school by her sixteen-year-old daughter. It is as impossible to buy envelopes at the grocery counter as it is to buy a tin of tuna and a bag of apples at the Post Office counter, and so you must wait as Nerys locks the till and shuffles from one side of the shop to the other. Today the daughter is behind the grocery counter. I fill a basket with eggs, milk and fruit, pick up a bag of dog food and place my shopping on the counter. I smile at the girl, who has always been friendly enough, and she glances up from her magazine but doesn't speak. Her eyes flick over me, then drop down to the counter again.

'Hello?' I say. My growing unease turns it into a question.

The little bell above the door rings as an elderly woman I recognise comes into the shop. The girl stands up and calls through into the next room. She says something in Welsh, and a few seconds later Nerys joins her behind the till.

'Hi, Nerys, I'll take these, please,' I say. Nerys's face is as stony as her daughter's, and I wonder if they have had an argument. She looks straight past me and addresses the woman behind.

'*Alla i eich helpu chi?*'

They begin a conversation. The Welsh words are as foreign to me as always, but the occasional glances in my direction, and the distaste on Nerys's face, make their meaning clear. They are talking about me.

The woman reaches around me to hand over the change for her newspaper and Nerys rings through the sale. She picks up my basket of groceries and dumps it behind the counter by her feet, then turns away from the shop floor.

The heat from my cheeks burns my face. I put my purse back in my bag and turn round, so desperate to get out of the shop that I knock into a display and cause packets of gravy mix to come tumbling down. I hear a tut of disapproval before I can wrench open the door. I walk swiftly through the village, not looking left or right for fear of another confrontation, and by the time I reach the caravan park I am crying uncontrollably. The blind on the shop window is up, meaning Bethan is there, but I can't bring myself to go and see her. I continue along the footpath to my cottage and only then realise that Patrick's car wasn't in the caravan park car park. I don't know why I expected it to be there – I didn't call him from the police station, so he has no way of knowing I have come back – but its absence leaves me with a feeling of misgiving. I wonder if he stayed at all, or if he left as soon as the police took me away; if he wanted nothing more to do with me. I console myself with the fact that even if he found it easy to walk away from me, he wouldn't abandon Beau.

I have the key in my hand before I realise that the red on

the door isn't an optical illusion, caused by the setting sun, but smears of paint, crudely brushed on with a clump of grass that now lies abandoned at my feet. The words have been written in a hurry; splashes of paint covering the stone doorstep.

GET OUT.

I look around, half expecting to find someone watching me, but dusk is creeping in and I can't see further than a few feet. I shiver and battle with the key, losing my patience with the temperamental lock and kicking the door hard in frustration. A shard of dried paint flies off and I kick it again, my pent-up emotion venting itself in a sudden and irrational rage. It doesn't help with the lock, of course, and eventually I stop, leaning my forehead against the wooden door until I'm calm enough to try the key again.

The cottage feels cold and inhospitable, as if it is joining the village in wanting me out. I know without calling for him that Beau isn't here, and when I go into the kitchen to check that the range is on I see a note on the table.

Beau is in the kennels at the surgery. Text me when you're back.

P.

It's enough for me to know that it's over. I can't help the tears welling up and I screw my eyes tightly shut to stop them from spilling on to my cheeks. I remind myself that I chose this path and now I have to walk it.

Aping Patrick's curtness I send him a one-line text message and he replies to say that he will bring Beau over after work. I had half expected him to send someone else, and I feel both eager and apprehensive at the thought of seeing him.

I have two hours before he arrives. It's dark out, but I don't want to stay here. I put my coat back on and go outside.

The beach is a curious place to be at night. There is no one up on the clifftop, and I walk down to the water's edge and stand in the shallows, my boots disappearing for a few seconds as the tail end of each wave reaches me. I take a step forward and the water licks at the hem of my trousers. I feel the damp creep up my legs.

And then I keep walking.

The slope of the sand at Penfach is gradual, leading a hundred metres or more out to sea before the shelf ends and it falls away. I watch the horizon and put one foot in front of the other, feeling the sand sucking at my feet. The water passes my knees and splashes my hands, and I think of playing in the sea with Eve, clutching buckets filled with seaweed, and jumping over foam-tipped waves. It is icy cold, and as the water swirls around my thighs my breath catches but I keep on moving. I'm not thinking any more; just walking, walking into the sea. I hear a roaring, but if it's coming from the sea I don't know if it is warning me or calling to me. It's harder to move now: I'm chest-high in the waves and dragging each leg forward against the weight of water. And then I'm falling; stepping into open space, and slipping under the surface. I tell myself not to swim, but the voice goes unheeded and my arms begin thrashing of their own accord. I suddenly think of Patrick, forced to search for my body until the tide throws it up, broken by the rocks and eaten by fish.

As though slapped on the face I shake my head violently and take a gasp of air. I can't do this. I can't spend my whole life running from the mistakes I've made. In my panic I've lost sight of the shore and I flail in a circle, before the clouds shift and the moon shows the cliffs high above the beach. I begin to swim. I've drifted further out since I stepped off the shelf, and although I kick downwards, searching for a foothold, I feel nothing but freezing water. A wave hits me and I choke on a mouthful of salty water, retching as I try to breathe through my coughs. My wet clothes drag in the sea, and I can't kick off my laced boots, which weigh heavily downwards.

My arms are aching and my chest feels tight, but my head is still clear and I hold my breath and push under the water, focusing on slicing my hands cleanly through the waves. When I look up and take a breath, I think I am a little closer to the shore, and I repeat the movement again, and again. I kick a foot downwards and feel something on the toe of my boot. I swim another few strokes and kick again, and this time I step on to solid ground. I swim and run and crawl my way out of the sea, salt water in my lungs and ears and eyes, and when I reach dry sand I crouch down on all fours and anchor myself before standing up. I am shaking uncontrollably: from the cold, and from the realisation that I'm capable of something so unforgivable.

When I reach the cottage I strip off my clothes and leave them on the floor in the kitchen. I pull on warm, dry layers, then go back downstairs and light the fire. I don't hear Patrick approach but I hear Beau bark, and before Patrick knocks at the door I have thrown it open. I crouch down to say hello to Beau, and to hide my uncertainty at seeing Patrick again.

'Will you come in?' I say, when I eventually stand up.

'I should get back.'

'Just for a minute. Please.'

He pauses, then comes inside and pulls the door closed behind him. He makes no move to sit down, and we stand for a moment or two, Beau on the floor between us. Patrick looks past me to the kitchen, where a pool of water has seeped from my sodden clothes. A hint of confusion clouds his expression, but he says nothing, and that's when I realise any feelings he had for me have evaporated. He doesn't care why my clothes are soaked; why even the coat he gave me is dripping wet. All he cares about is the terrible secret I kept from him.

'I'm sorry.' Inadequate, but heartfelt.

'What for?' He's not going to let me off so lightly.

'For lying to you. I should have told you I had . . .' I can't finish the sentence, but Patrick takes over.

'Killed someone?'

I close my eyes. When I open them Patrick is walking away.

'I didn't know how to tell you,' I say, the words falling over themselves in my hurry to speak. 'I was frightened of what you might think.'

He shakes his head, as though he doesn't know what to make of me. 'Tell me one thing: did you drive away from that boy? The accident I can understand, but did you drive away without stopping to help?' His eyes search mine for an answer I can't give him.

'Yes,' I say. 'Yes, I did.'

He pulls open the door with such force I take a step back, and then he is gone.

28

You stayed the night, that first time. I pulled the duvet around us both, and lay beside you watching you sleep. Your face was smooth and untroubled; tiny flickers of movement beneath the translucent skin on your eyelids. When you slept I didn't have to pretend, keeping my distance in case you realised how hard I was falling for you. I could smell your hair; kiss your lips; feel your soft breath on mine. When you slept you were perfect.

You smiled before you had even opened your eyes. You reached for me without prompting, and I lay back and let you make love to me. For once, I was glad to find someone in my bed in the morning, and I realised I didn't want you to leave. If it had not been absurd, I would have told you right then and there that I loved you. Instead I made you breakfast, then I took you back to bed, so that you would know how much I wanted you.

I was pleased when you asked to see me again. It meant I didn't have to spend another week on my own, waiting for the right time to call you. So I let you think you were calling the shots, and we went out again that night, and again two nights later. Before too long you were coming over every evening.

'You should leave some things here,' I said, one day.

You looked surprised, and I realised I was breaking the rules: it is not the men who fast-forward relationships. But when I returned from work each day only an upturned mug on the drainer told me you had been there at all, and I found the impermanence unsettling. There was no reason for you to come back; nothing to keep you here.

That night you brought a small bag with you: dropped a new toothbrush into the glass in the bathroom; clean underwear in the drawer I had cleared for you. In the morning I brought you tea and kissed you before leaving for work, and I tasted you on my lips as I drove to the office. I called home when I got to my desk, and could tell from the thickness when you spoke that you had gone back to sleep again.

'What's up?' you said.

How could I tell you I just wanted to hear your voice again?

'Could you make the bed today?' I said. 'You never do.'

You laughed, and I wished I hadn't called. When I got home I went straight upstairs without taking off my shoes. But it was fine: your toothbrush was still there.

I made space for you in the wardrobe and gradually you moved in more of your clothes.

'I won't be staying tonight,' you said one day, as I sat on the bed to put on my tie. You were sitting up in bed drinking tea, your hair tangled and last night's make-up still around your eyes. 'I'm going out with some of the guys from my course.'

I didn't say anything; concentrated on tying the perfect knot in my dark-blue tie.

'That's okay, isn't it?'

I turned around. 'Do you know it's exactly three months today since we met in the Student Union?'

'Is it really?'

'I booked a table at Le Petit Rouge for tonight. That place I took you on our first date?' I stood up and put on my jacket. 'I should have checked with you beforehand, there's no reason why you would have remembered something as silly as that day.'

'I do!' You put down your tea and pushed the duvet aside, climbing across the bed to kneel next to where I stood. You were naked, and when you threw your arms around me I could feel the warmth of your breasts through my shirt. 'I remember everything about that day: what a gentleman you were, and how much I wanted to see you again.'

'I've got something for you,' I said suddenly. I hoped it was still in the drawer of my bedside table. I felt around and found it at the back, under a packet of condoms. 'Here.'

'Is that what I think it is?' You grinned, and dangled the key in the air. I realised I hadn't thought to take off Marie's key fob, and the silver heart spun in the light.

'You're here every day. You might as well have a key.'

'Thank you. That means a lot to me.'

'I need to go to work. Have a great time tonight.' I kissed you.

'No, I'll cancel. You've gone to so much trouble – I'd love to go out for dinner. And now that I have this,' you held up the key, 'I'll be here when you get back from work.'

My headache began to lift as I drove to work, but it didn't go completely until I had called Le Petit Rouge and booked a table for that evening.

True to your word, you were waiting for me when I got home, in a dress that clung provocatively to your curves and exposed long tanned legs.

'How do I look?' You gave a twirl and stood smiling at me, one hand on your hip.

'Lovely.'

The flatness in my voice was unmissable and you abandoned the pose. Your shoulders dropped slightly and one hand fluttered across the front of the dress.

'Is it too tight?'

'You look fine,' I said. 'What else have you got with you?'

'It's too tight, isn't it? I've only got the jeans I was wearing yesterday, and a clean top.'

'Perfect,' I said, stepping forward to kiss you. 'Legs like yours are better in trousers, and you look fantastic in those jeans. Run and get changed and we'll go for a drink before dinner.'

I had worried that giving you a key may have been a mistake, but you seemed to find the novelty of keeping house appealing. I came home most days to the smell of freshly baked cakes, or roast chicken, and although your cooking was basic, you were learning. When what you made was unpalatable, I would leave it, and you soon tried harder. I found you reading a recipe book one day, a pen and paper by your side.

'What's a roux sauce?' you said.

'How would I know?' It had been a difficult day, and I was tired.

You didn't seem to notice. 'I'm making lasagne. Properly, without jars. I've got all the ingredients, but it's like the recipe is written in another language.'

I looked at the food laid out on the work surface: shiny red peppers, tomatoes, carrots, and raw minced beef. The vegetables were in the brown paper bags from the greengrocer, and even the meat looked as though it was from the butcher, not the supermarket. You must have spent all afternoon getting it ready.

I don't know what made me spoil it for you. It was something to do with the pride on your face, or perhaps the way you seemed so comfortable, so secure. Too secure.

'I'm not really that hungry.'

Your face fell and I felt instantly better, as though I had ripped off a plaster, or picked a troublesome scab.

'I'm sorry,' I said. 'Did you go to a lot of trouble?'

'No, it's fine,' you said, but it was clear you were offended. You closed the book. 'I'll make it another time.' I hoped you weren't going to spend the evening sulking, but you seemed to shake it off and opened a bottle of the cheap wine you liked. I poured myself a finger of whisky and sat down opposite you.

'I can't believe I graduate next month,' you said. 'It's gone so fast.'

'Have you had any more thoughts about what you'll do?'

You wrinkled your nose. 'Not really. I'll take the summer off, maybe do some travelling.'

It was the first I had heard of any desire to go travelling and I wondered who had put the idea in your head; who you were planning to go with.

'We could go to Italy,' I said. 'I'd love to take you to Venice. You'd love the architecture, and there are some incredible art galleries.'

'That would be amazing. Sarah and Izzy are going to India for a month, so I might join them for a couple of weeks, or maybe do some Inter-railing around Europe.' You laughed. 'Oh, I don't know. I want to do everything, that's the problem!'

'Maybe you should wait a while.' I swirled the rest of my whisky around my glass. 'After all, everyone will be off travelling during the summer, then you'll all be coming back and hitting the job market at the same time. Maybe you should get ahead of the others while they're gallivanting around the world.'

'Maybe.'

I could tell you weren't convinced.

'I've been thinking about when you leave uni, and I think you should move in here properly.'

You raised an eyebrow, as though there might be a catch.

'It makes sense: you're practically living here anyway, and you'll never be able to afford a place of your own with the sort of job you're looking at getting, so you'll end up with some grotty flat-share.'

'I was going to move back home for a bit,' you said.

'I'm surprised you want anything more to do with your mother, after she stopped you from seeing your dad.'

'She's okay,' you said, but you were a little less certain now.

'We're good together,' I said. 'Why change that? Your mum

lives over an hour away – we'd hardly see each other. Don't you want to be with me?'

'Of course I do!'

'You could move in here and you wouldn't have to worry about money at all. I'd take care of the bills and you could concentrate on getting your portfolio together and selling your sculptures.'

'But that wouldn't be fair on you – I'd have to contribute something.'

'You could do a bit of cooking, I suppose, and help keep the house tidy, but really you wouldn't have to. It would be enough just to wake up with you every morning, and have you here when I get home from work.'

A smile spread across your face. 'Are you sure?'

'I've never been more sure about anything in my life.'

You moved in on the last day of term, stripping your walls of posters and packing up your belongings into a car you borrowed from Sarah.

'I'll get the rest of my stuff from Mum next weekend,' you said. 'Hang on, there's one more thing in the car. It's a sort of surprise for you. For us.'

You ran out of the door and opened the passenger door of the car, where a cardboard box rested in the footwell. You carried it so carefully back to the house that I assumed it must be something breakable, but when you handed it to me it was far too light to be china or glass.

'Open it.' You were almost bursting with excitement.

I lifted the cardboard flap on top of the box and a tiny bundle of fluff looked up at me. 'It's a cat.' I said flatly. I had never understood the appeal of animals, particularly domestic dogs and cats, who leave hair everywhere and demand walks and affection and company.

'It's a kitten!' you said. 'Isn't he the most gorgeous thing?'

You scooped it up from inside the box and held it to your chest. 'Eve's cat had surprise kittens, and she's farmed them all out now, but she kept this one for me. He's called Gizmo.'

'Did it not occur to you to ask me before bringing a kitten into my house?' I didn't bother tempering my tone, and you began crying instantly. It was such a pathetic, obvious tactic that I became even angrier. 'Haven't you seen any of those adverts about thinking things through before getting a pet? It's no wonder so many animals are abandoned – it's people like you making impulsive decisions!'

'I thought you might like him,' you said, still crying. 'I thought it would be company for me while you're out at work – he can watch me paint.'

I stopped. It occurred to me that the cat might well be entertainment for you while I was out of the house. Perhaps I could cope with a cat, if it made you content.

'Just make sure you keep it away from my suits,' I said. I went upstairs and when I came down again you had laid out a cat bed and two bowls in the kitchen, and a litter tray by the door.

'It's only until he can go outside,' you said. Your eyes were wary and I hated that you had seen me lose control. I made myself stroke the kitten and heard you sigh with relief. You came up to me and snaked your arms around my waist. 'Thank you.' You kissed me in that way that was always a precursor to sex, and when I pushed ever so gently down on your shoulder you sank to your knees without a murmur.

You became obsessed with the kitten. Its food, its toys, even its shitty litter tray were somehow more interesting than tidying the house or cooking the dinner. Far more interesting than talking to me. You spent entire evenings playing with it, dragging stuffed mice across the floor on pieces of string. You told me you were working on your portfolio during the day, but when I came home from work I'd find your stuff strewn about the living room, as it had been the previous day.

A fortnight or so after you moved in, I came home to find a note on the kitchen table.

Out with Sarah. Don't wait up!

We had spoken, as we always did, two or three times that day, but you hadn't thought to mention it. You had left nothing out to eat, so presumably you were eating with Sarah and hadn't concerned yourself with what I might have. I took a beer from the fridge. The kitten mewed and tried to climb up my trousers, digging its claws into my leg. I shook it off and it fell on to the floor. I shut it in the kitchen and turned on the television, but I couldn't concentrate. All I could think about was the last time you and Sarah went out: the speed with which she disappeared with a guy she had only just met, and the ease with which you came home with me.

Don't wait up.

I hadn't asked you to live with me in order to spend my evenings sitting on my own. I had already been taken for a fool by one woman – I wasn't about to let it happen again. The mewling continued and I went to fetch another beer. I could hear the kitten inside the kitchen, and I pushed open the door sharply, sending it skidding across the floor. It was comical, and cheered me up momentarily, until I returned to the living room and looked at the mess you had left on the floor. You had made some half-hearted attempt to stack it in one corner of the room, but there was a lump of clay on a sheet of newspaper – no doubt transferring its ink on to the wooden floor – and jam jars filled with murky substances piled into a handyman's tray.

The kitten mewed. I took a swig of my beer. The television was showing a wildlife documentary, and I watched as a fox tore a rabbit to pieces. I turned up the volume but still I could hear the kitten mewing. The sound twisted itself into my head until each cry made the anger rise up inside me a little more;

a white-hot rage I recognised but over which I had no control. I stood up and went to the kitchen.

It was past midnight when you got home. I was sitting in the dark in the kitchen, an empty bottle of beer in my hand. I heard you close the front door oh-so-carefully, unzip your boots and tiptoe through the hall and into the kitchen.

'Did you have fun?'

You cried out, and it would have been funny, had I not been so angry with you.

'Jesus, Ian, you scared the life out of me! What are you doing sitting here in the dark?' You switched on the light and the fluorescent bulb flickered into life.

'Waiting for you.'

'I told you I'd be late.'

There was a faint slur in your voice and I wondered how much you had drunk.

'We all went back to Sarah's after the pub, and . . .' You saw the expression on my face and stopped. 'What's wrong?'

'I waited up for you so you didn't have to find out on your own,' I said.

'Find out what?' You suddenly sobered up. 'What's happened?'

I pointed to the floor by the litter tray, where the kitten lay prone and immobile. He had stiffened up in the last hour or two, and one leg pointed into the air.

'Gizmo!' Your hands flew to your mouth and I thought you were going to be sick. 'Oh my God! What happened?'

I stood up to comfort you. 'I don't know. I came home from work and he threw up in the living room. I looked online for advice, but within half an hour he was dead. I'm so sorry, Jennifer, I know how much you loved him.'

You were crying now, weeping into my shirt as I held you tightly.

'He was fine when I went out.' You looked up at me,

212

searching for answers in my face. 'I don't understand why it happened.'

You must have caught the hesitation on my face, because you pulled away. 'What? What aren't you telling me?'

'It's probably nothing,' I said. 'I don't want to make this worse for you.'

'Tell me!'

I sighed. 'When I came home I found him in the living room.'

'I shut him in the kitchen, like I always do,' you said, but already you were doubting yourself.

I shrugged. 'The door was open when I got home. And Gizmo had torn up pieces of newspaper from the pile next to your work. He was obviously fascinated by it all. I don't know what was in that jam jar with the red label, but the lid was off, and Gizmo had his nose in it.'

You went pale. 'It's the glaze for my models.'

'Is it toxic?'

You nodded. 'It's got barium carbonate in it. It's really dangerous stuff and I always, always make sure it's safely put away. Oh God, it's all my fault. Poor, poor Gizmo.'

'Darling, you mustn't blame yourself.' I pulled you into my arms and held you close, kissing your hair. You stank of cigarette smoke. 'It was an accident. You're trying to do too much. You should have stayed and finished your model while you had everything out – surely Sarah would have understood that?' You leaned into me and your sobs began to subside. I took off your coat and put your bag on the table. 'Come on; let's get you upstairs. I'll be up before you in the morning and I'll deal with Gizmo then.'

In the bedroom you were quiet, and I let you clean your teeth and wash your face. I turned out the light and got into bed, and you cuddled up to me like a child. I loved that you needed me so much. I began stroking your back in circles, and kissing your neck.

213

'Do you mind if we don't, tonight?' you said.

'It'll help,' I said. 'I want to make you feel better.'

You lay still beneath me, but when I kissed you there was no response. I pushed my way inside you and thrust hard, wanting to provoke a reaction – any reaction – but you closed your eyes and didn't make a sound. You took all the pleasure out of it for me, and your selfishness just made me fuck you harder.

29

'What's that?' Ray stood behind Kate and looked at the card she was turning over in her hands.

'Something Gray had in her purse. When I took it out she went quite white, as though she was shocked to see it there. I'm trying to figure out what it is.'

The card was the size of a standard business card. It was pale blue, with two lines of a central Bristol address, and no other writing. Ray took it from Kate's hand and rubbed it between his finger and thumb.

'It's very cheap card,' he said. 'Any idea what the logo is?' At the top of the card, printed in black ink, were what looked like two incomplete figures of eight, one inside the other.

'No idea. I don't recognise it.'

'I take it the address doesn't bring anything up on our systems?'

'No intelligence, and nothing on Voters.'

'An old business card of hers?' He scrutinised the logo again.

Kate shook her head. 'Not the way she reacted when I picked it up. It triggered something – something she didn't want me to know about.'

'Right, come on, then.' Ray strode over to the metal cabinet on the wall and took out a set of car keys. 'Only one way to solve this.'

'Where are we going?'

Ray held up the blue card in reply, and Kate grabbed her coat and ran after him.

*   *   *

It took some time for Ray and Kate to find 127 Grantham Street, an unprepossessing redbrick semi in a seemingly endless row in which odd numbers were inexplicably far from their even counterparts. They stood outside for a moment, contemplating the scrubby front garden and the greying nets at every window. In the neighbouring garden two mattresses provided a resting place for a watchful cat, which meowed as they made their way up the path to the front door. Unlike the adjacent houses, which had cheap UPVC doors, 127 had a smartly painted wooden door with a spyhole. There was no letterbox, but fixed to the wall by the side of the door was a metal post-box, its door secured with a padlock.

Ray rang the bell. Kate reached into her jacket pocket for her warrant card, but Ray put his hand on her arm. 'Best not,' he said, 'not till we know who lives here.'

They heard the sound of footsteps on a tiled floor. The footsteps stopped, and Ray looked directly at the tiny spyhole in the centre of the door. Whatever test was applied, they clearly passed, because after a couple of seconds Ray heard the door unlock. A second lock was turned, and the door opened by about four inches, stopped by a chain. The excessive security measures had led Ray to expect someone elderly, but the woman looking through the gap in the door was roughly the same age as him. She wore a patterned wraparound dress under a navy blue cardigan, with a pale yellow scarf looped around her neck and tied in a knot.

'Can I help you?'

'I'm looking for a friend,' Ray said. 'Her name's Jenna Gray. She used to live in this road but I can't for the life of me remember which house. I don't suppose you know her, do you?'

'I'm afraid not.'

Ray glanced over the woman's shoulder to see into the house, and she closed the door a fraction, making eye contact with him and holding his gaze.

'Have you lived here long?' Kate said, ignoring the woman's reticence.

'Long enough,' the woman said briskly. 'Now, if you'll excuse me . . .'

'I'm sorry we disturbed you,' Ray said, taking Kate's arm. 'Come on, honey, let's go. I'll make some calls – see if I can track down her address.' He brandished his phone in front of them.

'But—'

'Thanks anyway,' Ray said. He nudged Kate.

'Right,' she said, finally picking up on his cue. 'We'll make some calls. Thanks for your time.'

The woman closed the door firmly and Ray heard two keys turn, one after another. He kept his arm through Kate's until they were safely out of view of the house, feeling acutely conscious of the closeness.

'What do you reckon?' Kate said, as they got into the car. 'Somewhere Gray once lived? Or does the woman there know more than she's letting on?'

'Oh, she knows something, all right,' Ray said. 'Did you notice what she was wearing?'

Kate thought for a moment. 'A dress, and a dark-coloured cardigan.'

'Anything else?'

Kate shook her head, confused.

Ray pressed a button on his phone, and the screen burst into life. He handed it to Kate.

'You took a photo of her?'

Ray grinned. He reached across and zoomed in on the photo, pointing to the knot of the woman's yellow scarf, where there was a small circular mark.

'It's a pin badge,' he said. He zoomed in a second time, and finally there it was. Thick black lines like two figures of eight, one nestling inside the other.

'The symbol on the card!' Kate said. 'Nice work.'

'There's no doubt Jenna's connected in some way to this house,' Ray said. 'But how?'

30

I never understood why you were so keen for me to meet your family. You hated your mother, and although you spoke to Eve once a week or so, she never made the effort to come to Bristol, so why should you trek to Oxford every time she wanted you there? But off you went, like a good little girl, leaving me for a night – sometimes more – while you cooed over her burgeoning bump and, no doubt, flirted with her rich husband. Each time you asked me to go with you, and each time I refused.

'They're going to think I've been making you up,' you said. You smiled to show you were joking, but there was a desperation in your voice. 'I want to spend Christmas with you – it wasn't the same without you last year.'

'Then stay here with me.' It was a simple choice to make. Why wasn't I enough for you?

'But I want to be with my family too. We don't even have to stay the night – we can just go for lunch.'

'And not have a drink? Some Christmas lunch that'll be!'

'I'll drive. Please, Ian, I really want to show you off.'

You were virtually begging. You had gradually toned down the make-up you used to wear, but that day you were wearing lipstick, and I watched the red curve of your mouth as you pleaded with me.

'Fine.' I shrugged. 'But next Christmas it's just you and me.'

'Thank you!' You beamed and threw your arms around me.

'I suppose we'll need to take presents. Bit of a joke, considering how much money they've got.'

'It's all sorted,' you said, too happy to notice my barbed tone. 'Eve only ever wants smellies, and Jeff's happy with a bottle of Scotch. Honestly, it'll be fine. You'll love them.'

I doubted it. I had heard more than enough about 'Lady Eve' to make my own judgement on her, although I was intrigued to see what made you so obsessed with her. I had never felt the absence of siblings to be a loss, and found it irritating that you spoke to Eve so often. I would come into the kitchen when you were on the phone to her, and if you abruptly stopped talking I'd know you'd been discussing me.

'What did you get up to today?' I said, changing the subject.

'I had a great day. I went to an artisans' lunch at the Three Pillars – one of these networking groups, but for people working in creative industries. It's amazing how many of us there are, all working on our own at home in little offices. Or on kitchen tables . . .' You gave me an apologetic look.

It had become impossible to eat in the kitchen, thanks to the constant layer of paint, clay dust and scribbled drawings scattered on the table. Your things were everywhere, and there was no longer a place in which I felt relaxed. The house hadn't seemed small when I bought it, and even when Marie was here there had been sufficient room for the two of us. Marie was quieter than you. Less exuberant. Easier to live with, in a way, apart from the lying. But I learned how to deal with that, and I knew I wouldn't be caught out again.

You were still talking about the lunch you had been to, and I tried to concentrate on what you were saying.

'So we think that between the six of us, we can probably afford the rent.'

'What rent?'

'The rent on a shared studio. I can't afford one on my own, but I'm bringing in enough money from teaching to go in with the others, and this way I'll be able to have a proper kiln, and I can get all this stuff out of your way.'

I hadn't realised you were making any sort of income from your teaching. I had suggested you run pottery classes because it seemed a more sensible use of your time than making figurines that you sold for a pittance. I would have expected you to have offered a contribution towards my mortgage before agreeing to go into some sort of business partnership. After all, you had been living rent-free all this time.

'It sounds great in principle, darling, but what happens when someone moves away? Who picks up the extra rent?' I could see you hadn't thought it through.

'I need somewhere to work, Ian. Teaching's all well and good, but it's not what I want to do for ever. My sculptures are starting to sell, and if I could make them faster, and do more commissions, I think I could build a decent business.'

'How many sculptors and artists actually do that, though?' I said. 'I mean, you have to be realistic about it – it might never be more than a hobby that brings you in a bit of pocket money.'

You didn't like hearing the truth.

'But by working as a cooperative we can all help each other. Avril's mosaics would fit well with the sort of stuff I make, and Grant does the most incredible oil paintings. It would be great to involve some of my uni friends too, but I haven't heard from anyone for ages.'

'It's fraught with problems,' I said.

'Maybe. I'll give it some more thought.'

I could see you had already made up your mind. I would lose you to this new dream. 'Listen,' I said, my voice belying the anxiety I felt, 'I've been thinking for a while about moving house.'

'Have you?' You looked dubious.

I nodded. 'We'll find a place with enough outside space, and I'll build you a studio in the garden.'

'My own studio?'

'Complete with kiln. You can make as much mess as you like.'

'You'd do that for me?' A broad smile spread across your face.

'I'd do anything for you, Jennifer, you know that.'

It was true. I would have done anything to have kept you.

While you were in the shower the phone rang.

'Is Jenna there? It's Sarah.'

'Hi, Sarah,' I said. 'I'm afraid she's out with friends at the moment. Did she not call you back the last time you rang? I passed on your message.'

There was a pause.

'No.'

'Ah. Well, I'll tell her you called.'

While you were still upstairs, I went through your handbag. There was nothing out of the ordinary; your receipts were all for places you had told me you had been. I felt the bubble of tension inside me dissipate. Out of habit I checked the notes section of your purse, and although it was empty I felt a thickness under my fingers. I looked more carefully and saw there was a slit in the lining, into which had been slipped a small fold of notes. I pocketed it. If it was housekeeping, tucked away for safe-keeping, you would ask if I had seen it. If not, then I would know you were keeping secrets from me. Stealing my money.

You never mentioned it.

When you left me, I didn't even notice you had gone. I waited for you to come home, and it was only when I eventually went to bed that I realised your toothbrush had disappeared. I looked for the suitcases, and found nothing missing but a small bag. Did he offer to buy you what you needed? Did he tell you he'd give you anything you wanted? And what did you offer in return? You disgust me. But I let you go. I told myself I was better off without you, and that as long as you didn't go running to the police with accusations of what they'd no doubt call *abuse*, I would let you run off to wherever you were going. I could have come after you, but I didn't want to. Do you understand that? I didn't want you. And I would have left you alone, were it not for a tiny piece in today's *Bristol Post*. They didn't print your name, but did you think I wouldn't know it was you?

I imagined the police asking about your life; your relationships. I saw them testing you; putting words in your mouth. I saw you crying and telling them everything. I knew you'd break down and it wouldn't be long before they came knocking at my door, asking questions about matters that are no concern of theirs. Calling me a bully; an abuser; a wife-beater. I was none of those things: I never gave you anything you didn't ask for.

Guess where I went today. Go on, take a guess. No? I went to Oxford to pay a visit to your sister. I reckoned if anyone knew where you were now, it would be her. The house hasn't changed much in the last five years. Still the perfectly clipped bay trees either side of the front door; still the same irritating chiming door bell.

Eve's smile faded pretty quickly when she saw me.

'Ian,' she said flatly. 'What a surprise.'

'Long time, no see,' I said. She never had had the balls to tell me outright what she thought of me. 'You're letting all the warmth out,' I said, stepping forward on to the black-and-white tiles of the hall. Eve had no choice but to step aside, and I let my arm brush against her breasts as I passed her and made my way into the sitting room. She scurried after me, trying to show me she was still mistress of her own house. It was pathetic.

I sat in Jeff's chair, knowing she would hate it, and Eve sat opposite. I could see her fighting with herself, wanting to ask me what I was doing there.

'Jeff not here?' I asked. I caught a flash of something in Eve's eyes. She was frightened of me, I realised, and the thought was peculiarly arousing. Not for the first time I wondered what Lady Eve would be like in bed; if she would be as buttoned-up as you.

'He's taken the children into town.'

She shifted in her chair and I let the silence hang between us until she couldn't bear it any longer.

'Why are you here?'

'I was just passing,' I said, looking around the big sitting room. She's had it redecorated since we were last there – you'd like it. They've gone for those bland, chalky colours you wanted in our kitchen. 'It's been a long time, Eve.'

Eve gave a tiny nod of acknowledgement, but didn't reply.

'I'm looking for Jennifer,' I said.

'What do you mean? Don't tell me she finally left you?' She spat the words with more passion than I had ever seen her muster.

I let the dig pass. 'We split up.'

'Is she okay? Where is she living?'

She has the gall to be worried about you. After everything she said. Hypocritical bitch.

'You mean she didn't come running to you?'

'I don't know where she is.'

'Oh really?' I said, not believing her for a second. 'But you two were so close – you must have some idea.' A muscle began to twitch in the corner of my eye, and I rubbed it to make it stop.

'We haven't spoken in five years, Ian.' She stood up. 'I think you should go now.'

'Are you telling me you haven't heard from her in all that time?' I stretched out my legs and leaned back in my chair. I would decide when to leave.

'No,' Eve said. I saw her eyes flick briefly to the mantelpiece. 'Now I'd like you to go.'

224

The fireplace was a characterless affair, with a polished gas fire and fake coals. On top of the white-painted surround were a handful of cards and invitations, propped up either side of a carriage clock.

I knew at once what she hadn't meant me to see. You should have thought a little more carefully, Jennifer, before sending something so obvious. There it was, incongruous amongst the gilt-edged invitations: a photograph of a beach taken from the top of a cliff. On the sand were letters spelling out *Lady Eve*.

I stood up, allowing Eve to usher me towards the front door. I bent down and kissed her cheek, feeling her recoil from me and fighting the urge to slam her against the wall for lying to me.

She opened the door and I made a play of looking for my keys. 'I must have put them down,' I said. 'I won't be a second.'

I left her in the hall and went back to the sitting room. I picked up the postcard and turned it over, but didn't find the address I had hoped to see, only some saccharine message to Eve in your familiar untidy writing. You used to write notes to me; leave them under my pillow and in my briefcase. Why did you stop? A muscle tightened in my throat. I studied the photo. Where were you? The tension I felt threatened to burst out of me, and I ripped the card in half and then in half again, and again, feeling instantly better. I pushed the pieces behind the carriage clock just as Eve came into the room.

'Found them,' I said, patting my pocket.

She looked around the room, doubtless expecting to see something out of place. Let her look, I thought. Let her find it.

'A pleasure to see you again, Eve,' I said. 'I'll be sure to drop in next time I'm in Oxford.' I walked back towards the front door.

Eve opened her mouth but no words came, so I spoke for her:

'I'll look forward to it.'

*   *   *

I began looking online as soon as I got home. There was something obviously British about those high cliffs, reaching around the beach on three sides, and about the grey sky with its ominous clouds. I searched for 'UK beaches' and began scrolling through images. Again and again I clicked on to the next page, but all I found were holiday guide photos of sandy beaches filled with laughing children. I changed my search to 'UK beaches with cliffs' and continued scrolling. I will find you, Jennifer. Wherever you've gone to, I'll find you.

And then I will come for you.

31

Bethan strides towards me, a knitted hat pulled low over her hair. She begins speaking when she's still some distance from me. It's a clever trick: I can't hear what she's saying, but I can't walk away when she's talking to me. I stand and wait for her to reach me.

We've been walking across the fields, Beau and I, steering clear of the clifftops and the rolling sea. I'm too frightened to go near the sea again, although it's not the water I am scared of but my own mind. I can feel myself going mad, and no matter how much I walk I can't escape it.

'I thought it was you, up here.'

The caravan park is barely visible from here: I can only have been a speck on the hillside. Bethan's smile is still open and warm, as though nothing has changed since the last time we spoke, but she must know I'm on police bail. The whole village knows.

'I was going for a walk,' she says. 'Do you want to come?'

'You never go for walks.'

Bethan's mouth twitches slightly. 'Well then, that's how much I wanted to see you, isn't it?'

We fall into step together, Beau racing ahead in an endless search for rabbits. The day is crisp and clear, and our breath mists in front of us as we walk. It's almost noon, but the ground is still hard from this morning's frost, and spring feels a long way away. I have taken to scoring out the days on the calendar; the day I answer bail marked with a big black cross. I have ten days left. I know from the leaflet I was handed in custody that I might have to wait some time for my trial, but that I am unlikely to see another summer here in Penfach. I wonder how many I will miss.

'I suppose you've heard,' I say, unable to bear the silence any longer.

'Hard not to, in Penfach.' Bethan's breath is laboured, and I slow my pace a little. 'Not that I take much notice of gossip,' she continues. 'I'd rather hear it from the horse's mouth, but I get the distinct impression you've been avoiding me.'

I don't deny it.

'Do you want to talk about it?'

Instinctively I say no, but then realise that I do. I take a breath.

'I killed a boy. His name was Jacob.'

I hear a tiny sound from Bethan – a breath, perhaps, or a shake of the head – but she says nothing. I catch a glimpse of the sea as we draw closer to the cliffs.

'It was dark and it had been raining. I didn't see him until it was too late.'

Bethan lets out a long breath. 'It was an accident.'

It's not a question, and I am touched by her loyalty.

'Yes.'

'That's not all, is it?'

The Penfach gossip mill is impressive.

'No, that's not all.'

We reach the clifftop, and we turn left and begin walking towards the bay. I can hardly bring myself to speak.

'I didn't stop. I drove away and I left him there on the road, with his mother.' I can't look at Bethan, and she doesn't speak for several minutes. When she does, it's straight to the point.

'Why?'

It is the hardest question to answer, but here, at least, I can tell the truth. 'Because I was frightened.'

I finally steal a look at Bethan, but can't read her expression. She looks out to sea and I stop and stand beside her.

'Do you hate me for what I've done?'

She gives a sad smile. 'Jenna, you've done something terrible, and you'll pay for it every day for the rest of your life. I think that's punishment enough, don't you?'

'They won't serve me in the shop.' I feel petty, complaining about my groceries worries, but the humiliation hurt me more than I like to admit.

Bethan shrugs. 'They're a funny lot. They don't like incomers, and if they find an excuse to rally against them, well . . .'

'I don't know what to do.'

'Ignore them. Do your shopping out of town and hold your head up high. What's happened is between you and the court, and it's no one else's business.'

I give her a grateful smile. Bethan's practicality is very grounding.

'I had to take one of the cats to the vet's yesterday,' she says casually, as though changing the subject.

'You spoke to Patrick?'

Bethan stops walking and turns to face me. 'He doesn't know what to say to you.'

'He seemed to manage fine last time I saw him.' I recall the coldness in his voice, and the lack of emotion in his eyes as he left.

'He's a man, Jenna, they're simple creatures. Talk to him. Talk to him the way you've talked to me. Tell him how frightened you were. He'll understand how much you regret what you did.'

I think of how close Patrick and Bethan were when they were growing up, and for a brief moment I wonder if Bethan could be right: might there still be a chance for me with Patrick? But she didn't see the way he looked at me.

'No,' I say. 'It's over.'

We've reached the bay. A couple are walking their dog down by the sea, but it is otherwise deserted. The tide is coming in, licking at the sand as it creeps up the beach, and a gull stands in the middle of the beach, pecking at a crab shell. I'm about to say goodbye to Bethan when I catch sight of something on the sand, close to the incoming tide. I screw up my eyes and look again, but the surf blurs the surface of the sand and I can't read what it says. Another wave and it's gone completely, but I'm certain I saw something, just certain of it. I'm suddenly cold, and I pull my coat closer to me. I hear a noise on the path behind us and I whirl round, but there is nothing there. My eyes scan the coastal path, the clifftops, down on the beach again. Is Ian there, somewhere? Is he watching me?

Bethan looks at me, alarmed. 'What is it? What's wrong?'

I look at her, but I don't see her. I see the writing: writing I'm not sure if I saw on the beach or in my head. The white clouds seem to swirl around me, blood roaring in my ears till I can hardly make out the sound of the sea.

'Jennifer,' I say softly.

'Jennifer?' Bethan asks. She looks down at the beach, where the sea washes over smooth sand. 'Who's Jennifer?'

I try to swallow but the moisture sticks in my throat.

'I am. I'm Jennifer.'

32

'I'm sorry,' Ray said. He sat on the edge of Kate's desk and handed her a piece of paper.

Kate put it on the desk, but didn't look at it. 'Charge decision from the CPS?'

Ray nodded. 'There's no evidence to support the theory that Jenna's hiding something, and we can't delay things any more. She's due to answer bail this afternoon and we'll be charging her.' He caught sight of Kate's face. 'You did a good job. You looked beyond the evidence, and that's exactly what a good detective does. But a good detective also knows when to stop.'

He stood up and squeezed her shoulder gently, before leaving her to read through the CPS decision. It was frustrating, but that was the risk you took when you followed your instincts – they weren't always reliable.

At two o'clock the front desk rang to say Jenna had arrived. Ray booked her into custody and directed her to the metal bench by the wall, while he prepared the charge sheet. Her hair was swept back into a ponytail, exposing high cheekbones and pale, clear skin.

Ray took the printed charges from the custody sergeant and walked across to the bench. 'You are charged under Section 1 of the Road Traffic Act 1988 with causing death by dangerous driving of Jacob Jordan, on the twenty-sixth of November 2012. You are further charged under section 170(2) of the Road Traffic Act 1988, with failing to stop and report an accident. Do you have anything to say?' Ray watched her intently for any sign of fear, of shock, but she closed her eyes and shook her head.

'Nothing.'

'I am remanding you in custody, to appear before Bristol Magistrates' Court tomorrow morning.'

The waiting gaoler stepped forward, but Ray intervened.

'I'll take her.' He held Jenna's arm lightly above the elbow, and walked her into the female wing. The sound of their rubber soles provoked a cacophony of requests as they made their way down the cell block.

'Can I go out for a fag?'

'Is my brief here yet?'

'Can you get me another blanket?'

Ray ignored them, knowing better than to interfere in the custody sergeant's domain, and the voices settled into disgruntled grumbles. He stopped outside number 7.

'Shoes off, please.'

Jenna untied her laces and used the toe of each foot to ease her boots over her heel. She put them down outside the door, where a sprinkling of sand fell from them on to the glossy grey floor. She looked at Ray, who nodded towards the empty cell, and then walked inside and sat on the blue plastic mattress.

Ray leaned against the door frame.

'What aren't you telling us, Jenna?'

She turned her head sharply to face him. 'What do you mean?'

'Why did you drive away?'

Jenna didn't answer. She pushed her hair away from her face and he saw again that awful scar across the palm of her hand. A burn, perhaps. Or some sort of industrial accident.

'How did that happen?' he asked, pointing at her injury.

She looked away, avoiding the question. 'What will happen to me in court?'

Ray sighed. He wouldn't get any more out of Jenna Gray, that much was clear. 'Tomorrow's just the initial hearing,' he said. 'You'll be asked to enter a plea and the case will be sent to Crown Court.'

'And then?'

'You'll be sentenced.'

'Will I go to prison?' Jenna said, lifting her eyes to look at Ray.

'Perhaps.'

'For how long?'

'Anything up to fourteen years.' Ray watched Jenna's face, finally seeing the fear creeping across it.

'Fourteen years,' she repeated. She swallowed hard.

Ray held his breath. For a second he thought he was about to hear whatever it was that had made her drive off that night and not stop. But she turned away from him and lay on the blue plastic mattress, her eyes tightly closed.

'I'd like to try and sleep now, please.'

Ray stood watching her for a moment, then left, the slam of the cell door echoing behind him.

'Well done.' Mags kissed Ray's cheek as he came through the door. 'I saw it on the news. You were right not to give up on that job.'

He gave a non-committal response, still unsettled by Jenna's behaviour.

'Is the chief pleased with the result?'

Ray followed Mags into the kitchen, where she opened a can of bitter, pouring it into a glass for him.

'Delighted. Of course, the anniversary appeal was all her idea . . .' He flashed a wry smile.

'Doesn't that bother you?'

'Not really,' Ray said, taking a sip of his pint and setting it down with a satisfied sigh. 'I don't care who gets the credit for a job, so long as it's investigated properly and we get a result at court. Besides,' he added, 'it's Kate who did the hard work on this one.'

He might have imagined it, but Mags seemed to bridle slightly at the mention of Kate's name. 'What do you think Gray will get in court?' she said.

'Six or seven years, maybe? Depends who the judge is, and whether they decide to make an example of her. It's always an emotive issue, when there's a child involved.'

'Six years is nothing.' Ray knew she was thinking about Tom and Lucy.

'Except when it's six years too long,' Ray said, half to himself.

'What do you mean?'

'There's something a bit strange about it all.'

'In what way?'

'We thought there might be more to her story than she's letting on. But we've charged her now, so that's the end of it: I'd let Kate have all the time I could.'

Mags looked at him sharply. 'I thought you were the one leading on this job. Was it Kate who felt there was more to it? Is that why you bailed Gray?'

Ray looked up, surprised by the harshness in Mags' tone. 'No,' he said slowly. 'I bailed her because I could see a valid argument for taking time to establish the facts and ensure we were charging the right person.'

'Thank you, DI Stevens, I do know how it works. I might spend my days ferrying kids around and making packed lunches, but I was once a DC, so please don't speak to me as though I'm stupid.'

'Sorry. Guilty as charged.' Ray held up his hands in mock self-defence, but Mags didn't laugh. She ran a cloth under the hot tap and began briskly wiping down the kitchen surfaces.

'I'm surprised, that's all. This woman runs from the scene of an accident, dumps her car and hides out in the middle of nowhere, then when she's found a year later she admits the whole thing. It seems cut and dried, to me.'

Ray was struggling to hide his irritation. It had been a long day and all he wanted was to sit down with a beer and relax. 'There's a bit more to it than that,' he said. 'And I trust Kate – she's got good instincts.' He felt himself blush, and wondered if he was defending Kate a little too much.

'Has she?' Mags said tightly. 'Good for Kate.'

Ray let out a big breath. 'Has something happened?'

Mags carried on cleaning.

'Is it Tom?'

Mags started crying.

'Oh God, Mags, why didn't you say so earlier? What's happened?' He stood up and put his arm around her, turning her away from the sink and taking the cloth gently out of her hand.

'I think he might be stealing.'

The fury Ray felt was so overwhelming that for a second he couldn't speak.

'What makes you say that?' This was the final straw. It was one thing cutting school and stomping about the house in a hormonal temper tantrum, but *stealing*?

'Well, I'm not sure,' Mags said. 'I haven't said anything to him yet . . .' She caught sight of Ray's face, and raised a warning hand. 'And I don't want to. Not until I know the facts.'

Ray took a deep breath. 'Tell me everything.'

'I was cleaning his room earlier' – Mags closed her eyes briefly, as though even the memory of it was unbearable – 'and I came across a box of stuff under his bed. There's an iPod, some DVDs, a load of sweets, and a brand-new pair of trainers.'

Ray shook his head but remained silent.

'I know he hasn't got any money,' Mags said, 'because he's still paying us back for that broken window, and I can't think how else he would have got it all, unless he stole it.'

'Terrific,' Ray said. 'He's going to end up getting nicked. That's going to look good, isn't it? The DI's son in custody for shoplifting.'

Mags looked at him with dismay. 'Is that all you can think about? Your son has spent the last eighteen months being utterly miserable. Your previously happy, settled, clever son is now bunking off school and stealing, and your first thought is "How will it affect my career prospects?"' She stopped, mid-flow, and held up her hands as though warding him off. 'I can't talk to you about this now.'

She turned and walked towards the door, then spun to face Ray. 'Leave Tom to me. You'll only make matters worse. Besides, you've clearly got more important things to worry about.'

There was the sound of running feet on the stairs, followed by the slam of the bedroom door. Ray knew there was no point following her – she was clearly in no mood for a discussion. His career hadn't been his *first* consideration, it was just *a* consideration. And since he was the only one bringing any money into the family, it was a bit rich of Mags to dismiss it out of hand like that. As for Tom, he would let her deal with it if that was what she wanted. Besides, if he were honest, he didn't know where to start.

33

The house in Beaufort Crescent was much bigger than the old one. They wouldn't give me a mortgage for the full amount, so I took out a loan and hoped I would be able to pay it off. The repayments were going to be a stretch, but it was worth it. The house had a long garden for your studio, and I saw your eyes shine when we marked out where it could go.

'It's perfect,' you said. 'I'll have everything I need, right here.'

I took some time off work and began building the studio the week we moved in, and you couldn't do enough for me in return. You brought mugs of steaming tea down to the end of the garden, and called me in for bowls of soup with home-made bread. I didn't want it to stop, and almost without thinking I began to slow down. Instead of being out in the garden by nine each morning, I started work at ten. I stopped longer for lunch, and in the afternoon I sat in the wooden shell of the studio and let the time tick by until you called me in.

'You can't work in this light, honey,' you'd say. 'And look, your hands are freezing! Come in and let me warm you up.' You would kiss me and tell me how excited you were about having your own space to work; that you had never been looked after so well; that you loved me.

I went back to work and promised to fit out the interior at the weekend. But when I came home that first day you had dragged an old desk inside and spread out your glazes and tools. Your new kiln sat in the corner, and your wheel squatted in the centre of the room. You were sitting on a small stool, intent on the clay spinning between your hands. I watched you through the window as the pot took shape with the barest of touches. I hoped you might sense my presence, but you didn't look up and I opened the door.

'Isn't this fantastic?'

Still you didn't look at me.

'I love being out here.' You took your foot off the pedal and the wheel slowed and finally stopped. 'I'll go and change out of this shirt, then put supper on.' You kissed me lightly on the cheek, holding your hands carefully out of the way of my clothes.

I stood in the studio for a while, looking at the walls I had envisaged covered with shelves; at the corner where I had planned to build you a special desk. I took a step forward and pushed my foot briefly on to the pedal of your wheel. The wheel jerked round, barely a full revolution, and without your guiding hands the pot lurched to one side and sank in on itself.

After that it felt as though I went days without seeing you. You rigged up a heater so you could spend longer in your studio, and even at weekends I would find you pulling on clay-spattered clothes to head down there at first light. I did build your shelves, but I never made the desk I had planned, and the sight of your junk-shop table always irritated me.

We had been in the house for a year or so, I suppose, when I had to go to Paris with work. Doug had a lead on a potential new client, and we planned to make enough of an impression for them to place a big software order. Business was slow, and dividends smaller and less frequent than I had been promised. I had taken out a credit card so I could carry on taking you out for dinner, and buying you flowers, but the repayments were getting harder and harder to make. The Paris client would have got us back on an even keel.

'Can I come?' you asked. It must have been the only time I ever saw you show interest in my business. 'I love Paris.'

I had seen the way Doug leered when I once took Marie to an office party, and the way she behaved in return. I was not about to repeat that mistake.

'I'll be working non-stop; it won't be any fun for you. Let's go together when I'm not so busy. Besides, you've got your vases to finish.'

You had spent what seemed like weeks trudging round the city's gift shops and galleries with samples of your work, and all you had to show for it were two shops, each wanting a dozen or so pots and vases to sell on a commission basis. You were as pleased as if you had won the lottery, spending far more effort on each vase than on anything you had done before.

'The longer you spend, the less you're earning for your time,' I had reminded you, but it seemed my business experience was wasted on you, and you continued to spend hours painting and glazing.

I called you when I landed in Paris and felt a sudden pang of homesickness when I heard your voice. Doug took the client out for dinner, but I pleaded a migraine and remained in my room, where I picked at a room-service steak and wished I had brought you after all. The immaculately made bed seemed vast and unappealing, and at eleven o'clock I went down to the hotel bar. I ordered a whisky and stayed at the bar, ordering another before I had finished the first. I sent you a text message but you didn't answer: I supposed you were in your studio, oblivious to my calls.

There was a woman at a table near to where I sat at the bar. She was dressed for business in a grey pinstriped suit with black high heels, and an open briefcase lay on the chair beside her. She was going through paperwork, and when she looked up and caught my eye she gave a rueful smile. I smiled back.

'You're English,' she said.

'Is it that obvious?'

She laughed. 'When you travel as much as I do, you learn

to spot the signs.' She picked up the papers she was working on and dropped them into her briefcase, closing it with a thud. 'That's quite enough for one day.'

She didn't make any move to leave.

'May I join you?' I asked.

'I'd be delighted.'

I hadn't planned it, but it was exactly what I needed. I didn't ask her name until the morning, when she came out of the bathroom wrapped in a towel.

'Emma,' she said. She didn't ask mine and I wondered how often she did this, in anonymous hotel rooms in anonymous cities.

When she had gone, I called you and let you tell me about your day; about how pleased the gift-shop owner had been with the vases, and how you couldn't wait to see me. You told me you missed me, and that you hated us being apart, and I felt the reassurance seep into me and make me safe again.

'I love you,' I said. I knew you needed to hear it: that it wasn't enough for you to see everything I did for you; the way I looked after you. You gave a tiny sigh.

'I love you too.'

Doug had obviously worked hard on the client over dinner, and from the jokes at our morning meeting it was clear they had gone on to a strip club. By midday we'd clinched the deal, and Doug was on the phone to the bank to reassure them we were solvent once more.

I had the hotel receptionist call me a taxi. 'Where will I find the best jewellery shops?' I asked.

He gave a knowing smile that irritated me. 'A little something for a lady, sir?'

I ignored him. 'The best place?'

His smile became a little more fixed. 'Faubourg Saint-Honoré, monsieur.' He remained solicitous as I waited for the taxi to arrive, but his presuming air cost him a tip, and it took me the full cab ride to shake off my annoyance.

I walked the length of Faubourg Saint-Honoré before settling on a small jeweller's unimaginatively called 'Michel', where black trays were studded with sparkling diamonds. I wanted to take my time choosing, but staff in discreet suits hovered around, offering assistance and suggestions, and I found it impossible to concentrate. In the end I chose the biggest: a ring you couldn't possibly refuse. A square-set white diamond on a simple platinum ring. I handed over my credit card and told myself you were worth it.

I flew home the following morning, the small leather box burning a hole in my coat pocket. I had it in mind to take you out for dinner, but as I opened the front door you ran to me and squeezed me so tight that I couldn't wait another moment.

'Marry me.'

You laughed, but you must have caught the sincerity in my eyes, because you stopped and put your hand to your mouth.

'I love you,' I said. 'I can't be apart from you.'

You didn't say anything, and I faltered. This hadn't been part of my plan. I had expected you to fling your arms around me, kiss me, to cry, perhaps, but above all: to say yes. I scrabbled for the jewellery box and thrust it into your hand. 'I mean it, Jennifer. I want you to be mine, always. Say you will, please say you will.'

You gave a tiny shake of your head, but you opened the box and your mouth fell open a fraction. 'I don't know what to say.'

'Say yes.'

There was a pause long enough for me to feel the fear in my chest that you might refuse. And then you said yes.

34

A metallic thud makes me jump. After DI Stevens left my cell last night, I stared at the flaking paint on the ceiling, feeling the cold seep through the mattress from the concrete plinth below until sleep crept up on me unwittingly. As I push myself upright on the bed, my limbs ache and my head pounds.

Something rattles at the door, and I realise the thud was the drop of the square hatch in the centre of the door, through which a hand is now thrusting a plastic tray.

'Come on, I haven't got all day.'

I take the tray. 'May I have some painkillers?'

The gaoler is standing to the side of the hatch, and I can't see her face, just a black uniform and a straggle of blonde hair.

'The doctor's not here. You'll have to wait till you get to court.' She has barely finished speaking before the hatch slides up with a clunk that echoes round the cell block, and I hear her heavy footsteps retreating.

I sit on the bed and drink the tea, which has slopped messily on to the tray. It's tepid and sugary but I drink thirstily, realising I have had nothing since lunchtime yesterday. Breakfast is sausage and beans in a microwavable container. The plastic has melted around the edges, and the beans are crusted with bright orange sauce. I leave the offering on the tray with my empty cup and use the toilet. There is no loo seat, only a metal basin, and sheets of scratchy paper. I rush to finish before the gaoler comes back.

My abandoned food is long cold by the time I hear footsteps

again. They pause outside my cell and I hear the sound of keys jangling, then the heavy door swings open and I see a surly girl barely into her twenties. The black uniform and greasy blonde hair mark her out as the gaoler who brought my breakfast, and I indicate the tray resting on my mattress.

'I couldn't eat it, I'm afraid.'

'I'm not surprised,' says the gaoler, with a snort of laughter. 'I wouldn't touch it if I was starving.'

I sit on the metal bench opposite the custody desk and put on my boots. I have been joined by three others: all men, and all dressed in tracksuit bottoms and hooded tops so similar that I think at first they are wearing some kind of uniform. They sit slouched against the wall, as at home here as I am out of place. I twist around to see the myriad notices on the wall above our heads, but none of it makes sense. Information about solicitors, interpreters, offences 'taken into consideration'. Am I supposed to know what is happening? Each time a wave of fear hits me, I remind myself what I did, and that I have no right to be frightened.

We wait for what must be half an hour or more, until a buzzer sounds and the custody sergeant looks up at the CCTV screen on the wall, now filled with a large white lorry.

'Limo's here, lads,' he says.

The boy next to me sucks his teeth and mutters something I can't make out and don't want to.

The custody sergeant opens the door to a pair of Reliance security officers. 'Four for you today, Ash,' he says to the male officer. 'Hey, City took a bit of a pounding last night, didn't they?' He gives a slow shake of his head, as though in sympathy, but he is grinning broadly, and the man called Ash thumps him good-naturedly on the shoulder.

'We'll have our day,' he says. He glances across at us for the first time. 'Got the paperwork for these, then?'

The men continue talking football, and the female Reliance officer comes over to me.

'All right, love?' she says. She has a plump, maternal air, at odds with her uniform, and I feel a ridiculous urge to cry. She tells me to stand, running the flat of her hand over my arms, back and legs. She sweeps a finger around the inside of my waistband and checks the elastic of my bra through my shirt. I am aware of nudges from the boys on the bench and I feel as exposed as if I had been naked. The officer handcuffs my right wrist to her left one, and takes me outside.

We are driven to court in a partitioned lorry that reminds me of the horseboxes at the county shows to which my mother used to take me and Eve. I fight to stay on the narrow bench seat as the lorry turns a corner, my wrists cuffed to a chain that runs the width of the cubicle. The lack of space makes me claustrophobic and I stare through the obscured glass window which sends Bristol's buildings past me in a kaleidoscope of shapes and colours. I try to make sense of the twists and turns, but the motion has me feeling seasick and I close my eyes, resting my forehead against the cool glass.

My moving cell is replaced by a stationary one in the depths of the Magistrates' Court. They give me tea – hot, this time – and toast that splinters into matchsticks in my throat. My solicitor will be with me at ten, they tell me. How can it not yet be ten o'clock? I've lived a lifetime today already.

'Ms Gray?'

The solicitor is young and disinterested, his suit expensive and confidently striped.

'I didn't ask for a solicitor.'

'You have to have legal representation, Ms Gray, or represent yourself. Do you want to represent yourself?' His arched eyebrow suggests that only the very foolish would consider such an option.

I shake my head.

'Good. Now, I understand you have admitted in interview the offences of causing death by dangerous driving, and of failing to stop and give details after an accident. Am I correct?'

'Yes.'

He rifles through the file he has brought with him, its red ribbon untied and thrown carelessly on to the table. He hasn't yet looked at me.

'Do you want to plead guilty or not guilty?'

'Guilty,' I say, and the word seems to linger in the air; the first time I have said it out loud. I am guilty.

He writes down something far longer than one word, and I want to peer over his shoulder to read it. 'I shall apply for bail on your behalf and you stand a good chance of getting it. No previous convictions, abiding by your current bail conditions, answering bail on time . . . Clearly the initial abscond will work against us . . . Do you have any mental health issues?'

'No.'

'Pity. Never mind. I'll do my best. Now, do you have any questions?'

Dozens, I think.

'None,' I say.

'Court rise.'

I expected more people, but apart from a bored-looking man with a notebook, in a section of the court the usher explains to me is for press, there are very few. My solicitor sits in the middle of the room with his back to me. A young woman in a navy-blue skirt is next to him, passing a highlighter over a printed page. At the same long table, but several feet away, is an almost identical pairing – the prosecution.

The usher next to me tugs at my sleeve and I realise I am the only one still standing. The magistrate, a pinch-faced man with wispy hair, has arrived, and court is now in session. My heart is pounding and my face is hot with shame. The few people in the public gallery are looking at me curiously, as though I were an exhibit in a museum. I recall something I once read about public executions in France: the guillotine mounted in the town square for all to see; women clicking their knitting needles as they waited for the performance. A shiver runs through me as I realise I am today's entertainment.

'Will the defendant please rise?'

I get to my feet again and give my name when the clerk asks for it.

'How do you plead?'

'Guilty.' My voice sounds reedy and I cough to clear my throat, but I'm not asked to speak again.

The lawyers argue over bail in a verbose rally that makes my head spin.

There is too much at stake; the defendant will run.

The defendant has kept her bail conditions; she will continue to abide by them.

There is a life sentence to consider.

There is a life to consider.

They speak to each other through the magistrate, like warring children communicating through a parent. Their words are extravagantly emotive, illustrated with flamboyant gestures that are wasted on the empty courtroom. They argue over bail: over whether I should be remanded in prison until the Crown Court trial, or released on bail to wait for my trial at home. I realise my lawyer is arguing for my release, and I want to tug at his sleeve and tell him I have no interest in bail. Except for Beau, there is no one at home for me. No one to miss me. In prison I will be safe. But I sit mutely, my hands in my lap, unsure of what picture I should be portraying. Not that anyone is looking at me. I am invisible. I try to follow the lawyers' argument, to work out who is winning this war of words, but am quickly lost in the theatrics.

A hush descends on the court and the magistrate fixes me with an unsmiling gaze. I have the absurd urge to tell him that I'm not like the usual occupants of his court. That I grew up in a house like his, and that I went to university; held dinner parties; had friends. That I was once confident and outgoing. That before last year I had never broken the law, and that what happened was a terrible mistake. But his eyes are disinterested and I realise he doesn't care who I am, or how many dinner parties I have held. I'm just another criminal through his doors; no different from any other. I feel my identity being stripped away from me once more.

'Counsel has passionately defended your right to bail, Ms Gray,' the magistrate says, 'assuring me that you would no sooner abscond again than you would fly to the moon.' There is a titter from the public gallery, where a pair of old women are wedged into the second row with a Thermos flask. My modern-day *tricoteuses*. The corners of the magistrate's mouth twitch appreciatively. 'He tells me your initial flight from the scene of this truly abhorrent crime was a moment of madness, out of character and never to be repeated. I hope, Ms Gray, for all our sakes, he is correct.' He pauses, and I hold my breath.

'Bail is granted.'

I let out a sigh which might be taken for relief.

There is a noise from the press box and I see the young man with the notebook sidle out of the row of seats, his book stuffed messily into his jacket pocket. He gives a bob of his head in the direction of the bench before exiting, leaving the door swinging behind him.

'Court rise.'

As the magistrate leaves court, the hum of conversation grows louder, and I see my solicitor lean over towards the prosecution. They laugh about something, then he comes over to the dock to speak to me.

'A good result,' he says, all smiles now. 'The case has been adjourned for sentencing at Crown Court on the seventeenth of March – you'll be given information about legal aid and your options for representation. Safe trip home, Ms Gray.'

It feels strange to walk freely out of the courtroom, after twenty-four hours in a cell. I go to the canteen and buy a take-away coffee, burning my tongue in my impatience to taste something stronger than police station tea.

There is a glass roof above the entrance to Bristol Magistrates' Court, which gives shelter from the drizzle to small groups of people, speaking urgently to each other between drags of cigarettes. As I walk down the steps I'm jostled by a woman heading in the opposite direction, and coffee seeps through the ill-fitting plastic lid and on to my hand.

'Sorry,' I say automatically. But as I stop and glance up I see that the woman has stopped too, and that she is holding a microphone. A sudden flash of light startles me and I look up to see a photographer a few feet away from me.

'How do you feel about the prospect of prison, Jenna?'

'What? I—'

The microphone is thrust so close it almost brushes my lips.

'Will you be sticking by today's guilty plea? How do you think Jacob's family are feeling?'

'I, yes, I—'

People are pushing me from every angle, the reporter's questions shouted over a chanting I can't decipher. There is so much noise it's like being in a football stadium, or a concert arena. I can't breathe, and when I try to turn I'm pushed in the opposite direction. Someone pulls at my coat, and I lose my balance, falling heavily against someone who pushes me roughly upright. I see a placard, clumsily made and brandished high above the small throng of protesters. Whoever has written it has started too large, and the last few letters have been squeezed together to make it fit. *Justice for Jacob!*

That's it. That's the chant I can hear.

'Justice for Jacob! Justice for Jacob!' Over and over, until the shouts seem to come from behind and all around me. I look to the side for a space but there are people there too, and my coffee falls from my hand and loses its lid as it hits the ground, liquid splashing my shoes and running down the steps. I stumble again, and for a second I think I'm going to fall and be crushed underfoot by this furious mob.

'Scum!'

I make out an angry twisted mouth and a pair of enormous hooped earrings that swing from side to side. The woman makes a primitive sound at the back of her throat, then spits the glutinous result at my face. I turn my face just in time, and feel the warm saliva land on my neck and slide beneath the collar of my coat. It shocks me as much as if she had punched me, and I cry out and hide my face behind raised arms, waiting for the next offensive.

'Justice for Jacob! Justice for Jacob!'

I feel an arm grip my shoulder and I tense, twisting away and looking frantically for a way out.

'Let's take the scenic route, shall we?'

It's DI Stevens, his face grim and determined as he pulls me firmly back up the steps and into the court. He lets go of me once we are safely past security, but doesn't say anything, and I follow him mutely through a set of double doors and out into a quiet courtyard at the back of the courts. He gestures towards a gate.

'That'll take you into the bus station. Are you all right? Is there anyone I can call for you?'

'I'm fine. Thank you – I don't know what I would have done if you hadn't been there.' I close my eyes for a second.

'Bloody vultures,' DI Stevens says. 'The press argue they're doing their job, but they won't stop till they get a story. As for the protesters – well, let's just say there are a couple of soap-dodgers in that lot with placards like revolving doors; doesn't matter what the issue is, you'll find them on the court steps protesting about it. Don't take it personally.'

'I'll try not to.' I smile awkwardly and turn to leave, but he stops me.

'Ms Gray?'

'Yes?'

'Have you ever lived at 127 Grantham Street?'

I feel the blood drain out of my face and I force a smile on to my face.

'No, Inspector,' I say carefully. 'No, I've never lived there.'

He nods thoughtfully, and raises one hand to say goodbye. I look over my shoulder as I walk through the gate and see that he is still standing there, watching me.

Much to my relief, the train to Swansea is nearly empty, and I sink back into my seat and close my eyes. I'm still shaking from my encounter with the protesters. I look out of the window and breathe a sigh of relief to be heading back to Wales.

Four weeks. I have four weeks left before I go to prison. The thought is unimaginable, and yet it couldn't be more real. I call Bethan and tell her I will be home tonight after all.

'You got bail?'

'Till March seventeenth.'

'That's good. Isn't it?' She is confused by my lack of enthusiasm.

'Have you been down to the beach today?' I ask Bethan.

'I took the dogs along the clifftop at lunchtime. Why?'

'Was there anything on the sand?'

'Nothing that isn't there usually,' she said, laughing. 'What were you expecting?'

I breathe a sigh of relief. I'm beginning to doubt that I ever saw the letters in the first place. 'Nothing,' I say. 'I'll see you in a little while.'

*   *   *

250

When I get to Bethan's she invites me to stop and eat, but I wouldn't make good company, and I excuse myself. She insists on sending me home with something, so I wait while she spoons soup into a plastic tub. It's almost an hour later when I finally kiss her goodbye, and take Beau along the path to the cottage.

The door has warped so much in the bad weather that I can neither turn the key nor open it. I drive my shoulder into the wood and it gives a fraction, enough to free the lock and enable me to turn the key, which now spins uselessly in the mechanism. Beau begins to bark furiously, and I tell him to be quiet. I suspect I've broken the door, but I'm past caring. Had Iestyn come to mend the door when I first told him it was sticking, it might have been a simple job. Now my constant forcing of the key in the lock has made more work for him.

I pour Bethan's soup into a saucepan and put it on the range, leaving the bread on the side. The cottage is cold and I look for a jumper to put on, but there's nothing downstairs. Beau is agitated, running from side to side in the sitting room, as though he's been away far longer than twenty-four hours.

There's something different about the stairs today, and I can't place it. It wasn't yet fully dark when I came inside, and yet there's no light coming from the tiny window at the top of the stairs. Something is blocking the way.

I'm at the top of the stairs before I realise what it is.

'You broke your promise, Jennifer.'

Ian bends one knee and pushes the flat of his foot hard against my chest. The wooden handrail slips from my grasp and I fall backwards, crashing down the stairs until I hit the stone floor at the bottom.

35

You took the ring off after three days, and it felt as though you had punched me. You said you were worried about damaging it, and that you had to take it off so often to work that you thought you might lose it. You began wearing it on a delicate gold chain around your neck and I took you shopping for a wedding ring; something flat and plain you could wear all the time.

'You could wear it now,' I said, when we left the jeweller's.

'But the wedding isn't for six months.'

You were holding my hand, and I squeezed it tight as we crossed the road. 'Instead of your engagement ring, I mean. So you have something on your finger.'

You misunderstood me.

'I don't mind, Ian, really. I can wait till we get married.'

'But how will people know you're engaged?' I couldn't let it go. I stopped you and put my hands on your shoulders. You looked around, at all the busy shoppers, and tried to shake me off, but I held you fast. 'How will they know you're with me,' I said, 'if you're not wearing my ring?'

I recognised the look in your eyes. I used to see it in Marie's – that mixture of defiance and wariness – and it made me as angry to see it on you as it did to see it on her. How dare you be afraid of me? I felt myself tense, and when a flicker of pain passed across your face, I realised my fingers were digging into your shoulders. I let my hands drop to my sides.

'Do you love me?' I said.

'You know I do.'

'Then why don't you want people to know we're getting married?'

I reached into the plastic bag for the small box and opened it. I wanted to take away that look in your eyes, and on impulse I dropped to one knee and held out the open box towards you. There was an audible buzz from the passing shoppers, and a crimson flush spread across your face. The movement around us slowed, as people stopped to watch, and I felt a burst of pride that you were with me. My beautiful Jennifer.

'Will you marry me?'

You looked overwhelmed. 'Yes.'

Your response was far faster than the first time I had asked, and the tightness in my chest evaporated instantly. I slipped the ring on to your fourth finger and stood up to kiss you. There were cheers around us, and someone slapped me on the back. I found I couldn't stop grinning. This is what I should have done the first time, I thought: I should have given you more ceremony, more celebration. You deserved more.

We walked hand-in-hand through the busy Bristol streets and I rubbed the metal of your wedding ring with the thumb of my right hand.

'Let's get married now,' I said. 'Let's go to a registry office, pull some witnesses off the street, and do it.'

'But it's all fixed for September! All my family will be there. We can't just go ahead and do it now.'

You had taken some persuading that a big church wedding would be a mistake: you had no father to walk you down the aisle, and why waste money on a party for friends you didn't see any more? We booked a civil ceremony at the Courtyard Hotel, with lunch afterwards for twenty people. I had asked Doug to be my best man, but the other guests would be yours. I tried to imagine my parents standing beside us, but could only picture the look on my dad's face the last time I saw him.

The disappointment. The disgust. I shook the image from my mind.

You were firm. 'We can't change our plans now, Ian. It's only six months – it's not long to wait.'

It wasn't, but I still counted off the days until you would be Mrs Petersen. I told myself I would feel better then: more secure. I would know you loved me, and that you would stay with me.

The night before our wedding you insisted on staying with Eve at the hotel, while I suffered an awkward evening in the pub with Jeff and Doug. Doug made a half-hearted attempt to make a proper stag night of it, but no one resisted when I suggested I should get to bed early ahead of the big day.

At the hotel I calmed my nerves with a double whisky. Jeff patted my arm and called me a great chap, although we had never had anything in common. He wouldn't join me in a drink, and half an hour before the ceremony he nodded over to the door, where a woman in a navy hat had arrived.

'Ready to meet the mother-in-law?' Jeff said. 'She's not that bad, I promise.' On the few occasions I had met Jeff I had found his forced joviality intensely irritating, but that day I was grateful for the distraction. I wanted to call you, to make sure you were going to be there, and I couldn't quell the feeling of panic in my stomach that you might leave me standing there; that you might humiliate me in front of all these people.

I walked with Jeff across the bar. Your mother put out a hand and I took it, then leaned into her and kissed her dry cheek.

'Grace, it's a pleasure to meet you. I've heard so much about you.'

You told me you looked nothing like your mother, but I could see your high cheekbones in hers. You might have had your father's colouring, and his artistic genes, but you had Grace's lean frame and watchful expression.

'I wish I could say the same,' Grace said, with a flicker of amusement at the corner of her lips. 'But if I want to know what's happening in Jenna's life, it's Eve I have to speak to.'

I gave what I hoped was an expression of solidarity, as though I too was at the mercy of your failure to communicate. I offered Grace a drink, and she accepted a glass of champagne. 'In celebration,' she said, although she didn't propose a toast.

You kept me waiting for fifteen minutes, as was your right, I suppose. Doug made a play of having lost the ring, and we must have looked like every other wedding party in every other hotel in the country. But when you walked down the aisle there could have been no other bride as beautiful as you. Your dress was simple: a heart-shaped neckline and a skirt that skimmed your hips and fell to the floor in a shimmer of satin. You carried a spray of white roses, and your hair had been swept up on to your head in glossy curls.

We stood next to each other, and I stole glances at you as you listened to the registrar lead the ceremony. When we said our vows you looked into my eyes and I didn't care about Jeff, or Doug, or your mother. There could have been a thousand people in the room with us: all I could see was you.

'I now pronounce you husband and wife.'

There was a hesitant smattering of applause, and I kissed you on the lips before we turned and walked back up the aisle together. The hotel had set out drinks and canapés in an area off the bar, and I watched you move round the room taking compliments and holding out your ring hand to be admired.

'She looks beautiful, doesn't she?'

I hadn't noticed Eve coming to stand next to me. 'She *is* beautiful,' I said, and Eve nodded to concede the correction.

When I turned, I realised Eve was no longer watching you, but staring at me. 'You won't hurt her, will you?'

I laughed. 'What sort of thing is that to ask on a man's wedding day?'

'The most important thing, surely?' Eve said. She took a sip of champagne and studied me. 'You remind me a lot of our father.'

'Well then, that's probably what Jennifer sees in me,' I replied shortly.

'Probably,' Eve said. 'I just hope you don't let her down too.'

'I have no intention of leaving your sister,' I said, 'not that it is any business of yours. She's a grown woman, not some child upset by a philandering father.'

'My father was not a philanderer.' She was not defending him, merely stating a fact, but I was interested. I had always assumed he had left your mother for another woman.

'Then why did he leave?'

She ignored my question. 'Look after Jenna – she deserves to be treated well.'

I couldn't bear to see her smug face any longer, or listen to her ridiculous, patronising pleas. I left Eve standing at the bar, and went to slip my arm around you. My new wife.

I had promised you Venice and I couldn't wait to show it to you. At the airport you proudly handed over your new passport and grinned as they read out your name.

'It sounds so strange!'

'You'll soon get used to it,' I said, 'Mrs Petersen.'

When you realised I had organised an upgrade you were ecstatic, insisting on making the most of everything on offer. The flight was only two hours, but in that time you tried on the eye mask, flicked between films and drank champagne. I watched you, loving the fact that you were so happy, and that it was because of me.

Our transfer was delayed, and we didn't get to our hotel until late. The champagne had given me a headache, and I was tired and unimpressed by the poor service. I made a mental note to insist on a refund on the transfer when we returned home.

256

'Let's leave the cases and go straight out,' you said, when we arrived in the marble-clad lobby.

'We're here for a fortnight. We'll order room service and unpack – it'll all still be here in the morning. Besides,' I slipped an arm around you and squeezed your bottom, 'it's our wedding night.'

You kissed me, your tongue darting into my mouth, but then you pulled away and held my hand instead. 'It's not even ten o'clock! Come on, a walk around the block, and a drink somewhere, then I promise we'll call it a night.'

The receptionist smiled, making no attempt to hide his appreciation of our impromptu show. 'A lover's tiff?' He laughed, despite the look I gave him, and I was appalled to see you laughing with him.

'I'm trying to convince my *husband*' – you smiled as you said the word, and winked at me as though it would make a difference – 'that we need to take a stroll around Venice before we see our room. It looks so beautiful.' You closed your eyes for a fraction too long when you blinked, and I realised you were a little drunk.

'It is beautiful, *signora*, but not as beautiful as you.' The receptionist gave a ridiculous little bow.

I looked at you, expecting to see you roll your eyes at me, but you were blushing, and I saw that you were flattered. Flattered by this gigolo; this oily man with his manicured hands and buttonhole flower.

'Our key, please,' I said. I stepped in front of you and leaned forward on to the desk. There was a moment's pause, before the receptionist handed me a cardboard wallet in which were two credit-card-sized swipe cards.

'*Buona sera, signore.*'

He wasn't smiling now.

I refused help with our cases and let you drag your own to the lift, where I pressed the button for the third floor. I watched you in the mirror. 'He was nice, wasn't he?' you said, and I tasted bile in the back of my throat. It had been so good at the airport; so much fun on the plane; and now you had ruined it. You were talking, but I wasn't listening: I was thinking of the way you had simpered; the way you had blushed and let him flirt with you; the way you had *enjoyed* it.

Our room was at the end of a carpeted corridor. I pushed the key card into the reader and pulled it out, waiting impatiently for the click that told me the lock had been released. I shoved open the door and wheeled my suitcase through, not caring whether the door banged in your face. It was hot in the room – too hot – but the windows didn't open, and I pulled at my collar to get some air. Blood pulsed in my ears but still you talked; still you chattered as if nothing were wrong; as if you hadn't humiliated me.

My fist furled without instruction, the skin stretched tightly over tensed knuckles. The bubble of pressure began to expand in my chest, filling every available space, pushing my lungs to one side. I looked at you, still laughing, still jabbering, and I raised my fist and slammed it into your face.

Almost immediately the bubble burst. Calm washed over me, like the adrenalin release after sex, or a session in the gym. My headache eased, and the muscle at the corner of my eye ceased to twitch. You made a bubbling, strangled noise, but I didn't look at you. I left the room and took the lift back down to reception, walking straight out on to the street without looking behind the desk. I found a bar and drank two beers, ignoring the barman's attempts to engage me in conversation.

An hour later I returned to the hotel.

'Could I have some ice, please?'

'*Si, signore.*' The receptionist disappeared and came back with an ice bucket. 'Wine glasses, *signore*?'

'No thank you.'

I was calm now, my breathing measured and slow. I took the stairs, delaying my return.

When I opened the door you were curled up on the bed. You sat up and pushed yourself to the end of the bed, backing up against the headboard. A wad of bloody tissues lay on the bedside table, but despite your efforts to clean yourself up there was dried blood on your top lip. A bruise was already forming on the bridge of your nose and across one eye. When you saw me you began to cry, and the tears took on the colour of blood as they reached your chin, dripping on to your shirt and staining it pink.

I put the ice bucket on the table and spread out a napkin, spooning ice into it before wrapping it into a parcel. I sat down next to you. You were shivering, but I gently put the ice pack against your skin.

'I found a nice bar,' I said. 'I think you'll like it. I took a walk around and saw a couple of places you might like for lunch tomorrow, if you're feeling up to it.'

I took the ice pack away and you stared at me, your eyes big and guarded. You were still shaking.

'Are you cold? Here, wrap this around you.' I pulled the blanket off the end of the bed and placed it around your shoulders. 'You're tired, it's been a long day.' I kissed your forehead but still you cried, and I wished so much you hadn't spoilt our first night. I had thought that you were different, and that perhaps I wouldn't ever need to feel that release again: that blissful sense of peace that comes after a fight. I was sorry to see that, after everything, you were just the same as all the others.

36

I struggle to breathe. Beau begins whining, licking my face and pushing his nose against me. I try to think, try to move, but the force of the impact has winded me and I can't get up. Even if I could make my body work, something is happening inside me, spinning my world smaller and smaller. I'm suddenly back in Bristol, not knowing what mood Ian will come home in. I'm making his supper, bracing myself to have it thrown in my face. I'm doubled over on the floor of my studio, trying to protect my head from the punches raining down on me.

Ian walks carefully down the stairs, shaking his head as though admonishing a rebellious child. I have always disappointed him; never known the right things to say or do, no matter how hard I tried. He speaks softly, and if you didn't hear the words you would think him solicitous. But the sound of his voice is enough to make me shake violently, as though I am lying in ice.

He stands over me – his legs straddling me – and lets his eyes trail lazily along my body. The creases in his trouser-legs are knife-sharp; his belt buckle so polished I can see my own terrified face in it. He catches sight of something on his jacket, and picks off a loose thread, letting it float down on to the floor. Beau is still whining and Ian aims a sharp kick at his head that sends Beau three feet across the floor.

'Don't hurt him, please!'

Beau whimpers, but stands up. He slinks into the kitchen out of my view.

'You've been to the police, Jennifer,' Ian says.

'I'm sorry.' It comes out as a whisper and I'm not certain he's heard, but if I repeat it and Ian feels I am pleading it will make him angry. It's strange how quickly it all comes back to me: the need to walk a tightrope of doing as I am told without offering up the pathetic figure that infuriates him. Over the years I've got it wrong more often than I've got it right.

I swallow. 'I'm – I'm sorry.'

His hands are in his pockets. He looks relaxed, laid-back. But I know him. I know how quickly he can—

'You're fucking sorry?'

In an instant he is crouched over me, his knees pinning my arms to the floor. 'You think that makes it all right?' He leans forward, grinding his kneecaps into my biceps. I bite my tongue too late to stop the cry of pain that makes him curl his lips in disgust at my lack of control. I feel bile in the back of my throat and I swallow it down.

'You've told them about me, haven't you?' The corners of his mouth are edged with white, and specks of saliva moisten my face. I have a sudden memory of the protester outside court, although it feels far longer ago than a few hours.

'No. No, I haven't.'

We're playing that game again; the one where he lobs a question and I try to volley. I used to play it well. At first I used to think I saw a glimmer of respect in his eyes: he would abruptly break off mid-rally, and turn on the television, or go out. But I lost my edge, or perhaps he changed the rules, and I began to misjudge it every time. For now, however, he seems to be satisfied with my answer, and he changes the subject abruptly.

'You're seeing someone, aren't you?'

'No, I'm not,' I say quickly. I'm glad I can tell the truth, although I know he won't believe me.

'Liar.' He hits me across the cheek with the back of his hand. It makes a sharp cracking noise, like a whip, and when he speaks again the sound rings in my ears. 'Someone helped you set up a website, someone found you this place. Who is it?'

'No one,' I say, tasting blood in my mouth. 'I did it by myself.'

'You can't do anything by yourself, Jennifer.' He leans forward until his face is almost touching mine. I steel myself not to move, knowing how much he hates me flinching.

'You couldn't even run away properly, could you? Have you any idea how easy it was to find you once I knew where you were taking your photos? It seems the people of Penfach are more than happy to help a stranger looking for an old friend.'

It hadn't crossed my mind to wonder how Ian had found me. I always knew he would.

'That was a lovely card you sent your sister, by the way.'

The throwaway comment is like another slap to the face, making me reel anew. 'What have you done to Eve?' If anything happens to Eve and the children because of my carelessness I will never forgive myself. I was so desperate to show her I still cared that I didn't give a second thought to whether I was putting her in danger.

He laughs. 'Why would I do anything to her? She's of no more interest to me than you. You're a pathetic, worthless slut, Jennifer. You're nothing without me. Nothing. What are you?'

I don't answer.

'Say it. What are you?'

Blood trickles down the back of my throat and I struggle to speak without choking. 'I'm nothing.'

He laughs then, and shifts his weight to release the pressure so the pain in my arms dulls a little. He runs a finger across my face; down my cheek and over my lips.

I know what's coming, but it doesn't make it any easier. Slowly he undoes my buttons, peeling back my shirt inch by inch and pushing up my vest top so my breasts are exposed. His eyes run over me dispassionately, without so much as a flicker of desire, and then he reaches for the fastening on his

262

trousers. I close my eyes and disappear inside myself, unable to move, unable to speak. I wonder briefly what would happen if I cried out, or said no. If I fought him, or simply pushed him away. But I don't, and I never have, and so I only have myself to blame.

I have no idea how long I've been lying here, but the cottage is dark and cold. I pull up my jeans, and roll on to my side, hugging my knees to my body. There's a dull ache between my legs and a wetness I suspect is blood. I'm not sure if I blacked out, but I can't remember Ian leaving.

I call Beau. There is an agonising second of silence, before he creeps warily out of the kitchen, his tail clamped between his legs and his ears flat against his head.

'I'm so sorry, Beau.' I coax him towards me, but as I am reaching a hand out, he barks. Just once – a warning bark, with his head turned towards the door. I struggle to my feet, wincing as a sharp pain shoots through me, and there is a knock at the door.

I stand, half-crouched, in the centre of the room, with my hand on Beau's collar. He gives a low growl but doesn't bark again.

'Jenna? Are you in there?'

Patrick.

I feel a rush of relief. The door is unlocked and when I swing it open I have to choke back a sob at the sight of him. I leave the sitting-room light off, and hope that the darkness is enough to hide the face I suspect is already showing marks.

'Are you okay?' Patrick says. 'Has something happened?'

'I – I must have fallen asleep on the sofa.'

'Bethan told me you were back.' He hesitates, and looks briefly down at the floor before looking at me again. 'I came to apologise. I should never have spoken to you like that, Jenna, it was all such a shock.'

'It's fine,' I say. I look past him to the dark clifftop, wondering if Ian is somewhere there, watching us. I can't let him see me with Patrick – I can't let Patrick get hurt along with Eve; along with everyone else who means something to me. 'Is that all?'

'Can I come in?' He moves forward, but I shake my head.

'Jenna, what's wrong?'

'I don't want to see you, Patrick.' I hear myself say the words and I don't let myself take them back.

'I don't blame you,' he says. His face is crumpled and he looks as though he hasn't slept properly in days. 'I behaved atrociously, Jenna, and I don't know how to make it up to you. When I heard what you'd . . . what had happened, I was so shocked I couldn't think straight. I couldn't be around you.'

I start to cry. I can't help it. Patrick takes my hand and I don't want him to let it go.

'I want to understand, Jenna. I can't pretend I'm not shocked – that I'm not finding this hard – but I want to know what happened. I want to be there for you.'

I don't speak, although I know there is only one thing I can say. Only one way to keep Patrick from getting hurt.

'I miss you, Jenna,' he says quietly.

'I don't want to see you any more.' I pull my hand away and force myself to add conviction to my words. 'I don't want anything to do with you.'

Patrick takes a step back as though I have punched him, and the colour drains from his face. 'Why are you doing this?'

'It's what I want.' The lie is torture.

'Is this because I left?'

'It's got nothing to do with you. None of this has anything to do with you. Just leave me alone.'

Patrick looks at me and I make myself meet his eyes, praying he can't read the conflict I feel sure must be written in my own. Finally he puts up his hands, admitting defeat as he turns away from me.

He stumbles on the path and breaks into a run.

I shut the door and sink to the floor, pulling Beau to me and crying noisily into his coat. I wasn't able to save Jacob, but I can save Patrick.

As soon as I feel able, I call Iestyn to ask him to fix the broken lock. 'I can't turn the key at all now,' I say. 'It's completely broken, so there's no way of securing the door from the outside.'

'Don't you worry about it,' Iestyn says. 'There's no one'll be stealing anything round here.'

'I need it fixed!' The strength of my demand shocks us both, and there is silence for a second.

'I'll be up shortly.'

He's here within the hour, getting swiftly to work, but refusing the tea I offer. He whistles quietly to himself as he removes the lock and oils the mechanism, before refitting it and showing me how smoothly the key now turns.

'Thank you,' I say, almost sobbing with relief. Iestyn eyes me curiously and I pull my cardigan more tightly around me. Mottled bruises are spreading across my upper arms, their edges bleeding outwards like ink-stains on blotting paper. I ache as though I've run a marathon, my left cheek is swollen and I can feel a tooth has come loose. I let my hair fall forward over my face to hide the worst of it.

I see Iestyn looking at the red paint on the door.

'I'll clean it off,' I say, but he doesn't reply. He nods a goodbye, then seems to think better of it, turning back to face me. 'It's a small place, Penfach,' he says. 'Everyone knows everyone else's business.'

'So I understand,' I say. If he expects me to defend myself, he'll be disappointed. I'll take my punishment from the court, not the villagers.

'I'd keep yourself to yourself, if I were you,' Iestyn says. 'Let it all blow over.'

'Thank you for the advice,' I say tightly.

I close the door and go upstairs to run a bath. I sit in the scalding water with my eyes squeezed shut so that I can't see the marks emerging on my skin. Across my chest and thighs run tiny fingerprint bruises, deceptively delicate against my pale skin. I was stupid to think I could escape the past. However fast I run, however far: I will never outrun it.

37

'Do you want a hand with anything?' Ray offered, although he knew Mags would have it all under control. She always did.

'It's all done,' she said, taking off her apron. 'Chilli and rice in the oven, beers in the fridge and chocolate brownies for afters.'

'Sounds great,' Ray said. He hovered awkwardly in the kitchen.

'You can unload the dishwasher, if you're looking for a job.'

Ray began taking out the clean plates, trying to think of a neutral topic of conversation that wouldn't result in an argument.

Tonight's get-together had been Mags's idea. Something to celebrate the conclusion of a job well done, she had said. Ray wondered if it was her way of showing him that she was sorry for arguing.

'Thanks again for suggesting this,' he said, when the silence became uncomfortable. He lifted the cutlery tray from the dishwasher, leaving a trail of water on the floor. Mags handed him a cloth.

'It's one of the most high-profile cases you've done,' she said. 'You should celebrate.' She took the cloth from him and dropped it in the sink. 'Besides, if it's a choice between the three of you spending the night in the Nag's Head, or coming round here for a meal and a few beers, well . . .'

Ray took the criticism on the chin. So that was the real reason for the dinner.

The two of them moved carefully around each other in the

kitchen as though walking on ice; as though Ray hadn't spent the night on the sofa; as though their son didn't have a stash of stolen goods in his bedroom. He risked a glance at Mags but couldn't read her expression and decided it would be best to keep quiet. Lately, everything he said seemed to be wrong.

It was unfair to compare Mags to Kate, Ray knew, but things were so much easier at work. Kate never seemed to take umbrage, and so he didn't find himself rehearsing in his head before talking to her, as he had started doing before broaching a difficult subject with Mags.

He hadn't been certain Kate would want to come to the dinner tonight.

'I'll understand if you'd rather not,' he had said, but Kate had looked confused.

'Why would I—' She bit her lip. 'Oh, I see.' She had tried to match Ray's serious face, but couldn't quite manage it, and her eyes twinkled. 'I told you, it's all forgotten. I can handle it if you can.'

'I can handle it,' Ray had said.

He hoped he could. He suddenly felt very uncomfortable at the thought of both Mags and Kate in the same room. Lying awake on the sofa the previous night he hadn't been able to shake off the notion that Mags knew he had kissed Kate and had invited her with the express intention of telling him so. Even though he knew that a public showdown wasn't Mags's style, the prospect of a confrontation tonight still brought him out in a cold sweat.

'The school sent a letter home with Tom today,' Mags said. It burst out of her quite suddenly, and Ray had the impression she had been holding on to the news since he got home from work.

'What about?'

Mags took it from her apron pocket and handed it to him.

Dear Mr and Mrs Stevens,

I would be grateful if you could make an appointment with my office to come in and discuss an issue that has arisen within the school.

Yours faithfully,
Ann Cumberland
Head Teacher, Morland Downs Secondary School

'Finally!' Ray said. He smacked the back of his hand against the letter. 'They're admitting they've got a problem, then? About bloody time.'

Mags opened the wine.

'We've been saying for – what, over a year? – that Tom's being bullied, and they wouldn't even entertain the idea, would they?'

Mags looked at him, and for a moment her face crumpled and the defensiveness disappeared.

'How did we miss this?' She fished in vain for a tissue up the sleeve of her cardigan. 'I feel like such a useless mother!' She fished up her other sleeve, but found nothing.

'Hey, Mags, stop it,' Ray pulled out his handkerchief and gently wiped away the tears that were spilling over her bottom lashes. 'You didn't miss it. Neither of us did. We've known something was wrong ever since he started at that school, and we've been banging on at them to get it sorted out from day one.'

'But it's not their job to sort it out.' Mags blew her nose. 'We're the parents.'

'Maybe, but the problem isn't here, is it? It's at school, and perhaps now they've admitted it, something will actually be done.'

'I hope it doesn't make things worse for Tom.'

'I could speak to the PCSO who covers Morland Downs,' Ray said. 'See if they could pop in and do a session on bullying.'

'No!'

Mags's vehemence stopped him in his tracks.

'Let's work with the school to get it resolved. Not everything has to be a police matter. For once, let's keep this in the family, shall we? I'd really rather you didn't talk about Tom at work.'

On cue, the doorbell rang.

'Are you okay to do this?' Ray asked.

Mags nodded, scrubbing at her face with the handkerchief, and handing it back to Ray. 'I'm fine.'

Ray glanced at himself in the hall mirror. His skin looked grey and tired, and he had a sudden urge to send Kate and Stumpy away, and spend the night with Mags. But Mags had been cooking all afternoon – she wouldn't thank him for wasting her efforts. He sighed and opened the door.

Kate was wearing jeans with knee-length boots and a black V-neck top. There was nothing particularly glamorous about her outfit, but she looked younger and more relaxed than at work, and the whole effect was rather unsettling. Ray stepped back to allow her into the hall.

'This is such a great idea,' Kate said. 'Thanks so much for inviting me.'

'My pleasure,' Ray said. He showed her into the kitchen. 'You and Stumpy have worked really hard over the last few months: I just wanted to show you both I appreciate your efforts.' He grinned. 'And to be fair, it was Mags's idea – I can't take any of the credit.'

Mags acknowledged his comment with a small smile. 'Hi, Kate, it's good to finally meet you. Did you find us okay?' The two women faced each other, and Ray was struck by the contrast between them. Mags hadn't got round to getting changed, and her sweatshirt had a pattern of tiny sauce spatters across the chest. She looked the way she always looked – warm, familiar, kind – but next to Kate she was somehow . . . he grappled for the word. Less *polished*. Immediately Ray felt a stab of guilt and stepped nearer to Mags, as though proximity were a cure for disloyalty.

'What a gorgeous kitchen.' Kate looked at the rack of brownies on the side, fresh from the oven and drizzled with white chocolate. She held up a cheesecake in a cardboard packet. 'I brought a pudding, but I'm afraid it looks a bit pitiful now.'

'How kind of you,' Mags said, stepping forward to take the package from Kate. 'I always think cakes taste so much nicer when someone else has made them, don't you agree?'

Kate gave a grateful smile and Ray let out a slow breath. Perhaps the evening wasn't going to be as uncomfortable as he had feared, although the sooner Stumpy got here, the better.

'Now, what can I get you to drink?' Mags said. 'Ray's on beer, but I have wine, if you'd rather have that.'

'Lovely.'

Ray shouted up the stairs. 'Tom, Lucy, come and say hello, you unsociable pair.'

There was a series of thumps and the children raced down the stairs. They came into the kitchen and stood awkwardly in the doorway.

'This is Kate,' Mags said. 'She's a trainee detective on Dad's team.'

Ray's eyes widened at the put-down, but Kate seemed unperturbed.

'Another few months,' she grinned, 'and I'll be a proper detective. How are you guys?'

'Fine,' Lucy and Tom said in unison.

'You must be Lucy,' Kate said.

Lucy had her mother's fair hair, but the rest was pure Ray. Everyone commented on how much both children looked like him. He could never see the resemblance while the children

271

were awake – there was too much of their own personality in them – but when they slept, and their features were still, Ray could see his own face reflected in his children. He wondered if he ever looked as belligerent as his son did now: scowling at the floor as though he had a grudge against the tiles. He had gelled his hair so it stood up in spikes as angry as his expression.

'This is Tom,' Lucy offered.

'Say hello, Tom,' said Mags.

'Hello, Tom,' he repeated, still looking at the floor.

Mags flicked a tea-towel at him in exasperation. 'Sorry, Kate.'

Kate grinned at Tom, and he glanced at Mags to see if she was going to make him stick around.

'Kids!' Mags said, exasperated. She took the cling-film off a plate of sandwiches and handed it to Tom. 'You two can go and eat this upstairs, if you don't want to be with us *old people*.' She widened her eyes in mock horror at the term, making Lucy giggle. Tom rolled his eyes, and the pair disappeared back up to their rooms in an instant.

'They're good kids,' Mags said, 'most of the time.' She finished the sentence so quietly it wasn't clear whether she was speaking to herself or to the others.

'Have there been any more problems with bullying?' Kate said.

Ray groaned inwardly. He looked at Mags, who resolutely avoided his gaze. Her jaw tightened.

'Nothing we can't handle,' she snapped.

Ray winced and looked at Kate, trying to convey an apology without Mags noticing. He should have warned Kate how sensitive Mags was about Tom. There was an uncomfortable pause, then Ray's mobile pinged with a text message. He fished it from his pocket gratefully but his heart sank as he saw the screen.

'Stumpy can't make it,' he said. 'His mum's had another fall.'

'Is she okay?' Mags asked.

'I think so – he's on his way to the hospital now.' Ray sent a message to Stumpy, and put the phone back in his pocket. 'Just the three of us, then.'

Kate looked at Ray and then at Mags, who turned away and began stirring the chilli.

'Look,' Kate said, 'why don't we do this another time, when Stumpy can make it?'

'Don't be silly,' Ray said, with a cheeriness that sounded false, even to himself. 'Besides, we've got all this chilli: we'll never get through it without help.' He looked at Mags, half wanting her to agree with Kate and cancel the evening altogether, but she carried on stirring.

'Absolutely,' she said briskly. She handed a pair of oven gloves to Ray. 'Can you bring the casserole dish? Kate, why don't you grab those plates and come through to the dining room?'

There were no places laid, but Ray sat automatically at the head of the table, Kate on his left. Mags put a pan of rice on the table, then returned to the kitchen for a bowl of grated cheese and a tub of soured cream. She sat opposite Kate, and for a while the three of them were busy passing dishes and filling their plates.

As they settled down to eat, the clink of cutlery on china made the lack of conversation even more obvious, and Ray searched his mind for something to talk about. Mags wouldn't want them banging on about work, but perhaps it was the safest topic of conversation. Before he could make up his mind, Mags rested her fork on the side of her plate.

'How are you finding CID, Kate?'

'I love it. The hours are a killer, but the work's great, and it's what I've always wanted to do.'

'I hear the DI's a nightmare to work for.'

Ray looked sharply at Mags, but she was smiling pleasantly at Kate. It did nothing to diminish the feeling of unease that had crept over him.

'He's not too bad,' Kate said, with a sidelong glance at Ray. 'Although I don't know how you put up with the mess: his office is a disgrace. Half-drunk coffee cups all over the place.'

'That's because I'm working too hard to drink a full one,' Ray countered. Banter at his expense was a small price to pay under the circumstances.

'He's always right, of course,' Mags said.

Kate pretended to consider this. 'Except when he's wrong.'

They both laughed, and Ray allowed himself to relax a little.

'Does he hum "Chariots of Fire" under his breath all the time,' Kate said, 'like he does at work?'

'I wouldn't know,' Mags said smoothly. 'I never see him.'

The light mood evaporated and for a while they ate in silence. Ray coughed and Kate looked up. He gave her an apologetic smile and she shrugged it off, but when he turned back he realised Mags was watching them, a faint furrow across her brow. She put down her fork and pushed her plate away from the edge of the table.

'Do you miss being in the job, Mags?' Kate asked.

Everyone asked Mags that, as though they expected her to still be hankering after the paperwork; the shitty hours; the filthy houses where you wiped your feet on the way out.

'Yes,' she said, without hesitation.

Ray looked up. 'Do you?'

Mags continued talking to Kate as though he hadn't spoken. 'I don't miss the job, exactly, but I miss the person I was back then. I miss having something to say, something to teach people.' Ray stopped eating. Mags was the same person she had always been. The same person she always would be. Carrying a warrant card didn't change that, surely?

Kate nodded as though she understood, and Ray was grateful for the effort she was making. 'Would you ever go back?'

'How could I? Who would look after that pair?' Mags rolled her eyes upwards towards the bedrooms. 'Not to mention him.'

She looked at Ray, but she wasn't smiling, and he tried to decipher the look in her eyes. 'You know what they say: behind every great man . . .'

'It's true,' Ray said suddenly, with more vigour than the quiet conversation warranted. He looked at Mags. 'You hold everything together.'

'Pudding!' Mags said abruptly, standing up. 'Unless you'd like some more chilli, Kate?'

'I'm fine, thank you. Can I give you a hand?'

'You stay there, it won't take a moment. I'll clear these away then I'll nip upstairs and make sure the kids aren't up to mischief.' She carried everything out to the kitchen, then Ray heard light footsteps running upstairs, and the soft murmur of voices from Lucy's bedroom.

'I'm sorry,' he said. 'I don't know what's got into her.'

'Is it me?' Kate said.

'No, don't think that. She's been in a funny mood recently. She's worried about Tom, I think.' He gave a reassuring smile. 'It'll be my fault – it usually is.'

They heard Mags come back downstairs, and when she next appeared she was carrying a plate of brownies and a jug of cream.

'Actually, Mags,' Kate said, standing up, 'I think I'm going to pass on dessert.'

'Would you rather have some fruit? I've got melon, if you'd prefer?'

'No, it's not that. I'm just knackered. It's been a long old week. Dinner was lovely, though, thank you.'

'Well, if you're sure.' Mags put down the brownies. 'I never congratulated you on the Gray job – Ray tells me it was all down to you. That's a good result to have on your CV this early on.'

'Oh well, it was a joint effort, really,' Kate said. 'We're a good team.'

Ray knew she meant the whole CID team, but she glanced at Ray as she said it, and he didn't dare look at Mags.

They stood in the hall and Mags kissed Kate on the cheek. 'Come and see us again, won't you? It was lovely meeting you.' Ray hoped he was the only one who could hear the insincerity in his wife's voice. He said goodbye to Kate, having a moment of indecision over whether to kiss her. He decided it would be odd if he didn't, and kept it as brief as possible, but he felt Mags's eyes on him and was relieved when Kate set off down the path and the door was shut and locked behind her.

'Well, I don't think I can resist those brownies,' he said with a cheeriness he didn't feel. 'Are you having some?'

'I'm dieting,' Mags said. She went into the kitchen and unfolded the ironing board, filling the iron with water and waiting for it to heat up. 'I've put a Tupperware in the fridge with rice and chilli for Stumpy – will you take it in tomorrow? He won't have eaten properly if he's at the hospital all night tonight, and he won't feel like cooking tomorrow.'

Ray brought his bowl through to the kitchen, and ate standing up. 'That's good of you.'

'He's a nice guy.'

'He is. I work with a great bunch of people.'

Mags was silent for a while. She picked up a pair of trousers and began ironing them. When she spoke it was casual, but she pressed the tip of the iron hard against the fabric.

'She's pretty.'

'Kate?'

'No, Stumpy.' Mags looked at him, exasperated. 'Of course Kate.'

'I suppose so. I've never really thought about it.' It was a ridiculous lie – Mags knew him better than anyone.

She raised an eyebrow, but Ray was relieved to see her smile. He risked a gentle tease. 'Are you jealous?'

'Not a jot,' Mags said. 'In fact, if she'll do the ironing, she can move in.'

'I'm sorry I told her about Tom,' Ray said.

Mags pressed a button on the iron and a cloud of steam hissed on to the trousers. She kept her eyes on the iron as she spoke. 'You love your job, Ray, and I love that you love it. It's a part of you. But it's as though the kids and I exist in the background. I feel invisible.'

Ray opened his mouth to protest, but Mags shook her head.

'You talk more to Kate than you do to me,' she said. 'I could see it this evening – that connection between you. I'm not daft, I know what it's like when you're working all hours with someone: you talk to them, of course you do. But that doesn't mean you can't talk to me too.' She forced out another burst of steam and pushed the iron harder across the board, back and forth, back and forth. 'Nobody's ever laid on their death bed wishing they had spent more time at work,' she said. 'But our kids are growing up and you're missing it. And before too long they'll be gone and you'll be retired, and it'll be me and you, and we won't have anything to say to each other.'

It wasn't true, Ray thought, and he tried to find the words to say so, but they stuck in his throat and he found himself simply shaking his head as though he could make her words go away. He thought he heard Mags sigh, but it might have just been another cloud of steam.

38

You never forgave me for that night in Venice. You never lost that watchfulness, and you never again gave yourself up to me completely. Even when the bruise had faded from the bridge of your nose, and we could have forgotten all about it, I knew you were still thinking about it. I knew from the way your eyes followed me across the room when I went to get a beer, and from the hesitation in your voice before you answered me, although you told me constantly you were fine.

We went out for dinner on our anniversary. I had found you a leather-bound book on Rodin, in the antique bookshop in Chapel Road, and I wrapped it in the newspaper I had saved from our wedding day.

'The first anniversary is paper,' I reminded you, and your eyes lit up.

'It's perfect!' You folded the newspaper carefully and slipped it inside the book, where I had written a note: *For Jennifer, who I love more each day*, and you kissed me hard on the lips. 'I do love you, you know,' you said.

Sometimes I wasn't sure, but I never doubted the way I felt about you. I loved you so much it frightened me; I didn't realise it was possible to want someone so badly you would do anything to keep them. If I could have taken you away to a desert island, away from everyone, I would have done it.

'I've been asked to take a new adult education class,' you said, as we were shown to our table.

278

'What's the money like?'

You screwed up your nose. 'Pretty dreadful, but it's a therapy course offered at a subsidised rate to people with depression. I think it'll be a really worthwhile thing to do.'

I snorted. 'That sounds like a bundle of laughs.'

'There's a strong link between creative pursuits and people's moods,' you said. 'It would be great to know I was helping their recovery, and it's only for eight weeks. I should be able to fit it in around my other classes.'

'As long as you still have time for your work.' Your pieces were in five shops in the city now.

You nodded. 'It'll be fine. My regular orders are all manageable, and I'll limit the number of commissions I take for a while. Mind you, I didn't expect to end up doing quite so much teaching – I shall have to cut down next year.'

'Well, you know what they say,' I said, with a laugh. 'Those who can, do, and those who can't, teach!'

You said nothing.

Our food arrived and the waiter made a fuss of pulling out your napkin and pouring the wine.

'I was thinking it might be a good idea for me to open a separate bank account for the business,' you said.

'Why do you need to do that?' I wondered who had suggested that to you, and why you had been discussing our finances with them.

'It might be easier when I do my tax return. You know, if everything's in one account.'

'It'll only mean extra paperwork for you,' I said. I cut my steak in half to check it was cooked the way I liked it, and carefully removed the fat to place on the side of my plate.

'I don't mind.'

'No, it's easier if it all carries on going into mine,' I said. 'After all, I'm the one who pays the mortgage and the bills.'

'I suppose so.' You picked at your risotto.

'Do you need more cash?' I said. 'I can give you more house-keeping money this month if you like.'

'Maybe a little.'

'What do you need it for?'

'I thought I might go shopping,' you said. 'I could do with some new clothes.'

'Why don't I come with you? You know what you're like when you buy clothes – you'll choose things that look awful when you get home, and you'll end up taking half of them back.' I laughed, and reached across the table to squeeze your hand. 'I'll take some time off work and we'll make a day of it. We'll have lunch somewhere nice and then we'll hit the shops and you can hammer my credit card as much as you like. Does that sound good?'

You nodded, and I concentrated on my steak. I ordered another bottle of red wine, and by the time I had finished it we were the last couple in the restaurant. I left too big a tip and fell against the waiter when he brought my coat.

'I'm sorry,' you said, 'he's had a bit too much to drink.'

The waiter smiled politely, and I waited until we were outside before I took your arm and pinched it between my thumb and forefinger. 'Don't ever apologise for me.'

You were shocked. I don't know why – wasn't this what you had been expecting since Venice?

'I'm sorry,' you said, and I released your arm and took your hand instead.

It was late when we got home, and you went straight upstairs. I turned off the downstairs lights and joined you, but you were already in bed. When I got in next to you, you turned to me and kissed me, running your hands down my chest.

'I'm sorry, I love you,' you said.

I closed my eyes and waited for you to slip beneath the duvet. I knew it was pointless: I had drunk two bottles of wine and felt not so much as a stirring when you took me in your mouth. I let you try for a few moments, then pushed your head away.

'You don't turn me on any more,' I said. I rolled over to face the wall, and shut my eyes. You got up for the bathroom, and I could hear you crying as I went to sleep.

I didn't plan to cheat on you once we were married, but you stopped making an effort in bed completely. Do you blame me for looking elsewhere, when the alternative is missionary position with a wife who keeps her eyes shut the entire time? I started going out on a Friday after work, coming home in the early hours whenever I'd had enough of whoever I had ended up in bed with. You didn't seem to care, and after a while I didn't bother coming home at all. I would roll in at lunchtime on Saturday and find you in your studio, and you never asked where I'd been or who I'd been with. It became like a game, seeing how far I could push you before you accused me of being unfaithful.

The day you did I was watching football. Man U were playing Chelsea, and I was sitting with my feet up and a cold beer. You stood in front of the television.

'Get out of the way – they're into extra time!'

'Who's Charlotte?' you said.

'What do you mean?' I craned my neck to see past you.

'It's written on a receipt in the pocket of your coat, with a phone number. Who is she?'

There was a cheer from the television as Man U scored in time for the final whistle. I sighed and reached for the remote to turn it off.

'Happy now?' I lit a cigarette, knowing it would infuriate you.

'Can't you smoke that outside?'

'No, I can't,' I said, blowing a stream of smoke towards you. 'Because this is my house, not yours.'

'Who is Charlotte?' You were shaking, but you stayed standing in front of me.

I laughed. 'I have no idea.' It was true: I didn't remember her at all. She could have been any number of girls. 'She's probably some waitress who took a shine to me – I must have shoved the receipt in my pocket without looking at it.' I spoke easily, without a trace of defensiveness, and I saw you falter.

'I hope you're not accusing me of anything.' I held your gaze challengingly, but you looked away and didn't speak again. I almost laughed. You were so easy to beat.

I stood up. You were wearing a vest-top with no bra underneath and I could see the spread of your cleavage, and the shape of your nipples beneath the fabric. 'Have you been out like that?' I asked.

'Just to the shops.'

'With your tits on show?' I said. 'Do you want people to think you're some sort of slapper?'

You brought your hands up across your chest and I pushed them away. 'It's all right for complete strangers to see them, but not me? You can't pick and choose, Jennifer: either you're a tart or you're not.'

'I'm not,' you said quietly.

'That's not how it looks from where I'm standing.' I brought up my hand and pushed my cigarette end into your chest, grinding it out between your breasts. You screamed, but I had already left the room.

39

As Ray strode through back to his office after the morning meeting, he was collared by the station duty officer. Rachel was a slim woman in her early fifties, with neat, bird-like features and closely cropped silver hair.

'Are you duty DI today, Ray?'

'Yes,' Ray said, suspiciously, in the knowledge that nothing good ever followed that question.

'I've got a woman called Eve Mannings at the front counter who wants to report a fear for welfare: she's concerned about her sister.'

'Can't shift deal with it?'

'They're all out, and she's very worried. She's already been waiting an hour to see someone.' Rachel didn't say anything else; she didn't need to. She simply looked at Ray over plain, wire-framed glasses, and waited for him to do the right thing. It was like being told off by a kindly but intimidating aunt.

He peered through the SDO to the front counter, where a woman was doing something on a mobile phone.

'Is that her?'

Eve Mannings was the sort of woman more at home in a coffee shop than a cop shop. She had sleek brown hair that swished around her shoulders as she bent her head to look at her phone, and a bright yellow coat with over-sized buttons and a flowery lining. She was flushed, although that was not necessarily a reflection of her state of mind. The central heating in the station only seemed to have two settings: arctic or tropical, and today was obviously a tropical day. Ray silently cursed the protocol that dictated that fear-for-welfare reports should be dealt with by a police officer. Rachel would have been more than capable of taking a report.

He sighed. 'All right, I'll send someone down to see her.'

Satisfied, Rachel went back to her counter.

Ray made his way upstairs and found Kate at her desk. 'Can you nip down and deal with a fear for welfare at the front desk?'

'Can't shift deal?'

Ray laughed at the face she pulled. 'Already tried that. Go on, it'll take twenty minutes, max.'

Kate sighed. 'You're only asking because you know I never say no.'

'You want to be careful who you say that to.' Ray grinned. Kate rolled her eyes, but an attractive blush spread across her cheeks.

'Go on, then, what's the job?'

Ray handed her the piece of paper Rachel had given him. 'Eve Mannings. She's waiting for you downstairs.'

'Okay, but you owe me a drink.'

'Fine by me,' Ray called, as she left CID. He had apologised for the awkwardness at dinner, but Kate had shrugged it off as unimportant and they hadn't spoken about it again.

He made his way to his office. When he opened his briefcase he found a Post-it note from Mags on his diary with the date and time of their meeting with the school the following week. Mags had drawn a circle around it in red felt-tip pen, in case he had missed it. Ray stuck it to the front of his computer with the other Post-it notes, each carrying supposedly important bits of information.

He was still midway through his in-tray when Kate knocked on his door.

'Don't stop me,' Ray said. 'I'm on a roll.'

'Can I fill you in on this fear for welfare?'

Ray stopped and gestured for Kate to sit down.

'What are you doing?' she said, looking at the mountain of paper on his desk.

'Admin. Filing, mostly, and my expenses for the last six months. Finance say that if I don't get them in today they won't authorise them.'

'You need a PA.'

'I need to be allowed to get on with being a police officer,' he said, 'instead of all this crap. Sorry. Tell me how you got on.'

Kate looked at her notes. 'Eve Manning lives in Oxford, but her sister Jennifer lives here in Bristol with her husband, Ian Petersen. Eve and her sister fell out about five years ago and she hasn't seen her or her brother-in-law since. A few weeks ago Petersen popped round to see Eve out of the blue, asking where her sister is.'

'She's left him?'

'Apparently so. Mrs Manning got a card from her sister several months ago but she couldn't make out the postmark and she's thrown away the envelope. She's just found the card torn into pieces and hidden behind a clock on her mantelpiece, and she's convinced her brother-in-law did it when he visited.'

'Why would he do that?'

Kate shrugged. 'No idea. Mrs Manning doesn't know either, but it's put the wind up her for some reason. She wants to report her sister missing.'

'But she isn't missing, clearly,' Ray said, exasperated. 'Not if she's sent a card. She just doesn't want to be found. The two things are entirely different.'

'That's what I told her. Anyway, I've written it up for you.' She handed a plastic sleeve to Ray, containing a couple of handwritten pages.

'Thanks. I'll take a look.' Ray took the report and put it on his desk among the sea of paperwork. 'Assuming I can get through this lot, are you still up for a drink later? I think I'm going to need it.'

'Looking forward to it.'

'Great,' Ray said. 'Tom's going somewhere after school and I've said I'll pick him up at seven, so it'll just be a quick one.'

'No worries. Does that mean Tom's making friends?'

'I think so,' Ray said. 'Not that he'll tell me who they are. I'm hoping we'll find out more when we see the school next week, but I'm not holding my breath.'

'Well, if you need a sounding board in the pub, feel free to offload.' Kate said. 'Not that I can offer any advice about teenage kids, mind.'

Ray laughed. 'To be honest, it's nice to talk about something *other* than teenage kids.'

'Then I'm happy to provide a distraction.' Kate grinned, and Ray had a sudden picture in his mind of that night outside her flat. Did Kate ever think about it? He considered asking her, but Kate was already heading back to her desk.

Ray got out his phone to text Mags. He stared at the screen, trying to come up with some wording that wouldn't antagonise Mags or be an out and out lie. He shouldn't have to bend the truth at all, he thought; going for a drink with Kate should be no different to going for a pint with Stumpy. Ray ignored the voice in his head that told him precisely why it wasn't the same.

He sighed and put the phone back in his pocket, text message unwritten. Easier not to say anything at all. Glancing through his open office door, he could see the top of Kate's head as she sat at her desk. She was certainly providing a distraction, Ray thought. He just wasn't sure it was the right kind.

40

It's two weeks before I dare risk being seen in public; when the violent purple bruises on my arms have faded to a pale green. It jolts me to realise how shocking the contusions look against my skin, when two years ago they were as much a part of me as the colour of my hair.

I'm forced out by the need for dog food, and I leave Beau at home so I can take the bus into Swansea, where no one will notice a woman in the supermarket with her eyes to the floor, a scarf around her neck despite the mild weather. I take the footpath towards the caravan park, but can't shake off the feeling that someone's watching me. I look behind me, then panic that I've chosen the wrong direction, so I turn once more, but there is nothing there either. I spin in circles, unable to see for the black spots that have appeared in my eyes and seem to move infuriatingly wherever I want to look. I teeter on the brink of panic, the fear in my chest so intense it hurts, and I half walk, half run until I can see the static caravans and the low building of Bethan's shop. Finally my heart begins to slow and I fight to get myself back under control. It is times like this when prison becomes a welcome alternative to this life I'm living.

The car park at Bethan's is for people staying at the caravan park, but its proximity to the beach makes it an attractive option for walkers heading off up the coastal path. Bethan doesn't mind, except in high season when she puts up big signs saying 'private parking', and charges out of the shop when she sees a family unpacking picnics from their car. At this time of year, when the park is closed, the occasional cars left there belong to dog-walkers or hardy ramblers.

'You can use it, of course,' Bethan said to me when I first met her.

'I don't have a car,' I explained.

She told me my visitors could park there, and never remarked on the fact that I had none, apart from Patrick, who would leave his Land Rover at the park before walking to see me. I force the memory from my mind before it can take hold.

There are few cars there now. Bethan's battered Volvo; a van I don't recognise; and – I screw up my eyes and shake my head. This isn't possible. That can't be my car. I start to sweat and I take a gulp of air as I try to make sense of what I am seeing. The front bumper is cracked and in the centre of the windscreen is a spider-web pattern of cracks, the size of a fist.

It is my car.

Nothing makes sense. When I left Bristol I left my car behind. Not because I thought the police would trace it – although it crossed my mind – but because I couldn't bear to see it. For one wild moment I wonder if the police have found it and brought it here to test my reaction, and I look around the car park as though armed officers might leap out at me.

In my confused state I can't work out how important this is; if it matters. But it must, or the police wouldn't have insisted I tell them what I did with the car. I need to get rid of it. I think of films I've seen. Could I push it off a cliff? Or set fire to it? I'd need matches and lighter fuel or maybe petrol – but how would I set it alight without Bethan seeing?

I glance at the shop but can't see her in the window, so I take a deep breath and cross the car park to my car. The keys are in the ignition and I don't hesitate. I open the car door and sit in the driver's seat. Immediately I'm assaulted by memories of the accident: I can hear the scream from Jacob's mother, and my own horrified cry. I start to shake and try to pull myself together. The car starts first time and I speed out of the car park. If Bethan looks out now, she won't see me, only the car and the cloud of dust in its wake as I head for Penfach.

'Nice to be behind the wheel again?'

Ian's voice is measured and dry. I slam on the brakes, and the car veers sharply to the left as my hands slip on the steering wheel. I have my hand on the car door handle when I realise the sound is coming from the CD player.

'I expect you've missed your little run-about, haven't you? No need to thank me for returning it to you.'

The effect of his voice on me is immediate. I become instantly smaller, shrinking back into my seat as though I can disappear into it, and my hands are hot and clammy.

'Have you forgotten our wedding vows, Jennifer?'

I put my hand on my chest and press against it, trying to slow the frantic pounding of my heart.

'You stood next to me, and you promised to love, honour and obey me as long as we both shall live.'

He's taunting me, the sing-song pace of the vow I made so many years ago at odds with the coldness in his voice. He is insane. I can see that now, and it terrifies me to think of the years I spent lying next to him, not knowing what he was truly capable of.

'Running to the police with your stories isn't honouring me, is it, Jennifer? Telling them what goes on behind closed doors isn't obeying me. Just remember, I only ever gave you what you asked for . . .'

I can't hear any more. I jab at the stereo controls and the CD ejects with agonising slowness. I snatch it from the slot and try to snap it in half, but it won't bend and I scream at it, my twisted face reflected in its shiny surface. I get out of the car and hurl the CD into the hedge.

'Leave me alone!' I scream. 'Just leave me alone!'

I drive frantically, dangerously, along the high-hedged rows, heading out of Penfach and into the countryside. I'm shaking violently and it is beyond my capabilities to change gear, so I stay in second and the car whines in protest. I hear Ian's words over and over in my head.

As long as we both shall live.

There is a collapsed barn a little way from the road, and no other houses nearby that I can see. I turn down the bumpy farm track towards it. As I draw near I see that the barn has no roof, and naked rafters reach towards the sky. There's a pile of tyres at one end, and a collection of rusting machinery. It will do. I drive into the far end of the barn, tucking the car into the corner. There is a tarpaulin heaped on the floor and I drag it open, covering myself in fetid water that has collected in its folds. I pull it over my car. It's a risk, but under the dark green sheet the car disappears into the rest of the barn, and it doesn't look as though anything has been moved for some time.

I begin the long walk home, and I'm reminded of the day I arrived in Penfach, when what was ahead of me was so much more uncertain that what lay behind. Now I know what the future holds: I have two more weeks in Penfach, then I'll return to Bristol for sentencing, and I'll be safe.

There is a bus stop ahead of me but I keep walking, taking comfort in the rhythm of my feet. Gradually I begin to feel calmer. Ian's playing games, that's all. If he were going to kill me he would have done so when he came to the cottage.

It's late in the afternoon when I reach the cottage, and dark clouds are gathering overhead. I go inside only long enough to put on my waterproof jacket and to call Beau outside, and I take him down to the beach for a run. Down by the sea I can breathe again, and I know I will miss this most of all.

The feeling of being watched is overpowering and I turn and keep my back to the sea. I feel a clutch of fear as I see a figure standing on the clifftop, facing me, and my heart quickens. I call for Beau and place my hand on his collar, but he barks and pulls away from me, running across the sand towards the footpath leading up to where the man is standing, silhouetted against the sky.

'Beau, come back!'

He races on, oblivious, but I am rooted to the spot. It is only when Beau reaches the end of the beach, and bounds easily up the footpath, that the figure moves. The man bends to stroke Beau, and I instantly recognise the familiar movements. It's Patrick.

I might have been more reluctant to encounter him, after our last meeting, but the relief I feel is so great that before I know it I am following the scuff marks left by Beau in the sand, and walking to join them.

'How are you?' he says.

'I'm fine.' We're strangers, walking in conversational circles around each other.

'I left messages.'

'I know.' I've ignored them all. At first I listened to them, but I couldn't bear to hear what I'd done to him, and so I deleted the others without playing them. Eventually I simply turned off my phone.

'I miss you, Jenna.'

I found his anger understandable and easier to deal with, but now he is quiet and beseeching, and I feel my resolve crumbling. I start walking back to the cottage. 'You shouldn't be here.' I resist the temptation to look around to see if we are being watched, but I'm terrified Ian will see us together.

I feel a drop of rain on my face, and I pull up my hood. Patrick strides alongside me.

'Jenna, talk to me. Stop running away!'

It is so exactly what I have done all my life that I can't defend myself.

There's a flash of lightning and the rain falls so hard it takes

291

my breath away. The skies darken so suddenly our shadows vanish, and Beau presses himself into the ground, flattening his ears. We run to the cottage and I wrench the door open just as thunder crashes overhead. Beau races past our legs and shoots up the stairs. I call for him, but he doesn't come.

'I'll go and see if he's okay.' Patrick goes up the stairs and I bolt the front door, following a minute later. I find him on the floor of my bedroom, a quivering Beau in his arms. 'They're all the same,' he says with a half-grin, 'highly strung poodles or macho mastiffs – they all hate thunder and fireworks.'

I kneel down beside them and stroke Beau's head. He whines a little.

'What's this?' Patrick says. My wooden box is sticking out from beneath the bed.

'It's mine,' I say abruptly, and I kick it violently back under the bed.

Patrick's eyes widen but he says nothing, getting to his feet awkwardly and carrying Beau downstairs. 'It might be an idea to put the radio on for him,' he tells me. He speaks as though he is the vet and I'm the customer, and I wonder if it's out of habit, or whether he has decided enough is enough. But when he has settled Beau on the sofa, with a blanket around him and Classic FM on loud enough to drown out the quietest rumbles, he speaks again, and his voice is more gentle now.

'I'll look after him for you.'

I bite my lip.

'Leave him here when you go,' he says. 'You don't have to see me, or speak to me. Just leave him here and I'll come and get him, and I'll have him while you're . . .' he pauses. 'While you're away.'

'It could be years,' I say, and my voice cracks on the final word.

'Let's just take each day as it comes,' he says. He leans forward and drops the softest of kisses on my forehead.

I give him the spare key from the kitchen drawer and he leaves without another word. I fight back the tears that have no right to spring from my eyes. This is of my own making and however much it hurts it has to be done. But my heart still leaps when there is a knock at the door barely five minutes later, and I imagine Patrick has come back for something.

I fling open the door.

'I want you out of the cottage,' Iestyn says, without preamble.

'What?' I put my hand flat against the wall to anchor myself. 'Why?'

He doesn't look me in the eye, reaching down instead to pull Beau's ears and fuss his mouth. 'You need to be out by the morning.'

'But, Iestyn, I can't! You know what's going on. My bail conditions state I have to stay at this address until my trial.'

'It's not my problem.' Iestyn finally looks at me and I see he isn't enjoying this task. His face is set hard, but his eyes are pained and he shakes his head slowly. 'Look, Jenna, the whole of Penfach knows you've been arrested for running over that little lad, and they all know you're only here in the bay because you're renting my cottage. As far as they're concerned, I might as well have been driving that car myself. It's only a matter of time before there's more of this' – he gestures to the graffiti on the door, which despite my scrubbing has stubbornly remained – 'or worse. Dog mess through the letter box, fireworks, petrol – you read it in the papers all the time.'

'I've got nowhere to go, Iestyn,' I try to appeal to him, but his determination doesn't waver.

'The village shop won't stock my produce any more,' he says, 'so disgusted they are that I'm putting a roof over the head of a murderer.'

I take a sharp breath.

'And this morning they refused to serve Glynis. It's one thing getting at me, but when they start on my wife . . .'

'I just need a few more days, Iestyn,' I plead. 'I'm due in court for sentencing in a fortnight, and then I'll be gone for good. Please, Iestyn, just let me stay until then.'

Iestyn thrusts his hands in his pockets and stares out at the sea for a moment. I wait, knowing there is nothing else I can say to make him change his mind.

'Two weeks,' he says, 'but not a day longer. And if you've got any sense you'll stay away from the village until then.'

41

You stayed in your studio all day and would disappear back there of an evening, unless I told you not to. You didn't seem to care that I worked hard during the week, and that I might like a little comfort in the evenings, someone to ask about my day. You were like a mouse, scurrying down to your shed whenever you got the chance. You had somehow become well known as a local sculptor; not for your thrown pots, but for the hand-sculpted figurines that stood eight inches tall. They had no appeal for me, with their warped faces and disproportionate limbs, but it seemed there was a market for such things, and you could hardly make them fast enough.

'I bought a DVD to watch tonight,' I said, when you came into the kitchen one Saturday to make a coffee.

'Okay.' You didn't ask what the film was, and I didn't know. I would go out later to choose one.

You leaned against the worktop as the kettle boiled, hooking your thumbs into the pockets of your jeans. Your hair was loose, but tucked behind your ears, and I caught sight of the graze on the side of your face. You saw me looking and flicked your hair forward until it fell across your cheek.

'Would you like coffee?' you said.

'Please.' You poured water into two mugs, but only added coffee to one. 'Aren't you having one?'

'I don't feel very well.' You sliced a lemon and dropped a piece into your mug. 'I haven't felt right for a few days.'

'Darling, you should have said. Here, sit down.' I pulled out a chair for you, but you shook your head.

'It's okay, I'm just a bit off colour. I'll be fine tomorrow, I'm sure.'

I wrapped my arms around you and pressed my cheek against yours. 'Poor baby. I'll look after you.'

You returned the embrace and I rocked you gently, until you moved away. I hated it when you pulled away from me. It felt like a rejection, when all I was trying to do was comfort you. I felt my jaw tighten and instantly saw a watchfulness pass across your eyes. I was glad to see it – it showed me you still cared what I thought; what I did – but at the same time it annoyed me.

I raised my arm towards your head and heard the sharp intake of breath as you flinched, screwing your eyes tightly shut. I stilled my hand as it brushed your forehead and gently removed something from your hair.

'A money spider,' I said, opening my fist to show you. 'That's supposed to be lucky, isn't it?'

You were no better the following day, and I insisted you stay in bed. I brought you dry crackers to ease your churning stomach, and read to you until you told me your head was aching. I wanted to call the doctor, but you promised me you would go as soon as the surgery opened on Monday. I stroked your hair and watched your eyelids flicker in your sleep, and I wondered what you were dreaming of.

I left you in bed on Monday morning, with a note by your pillow reminding you to see the doctor. I called from work, but there was no answer, and although I rang every half-hour from that point, you didn't answer the house phone and your mobile was turned off. I became frantic with worry, and by lunchtime I decided I would go home to check you were okay.

Your car was outside the house, and when I put my key in

the door I realised it was still on the latch. You were sitting on the sofa with your head in your hands.

'Are you okay? I've been going out of my mind!'

You looked up but didn't say anything.

'Jennifer! I've been calling you all morning – why didn't you pick up?'

'I popped out,' you said, 'and then . . .' You tailed off without any explanation.

Anger bubbled inside me. 'Did it not occur to you how worried I would be?' I grabbed the front of your jumper and hauled you to your feet. You screamed, and the noise stopped me thinking straight. I pushed you backwards across the room and held you against the wall, my fingers pressing against your throat. I felt your pulse beat fast and hard against my own.

'Please don't!' you cried.

Slowly, gently, I pressed my fingers into your neck, watching my hand squeeze tighter as though it belonged to someone else. You made a choking noise.

'I'm pregnant.'

I let go of you. 'You can't be.'

'I am.'

'But you're on the pill.'

You began to cry, and you sank down to the floor and wrapped your arms around your knees. I stood over you, trying to make sense of what I'd heard. You were pregnant.

'It must have been that time I was sick,' you said.

I crouched down and put my arms around you. I thought of my father; how cold and unapproachable he had been all my life, and I vowed never to be like that with my own child. I hoped it would be a boy. He would look up to me – want to be like me. I couldn't stop the smile forming on my face.

You unwrapped your arms and looked at me. You were shaking, and I stroked your cheek. 'We're going to have a baby!'

297

Your eyes were still shiny, but slowly the tension left your face. 'You're not angry?'

'Why would I be angry?'

I felt euphoric. This would change everything. I imagined you full and taut with child, dependent on me to keep you healthy, grateful when I rubbed your feet or brought you tea. When the baby was born you would stop work, and I would provide for you both. I saw our future play out in my mind. 'It's a miracle baby,' I told you. I gripped your shoulders and you tensed. 'I know things haven't been perfect between us lately,' I said, 'but it will all be different now. I'm going to look after you.' You looked straight into my eyes and I felt a wave of guilt engulf me. 'Everything will be all right now,' I said. 'I love you so much, Jennifer.'

Fresh tears burst over your lower lids. 'I love you too.'

I wanted to say sorry – sorry for everything that I had done to you, for every time I had ever hurt you – but the unformed words stuck in my throat. 'Don't ever tell anyone,' I said instead.

'Tell them what?'

'About our arguments. Promise me you'll never tell anyone.' I could feel your flesh pushing up between my fingers as I held your shoulders, and your eyes grew wide and scared.

'Never,' you said, the sound little more than a breath. 'I'll never tell a soul.'

I smiled. 'Now stop crying – you mustn't stress the baby.' I stood up and held out a hand to help you to your feet. 'Do you feel sick?'

You nodded.

'Lie on the sofa. I'll get you a blanket.' You protested but I guided you to the sofa and helped you lie down. You were carrying my son, and I intended to look after you both.

You worried about the first scan. 'What if there's something wrong?'

'Why would there be anything wrong?' I said.

I took the day off work and drove you to the hospital.

'It can already close its fingers. Isn't that amazing?' you said, reading from one of your many baby books. You had become obsessed with the pregnancy, buying endless magazines and trawling the internet for advice on labour and breastfeeding. No matter what I said, the conversation would inevitably turn to baby names or lists of equipment we should be buying.

'Amazing,' I said. I had heard it all before. The pregnancy wasn't working out the way I had expected. You seemed hell-bent on continuing work in the same way as before, and although you accepted my offers of tea and foot massages, you didn't seem grateful for them. You paid more attention to our unborn child – a child who as yet had no idea he was even being spoken about – than to your own husband, standing right in front of you. I imagined you leaning over our newborn, oblivious to my own part in his creation, and I had a sudden memory of the way you played with that kitten for hours at a time.

You clutched my hand when the sonographer smeared gel on to your belly, and squeezed it tight until we heard the muffled sound of a heartbeat and saw a tiny flicker on the screen.

'There's the head,' the sonographer said, 'and you should be able to make out his arms – look, he's waving to you!'

You laughed.

'He?' I said, hopefully.

The sonographer looked up. 'Figure of speech. We won't be able to tell the sex for a good while yet. But everything looks healthy and it's the right size for your dates.' She printed off a picture and handed it to you. 'Congratulations.'

The midwife appointment was half an hour afterwards, and we sat in the waiting room with half a dozen other couples. There was a woman on the other side of the room with a grotesquely big stomach that forced her to sit with her legs wide open. I looked away, and was relieved when we were called in.

The midwife took your blue folder from you and looked through your notes, checking your details and producing fact sheets on diet and pregnancy health.

'She's already an expert,' I said. 'She's read so many books there can't be anything she doesn't know.'

The midwife looked at me appraisingly. 'And how about you, Mr Petersen? Are you an expert?'

'I don't need to be,' I said, meeting her gaze and holding it. 'I'm not the one having the baby.'

She didn't reply. 'I'll just check your blood pressure, Jenna. Roll up your sleeve and rest your arm on the desk for me.'

You hesitated and it took me a second to understand why. My jaw clenched but I leaned back in my chair, watching the proceedings with forced indifference.

The bruise on your upper arm was mottled green. It had faded significantly over the last few days, but it was stubborn, as they always were. Although I knew it was impossible, I sometimes felt that you deliberately hung on to them, to remind me what had happened; to provoke me into feeling guilty.

The midwife said nothing, and I relaxed slightly. She took your blood pressure, which was a little high, and noted down the figures. Then she turned to me.

'If you'd like to step into the waiting room, I'll just have a quick chat with Jenna on her own.'

'That won't be necessary,' I said. 'We don't keep anything from each other.'

'Standard practice,' the midwife said briskly.

I stared at her but she didn't back down, and I stood up. 'Fine.' I took my time leaving the room, and went to stand by the coffee machine where I could see the door to the midwife's room.

I looked around at the other couples: there were no men on

their own – no one else was being treated this way. I marched across to the consulting room and opened the door without knocking. You had something in your hand and you slipped it between the pages of your pregnancy notes. A small rectangular card: pale blue, with some kind of logo in the centre at the top.

'We need to move the car, Jennifer,' I said. 'We're only allowed to park for an hour.'

'Oh, okay. I'm sorry.' This last was directed at the midwife, who smiled at you and ignored me completely. She leaned forward and put her hand on your arm.

'Our number's on the front of your notes, so if you're worried about anything – anything at all – ask.'

We drove home in silence. You held the scan picture in your lap and every now and then I saw you put a hand to your stomach, as if trying to reconcile what you felt inside with what you held in your hand.

'What did the midwife want to talk to you about?' I said when we got home.

'Just my medical history,' you said, but it was too quick, too rehearsed.

I knew you were lying. Later that day, when you fell asleep, I went through your notes, looking for that pale-blue business card with the round logo, but it wasn't there.

I watched you change, as your stomach grew. I thought your need for me would increase, but if anything you became more self-sufficient, more resilient. I was losing you to this baby, and I didn't know how to get you back.

That summer was hot, and you seemed to revel in walking around the house with your skirt rolled down under your bump; a tiny T-shirt riding up above it. Your belly button popped out and I couldn't bear to look at it; couldn't understand why you were happy to wander around like that, answer the door, even.

You stopped working, even though you weren't due for weeks,

and so I cancelled the cleaner. It made no sense to pay for someone to clean the house when you were at home all day doing nothing.

I left you with the ironing one day, and when I returned you had finished it all and the house was spotless. You looked exhausted, and I was touched by your commitment. I decided I would run you a bath; pamper you a little. I wondered if you might like a takeaway, or perhaps I would cook for you. I carried the shirts upstairs and turned on the taps before calling you.

I was hanging the shirts in my wardrobe when I noticed something.

'What's this?'

You were immediately abashed. 'It's a scorch mark. I'm so sorry. The phone rang, and I got distracted. But it's on the bottom, I don't think it will show if you tuck it in.'

You looked so upset, but it really didn't matter. It was just a shirt. I put it down and stepped forward to give you a cuddle, but you flinched and drew an arm protectively across your stomach, your face turned away and screwed up in anticipation of something I had never even intended to happen.

But it did happen. And you had only yourself to blame.

42

Ray's mobile rang as he was manoeuvring his car into the last available space in the yard. He pressed 'accept' on the hands-free and twisted round to see how much further he could inch backwards.

Chief Constable Rippon got straight to the point. 'I want you to bring forward the Op Falcon briefing to this afternoon.'

Ray's Mondeo nudged the blue Volvo parked behind it.

'Shit.'

'That wasn't quite the reaction I was hoping for.' There was an amused note in the chief's voice that Ray had not heard before. He wondered what had happened to put her in such good humour.

'Sorry, ma'am.'

Ray got out of his car, leaving the keys in the ignition in case the owner of the Volvo needed to get out. He glanced at the bumper but could see no obvious mark. 'You were saying?'

'The Op Falcon briefing is scheduled for Monday,' Olivia said, with uncharacteristic patience, 'but I want to bring it forward. You might have seen on the news this morning that several other forces have been criticised for their apparently tolerant approach to drug possession.'

Ah, Ray thought. That explained the good mood.

'So it's the ideal time for us to launch our "tough on drugs" stance. We've already got the nationals lined up – I need you to pull the relevant resources together a few days early.'

Ray's blood ran cold. 'I can't do it today,' he said.

There was a pause.

Ray waited for the chief to speak, but the silence stretched unbearably between them until he felt he had to fill it. 'I have an appointment at my son's school at midday.'

It was rumoured that Olivia conducted parents' evenings at her children's school via telephone conferencing, so Ray knew this was unlikely to sway her.

'Ray,' she said, all traces of humour dispelled, 'as you know, I am extremely supportive of those with dependants, and in fact championed the introduction in this force of flexible working for parents. But unless I'm very much mistaken, you do have a *wife*, do you not?'

'I do.'

'And is she going to this meeting?'

'She is.'

'Then what, may I ask, is the problem?'

Ray leaned against the wall by the back door and looked up at the sky for inspiration, but all he saw were heavy black clouds.

'My son is being bullied, ma'am. Badly, I think. This is the first opportunity we have had to speak to the school since they admitted there was a problem, and my wife wants me there.' Ray cursed himself for pushing the blame on to Mags. 'I want to be there,' he said. 'I need to be there.'

Olivia's tone softened slightly. 'I'm sorry to hear that, Ray. Kids can be a worry. If you need to go to this meeting, then of course you should go. But the briefing will go ahead this morning, with the national coverage this force needs in order to cement itself as a progressive, zero-tolerance force. And if you can't lead it, then I'll have to find someone who can. I'll speak to you in an hour.'

'Talk about Hobson's choice,' Ray muttered, as he put the phone back in his pocket. It was as simple as that, then: career prospects on one side; family on the other. Upstairs in his office, he shut the door and sat at his desk, pressing the tips of his fingers together. Today's operation was a big deal, and he was under no illusions that this was a test. Did he have what it took to go further in the police? He wasn't sure himself, any more – he didn't even know if that was what he wanted. He thought about the new car they would need in a year or so; the foreign holidays the kids would start clamouring for before too long; the bigger house Mags deserved. He had two bright kids who would hopefully go on to university, and where was the money going to come from for that, unless Ray continued climbing the ladder? Nothing was possible without sacrifices.

Taking a deep breath, Ray picked up the phone to call home.

The launch of Operation Falcon was a triumph. Members of the press were invited to the conference room at headquarters for a half-hour briefing, during which the chief introduced Ray as 'one of the best detectives in the force'. Ray felt a surge of adrenalin as he answered questions on the scale of the drugs problem in Bristol, the force's approach to enforcement, and his own commitment to restoring community safety by eradicating on-street dealing. When the ITN reporter asked him for a final word, Ray looked directly into the camera and didn't hesitate. 'There are people out there who are dealing drugs with impunity, and who believe the police are powerless to stop them. But we do have powers, and we have resilience, and we won't rest until we have taken them off the streets.' There was a smattering of applause, and Ray glanced at the chief, who gave an almost imperceptible nod. The warrants had been executed earlier, with fourteen arrests made from six addresses. The house searches would take hours, and he wondered how Kate was getting on as Exhibits' Officer.

As soon as he had a chance, he called her.

'Perfect timing,' she said. 'Are you in the nick?'

'I'm in the office. Why?'

'Meet me in the canteen in ten minutes. I've got something to show you.'

He was there in five, waiting impatiently for Kate, who burst through the door with a grin on her face.

'Do you want a coffee?' Ray said.

'No time, I've got to get back. But take a look at this.' She handed him a clear plastic bag. Inside was a pale-blue card.

'It's the same card Jenna Gray had in her purse,' Ray said. 'Where did you get it from?'

'It was in one of the houses raided this morning. It's not exactly the same though.' She smoothed the plastic, so Ray could read the writing on the card. 'Same card, same logo, different address.'

'Interesting. Whose house was it in?'

'Dominica Letts. She won't talk till her brief gets here.' Kate looked at her watch. 'Shit, I've got to go.' She thrust the bag at Ray. 'You can keep that – I've got a copy.' She grinned again and disappeared, leaving Ray looking at the card. There was nothing distinctive about the address – it was a residential road like Grantham Street – but Ray felt he should be able to glean more from that logo. The figures of eight were broken at the bottom and stacked one on top of the other, like Russian dolls.

Ray shook his head. He needed to go and check on the custody team before he went home, and double-check that everything was in place for Gray's sentencing tomorrow. He folded the bag and tucked it into his pocket.

It was gone ten o'clock before Ray got in his car to go home, and the first time since that morning that he had felt any misgivings about his decision to put work before his family. He spent the drive home rationalising it to himself and by the time he reached his house he had convinced himself that he had made the right choice. The *only* choice, really. Until he put his key in the door and heard Mags crying.

'Oh my God, Mags, what happened?' He dropped his bag in the hall and came to crouch in front of the sofa, lifting up her hair to see her face. 'Is Tom okay?'

'No, he's not okay!' She pushed his hands away.

'What did the school say?'

'It's been going on for at least a year, they think, although the Head said she couldn't do anything about it until they had evidence.'

'Which they've now got?'

Mags gave a hard laugh. 'Oh, they've got it, all right. Apparently it's all over the internet. Shoplifting dares, "happy slapping", the works. All filmed and uploaded to YouTube for the world to see.'

Ray felt something grip his chest. The thought of what Tom had been put through made Ray physically sick.

'Is he asleep?' Ray nodded towards the bedrooms.

'I would have thought so. He's probably exhausted: I've spent the last hour and a half yelling at him.'

'Yelling at him?' Ray stood up. 'Jesus, Mags, don't you think he's been through enough?' He began walking towards the stairs, but Mags pulled him back.

'You've got no idea, have you?' she said.

Ray looked at her blankly.

'You've been so wrapped up in solving problems at work that you've completely ignored what's going on in your own family. Tom isn't being bullied, Ray. He's the bully.'

Ray felt as though he had been punched.

'Someone's making him . . .'

Mags interrupted, more gently. 'No one's making him do anything.' She sighed and sat back down. 'It seems Tom is the ring-leader of a small but influential "gang". There are about six of them – including Philip Martin and Connor Axtell.'

'That figures,' Ray said grimly, recognising the names.

'The one consistent piece of information is that Tom rules

the roost. His idea to bunk off school; his idea to lie in wait for the kids coming out of the Special Ed centre . . .'

Ray felt nauseous.

'And the stuff under his bed?' he asked.

'Stolen to order, apparently. And none of it by Tom – by all accounts he doesn't like to get his hands dirty.' Ray had never heard such bitterness in Mags's voice.

'What do we do now?' When something went wrong at work there were rules to fall back on. Protocols, laws, manuals. A team of people around him. Ray felt totally adrift.

'We sort it out.' Mags said simply. 'Apologise to the people Tom's hurt, return the things he had stolen, and – more than anything – find out why he's doing it.'

Ray was silent for a moment. He almost couldn't bring himself to say it, but once the thought was in his head he couldn't keep it to himself. 'Is this my fault?' he said. 'Is it because I haven't been there for him?'

Mags took his hand. 'Don't – you'll drive yourself mad. It's as much my fault as it is yours – I didn't see it either.'

'I should have spent more time at home, though.'

Mags didn't contradict him.

'I'm so sorry, Mags. It won't always be like this, I promise. I just need to get to superintendent, and—'

'But you love your job as a DI.'

'Yes, but—'

'So why go for promotion and leave it behind?'

Ray was momentarily floored. 'Well, for us. So we can have a bigger house, and so you don't need to go back to work.'

'But I want to go back to work!' Mags turned to him, exasperated. 'The kids are at school all day, you're at work . . . I want to do something for *me*. Planning a new career is giving me a focus I haven't had in years.' She looked at Ray and her expression softened. 'Oh, you daft sod.'

'I'm sorry,' Ray said again.

Mags bent down and kissed his forehead. 'Leave Tom for tonight. I'll keep him off school tomorrow and we'll talk to him in the morning. For now, let's talk about us.'

Ray woke up to see Mags putting a cup of tea gently by the side of the bed.

'I thought you'd probably want to be up early,' she said. 'It's Gray's sentencing today, isn't it?'

'Yes, but Kate can go.' Ray sat up. 'I'll stay home and talk to Tom with you.'

'And miss your moment of glory? It's fine, really. You go. Tom and I will potter about at home, like we used to when he was a baby. I've got a feeling it's not a talking-to he needs: it's listening.'

Ray thought how wise she was. 'You're going to be a brilliant teacher, Mags.' He took her hand. 'I don't deserve you.'

Mags smiled. 'Maybe not, but you're stuck with me, I'm afraid.' She squeezed his hand and went downstairs, leaving Ray to drink his tea. He wondered how long he had been putting work before his family, and was ashamed to realise he couldn't remember a time when that hadn't been the case. He had to change that. Had to start putting Mags and the kids first. How could he have been so blind to her needs, the fact that she actually *wanted* to go back to work? Clearly he wasn't the only one who found life a little dull at times. Mags had addressed this by looking for a new career. What had Ray done? He thought of Kate and felt himself blush.

Ray showered and dressed, and went downstairs to find his suit jacket.

'It's in here,' Mags called, coming out of the sitting room holding the jacket. She picked at the plastic bag protruding from his pocket. 'What's this?'

Ray pulled it out and handed it to her. 'It's something that may or may not be related to the Gray job. I'm trying to figure out what the logo might be.'

Mags held up the bag and looked at the card. 'It's a person, isn't it?' she said without hesitation. 'With their arms around someone.'

Ray's mouth fell open. He looked at the card and saw instantly what Mags had described. What had looked to him like an incomplete and out-of-proportion number eight was indeed a head and shoulders; the arms encircling a smaller figure that echoed the lines of the first.

'Of course!' he said. He thought of the house in Grantham Street, with its multiple locks, and net curtains stopping anyone looking in. He thought of Jenna Gray, and the ever-present fear in her eyes, and slowly a picture began to emerge.

There was a sound on the stairs, and seconds later Tom appeared, looking apprehensive. Ray stared at him. For months he had seen his son as a victim, but it turned out he wasn't the victim at all.

'I've got it all wrong,' he said out loud.

'Got what all wrong?' Mags said. But Ray had already gone.

43

The entrance to Bristol Crown Court is tucked away down a narrow road appropriately called Small Street.

'I'll have to drop you here, love,' my taxi driver tells me. If he recognises me from today's papers he isn't showing it. 'There's something going on outside the court today – I'm not taking the cab past that lot.'

He stops at the corner of the street, where a collection of self-satisfied suits trickles out of All Bar One after a liquid lunch. One of them leers at me. 'Fancy a drink, sweetheart?'

I look away.

'Frigid cow,' he mutters and his friends roar with laughter. I take a deep breath, fighting to keep my panic under control as I scan the streets for Ian. Is he here? Is he watching me right now?

The high buildings either side of Small Street lean towards each other, creating a shadowy, echo-filled walkway that makes me shiver. I haven't walked more than a few paces when I see what the taxi driver was talking about. A section of the road has been cordoned off with roadside barriers, behind which thirty or so protesters are grouped. Several have placards resting against their shoulders, and a huge painted sheet is draped over the barrier immediately in front of them. The word *MURDERER!* is written in thick red paint, each letter dripping down to the bottom of the sheet. A pair of police officers in fluorescent jackets stand to the side of the group, seemingly unfazed by the repetitive chant I can hear from the other end of Small Street.

'Justice for Jacob! Justice for Jacob!'

I walk slowly towards the court, wishing I had thought to bring a scarf, or some dark glasses. From the corner of my eye I notice a man on the opposite side of the pavement. He's leaning against the wall but when he sees me he straightens and pulls a phone out of his pocket. I quicken my steps, wanting to get inside the court as soon as I can, but the man keeps pace with me on the other side of the street. He makes a call that lasts seconds. The pockets of the man's beige waistcoat are rammed with what I now realise are camera lenses, and he has a black bag slung over his shoulders. He runs ahead, opening the bag and pulling out a camera; fitting a lens in a fluid movement born of years of practice; taking my picture.

I will ignore them, I think, my breath coming in hard lumps. I'll simply walk into court as if they aren't there. They can't hurt me – the police are there to keep them behind those barriers – so I'll just act as if they aren't there.

But as I turn towards the entrance to the court, I see the reporter who accosted me as I left the Magistrates' Court all those weeks ago.

'Quick word for the *Post*, Jenna? Chance to put your story across?'

I turn away and freeze as I realise I'm now directly facing the protesters. The chanting dissolves into angry shouts and jeers, and there's a sudden surge towards me. A barrier topples over and slams on to the cobbles, the sound ricocheting between the high buildings like a gunshot. The police move lazily across, their arms outstretched, ushering the protesters back behind the line. Some are still shouting but most are laughing, chatting with others as though they are going shopping. A fun day out.

As the group melts backwards, and the police replace the barriers around the designated protest area, one woman is left standing in front of me. She is younger than me – still in her twenties – and unlike the other protesters she holds no banner or placard, just something clutched in one hand. Her dress is brown and a little short, worn over black tights that end incongruously in grubby white plimsolls, and her coat flaps open despite the cold.

'He was such a good baby,' she says quietly.

At once I can see Jacob's features in hers. The pale-blue eyes with their slight tilt upwards; the heart-shaped face ending in a small pointed chin.

The protesters fall silent. Everyone is watching us.

'He hardly ever cried; even when he was sick he would just lie against me, looking up at me and waiting to get better.'

She speaks perfect English, but with an accent I can't place. Something Eastern European, perhaps. Her voice is measured, as though she's reciting something learnt by rote, and although she stands her ground I have the impression she is as frightened by this encounter as I am. Perhaps more so.

'I was very young when I had him. Only a child myself. His father didn't want me to keep the baby, but I couldn't bring myself to have a termination. I already loved him too much.' She speaks calmly, without emotion. 'Jacob was all I had.'

My eyes fill with tears and I despise myself for such a response, when Jacob's mother is dry-eyed. I force myself to stand still and don't let myself wipe my cheeks. I know that, like me, she's thinking of that night, when she stared at the rain-streaked windscreen, her eyes screwed up against the glare of the headlights. Today there is nothing between us, and she can see me as clearly as I can see her. I wonder why she doesn't rush at me: punch or bite or claw at my face. I don't know if I would have such self-restraint, were I in her shoes.

'Anya!' A man calls to her from within the crowd of protesters, but she ignores him. She holds out a photograph, thrusting it towards me until I take hold of it.

The picture isn't one I have seen in the newspapers or online; that gap-toothed grin in the school uniform, head

313

turned just so for the photographer. In this photo Jacob is younger – perhaps three or four. He nestles in the crook of his mother's arm, both lying on their backs in long grass scattered with dandelion clocks. The angle of the photo suggests Anya took it herself: her arm is outstretched as though reaching right outside the picture. Jacob is looking at the camera, squinting against the sun and laughing. Anya is laughing too, but she's looking at Jacob, and in her eyes are tiny reflections of him.

'I'm so sorry,' I say. I hate how weak the words sound, but I can't find any others, and I can't bear to offer only silence in response to her grief.

'Do you have children?'

I think of my son; of his weightless body wrapped in its hospital blanket; of the ache in my womb that has never left. I think that there should be a word for a mother with no children; for a woman bereft of the baby that would have made her whole.

'No.' I search for something to say, but there is nothing. I hold the photograph towards Anya, who shakes her head.

'I don't need it,' she says. 'I carry his face in here.' She places the flat of her palm against her chest. 'But you,' there is the briefest of pauses, 'you, I think, must remember. You must remember that he was a boy. That he had a mother. And that her heart is breaking.'

She turns and ducks under the barrier, disappearing into the crowd, and I draw in air as though I've been held under water.

My barrister is a woman in her forties. She looks at me with calculated interest as she sweeps into the small consultation room, where a security officer stands outside the door.

'Ruth Jefferson,' she says, holding out a firm hand. 'It's a simple process today, Ms Gray. You've already entered a plea, so today's hearing is merely for sentencing. We're first up after lunch, and I'm afraid you've got Judge King.' She sits opposite me at the table.

'What's wrong with Judge King?'

'Let's just say he's not known for his leniency,' Ruth replies, with a humourless laugh that shows perfect white teeth.

'What will I get?' I ask before I can stop myself. It doesn't matter. All that matters now is doing the right thing.

'It's hard to say. Failing to stop and report an accident is a straightforward driving ban, but since the minimum ban for death by dangerous driving is two years, that's irrelevant. It's the prison sentence that could go either way. Death by dangerous carries up to fourteen years; guidelines would suggest between two and six years. Judge King will be looking at the upper end, and it's my job to convince him two years would be more appropriate.' She takes the lid off a black fountain pen. 'Any history of mental illness?'

I shake my head and catch the flash of disappointment in the barrister's face.

'Let's talk about the incident, then. I understand conditions made visibility very poor – did you see the boy before the point of impact?'

'No.'

'Do you have any chronic medical conditions?' Ruth asks. 'They're useful in these cases. Or perhaps you were feeling unwell that particular day?'

I look at her blankly and the barrister tuts.

'You're making this very hard, Ms Gray. Do you have any allergies? Did you suffer from a fit of sneezes prior to the point of impact, perhaps?'

'I don't understand.'

Ruth sighs and speaks slowly, as though to a child. 'Judge King will have already looked at your pre-sentence report and have a sentence in mind. My job is to present this as nothing more than an unfortunate accident. An accident that couldn't be avoided, and for which you are extremely sorry. Now, I don't want to put words in your mouth, but if for example' – she looks pointedly at me – 'you were overcome by a sneezing fit—'

'But I wasn't.' Is this how it works? Lies upon lies upon lies, all designed to get the lowest possible punishment. Is our justice system so flawed? It sickens me.

Ruth Jefferson scans her notes and looks up suddenly. 'Did the boy run out in front of you with no warning? According to the mother's statement, she released his hand as they approached the road, so—'

'It's not her fault!'

The barrister raises carefully groomed eyebrows. 'Ms Gray,' she says smoothly, 'we're not here to agree whose fault this is. We're here to discuss the extenuating circumstances that led to this unfortunate accident. Please try not to get emotional.'

'I'm sorry,' I say. 'But there are no extenuating circumstances.'

'It's my job to find them,' Ruth replies. She puts down her file and leans forward. 'Believe me, Ms Gray, there's a big difference between two years in prison and six, and if there's anything at all that justifies you killing a five-year-old boy and driving away without stopping, you need to tell me now.'

We look at each other.

'I wish there was,' I say.

44

Not stopping to take off his coat, Ray marched into CID and found Kate scrolling through the overnight jobs. 'My office, now.'

She stood up and followed him. 'What's up?'

Ray didn't answer. He turned on his computer and put the blue business card on his desk. 'Remind me who had this card.'

'Dominica Letts. The partner of one of our targets.'

'Did she talk?'

'No comment.'

Ray folded his arms. 'It's a women's refuge.'

Kate looked at him, confused.

'The house in Grantham Street,' Ray said, 'and this one here.' He nodded at the pale-blue card. 'I think they're refuges for victims of domestic violence.' He sat back in his chair and put his hands behind his head. 'Dominica Letts is a known victim of domestic abuse – it's what nearly put Operation Falcon in jeopardy. I drove by the address on this card on my way into work and it's exactly the same as Grantham Street: motion sensors at the front; nets up at all the windows; no letter box at the door.'

'You think Jenna Gray's a victim too?'

Ray nodded slowly. 'Have you noticed how she won't make eye contact? She's got that jumpy, nervous look about her, and she clams up whenever she's challenged.'

Before he could continue with his theory, his phone rang and the screen flashed with the extension for the front desk.

'You've got a visitor, sir,' Rachel told him. 'A guy called Patrick Mathews.'

The name didn't ring any bells.

'I'm not expecting anyone, Rach. Can you take a message and get rid of him?'

'I've tried, sir, but he's insistent. Says he needs to talk to you about his girlfriend – Jenna Gray.'

Ray widened his eyes at Kate. Jenna's boyfriend. The checks Ray had done into his background hadn't revealed more than a caution for drunk and disorderly as a student, but was there more to him than met the eye?

'Bring him up,' he said. He filled Kate in while they waited.

'Do you think he's the abusive partner?' she said.

Ray shook his head. 'He doesn't look the type.'

'They never do,' Kate said. She stopped abruptly as Rachel arrived with Patrick Mathews. He wore a battered waxed jacket and carried a rucksack over one shoulder. Ray gestured to the chair next to Kate, and he sat down, perching on the edge as though he might stand up again at any time.

'I believe you have some information about Jenna Gray,' Ray said.

'Well, not information, really,' said Patrick. 'It's more of a feeling.'

Ray glanced at his watch. Jenna's case was listed for immediately after lunch and Ray wanted to be in court when she was sentenced. 'What sort of feeling, Mr Mathews?' He looked at Kate, who gave a barely noticeable shrug. Patrick Mathews wasn't the man Jenna was afraid of. But who was?

'Call me Patrick, please. Look, I know you'll think I'm bound to say this, but I don't think Jenna's guilty.'

Ray felt a spark of interest.

'There's something she's not telling me about what happened the night of the accident,' Patrick said. 'Something she's not telling anyone.' He gave a humourless laugh. 'I honestly thought there might be a future for us, but if she won't talk to me, how can there be?' He held up his hands in a gesture of hopelessness, and Ray was reminded of Mags. *You never talk to me*, she'd said.

'What do you think she's hiding from you?' Ray asked, with more sharpness than he intended. Did every relationship have secrets, he wondered?

'Jenna keeps a box under her bed.' Patrick looked uncomfortable. 'I wouldn't have dreamed of going through her things, only she wouldn't tell me anything about what happened, and then when I touched the box she snapped at me to leave it alone . . . I hoped it might give me some answers.'

'So you took a look.' Ray eyed Patrick thoughtfully. He didn't seem to be an aggressive man, but snooping through someone's possessions was the act of someone wanting control.

Patrick nodded. 'I have a key to the cottage: we agreed I'd go and pick up her dog this morning, after she left for court.' He sighed. 'I half wish I hadn't.' He handed Ray an envelope. 'Look inside.'

Ray opened the envelope and saw the distinctive red cover of a British passport. Inside, a younger Jenna looked back at him, unsmiling, her hair tied back in a loose ponytail. To the right, he saw a name: Jennifer Petersen.

'She's married.' Ray glanced at Kate. How had they missed that? Intelligence checks were run on anyone coming into custody – surely they wouldn't have missed something as basic as a name change? He looked at Patrick. 'Did you know?'

Court would be sitting in the next ten minutes. Ray drummed his fingers on his desk. Something about the name Petersen was nagging him. It felt familiar.

'She told me she was married once: I assumed she was divorced.'

Ray and Kate exchanged glances. Ray picked up the phone and called the court. 'Has R v Gray been called yet?' He waited while the desk clerk checked the court list.

Petersen, not Gray. What a cock-up.

'Okay, thanks.' He replaced the handset. 'Judge King's been delayed – we've got half an hour.'

Kate sat forward. 'That report I gave you the other day – after you sent me to deal with the woman at the front counter. Where is it?'

'Somewhere in my in-tray,' Ray said.

Kate began rifling through the paperwork on his desk. She picked up three files from the top of Ray's in-tray and, finding herself with no free space on the desk, dumped them on the floor. She leafed quickly through the remaining paperwork, discarding each unwanted page and picking up the next in seconds.

'That's it!' she said triumphantly. She pulled out the report from its plastic wallet and dropped it on to Ray's desk. A handful of torn photo pieces fluttered on top of it and Patrick picked one up. He looked at it curiously, then glanced up at Ray.

'May I?'

'Be my guest,' Ray said, not completely clear what he was giving permission for.

Patrick gathered up the sections of photograph and began piecing them together. As the photo of Penfach Bay took shape in front of them, Ray let out a low whistle. 'So Jenna Gray is the sister Eve Manning is so worried about.'

He sprang into action. 'Mr Mathews, thank you for bringing the passport. I'm afraid I'm going to have to ask you to wait for us at the court. Rachel at the front desk will direct you. We'll be there as fast as we can. Kate, meet me at DAU in five minutes.'

As Kate escorted Patrick downstairs, Ray picked up the phone. 'Natalie, it's Ray Stevens from CID. Can you see what you've got on an Ian Petersen? White male, late forties . . .'

* * *

Ray ran down a flight of stairs and along a corridor through a door marked Protective Services. A moment later Kate joined him, and together they rang a buzzer for the Domestic Abuse Unit. A cheery-looking woman with cropped black hair and chunky jewellery opened the door.

'Did you find anything, Nat?'

She showed them in and swivelled her computer screen to face them. 'Ian Francis Petersen,' she said, 'born twelfth April 1965. Previous for drink drive, aggravated assault and currently the subject of a restraining order.'

'Against a woman called Jennifer, by any chance?' Kate said, but Natalie shook her head.

'Marie Walker. We supported her to leave Petersen after six years of systematic abuse. She pressed charges, but he got off. The restraining order was granted at civil court and is still in place.'

'Any history prior to Marie?'

'Not with partners, no, but ten years ago he was cautioned for common assault. On his mother.'

Ray felt bile rise in his throat. 'We think Petersen is married to the woman involved in the Jacob Jordan hit-and-run,' he said. Natalie stood up and walked towards a wall full of grey metal filing cabinets. She pulled out a drawer and flicked through the contents.

'Here it is,' she said. 'This is everything we've got on Jennifer and Ian Petersen, and it doesn't make pleasant reading.'

45

The exhibitions you held were tedious. The venues were different: converted warehouses; studios; shop floors, but the people were always the same: ranting liberals in coloured scarves. The women were hairy and opinionated; the men insipid and under the thumb. Even the wine lacked personality.

During the week of your November exhibition you were particularly difficult. I helped you take your pieces to the warehouse three days early, and you spent the rest of the week there, getting ready.

'How long does it take to set out a few sculptures?' I said, when you came in late for the second night in a row.

'We're telling a story,' you said. 'The guests will move through the room from one sculpture to another, and the pieces have to speak in the right way to them.'

I laughed. 'You should hear yourself! What a load of rubbish. Just make sure the price tag is nice and easy to read, that's all that matters.'

'You don't have to come, if you don't want to.'

'Don't you want me there?' I eyed you suspiciously. Your eyes were a little too bright; your chin a little too defiant. I wondered what had caused such sudden joie de vivre.

'I just don't want you to be bored. We can manage.'

There it was: the flash of something unreadable in your eyes.

'We?' I said, raising an eyebrow.

You were flustered. You turned away and pretended to busy

yourself with the washing-up. 'Philip. From the exhibition. He's the curator.'

You began wiping a cloth around the inside of a pan I had left to soak. I moved to stand behind you, pressing you between my body and the sink so my mouth was level with your ear. 'Oh, he's the *curator*, is he? Is that what you call him when he's *fucking you*?'

'It's nothing like that,' you said. Ever since your pregnancy you had adopted a particular tone of voice when I spoke to you. It was excessively calm; the sort of voice you might use when talking to a screaming child, or the clinically insane. I hated it. I moved a fraction backwards, and felt you breathe out, then I pushed you forward again. I guessed from the sound you made that you were winded, and you put both hands on the edge of the sink to get your breath back.

'You're not fucking Philip?' I spat the words out on to the back of your neck.

'I'm not fucking anyone.'

'Well, you're certainly not fucking me,' I said, 'not lately, anyway.' I felt you tense, and I knew you expected me to slide a hand between your legs; wanted it, even. I was almost sorry to disappoint, but your skinny backside held little attraction for me by then.

On the day of the exhibition I was in our bedroom when you came upstairs to get changed. You hesitated.

'It's nothing I haven't seen before,' I said. I found a clean shirt and hung it on the back of the wardrobe door; you laid your outfit out on the bed. I watched you shrug off your track-suit bottoms and fold up your sweatshirt for the next day. You wore a white bra and matching pants, and I wondered if you had chosen the colour deliberately to contrast with the bruise on your hip. The swelling was still noticeable, and when you sat on the bed you winced, as though making a point. You put

323

on wide linen trousers and a voluminous top in the same fabric, which hung off your bony shoulders. I chose a necklace of fat green beads from the jewellery tree on your dressing table.

'Shall I put this on for you?'

You hesitated, then sat on the little stool. I put my arms over your head and held the necklace in front of you, and you lifted your hair out of the way. I moved my hands to the back of your neck, tightening the pressure of the necklace against your throat for a split-second, and feeling you tense in front of me. I laughed and fastened the clasp. 'Beautiful,' I said. I bent down and looked at you in the mirror. 'Try not to make a fool of yourself today, Jennifer. You always humiliate yourself at these things by drinking too much and fawning over the guests.'

I stood up to put on my shirt, choosing a pale pink tie to go with it. I slipped on my jacket and looked in the mirror, satisfied with what I saw. 'You may as well drive,' I said, 'as you won't be drinking.'

I had offered on several occasions to buy a new car for you, but you had insisted on keeping your battered old Fiesta. I went in it as little as possible, but I had no intention of letting you drive my Audi after you dented it trying to park, so I sat in the passenger seat of your filthy car and let you drive me to the exhibition.

When we arrived, there was already a crowd of people around the bar, and as we walked through the room there was a murmur of appreciation. Someone clapped and the others joined in, although there were too few people for it to be applause, and the resulting sound was embarrassing.

You handed me a glass of champagne and took one for yourself. A man with dark wavy hair approached us, and I knew from the way your eyes lit up that this was Philip.

'Jenna!' He kissed you on both cheeks and I saw your hand touch his so briefly you might have thought I wouldn't notice. So briefly it might almost have been by accident. But I knew it wasn't.

You introduced me, and Philip shook my hand. 'You must be very proud of her.'

'My wife is immensely gifted,' I said. 'Of course I'm proud of her.'

There was a pause before Philip spoke again. 'I'm sorry to steal Jenna away from you, but I really must introduce her to a few people. There's been a lot of interest in her work, and . . .' He stopped talking and rubbed his thumb and fingers together, winking at me.

'Far be it from me to stand in the way of possible sales,' I said.

I watched you work the room together, Philip's hand never leaving the small of your back, and I knew then you were having an affair. I don't know how I got through the rest of the exhibition, but my eyes never left you. When the champagne was finished, I drank wine, and I stood next to the bar to save the need to return. And all the time I watched you. You had a smile on your face I never saw any more, and I had a brief glimpse of the girl I saw in the Student Union all those years ago, laughing with her friends. You never seemed to laugh any more.

My bottle was empty and I asked for more. The bar staff exchanged looks, but did what I said. People began leaving. I watched you say goodbye to them: kissing some, shaking hands with others. None were treated as warmly as your *curator*. When there were only a handful of guests left, I went up to you. 'It's time to go.'

You looked uncomfortable. 'I can't go yet, Ian, there are still people here. And I need to help clear up.'

Philip stepped forward. 'Jenna, it's fine. Poor Ian's hardly seen you: he probably wants the chance to celebrate properly with you. I'll finish up here and you can come for your pieces tomorrow. It's been a huge success – well done!' He kissed your cheek, only once this time, but the rage inside me threatened to boil over, and I could not speak.

325

You nodded. You seemed disappointed with Philip: did you hope he would ask you to stay? Send me away and keep you there? I took your hand and squeezed it tight as you continued talking to him. I knew you would never say a word, and I slowly tightened my grip until I could feel the cartilage in your hand slipping under my fingers.

Finally Philip was finished. He extended a hand to shake mine and I had to release my grip on you. I heard you exhale and saw you wrap one hand in the other.

'Great to meet you, Ian,' Philip said. His eyes flicked to you, before looking at me again. 'Look after her, won't you?'

I wondered what you had told him.

'I always do,' I said smoothly.

I turned for the exit and put my hand on your elbow, my thumb digging into your flesh.

'You're hurting me,' you said under your breath. 'People can see.'

I don't know where you found this voice from, but I hadn't heard it before.

'How dare you make a fool of me?' I hissed. We walked down the stairs, passing a couple who smiled politely at us. 'Flirting with him in front of everyone, spending the whole evening touching him, kissing him!' As we got to the car park I didn't bother to keep my voice down, and the sound rang out in the night air. 'You're fucking him, aren't you?'

You didn't answer, and your silence made me even angrier. I grabbed your arm and twisted it behind you, bending it more and more until you cried out. 'You brought me here to make fun of me, didn't you?'

'I didn't!' Tears ran down your face and fell in dark spots on to your top.

My fist clenched of its own accord, but just as I felt the tremor in my forearm, a man walked past us.

'Good afternoon,' he said.

I stilled my arm, and we stayed like that, two feet apart, until his footsteps faded.

'Get in the car.'

You opened the driver's door and got in, taking three attempts to put the key in the ignition and turn it. It was only four o'clock, but it was dark already. It had been raining, and every time a car came towards you the lights bounced off the wet tarmac, making you screw up your eyes. You were still crying, and you rubbed your hand across your nose.

'Look at the state you're in,' I said. 'Does Philip know you're like this? A snivelling, pathetic mouse of a woman?'

'I'm not sleeping with Philip,' you said. You left a pause between each word to emphasise your point, and I slammed my fist on the dashboard.

You flinched. 'I'm not Philip's type,' you said. 'He's—'

'Don't talk to me as though I'm an idiot, Jennifer! I have eyes. I can see what's going on between you.'

You braked sharply at red lights, then jerked hard on the accelerator as they changed to green. I twisted in my seat so I could watch you. I wanted to read your face; see what you were thinking. Whether you were thinking about *him*. I could tell that you were, although you were trying to hide it.

As soon as we got home I would stop that. As soon as we got home I would stop you thinking at all.

46

Bristol Crown Court is older than the Magistrates' Court, and solemnity murmurs through its wood-panelled corridors. Ushers walk quickly in and out of the courtroom, their flapping black gowns causing papers on the clerk's desk to float upwards as they pass. The quiet is discomforting, like a library where the pressure of not talking makes you want to scream, and I press the heels of my hands hard into my eye sockets. When I remove them, the courtroom swims out of focus. I wish I could keep it that way: the blurred edges and foggy shapes seem less threatening, less serious.

Now that I'm here, I'm frightened. The bravado with which I have approached this day in my own mind has vanished, and although I'm terrified of what Ian would do to me if I walked free, I am suddenly just as frightened of what will be waiting for me in prison when I'm sentenced. I squeeze my hands together and dig my nails into the skin on my left hand. My mind fills with the echo of approaching footsteps on metal walkways; narrow bunks in grey cells with walls so thick no one will hear me scream. I feel a sharp pain in my hand and look down to see that I've drawn blood, and when I wipe it away it leaves a smear of pink across the back of my hand.

The enclosure into which I have been placed has space for several more people; two rows of chairs are bolted on to the floor, their seats flipped up as though in a cinema. A glass wall runs inharmoniously around three sides, and I twist self-consciously in my seat as the courtroom begins to fill with people. There are many, many more spectators here than at my initial hearing. On their faces isn't the mild curiosity of the magistrates' *tricoteuses*, but the violent hatred of those intent on justice. One man, olive-skinned and with a leather jacket two sizes too big for him, leans forward in his seat. He doesn't take his eyes off me, and his mouth twists in silent anger. I start to cry, and he shakes his head, curling his lip in disgust.

In my pocket is the photo of Jacob and I slip my hand around it, finding the corners with my fingers.

The legal teams have grown: each barrister has several people behind them, sitting at rows of desks, and leaning forward to mutter urgently to one another. The ushers and barristers are the only people who seem comfortable here. They joke amongst themselves in daringly raised tones, and I wonder why the court is like this; why a system would so intentionally seek to alienate those who need it. The door creaks open and another wave of people come in, uneasy and wary. My breath catches as I see Anya. She slides into the front row next to the man in the leather jacket, who takes her hand.

You must remember that he was a boy. That he had a mother. And that her heart is breaking.

The only empty area of the court is the jury box; its twelve seats redundant. I imagine the rows filled with men and women, hearing the evidence, watching me speak, deciding on my guilt. I have spared them that; spared them the torment of wondering whether they've made the right decision; spared Anya the pain of her son's death spread across a courtroom. Ruth Jefferson explained this would work in my favour: judges look more leniently on those who save the courts the expense of a trial.

'Court rise.'

The judge is old, the stories of a thousand families written across his face. His sharp eyes take in the full courtroom, but don't linger on me. I am just another chapter in a career full of difficult decisions. I wonder if he has already made up his mind about me – if he already knows how long I should serve.

'Your Honour, the Crown brings this case against Jenna Gray . . .' The Clerk reads from a piece of paper, her voice clear and matter-of-fact. 'Ms Gray, you are charged with causing death by dangerous driving, and with failing to stop and record an accident.' She looks up at me. 'How do you plead?'

I press my hand against the photo in my pocket. 'Guilty.'

There is a muffled sob from the public gallery.

Her heart is breaking.

'Please sit down.'

The Crown Prosecution barrister stands up. He lifts a carafe from the table in front of him and he pours slowly and deliberately from it. The sound of water filling his glass is the only noise in the courtroom, and when all eyes are on him, he begins.

'Your Honour, the defendant has pleaded guilty to causing the death of five-year-old Jacob Jordan. She has admitted that the standard of her driving on that night last November fell far below the standard expected by a reasonable person. In fact, police investigations showed that Ms Gray's car left the road and mounted the pavement immediately prior to the point of impact, and that she was travelling at between thirty-eight and forty-two miles per hour – far in excess of the thirty-mile-an-hour speed limit.'

I squeeze my hands together. I try to breathe slowly, evenly, but a hardness has formed in my chest and I can't take in air properly. The sound of my heart seems to echo inside my head and I close my eyes. I can see the rain on the windscreen, hear the scream – my scream – as I see the little boy on the pavement; running, turning his head to shout something to his mother.

'Furthermore, Your Honour, after hitting Jacob Jordan and – it is believed – killing him outright, the defendant failed to stop.' The barrister looks around the courtroom; his rhetoric wasted with no jury to impress. 'She did not get out of the car.

She did not call for help. She did not offer any remorse, or practical assistance. Instead, the defendant drove away, leaving five-year-old Jacob in the arms of his traumatised mother.'

She leaned over her son, I remember, her coat almost covering him, protecting him from the rain. The car headlights picked out every detail, and I covered my mouth with my hands, too frightened to breathe.

'You might imagine, Your Honour, that such an initial reaction could be attributed to shock. That the defendant may have panicked and driven away, and that minutes later, perhaps a few hours – maybe even a day later – she would come to her senses and do the right thing. But, Your Honour, the defendant instead fled the area, hiding in a village a hundred miles away, where nobody knew her. She didn't give herself up. She may have entered a guilty plea today, but it is a plea born from a realisation that there is nowhere left to run, and the Crown respectfully requests that this be taken into consideration when sentencing.'

'Thank you, Mr Lassiter.' The judge makes notes on a pad of paper, and the CPS barrister bows his head before taking his seat, flicking his gown out behind him as he does so. My palms grow damp. There is a wave of hatred from the public gallery.

The defence barrister gathers her papers. Despite my guilty plea, despite the knowledge that I have to pay for what has happened, I suddenly want Ruth Jefferson to fight my corner. Nausea rises in my stomach at the realisation that this is my last chance to speak out. In another few moments the judge will sentence me, and it will be too late.

Ruth Jefferson rises, but before she can speak, the courtroom door flies open with a bang. The judge looks up sharply, his disapproval evident.

Patrick seems so out of place in the courtroom that for a moment I don't recognise him. He looks at me, visibly shaken to see me handcuffed in a bullet-proof glass box. What is he doing here? I realise the man with him is DI Stevens, who nods his head briefly towards the judge, before making his way to the centre of the courtroom and leaning over to speak in a low voice to the CPS barrister.

The barrister listens intently. He scribbles a note, then stretches an arm across the long bench to pass it to Ruth Jefferson. There is a heavy silence, as though everybody is holding their breath.

My barrister reads the note and gets slowly to her feet. 'Your Honour, may I be permitted a short recess?'

Judge King sighs. 'Mrs Jefferson, do I need to remind you how many cases I have this afternoon? You have had six weeks to consult with your client.'

'I apologise, Your Honour, but information has come to light that may have material bearing on my client's mitigation.'

'Very well. You have fifteen minutes, Mrs Jefferson, after which time I fully expect to sentence your client.'

He nods to the clerk.

'Court rise,' she calls.

As Judge King leaves the courtroom, a security guard steps into the dock to take me back down to the cell block.

'What's going on?' I ask him.

'God knows, love, but it's always the same. Up and down like a bleedin' yoyo.'

He escorts me back to the airless room in which I spoke to my barrister less than an hour previously. Almost immediately Ruth Jefferson comes in, with DI Stevens behind her. Ruth begins talking before the door has closed behind them.

'You do realise, Ms Gray, that perverting the course of justice isn't something the courts take lightly?'

I say nothing, and the barrister sits down. She tucks a stray dark hair back beneath her wig.

DI Stevens reaches into his pocket and drops a passport on to the table. I don't need to open it to know that it's mine. I look at him, and at my exasperated barrister, then I put out my hand to touch the passport. I remember filling out the form to change my name ahead of our wedding. I tried out my signature a hundred times, asking Ian which one looked the most grown-up, the most *me*. When the passport arrived it was the first tangible proof of my change in status, and I couldn't wait to hand it over at the airport.

DI Stevens leans forward and rests his hands on the table, his face level with mine. 'You don't have to protect him any more, Jennifer.'

I flinch. 'Please don't call me that.'

'Tell me what happened.'

I say nothing.

DI Stevens speaks quietly, his calmness making me feel safer, more grounded.

'We won't let him hurt you again, Jenna.'

So they know. I let out a slow breath and look first at DI Stevens, and then Ruth Jefferson. I feel suddenly exhausted. The DI opens a brown file on which I see is written 'Petersen'; my married name. Ian's name.

'Lots of calls,' he says. 'Neighbours, doctors, passers-by, but never you, Jenna. You never called us. And when we came, you wouldn't speak to us. Wouldn't press charges. Why wouldn't you let us help you?'

'Because he would have killed me,' I say.

There is a pause before DI Stevens speaks again. 'When did he first hit you?'

'Is this relevant?' Ruth says, looking at her watch.

'Yes,' DI Stevens snaps, and she sits back in her chair, her eyes narrowed.

'It started the night we got married.' I close my eyes, remembering the pain that came out of nowhere and the shame that my marriage had failed before it had even begun. I remember how tender Ian was when he returned; how gently he soothed my aching face. I said I was sorry, and I went on saying it for seven years.

'When did you go to the refuge in Grantham Street?'

I'm surprised by how much he knows. 'I never went there. They saw my bruises at the hospital and asked about my marriage. I didn't tell them anything, but they gave me a card and said I could go there whenever I needed to, that I'd be safe there. I didn't believe them – how could I be safe so close to Ian? – but I kept the card. I felt a little less alone for having it.'

'You never tried to leave?' DI Stevens says. There is barely concealed anger in his eyes, but it isn't directed at me.

'Plenty of times,' I say. 'Ian would go to work and I'd start packing. I'd walk round the house picking up memories, working out what I could realistically take with me. I would put it all in the car – the car was still mine, you see.'

DI Stevens shakes his head, not following.

'It was still registered in my maiden name. Not intentionally, at first – it was just one of those things I forgot to do when we got married – but later it became really important. Ian owned everything else; the house, the business . . . I started to feel I didn't exist any more, that I'd become another one of his possessions. So I never re-registered my car. A small thing, I know, but . . .' I shrug. 'I would get everything packed, and then I would carefully take everything out and put it back the way it was. Every time.'

'Why?'

'Because he would have found me.'

DI Stevens is flicking through the file. It is astonishingly thick and yet all that can be listed within it are the incidents that resulted in a call to police. The broken ribs and the concussion that required a spell in hospital. For every mark seen there were a dozen others hidden.

Ruth Jefferson puts a hand on the file. 'May I?'

DI Stevens looks at me and I nod. He passes her the file and she begins looking through it.

'But you left after the accident,' DI Stevens said. 'What changed?'

I take a deep breath. I want to say that I had found my courage, but of course it wasn't that at all. 'Ian threatened me,' I say quietly. 'He told me that if I ever went to the police – if I ever told anyone what had happened – he would kill me. And I knew he meant it. That night, after the accident, he beat me so badly I couldn't stand, then he hauled me upright and pinned my arm across the sink. He poured boiling water over my hand, and I passed out from the pain. Then he dragged me out to my studio. He made me watch while he broke everything – everything I'd ever made.'

I can't look at DI Stevens. It is as much as I can do to get the words out. 'Ian went away then. I don't know where. I spent the first night on the kitchen floor, then I crawled upstairs and lay in bed, praying I would die in the night, so that by the time he came back he wouldn't be able to hurt me any more. But he didn't come back. He was gone for days, and gradually I got stronger. I started to fantasise that he was gone for good, but he had hardly taken anything with him, so I knew he could come back at any moment. I realised that if I stayed with him, that one day he would kill me. And that's when I left.'

'Tell me what happened to Jacob.'

I put my hand in my pocket and touch the photograph. 'We had an argument. I had an exhibition – the biggest I'd ever had – and I'd spent days setting it up with the man who curated it, a man called Philip. It was a day-time event, but even so Ian got drunk. He accused me of having an affair with Philip.'

'Were you?'

I redden at the personal question. 'Philip was gay,' I said, 'but Ian wouldn't accept it. I was crying and I couldn't see the road properly. It had been raining and the headlights kept shining in my eyes. He was shouting at me, calling me a slut and a whore. I went through Fishponds to avoid the traffic, but Ian made me pull over. He hit me and took the keys, even though he was too drunk to stand.

'He drove like a maniac, all the time shouting at me about how he was going to teach me a lesson. We were going through an estate, through residential roads, and Ian was driving faster and faster. I was terrified.' I twist my hands together in my lap.

'Then I saw the boy. I screamed, but Ian didn't slow down at all. We hit him and I saw his mother buckle as though she'd been hit too. I tried to get out of the car, but Ian locked the doors and started reversing. He wouldn't let me go back.' I take a gulp of air and when I exhale it comes out as a low wail.

There is silence in the small room.

'Ian killed Jacob,' I say. 'But I felt as though I had.'

47

Patrick drives carefully. I brace myself for a thousand questions, but he doesn't speak until the Bristol skyline is far behind us. As the towns give way to green fields, and the jagged lines of the coast appear, he turns to me.

'You could have gone to prison.'

'I meant to.'

'Why?' He doesn't sound judgemental, simply confused.

'Because someone had to pay for what happened,' I tell him. 'Someone had to go to court so that Jacob's mother could sleep at night knowing that someone had paid for her son's life.'

'But not you, Jenna.'

Before we left I asked DI Stevens what they would tell Jacob's mother, suddenly presented with the collapsed trial of the person she thought had killed her son.

'We'll wait till he's safely in custody,' he told me, 'then we'll tell her.'

I realise my actions now mean she will have to relive it all.

'In the box with your passport,' Patrick says suddenly, 'I saw – I saw a baby's toy.' He stops, not putting words around his question.

'It belonged to my son,' I say. 'Ben. I was terrified when I fell pregnant. I thought Ian would be furious, but he was ecstatic. He said it would change everything, and although he never said it I was certain he was sorry for the way he had treated me. I thought the baby might be a turning point for us: that it would make Ian realise we could be happy together. As a family.'

'But it didn't.'

'No,' I say, 'it didn't. At first he couldn't do enough for me. He waited on me hand and foot, and was always telling me what I should and shouldn't eat. But as my bump grew, he became more and more distant. It was as though he hated my pregnancy; resented it, even. When I was seven months pregnant I got a scorch-mark on his shirt while I was doing the ironing. It was stupid of me – I'd gone to answer the phone and got distracted, didn't notice till it was too late. Ian went mad. He punched me hard in the stomach, and I started to bleed.'

Patrick pulls the car over and switches off the engine. I gaze out of the windscreen at the waste ground by the side of the road. The litter bin is overflowing, and discarded wrappers dance around in the breeze.

'Ian called an ambulance. Told them I'd fallen. I don't think they believed him, but what could they do? The bleeding had stopped by the time we got to hospital, but I knew he had died even before they scanned me. I felt it. They offered me a Caesarean section, but I didn't want him taken from me like that. I wanted to give birth to him.'

Patrick puts his hand out to me but I can't touch him and he lets it fall back on to his seat.

'They gave me drugs to induce labour and I waited on the ward with all the other women. We went through it together: the early pains, the gas and air, the checks from midwives and doctors. The only difference was that my baby was dead. When I was finally wheeled through to the delivery suite the woman next to me waved and wished me luck.

'Ian stayed with me during labour, and even though I hated him for what he'd done, I held his hand as I pushed, and let him kiss my forehead, because who else did I have? And all I could think was that if I hadn't burnt that shirt, Ben would still be alive.'

I begin to shake and I press my palms on to my knees to

338

anchor myself. For weeks after Ben died my body tried to trick me into thinking I was a mother. Milk stung my nipples, and I would stand in the shower and press my flesh to relieve the pressure, the sweet smell of milk rising up through the scalding water. I looked up once and saw Ian watching me from the bathroom door. My stomach was still rounded from pregnancy, the skin stretched and slack. Blue veins ran across my swollen breasts and milk trickled down my body. I caught the look of revulsion on his face before he turned away.

I tried to talk to him about Ben. Just once – once when the pain of losing him was so intense I could hardly put one foot in front of the other. I needed to share my grief with someone – with anyone – and by then I had no one else to talk to. But he cut me off mid-sentence. 'It never happened,' he said. 'That baby never existed.'

Ben might not have taken a breath, but he lived. He lived in me, and breathed my oxygen and ate my food, and was a part of me. But I never spoke about him again.

I can't look at Patrick. Now that I have started, I can't stop, and the words tumble out of me. 'There was an awful silence when he was born. Someone read out the time, and then they put him in my arms so gently, as though they didn't want to hurt him, and left us alone with him. I lay there for ages like that, looking at his face, at his eyelashes, his lips. I stroked the palm of his hand and imagined I could feel him gripping my fingers, but eventually they came and took him away from me. I screamed then, hung on to him until they had to give me something to calm me down. But I didn't want to sleep, because I knew that when I woke up I'd be all alone again.'

When I finish, I look at Patrick and see he has tears in his eyes, and when I try to tell him it's okay, that I'm all right, I cry too. We cling to each other in the car by the side of the road, until the sun begins to dip, and then we drive home.

Patrick parks the car at the caravan park and walks with me

along the path to the cottage. The rent is paid until the end of the month, but my footsteps slow as I hear Iestyn's words in my head; his disgust as he told me to leave.

'I called him,' Patrick said, reading my mind. 'I explained everything.'

Patrick is calm and gentle, as though I'm a patient recovering from a long illness. I feel safe with my hand tucked into his.

'Will you go and get Beau?' I ask him, when we reach the cottage.

'If you want me to.'

I nod. 'I just want everything to get back to normal.' As I say it I realise I'm not certain what normality is.

Patrick draws the curtains and makes me tea, and when he is happy I am warm and settled he kisses me lightly on the lips and leaves me. I look around at the snapshots of my life here in the bay: the photos and the shells; Beau's water bowl on the floor in the kitchen. I feel more at home here than I ever did in Bristol.

On impulse I reach for the switch on the table lamp next to me. It's the only light on downstairs and it bathes the room in a warm apricot glow. I switch it off, and I am plunged into darkness. I wait, but my heart rate is steady; my palms dry; there is no prickle of fear across the back of my neck. I smile: I am no longer afraid.

48

'And there's no question that's the right address?' Ray directed the question at Stumpy, but widened his gaze to include the rest of the room. Within two hours of leaving the Crown Court, he had assembled a public order team, while Stumpy got Area Intelligence working on an address for Ian Petersen.

'None at all, boss,' Stumpy said. 'The Voters' Register shows him at 72 Albercombe Terrace, and AIT have cross-referenced that with the DVLA register. Petersen picked up three points for speeding a couple of months ago, and they returned his licence to the same address.'

'Right,' Ray said, 'then let's hope he's home.' He turned to brief the public order team, who were getting restless. 'Petersen's arrest is critical, not just for the resolution of the Jordan case, but to ensure Jenna's safety. There is a long history of domestic violence that culminated in Jenna leaving Petersen following the hit-and-run.'

There were nods from the officers in the room, their faces set with grim determination. They all knew what sort of man Ian Petersen was.

'PNC shows him – unsurprisingly – with warnings for violence,' Ray said, 'and he's also got previous convictions for drink-drive and disorder. I don't want to take any chances with him, so it's straight in, get him cuffed, and get out. Got it?'

'Got it,' came the chorus.

'Then let's go.'

* * *

Albercombe Terrace was a run-of-the-mill street with narrow pavements and too many parked cars. The only characteristics that marked out number 72 from its neighbours were the drawn curtains at every window.

Ray and Kate parked in a neighbouring street to wait for the confirmation that two of the public order team had reached the rear of Petersen's house. Ray killed the ignition and they sat in silence, the only sound a rhythmic ticking from the cooling engine.

'You okay?' Ray said.

'Yup,' Kate said tightly. Her face was set with a grim determination that gave no hint to how she might be feeling underneath. Ray felt fire coursing through his veins. In a few moments that adrenalin would get him through the job, but right now it had nowhere to go. He tapped his foot against the clutch pedal and glanced at Kate again.

'Got your vest on?'

In answer, Kate banged a clenched fist against her chest, and Ray heard the dull thud of body armour beneath her sweatshirt. Knives were easily concealed and swiftly employed, and Ray had seen too many close calls to take risks. He felt for the baton and spray on the harness he wore under his jacket, gaining comfort from their presence.

'Stay close to me,' he said. 'And if he pulls a weapon, get the hell out of there.'

Kate raised her eyebrows. 'Because I'm a woman?' She snorted derisively. 'I'll back off when you do.'

'To hell with political correctness, Kate!' Ray slapped the flat of his hand against the steering wheel. He fell silent and stared through the windscreen on to the empty street. 'I don't want you getting hurt.'

Before either of them could say anything else, their handsets crackled into life. 'Zero six, guv.'

The units were in situ.

'Copied,' Ray responded. 'If he comes out of the back door, nick him. We'll make for the front door.'

'Roger,' came the response, and Ray looked at Kate.

'Ready?'

'As I'll ever be.'

They rounded the corner on foot and walked smartly to the front of the house. Ray rapped on the door and stood on his toes to peer in through the small glass opening above the knocker.

'Can you see anything?'

'No.' He knocked again, and the sound echoed in the empty street.

Kate spoke into her radio. 'Tango Charlie 461 to Control, talk-through with Bravo Foxtrot 275?'

'Go ahead.'

She spoke directly to the pair of officers at the rear of the premises. 'Any sign of movement?'

'Negative.'

'Copied. Stay put for the time being.'

'Will do.'

'Obliged for talk-through, Control.' Kate slid the radio back into her pocket and turned to Ray. 'Time for the big red key.'

They watched as the Method of Entry team swung the red metal battering ram in a semi-circle towards the door. There was an almighty bang and a splintering of wood, and the door flew open, slamming against the wall of a narrow hallway. Ray and Kate stood back, and the public order officers ran in, fanning out in pairs to check each room for occupants.

'Clear!'

'Clear!'

'Clear!'

Ray and Kate followed them inside, keeping each other in sight and waiting for confirmation that Petersen had been located. Barely two minutes had passed before the public order sergeant came down the stairs, shaking his head.

'No joy, guv,' he said to Ray. 'Place is empty. The bedroom's been cleaned out – wardrobe's empty and there's nothing in the bathroom. Looks like he's done a runner.'

'Shit!' Ray thumped his fist on the banister. 'Kate, call Jenna's mobile. Find out where she is and tell her to stay put.' He strode out to the car, and Kate ran to keep up.

'It's switched off.'

Ray got into the driver's seat and started the engine.

'Where to now?' Kate said, putting on her seat belt.

'Wales,' Ray said grimly.

As he drove he barked instructions at Kate. 'Get on to AIT,' he said, 'and get them to pull anything they can on Petersen. Contact Thames Valley and make sure someone visits Eve Manning in Oxford: he's threatened her once already, and there's every chance he'll go back. Get in touch with South Wales and log a fear for welfare relating to Jenna Gr—' Ray corrected himself: 'Petersen. I want someone to go to the cottage and make sure she's okay.'

Kate scribbled down actions as Ray listed them, updating him after every call she made.

'There's no one on duty at Penfach tonight, so they'll send someone out from Swansea, but they've got Sunderland playing at home today and the whole place is rammed.'

Ray gave an exasperated sigh. 'They do know the history of domestic violence?'

'Yes, and they've said they'll make it a priority, they just can't guarantee when they'll be able to get to it.'

'Jesus,' Ray said. 'What a joke.'

Kate tapped her pen on the window as she tried Patrick's mobile. 'It's ringing out.'

'We need to get hold of someone else. Someone local,' Ray said.

'What about the neighbours?' Kate sat up and brought up the internet on her phone.

'There aren't any neighbours—' Ray looked at Kate. 'The caravan park, of course!'

'Got it.' Kate found the number and pressed it to dial. 'Come on, come on . . .'

'Put it on speakerphone.'

'Hello, Penfach Caravan Park, Bethan speaking.'

'Hi, this is Detective Constable Kate Evans, from Bristol CID. I'm looking for Jenna Gray – have you seen her today?'

'Not today, love. She's in Bristol though isn't she?' Bethan's voice took on a note of caution. 'Is something wrong? What happened at court?'

'She was acquitted. Look, I'm sorry to rush you, but Jenna left here about three o'clock and I need to make sure she arrived safely. She was being driven by Patrick Mathews.'

'I haven't seen either of them,' Bethan said, 'but Jenna's definitely back – she's been down to the beach.'

'How do you know?'

'I'm not long back from walking the dogs, and I saw some of her writing in the sand. Not her usual style though – it was most peculiar.'

Ray felt a sense of unease creep across him. 'What does the writing say?'

'What is it?' Bethan said sharply. 'What aren't you telling me?'

'What does it say?' He hadn't meant to shout, and for a moment he thought Bethan had hung up. When she eventually spoke, the hesitation in her voice told him she knew something was badly wrong.

'It just says, "Betrayed".'

49

I didn't mean to fall asleep, but the knock at the door makes my head jerk upwards, and I rub my stiff neck. It takes me a second to remember that I'm at home, and I hear another, more insistent knock. I wonder how long I have kept Patrick waiting. I clamber to my feet and wince as cramp seizes my calf.

As I turn the key I feel a whisper of fear, but before I can react the door flies open, slamming me into the wall. Ian is flushed and his breathing is ragged. I brace myself for his fist, but it doesn't come, and I count my heartbeats as he slowly draws the bolt across again.

One, two, three.

Fast and hard, banging against my chest.

Seven, eight, nine, ten.

And then he's ready, and he turns to me with a smile I know as well as my own. A smile that doesn't reach his eyes; that hints at what he has in store for me. A smile that tells me that, although the end is coming, it won't be swift.

He rubs the nape of my neck, his thumb pressing hard against the bone at the top of my spine. It's uncomfortable, but not painful.

'You gave my name to the police, Jennifer.'

'I didn't—'

He grabs a handful of my hair, yanking me towards him so fast I screw up my eyes, waiting for the explosion of pain as he breaks my nose with his forehead. When I open them again his face is an inch from mine. He smells of whisky and sweat.

'Don't lie to me, Jennifer.'

I close my eyes and tell myself I can survive this, although every part of me wants to beg him to kill me now.

He grips my jaw with his free hand, and strokes his forefinger over my lips, slipping a finger into my mouth. I fight the urge to gag as he presses down on my tongue.

'You double-crossing bitch,' he says, the words as smooth as if he is paying me a compliment. 'You made a promise, Jennifer. You promised you wouldn't go to the police, and what do I see today? I see you buying your own freedom by taking mine. I see my name – my fucking name! – all over the *Bristol Post*.'

'I'll tell them,' I say, the words thick around his finger. 'I'll tell them it's not true. I'll say I lied.' Saliva escapes my mouth to coat Ian's hand and he looks at it with revulsion.

'No,' he says. 'You won't say anything to anybody.'

With his left hand still gripping my hair, he releases my jaw and slaps me hard across the face. 'Get upstairs.'

I clench my fists by my sides, knowing I mustn't lift a hand to feel my face, which throbs in time with my pulse. I taste blood, and swallow quietly. 'Please,' I say, my voice sounding reedy and unnatural, 'please don't . . .' I search for the words to use, the words least likely to provoke him. *Don't rape me*, I want to say. It has happened enough times for it not to matter, and yet I can't bear the thought of his body pressing down on mine again, being inside me, forcing sounds from me that belie how much I hate him.

'I don't want to have sex,' I say, and I curse the cracking of my voice that will tell him how much this means to me.

'Have sex with you?' he spits, flecks of saliva hitting my face. 'Don't flatter yourself, Jennifer.' He releases his grip on me and looks me up and down. 'Get upstairs.'

My legs threaten to buckle under me as I walk the few paces to the stairs, and I cling to the banister on the way up, feeling his presence behind me. I try to calculate how long before Patrick will be back, but I've lost all sense of time.

Ian propels me into the bathroom.

'Get undressed.'

I'm ashamed of how easily I comply.

He folds his arms and watches me struggle with my clothes. I'm crying freely now, although I know it will anger him. I can't stop.

Ian puts the plug in the bath. He turns on the cold tap but doesn't touch the hot. I am naked now, standing shivering in front of him, and he looks at my body with distaste. I remember when he would kiss my shoulder blades, then trace a line so softly, reverently almost, down between my breasts and over my stomach.

'You've only yourself to blame,' he says with a sigh. 'I could have brought you back whenever I wanted, but I let you go. I didn't want you. All you had to do was keep your mouth shut and you could have lived out your pitiful life here.' He shook his head. 'But you didn't, did you? You went to the police and you blurted it all out.' He turns off the tap. 'Get in.'

I don't resist. There is no point now. I step into the bath and lower myself into it. The icy water takes my breath away and pain grips my insides. I try to fool myself that it's hot.

'Now get yourself clean.'

He picks up a bottle of bleach from the floor by the toilet and unscrews the top. I bite my lip. Once he made me drink bleach. Once when I came home late from a meal with the crowd from college. I told him time had run away with me, but he poured the thick liquid into a wine glass and watched while I put it to my lips. He stopped me after the first sip, bursting out laughing and telling me only an idiot would have drunk it. I threw up all night and had the chemical taste in my mouth for days.

Ian pours the bleach on to my flannel and it runs over the edges, dripping into the bath, where blue blooms fan across the surface of the water like ink on blotting paper. He hands me the flannel.

'Scrub yourself.'

I rub the flannel across my arms, trying to splash water on myself as I do so, in an effort to dilute the bleach.

'Now the rest of you,' he says. 'And don't forget your face. Do it properly, Jennifer, or I'll do it for you. Maybe this will wash away some of your badness.'

He directs me until I have washed every bit of my body with bleach, and my skin stings. I sink into the freezing water to relieve the burning sensation, unable to stop my teeth chattering. This pain, this humiliation; this is worse than death. The end cannot come soon enough.

I can't feel my feet any more. I reach out and rub them, but my fingers feel as though they belong to someone else. I am beyond cold now. I try to sit up, to keep at least half of my body out of the water, but he makes me lie down, my legs bent awkwardly to the side to accommodate the tiny bath tub. He runs the cold tap again until the water reaches the top. My heartbeat no longer thumps loudly in my ears, but taps tentatively in my chest. I feel dull and sluggish, hearing Ian's words as though from far away. My teeth are chattering and I bite my tongue, but barely register the pain.

Ian has been standing over me while I washed, but now he sits on the closed toilet seat. He watches me dispassionately. He is going to drown me, I suppose. It won't take long – I'm half-dead already.

'You were easy to find, you know.' Ian speaks casually, as though we are sitting in a pub, catching up, the way old friends do. 'It's not difficult to set up a website with no paper trail, but you were too stupid to realise anybody could look up your address.'

I don't say anything, but he doesn't seem to need a response.

'You women think you can cope on your own,' he says. 'You think you don't need men, but when we leave you to it, you're useless. You're all the same. And the lies! Jesus, the lies you women tell. One after another, tripping off your forked tongues.'

I'm so tired. So desperately tired. I feel myself slipping underneath the surface of the water, and I jerk myself awake. I dig my fingernails into my thigh, but I can barely feel them.

'You think we won't find you out, but we always do. The lies, the betrayal, the bare-faced treachery.'

His words wash over me.

'From the start I was perfectly clear about not wanting children,' Ian says.

I close my eyes.

'But we don't get a choice in it, do we? It's all about what the woman wants. Pro-fucking-choice? What about my choice?'

I think of Ben. He came so close to living. If I had only been able to keep him safe for a few more weeks . . .

'Suddenly I'm presented with a son,' Ian says, 'and I'm expected to celebrate! Celebrate the child I never asked for in the first place. The child who never would have existed if she hadn't tricked me into it.'

I open my eyes. The white tiles above the taps are crazed with grey lines, and I follow them until my eyes fill with water and they blur back into white. He's not talking sense. Or perhaps I'm not making sense of it. I want to speak but my tongue feels too big for my mouth. I didn't trick Ian into having a baby. It was an accident, but he was pleased. He said it changed everything.

Ian is leaning forward, his elbows resting on his knees and his mouth touching his closed hands, as though praying. But his fists are clenched and the muscle near his eye flickers uncontrollably.

'I told her what the score was,' he says. 'I told her no strings. But she ruined it.' He looks at me. 'It was supposed to be a one-off – a quick fuck with a meaningless girl. There was no reason for you ever to know about it. Except she got pregnant, and instead of fucking off back home, she decided to stay and make my life hell.'

I struggle to pull together the pieces of what Ian is saying. 'You have a son?' I manage to say.

He looks at me and gives a mirthless laugh. 'No,' he corrects me, 'he was never my son. He was the offspring of a Polish tart who used to clean the loos at work – I was just the sperm donor.' He stands up and straightens his shirt. 'She came knocking when she found out she was pregnant, and I made it quite clear that if she went ahead with it, she was on her own.' He sighs. 'I didn't hear from her again until the child started school. And then she wouldn't let it go.' His mouth twists as he does a poor impression of an Eastern European accent. '*He needs a father, Ian. I want Jacob to know who his father is.*'

I lift my head. With an effort that makes me cry out in pain, I push my hands against the bottom of the bath until I am sitting up. 'Jacob?' I say. 'You're Jacob's father?'

There is a moment's silence while Ian looks at me. Abruptly he takes hold of my arm. 'Get out.'

I fall over the side of the bathtub and collapse on to the floor, my legs useless after an hour in freezing water.

'Cover yourself up.' He throws my dressing gown on to me and I pull it on, hating myself for the gratitude I feel. My head is spinning: Jacob was Ian's son? But when Ian had found out it was Jacob in the accident, he must have . . .

When the truth finally hits me, it's like a knife to my stomach. Jacob's death was no accident. Ian killed his own son, and now he's going to kill me.

50

'Stop the car,' I said.

You made no move to pull over, and I grabbed the wheel.

'Ian, no!' You tried to get the wheel back from me, and we hit the kerb and then veered back into the middle of the road, just missing a car coming in the opposite direction. You had no choice but to take your foot off the accelerator and apply the brakes. We came to a stop, the car parked diagonally in the road.

'Get out.'

You didn't hesitate, but once out of the car you stood motionless by its door, a fine layer of drizzle covering you. I walked round to your side of the car. 'Look at me.'

You continued looking at the ground.

'I said look at me!'

Slowly you lifted your head but you stared behind me, over my shoulder. I shifted my position to fall within your gaze, and immediately you looked over the other shoulder. I grabbed hold of your shoulders and shook you hard. I wanted to hear you cry out: I told myself I'd stop when I heard you cry, but you made no sound. Your jaw clenched with the effort. You were playing games with me, Jennifer, but I would win. I would make you cry out.

I let go of you, and you couldn't hide the flash of relief that passed across your face. It was still there when I balled my fist and drove it into your face.

My knuckles caught the underside of your chin, and your

head snapped back and hit the roof of the car. Your legs buckled and you slid on to the road. Finally you made a sound, a whimpering, like a kicked dog, and I couldn't help but smile at this tiny victory. It wasn't enough though. I wanted to hear you beg for my forgiveness; admit you'd been flirting; admit you'd been fucking someone else.

I looked at you thrashing about on the wet tarmac. The usual sense of release wasn't there – the ball of white-hot fury inside me was still bubbling away, rising higher every second. I would finish this at home.

'Get in the car.'

I watched you struggle to your feet. Blood poured from your mouth and you stemmed it ineffectively with your scarf. You tried to get back in the driver's seat but I pulled you back. 'The other side.' I started the engine and drove off before you had even shut the door. You gave a cry of alarm, then slammed the door and fumbled for your seat belt. I laughed, but it still didn't soothe the rage inside me. I wondered briefly if I was having a heart attack: my chest was so tight, and my breath painful and laboured. You had done this to me.

'Slow down,' you said, 'you're going too fast.' The words bubbled through a mouthful of blood, and I saw it spatter on the glove box. I drove faster, to show you I wouldn't be governed by you. We were in a quiet residential street, with neat houses and a row of parked cars ahead taking up my side of the road. I moved out to overtake them, despite the headlights coming towards us, and put my foot down. I saw you pull your arms across your face; there was a blare of horn and a flash of colour as I swung back on to our side of the road seconds before it was too late.

The tightness in my chest eased a fraction. I kept my foot on the accelerator and we turned left, into a long straight road lined with trees. I felt a jolt of recognition, although I had only been there once before and I could not have told you the name of the street. It was where Anya lived. Where I fucked her. The wheel slipped between my hands and the car hit the kerb.

'Please, Ian, please slow down!'

There was a woman on the pavement, a hundred yards ahead, walking with a small child. The child wore a bobble hat, and the woman . . . I gripped the steering wheel tighter. I was seeing things. Imagining this woman was her, simply because we were in her street. It couldn't be Anya.

The woman looked up. Her hair was loose and she wore no hat or hood, despite the weather. She was facing me and laughing, the boy running by her side. I felt a crushing pain in my head. It was her.

I had sacked Anya after I fucked her. I had no interest in a repeat performance, and no wish to see her pretty but vacuous face around the office. When she turned up again last month I wouldn't have recognised her: now she wouldn't leave me alone. I watched her walk towards the glare of the headlights.

He wants to know about his father, he wants to meet you.

She would ruin everything. The boy would ruin everything. I looked at you, but your head was dropped to your lap. Why didn't you look at me any more? You used to put your hand on my thigh when I drove, twisting in the seat so you could watch me. Now you hardly ever looked me in the eye. I was already losing you, and if you found out about the boy I would never get you back.

They were crossing the road. My head pounded. You whimpered and the sound was like a fly, buzzing in my ear.

I pushed the accelerator flat to the floor.

51

'You killed Jacob?' I say, almost unable to form the words. 'But why?'

'He was ruining everything,' Ian says simply. 'If Anya had stayed away nothing would have happened to them. It's her own fault.'

I think of the woman outside the Crown Court, her feet in tatty plimsolls. 'Did she need money?'

Ian laughs. 'Money would have been easy. No, she wanted me to be a father. To see the boy at weekends, have him to stay, buy him fucking birthday presents—' He breaks off as I stand up, clinging on to the basin as I cautiously test the weight on my aching legs. My feet sting as they warm up. I look in the mirror and don't recognise what I see.

'You would have found out about him,' Ian says. 'About Anya. You would have left me.'

He stands behind me and puts his hands gently on my shoulders. I see the look on his face I have seen so many times the morning after a beating. I used to tell myself it was contrition – although he never once apologised – but now I realise it was fear. Fear that I would see him for the man he really is. Fear that I would stop needing him.

I think of how I would have loved Jacob like my own son; how I would have taken him in and played with him and chosen gifts just to see the pleasure on his face. And suddenly I feel as though Ian has taken not one but two children from me, and I find vigour from both their lost lives.

*   *   *

I feign weakness and look down towards the sink, then throw my head back with every last ounce of my strength. I hear a sickening crunch as the back of my skull hits bone.

He lets go of me, holding both hands to his face, blood seeping between his fingers. I run past him into the bedroom and on to the landing, but he's too quick, grabbing my wrist before I can get down the stairs. His bloody fingers slip against my wet skin and I fight to get free, elbowing him in the stomach and earning myself a punch that takes my breath away. The landing is pitch-black and I've lost my bearings – which way are the stairs? I feel around with my bare foot and my toes touch the metal stair rod on the top step.

I duck underneath Ian's arm, reaching out both hands towards the wall. I bend my elbows as though doing press-ups, then push back hard, slamming my whole weight against him. He gives a short cry as he loses his footing, then falls, crashing down the stairs.

There is silence.

I turn on the light.

Ian is lying at the foot of the stairs, not moving. He is face down on the slate floor and I can see a gash at the back of his head, from which a thin trickle of blood is oozing. I stand watching him, my whole body trembling.

Gripping the banister tightly, I make my way slowly down the stairs, never taking my eyes off the prone figure at the bottom. A step from the end, I stop. I can see the faintest movement from Ian's chest.

My own breath coming in shallow pants, I stretch out a foot and tread lightly on to the stone floor beside Ian, freezing like a child playing grandmother's footsteps.

I step across his outstretched arm.

His hand grips my ankle and I scream, but it is too late. I'm on the floor and Ian's on top of me, dragging himself up my body, blood on his face and on his hands. He tries to speak, but the words don't come; his face contorts with the effort.

He reaches his hands up to grip my shoulders, and as he pulls himself up level with my face, I bring up my knee hard into his groin. He roars, letting me go and doubling over with pain, and I scramble to my feet. I don't hesitate, running to the door and scrabbling for the bolt, which slips beneath my fingers twice before I am able to pull it across and throw open the door. The night air is cold, and clouds obscure all but a thin sliver of moon. I run blindly, and have barely begun when I hear Ian's heavy tread behind me. I don't look back to see how far behind me he is, but I can hear him grunt with each step, his breathing laboured.

The stony path is hard to run on with bare feet, but the noise behind me seems fainter and I think I'm gaining ground. I try to hold my breath as I run; to make as little sound as possible.

It's only when I hear the waves crashing against the shore that I realise I've missed the turning for the caravan park. I curse my stupidity. I have only two options now: take the path down on to the beach or turn right, and carry on along the coastal path away from Penfach. It's a path I've taken many times with Beau but never in the dark – it runs too close to the cliff edge and I've always worried he might lose his footing. I hesitate for a second, but the thought of being trapped down on the beach is terrifying: surely I have more chance if I keep running? I turn right and take the coastal path. The wind has picked up and as the clouds shift the moon lets out a little more light. I risk a quick glance behind me, but the path is clear.

I slow to a walk, and then stop to listen. It is silent, apart from the sounds of the sea, and my heart begins to calm a little. Waves crash rhythmically on the beach and I hear the distant blare of a ship far out to sea. I catch my breath and try to get my bearings.

'There's nowhere to run to, Jennifer.'

I whirl around but can't see him. I peer through the gloom and make out scrubby bushes; a stile; in the distance a small building I know to be a shepherd's hut.

'Where are you?' I call, but the wind whips my words away and carries them out to sea. I draw breath to scream but in an instant he's behind me, his forearm across my throat, drawing me up and backwards until I start to choke. I jab my elbow into his ribs and his grip relaxes enough for me to take a breath. I will not die now, I think. I have spent most of my adult life hiding; running; being afraid, and now, just as I'm feeling safe, he has come back to take it away from me. I will not let him. I feel a surge of adrenalin and I lean forward. The move unbalances him enough for me to twist away from him.

And I don't run. I have run enough from him.

He reaches for me and I push out my hand, smashing the heel of my palm into the underside of his chin. The impact pushes him backwards and he teeters for what feels like seconds on the edge of the cliff. He reaches for me, clawing for my dressing gown, and his fingers brush against the fabric. I cry out and step back, but I lose my balance and for a moment I think I am going with him, crashing against the cliff on the way down to the sea. But then I'm face down on the edge of the cliff, and he's falling. I look down and see a glimpse of his rolled-back eyes, before the waves suck him under.

52

Ray's phone rang as they were skirting Cardiff. He glanced at the screen.

'It's the South Wales DI.'

Kate watched Ray as he listened to the update from Penfach.

'Thank God for that,' Ray said into the phone. 'No problem. Thanks for letting me know.'

He ended the call and let out a long, slow breath. 'She's okay. Well, she's not okay, but she's alive.'

'And Petersen?' Kate said.

'Not so lucky. By all accounts Jenna was running along the coastal path when he came after her. They struggled and Petersen went over the edge.'

Kate winced. 'What a way to go.'

'No less than he deserved,' Ray said. 'Reading between the lines, I don't think he "fell" exactly, if you know what I mean, although Swansea CID have got the right approach: they're filing it as an accident.'

They fell silent.

'Do we go back to the nick now, then?' Kate asked.

Ray shook his head. 'No point. Jenna's in Swansea hospital and we'll be there in less than an hour. Might as well see the job through to the end, and we can grab a bite to eat before we head home.'

The traffic freed up as they got further into their journey, and it was a little after seven when they arrived at Swansea hospital. The entrance to A&E was thronged with smokers with hastily assembled slings, bandaged ankles and assorted unseen injuries. Ray sidestepped a man bent double with stomach pain, still managing to take a deep drag from the cigarette his girl-friend held to his lips.

The smell of smoke hanging in cold air was replaced with the clinical warmth of A&E, and Ray showed his warrant card to a weary-looking woman on reception. They were directed through a pair of double-doors to C ward, and from there to a side room, where Jenna lay propped up on a pile of pillows.

Ray was shocked to see the deep purple bruises that crept out of her hospital gown and up her neck. Her hair was loose and fell lankly on her shoulders, and her face was etched with tiredness and pain. Patrick sat next to her, a discarded paper open at the crossword.

'Hey,' Ray said softly, 'how are you doing?'

She gave a weak smile. 'I've had better days.'

'You've been through a lot.' Ray came to stand by the bed. 'I'm sorry we didn't get to him in time.'

'It doesn't matter now.'

'I hear you were the hero of the hour, Mr Mathews.' Ray turned to Patrick, who raised his hand in protest.

'Hardly. If I'd been an hour earlier I might have been some use, but I was held up at the surgery and by the time I got there . . . well . . .' He looked at Jenna.

'I don't think I'd have made it back to the cottage without you,' she said. 'I think I would still be lying there, staring down at the sea.' She shivered and Ray felt a chill, despite the stifling hospital air. What must it have felt like, out there on the edge of the cliff?

'Have they said how long you'll be in here?' he asked.

Jenna shook her head. 'They want to keep me in for obser-vation, whatever that means, but I'm hoping it won't be longer than twenty-four hours.' She looked between Ray and Kate. 'Will I be in trouble? For lying to you about who was driving?'

'There's a small issue of perverting the course of justice to think about,' Ray said, 'but I'm pretty confident we won't consider it to be in the public interest to pursue.' He smiled and Jenna gave a sigh of relief.

'We'll leave you in peace,' Ray said. He looked at Patrick. 'Take care of her, won't you?'

They left the hospital and drove the short distance to Swansea police station, where the local DI was waiting to speak to them. DI Frank Rushton was a few years older than Ray, with a physique that suggested he would be more at home on the rugby pitch than in the office. He welcomed them warmly and showed them into his office, offering coffee, which they declined.

'We need to get back,' Ray said. 'Otherwise DC Evans here will be putting undue strain on my overtime budget.'

'Pity,' Frank said. 'We're all heading out for a curry – one of our skippers is retiring and it's a bit of a send-off for him. You'd be welcome to join us.'

'Thanks,' Ray said, 'but we'd better not. Will you be keeping Petersen's body here, or do you need me to contact the coroner's office in Bristol?'

'If you've got the number on you, that would be great,' Frank said. 'I'll give them a ring once the body's recovered.'

'You haven't recovered it?'

'We haven't found it yet,' Frank said. 'He went off the edge about a half-mile from Gray's cottage, in the opposite direction to Penfach Caravan Park. I believe you've been to the premises?'

Ray nodded.

'The guy who found her, Patrick Mathews, took us out there and there's no doubt it's the right place,' Frank said. 'There are marks on the ground consistent with Gray's account of a struggle, and the edge of the cliff is freshly scuffed.'

'But there's no body?'

'To be honest, that's not unusual.' Frank noticed Ray's raised eyebrows and gave a short laugh. 'That is, not finding a body straight away isn't unusual. We get the odd jumper, or a walker slips when he's coming back from the pub, and it takes a few days – often longer – for them to be washed up. Sometimes they never come back at all; sometimes just a bit of them does.'

'What do you mean?' Kate asked.

'It's a two-hundred-foot drop from that part of the cliff to the sea,' Frank said. 'You might miss the rocks on the way down, but as soon as you land you'll be smashed against them again and again and again.' He shrugged. 'Bodies get broken up easily.'

'Christ,' Kate said, 'living by the sea doesn't sound quite so appealing now.'

Frank grinned. 'Now, are you sure we can't tempt you out for a curry? I contemplated a transfer to Avon and Somerset once – it would be good to hear what I missed out on.' He stood up.

'We did say we'd grab something to eat,' Kate said, looking at Ray.

'Go on,' Frank said. 'It'll be a good laugh. Most of CID will be there, and some uniform.' He took them out to the front desk, and shook hands with them both. 'We're knocking off now and we should be at the Raj on the High Street in about half an hour. This hit-and-run's a big result for your lot, isn't it? You should wangle an overnighter – celebrate in style!'

They said goodbye and Ray felt his stomach rumble as they walked out to the car. A chicken Jalfrezi and a beer were precisely what he needed after the day they'd had. He glanced at Kate, and thought how much he would enjoy an evening of easy conversation and some banter with the Swansea lads. It would be a shame to have to drive home, and Frank was right – he could probably swing an overnighter on the grounds that there were still some loose ends to tie up tomorrow.

'Let's go,' Kate said. She stopped walking and turned to face Ray. 'It'll be a laugh, and he's right, we should celebrate.' They

362

were standing so close to each other they were almost touching, and Ray imagined them leaving the Swansea boys after the curry; perhaps having a night-cap somewhere, then walking back to the hotel. He swallowed, imagining what might happen after that.

'Some other time,' he said.

There was a pause, then Kate nodded slowly. 'Sure.' She walked towards the car, and Ray pulled out his mobile phone to text Mags.

Coming home. Fancy a takeaway?

53

The nurses have been kind. They've treated my injuries with a quiet efficiency, seeming not to mind when I ask them to confirm for the hundredth time that Ian is dead.

'It's over,' the doctor says. 'Now get some rest.'

I don't feel any great sense of release or freedom. Just a crushing tiredness that refuses to go. Patrick doesn't leave my side. I wake with a jolt several times in the night to find him instantly there to soothe away my nightmares. Eventually I give in to the sedative the nurse offers me. I think I hear Patrick talking to someone on the phone, but I'm asleep again before I can ask who it is.

When I wake, daylight is pushing its way through the horizontal blinds at the window, painting sunshine stripes across my bed. There's a tray on the table next to me.

'The tea will be cold now,' Patrick says. 'I'll see if I can find someone to get you a fresh one.'

'It's fine,' I say, struggling to sit up. My neck is sore and I touch it gingerly. Patrick's phone beeps and he picks it up to read a text message.

'What is it?'

'Nothing,' he says. He changes the subject. 'The doctor says you'll be sore for a few days, but there's nothing broken. They've given you some gel to counteract the effects of the bleach, and you'll need to put it on every day to stop your skin drying out.'

I draw up my legs and make space for him to sit next to me on the bed. His brow is furrowed and I hate that I have caused him such worry. 'I'm okay,' I say. 'I promise. I just want to go home.'

I can see him searching for answers on my face: he wants to know how I feel about him, but I don't know myself yet. I only know that I can't trust my own judgement. I force a smile to prove I'm fine, then shut my eyes, more to avoid Patrick's gaze, than in any expectation of sleep.

I wake to footsteps outside my door and hope it's the doctor, but instead I hear Patrick speaking to someone. 'She's in here. I'll head off to the canteen for a coffee – give the two of you some time alone.'

I can't think who it could be, and even after the door has swung fully open, and I see the slim figure in the bright yellow coat with its big buttons, I still take a second to register what I am seeing. I open my mouth but the lump in my throat stops me from speaking.

Eve flies across the room, pressing me into the tightest of embraces. 'I've missed you so much!'

We cling to each other until our sobs subside, then sit cross-legged opposite each other on the bed, holding hands as though we were children again, sitting on the bottom bunk in the room we used to share.

'You've cut your hair,' I say. 'It suits you.'

Eve touches her sleek bob self-consciously. 'I think Jeff prefers it long, but I like it this length. He sends his love, by the way. Oh, and the children did this for you.' She rifles through her bag and produces a crumpled picture, folded in half to make a get-well card. 'I told them you were in hospital, so they think you've got chicken pox.'

I look at the drawing of myself in bed, covered in spots, and laugh. 'I've missed them. I've missed you all.'

'We've missed you too.' Eve takes a deep breath. 'I should never have said the things I did. I had no right.'

I remember lying in hospital after Ben had been born. No

one had thought to remove the Perspex cot from the side of my bed, and it taunted me from the corner of my eye. Eve had arrived before the news reached her, but I knew from her face that the nurses had intercepted her. A once beautifully wrapped present had been shoved into the recesses of her handbag, the paper creased and torn in her efforts to hide it from view. I wondered what she would do with the contents – if she would find another baby to wear whatever outfit she had handpicked for my son.

She didn't speak at first, and then she wouldn't stop.

'Did Ian do something to you? He did, didn't he?'

I turned away, saw the empty cot and closed my eyes. Eve had never trusted Ian, although he had taken care never to let anyone see his temper. I denied anything was wrong: first because I was too blinded by love to see the cracks in my relationship, and later because I was too ashamed to admit that I had stayed for so long with a man who hurt me so much.

I had wanted Eve to hold me. Just to hold me tight and press hard against the pain that hurt so badly I could hardly breathe. But my sister had been angry, her own grief demanding answers; a reason; someone to blame.

'He's trouble,' she said, and I closed my eyes tightly against her tirade. 'You might be blind to it, but I'm not. You should never have stayed with him when you fell pregnant, then maybe you'd still have your baby. You're just as much to blame as he is.'

I had opened my eyes in dismay, Eve's words burning into my very core. 'Get out,' I said, my voice broken but determined. 'My life is none of your business and you have no right to tell me what to do. Get out! I don't ever want to see you again.'

Eve had fled from the ward, leaving me distraught, pressing my hands on my empty belly. It wasn't Eve's words that hurt me as much as their honesty. My sister had simply told the truth. Ben's death was my fault.

In the weeks that followed, Eve had tried to contact me, but I refused to speak to her. Eventually she stopped trying.

'You realised what Ian was like,' I say to her now. 'I should have listened to you.'

'You loved him,' she says simply. 'Just like Mum loved Dad.'

I sit up. 'What do you mean?'

There is a pause and I see Eve trying to decide what to tell me. I shake my head, because suddenly I can see what I refused to acknowledge as a child. 'He hit her, didn't he?'

She nods mutely.

I think of my handsome, clever father; always finding funny things to share with me; twirling me round even when I was far too big for such games. I think of my mother; always quiet, unapproachable, cold. I think how I hated her for letting him leave.

'She put up with it for years,' Eve says, 'and then one day after school I came into the kitchen and saw him beating her. I screamed at him to stop, and he turned round and hit me across the face.'

'Oh God, Eve!' I'm sickened by the difference in our childhood memories.

'He was horrified. He said how sorry he was, that he hadn't seen me there, but I saw the look in his eyes before he hit me. For that moment he hated me, and I honestly believe he could have killed me. It was as though something suddenly switched in Mum: she told him to leave and he went without a word.'

'He was gone when I got home from ballet,' I say, remembering my grief when I realised.

'Mum told him she would go to the police if he ever came near us again. It broke her heart to send him away from us, but she said she had to protect us.'

'She never told me,' I say, but I know I never gave her the chance. I wonder how I could have read things so wrong. I wish Mum was still here so I could put them right.

A wave of emotion floods my heart and I start to sob.

'I know, my darling, I know.' Eve strokes my hair like she used to do when we were children, and then she wraps her arms around me and cries too.

She stays for two hours, while Patrick hovers between the canteen and my bedside, wanting to give us time together but anxious that I shouldn't become too tired.

Eve leaves me with a pile of magazines I won't read, and a promise that she will come again as soon as I'm back at the cottage, which the doctor has told me will be in a day or two.

Patrick squeezes my hand. 'Iestyn's sending two of the lads from the farm over to clean up the cottage,' he says, 'and they'll change the lock, so you know you're the only one with a key.' He must have seen the anxiety cross my face. 'They'll put everything straight,' he says. 'It'll be like it never happened.'

No, I think, it could never be like that.

But I squeeze his hand in return, and in his face I see nothing but honesty and kindness, and I think that, despite everything, life could go on with this man. Life could be good.

Epilogue

The evenings have grown longer, and Penfach has again found its natural tempo, broken only by the summer swell of families heading for the beach. The air is filled with the scents of sun cream and sea salt, and the bell above the door to the village shop seems never to be still. The caravan park opens for the season with a fresh coat of paint; the shop shelves stacked high with holiday essentials.

The tourists have no interest in local scandal, and to my relief the villagers quickly lose their enthusiasm for idle chatter. By the time the nights draw in again, the gossip has all but burned out, extinguished by a lack of fresh information, and by the fierce opposition of Bethan and Iestyn, who have made it their business to set straight anyone claiming to know what happened. Before long the last tent has been packed away, the last bucket and spade sold, the last ice-cream eaten, and it is forgotten. Where once I saw nothing but judgement and closed doors, I now find kindness and open arms.

True to his word, Iestyn cleared up the cottage. He changed the locks, fitted new windows, painted over the graffiti on the wooden door, and removed all traces of what happened there. And although I will never be able to erase that night from my mind, I still want to be there, high on the clifftop with nothing but the sound of the wind around me. I'm happy in my cottage and I refuse to let Ian destroy that part of my life too.

I pick up Beau's lead and he stands impatiently by the door

while I put on my coat to take him out for a final run before bed. I still can't bring myself to leave the door unlocked, but when I'm inside I no longer lock and bolt it, and I don't jump when Bethan comes in without knocking.

Patrick stays more often than not, although he recognises my occasional but urgent need for solitude almost before I can see it myself, discreetly taking himself back to Port Ellis and leaving me to my thoughts.

I look down on the bay at the tide coming in. The beach is scuffed with the prints of walkers and their dogs, and from the gulls that swoop down to pull lugworms from the sand. It's late, and there's no one else walking along the coastal path at the top of the cliff, where the newly built fence carries reminders to ramblers not to stray too close to the edge. I feel a sudden shiver of loneliness. I wish Patrick was coming back tonight.

The waves break on the beach, surf running up the sand in white foam that bubbles and disappears as the wave pulls back again. Each wave advances a little more, exposing smooth, glistening sand for a matter of seconds before another rushes forward to fill the space. I'm about to turn away when I catch sight of something etched in the sand. In the blink of an eye it is gone. The sea washes over the writing I'm now not certain I saw at all, and when the water catches the setting sun it sparkles against the dark, damp sand. I shake my head and turn towards the cottage, but something pulls me back and I return to the edge of the cliff, standing as close as I dare, to look down on the beach.

There is nothing there.

I pull my coat around myself to ward off the sudden chill that surrounds me. I'm seeing things. There's nothing written there on the sand; nothing carved in bold, straight letters. It is not there. I cannot see my name.

Jennifer.

The sea doesn't falter. The next wave breaks over the marks in the sand, and they are gone. A gull gives a final sweep of the bay as the tide comes in, and the sun slips beneath the horizon.

And then it is dark.

Author's note

I began my police training in 1999 and was posted to Oxford in 2000. In December that year a nine-year-old boy was killed by joyriders in a stolen car on the Blackbird Leys estate. It was four years before the inquest ruling of unlawful killing, during which time an extensive police investigation was carried out. The case formed the backdrop to my early years as a police officer, and was still generating enquiries when I joined CID, three years later.

A substantial reward was offered, as well as the promise of immunity from prosecution for the passenger travelling in the car, should they come forward and identify the driver. But despite several arrests, no one was ever charged.

The aftermath of this crime made a big impression on me. How could the driver of that Vauxhall Astra live with what they'd done? How could the passenger keep quiet about it? How could the child's mother ever come to terms with such a terrible loss? I was fascinated by the intelligence reports that came in following each anniversary appeal, and by the diligence of the police in sifting through every single piece of information in the hope of finding that one missing link.

Years later, when my own son died – in very different circumstances – I experienced first-hand how emotion can cloud one's judgement and affect behaviour. Grief and guilt are powerful feelings, and I began to wonder how they might affect two women, involved in very different ways in the same incident. The result is *I Let You Go*.

Acknowledgements

I always used to read the acknowledgements pages of books and wonder how on earth so many people could be involved in the creation of a single piece of work. Now I understand. I am hugely grateful to the early readers of *I Let You Go* – Julie Cohen, AJ Pearce, Merilyn Davies and others, who helped me see what was working and what wasn't, and to Peta Nightingale and Araminta Whitley, for believing in me. I am fortunate to have the wonderful Sheila Crowley as my literary agent, but I would never have met her had it not been for a chance conversation with Vivienne Wordley, who liked my manuscript enough to pass it on. Thank you Vivienne, Sheila, Rebecca and the rest of the Curtis Brown team, for everything that you do. You could not have found a better home for me than Little, Brown. I loved the brilliant Lucy Malagoni the moment I met her, and couldn't wish for a more insightful and enthusiastic editor. Thank you Lucy, Thalia, Anne, Sarah, Kirsteen, and the rest of Little, Brown, including the wonderful foreign rights team, all of whom are terribly busy, but manage to make me feel as though this is the only book they're working on.

Thank you to former colleagues Mary Langford and Kelly Hobson: Mary for reading an early draft, and Kelly for some last-minute help with procedure. Finally, thank you to the friends and family who always believed in me; who supported me when I decided to jack in a good career and write books instead, and who never once suggested I should go and get a proper job. I couldn't – and wouldn't – have done it without the support of my husband Rob, and our three children, Josh, Evie and Georgie, who have cheered me on from the sidelines, brought me cups of tea, and looked after themselves while I 'just finish this chapter'. Thank you all so much.

Now read on for the opening of
Clare Mackintosh's gripping second novel,

I
SEE
YOU

1

The man behind me is standing close enough to moisten the skin on my neck with his breath. I move my feet forward an inch and press myself into a grey overcoat that smells of wet dog. It feels as if it hasn't stopped raining since the start of November, and a light steam rises from the hot bodies jammed against each other. A briefcase jabs into my thigh. As the train judders around a corner I'm held upright by the weight of people surrounding me, one unwilling hand against the grey overcoat for temporary support. At Tower Hill the carriage spits out a dozen commuters and swallows two dozen more, all hell-bent on getting home for the weekend.

'Use the whole carriage!' comes the announcement.

Nobody moves.

The grey overcoat has gone, and I've shuffled into its place, preferable because I can now reach the handrail, and because I no longer have a stranger's DNA on my neck. My handbag has swung round behind my body, and I tug it in front of me. Two Japanese tourists are wearing gigantic rucksacks on their chests, taking up the space of another two people. A woman across the carriage sees me looking at them; she catches my eye and grimaces in solidarity. I accept the eye contact fleetingly, then look down at my feet. The shoes around me vary: the men's are large and shiny, beneath pinstriped hems; the women's heeled and colourful, toes crammed into impossible points. Amongst the legs I see a pair of sleek stockings; opaque black nylon ending in stark white trainers. The owner is hidden but

I imagine her to be in her twenties, a pair of vertiginous office heels stashed in a capacious handbag, or in a drawer at work.

I've never worn heels during the day. I was barely out of my Clark's lace-ups when I fell pregnant with Justin, and there was no place for heels on a Tesco checkout, or coaxing a toddler up the high street. Now I'm old enough to know better. An hour on the train on the way into work: another hour on the way home. Tripping up broken escalators. Run over by buggies and bikes. And for what? For eight hours behind a desk. I'll save my heels for high days and holidays. I wear a self-imposed uniform of black trousers and an array of stretchy tops that don't need ironing, and are just smart enough to pass as office-wear; with a cardigan kept in my bottom drawer for busy days when the door's forever opening and the heat disappears with every prospective client.

The train stops and I push my way on to the platform. I take the Overground from here, and although it's often as busy, I prefer it. Being underground makes me feel uneasy; unable to breathe, even though I know it's all in my head. I dream of working somewhere close enough to walk to, but it's never going to happen: the only jobs worth taking are in zone one; the only affordable mortgages in zone four.

I have to wait for my train and at the rack by the ticket machine I pick up a copy of the London Gazette, its headlines appropriately grim for today's date: Friday 13 November. The police have foiled another terrorism plot: the front three pages are rammed with images of explosives they've seized from a flat in North London. I flick through photos of bearded men, and move to find the crack in the tarmac beneath the platform sign, where the carriage door will open. My careful positioning means I can slide into my favourite spot before the carriage fills up; on the end of the row, where I can lean against the glass barrier. The rest of the carriage fills quickly, and I glance at the people still standing, guiltily relieved to see no one old, or obviously pregnant. Despite the flat shoes, my feet ache, thanks to standing by the filing cabinets for most of the day. I'm not supposed to do the filing. There's a girl who comes in to photocopy property details and keep the cabinets in order, but she's in Mallorca for a fortnight and from what I saw today she can't have done any filing for weeks. I found residential mixed up with commercial, and lettings muddled up with sales, and I made the mistake of saying so.

'You'd better sort it out, then, Zoe,' Graham said. So instead of booking viewings I stood in the draughty corridor outside Graham's office, wishing I hadn't opened my mouth. Hallow & Reed isn't a bad place to work. I used to do one day a week doing the books, then the office manager went on maternity leave and Graham asked me to fill in. I was a bookkeeper, not a PA, but the money was decent and I'd lost a couple of clients, so I jumped at the chance. Three years later, I'm still there.

By the time we reach Canada Water the carriage has thinned out and the only people standing are there by choice. The man sitting next to me has his legs so wide apart I have to angle mine away, and when I look at the row of passengers opposite I see two other men doing the same. Is it a conscious thing? Or some innate need to make themselves bigger than everyone else? The woman immediately in front of me moves her shopping bag and I hear the unmistakable clink of a wine bottle. I hope Simon has thought to put one in the fridge: it's been a long week and right now all I want to do is curl up on the sofa and watch telly.

A few pages into the London Gazette some former X Factor finalist is complaining about the 'pressures of fame', and there's a debate on privacy laws that covers the best part of a page. I'm reading without taking in the words: looking at the pictures and scanning the headlines so I don't feel completely out of the loop. I can't remember the last time I actually read a whole newspaper, or sat down to watch the news from start to finish.

It's always snatches of Sky News while I'm eating breakfast, or the headlines read over someone's shoulder on the way in to work.

The train stops between Sydenham and Crystal Palace. I hear a frustrated sigh from further up the carriage but don't bother looking to see who it's from. It's already dark and when I glance at the windows all I see is my own face looking back at me; even paler than it is in real life, and distorted by rain. I take off my glasses and rub at the dents they leave either side of my nose. We hear the crackle of an announcement but it's so muffled and heavily accented there's no telling what it was about. It could have been anything from signal failure to a body on the line.

I hope it's not a body. I think of my glass of wine, and Simon rubbing my feet on the sofa, then feel guilty that my first thought is about my own comfort, not the desperation of some poor suicidal soul. I'm sure it's not a body. Bodies are for Monday mornings, not Friday evenings, when work is a blissful three days away.

There's a creaking noise and then silence. Whatever the delay is, it's going to be a while.

'That's not a good sign,' the man next to me says.

'Hmm,' I say non-committally. I carry on turning the pages of my newspaper, but I'm not interested in sport and now it's mostly adverts and theatre reviews. I won't be home till after seven at this rate: we'll have to have something easy for tea, rather than the baked chicken I'd planned. Simon cooks during the week, and I do Friday evening and the weekend. He'd do that too, if I asked him, but I couldn't have that. I couldn't have him cooking for us – for my children – every night. Maybe I'll pick up a takeaway.

I skip over the business section and look at the crossword, but I don't have a pen with me. So I read the adverts, thinking I might see a job for Katie – or me, come to that, although I know I'll never leave Hallow & Reed. It pays well and I know what I'm doing, now, and if it wasn't for my boss it would be perfect. The customers are nice, for the most part. They're generally start-ups, looking for office space; or businesses that have done well, ready for a bigger place. We don't do much residential, but the flats above the shops work for the first-time buyers and the downsizers. I meet a fair number of recently separateds. Sometimes, if I feel like it, I tell them I know what they're going through.

'Did it all turn out okay?' the women always ask.

'Best thing I ever did,' I say confidently. It's what they want to hear.

I don't find any jobs for a nineteen-year-old wannabe actress, but I turn down the corner on a page with an advert for an office manager. It doesn't hurt to know what's out there. For a second I imagine walking into Graham Hallow's office and handing in my notice, telling him I won't put up with being spoken to like I'm dirt on the sole of his shoe. Then I look at the salary printed under the office manager position, and remember how long it's taken me to claw my way up to something I can actually live on. Better the devil you know, isn't that what they say?

The final pages of the Gazette are all compensation claims and finances. I studiously avoid the ads for loans – at those interest rates you'd have to be mad or desperate – and glance at the bottom of the page, where the chatlines are advertised.

Married woman looking for discreet casual action. Txt ANGEL to 69998 for pics.

I wrinkle my nose more at the exorbitant price per text than the services offered. Who am I to judge what other people do? I'm about to turn the page, resigned to reading about last night's footie, when I see the advert below 'Angel's'.

For a second I think my eyes must be tired: I blink hard but it doesn't change anything.

I'm so absorbed in what I'm looking at that I don't notice the train start up again. It sets off suddenly and I jerk to one side, putting my hand out automatically and making contact with my neighbour's thigh.

'Sorry!'

'It's fine – don't worry.' He smiles and I make myself return it. But my heart is thumping and I stare at the advert. It bears the same warning about call charges as the other boxed adverts, and a 0809 number at the top of the ad. A web address reads www.findtheone.com. But it's the photo I'm looking at. It's cropped close to the face, but you can clearly see blonde hair and a glimpse of a black strappy top. Older than the other women pimping their wares, but such a grainy photo it would be hard to give a precise age.

Except I know how old she is. I know she's forty.

Because the woman in the advert is me.

2

Kelly Swift stood in the middle of the Central line carriage, shifting to one side to keep her balance as the train took a bend. A couple of kids – no more than fourteen or fifteen years old – jostled on to the train at Bond Street, engaged in competitive swearing that jarred with their middle-class vowels. Too late for after-school clubs, and it was already dark outside; Kelly hoped they were on their way home, not heading out for the evening. Not at their age.

'Fucking mental!' The boy looked up, his swagger giving way to self-consciousness as he saw Kelly standing there. Kelly assumed the sort of expression she remembered her mother sporting on many an occasion, and the teenagers fell silent, blushing furiously and turning away to examine the inside of the closing doors. She probably was old enough to be their mother, she thought ruefully, counting backwards from thirty and imagining herself with a fourteen-year-old. Several of her old school friends had children almost that age; Kelly's Facebook page regularly filled up with proud family photos, and she'd even had a couple of friend requests from the kids themselves. Now there was a way to make you feel old.

Kelly caught the eye of a woman in a red coat on the opposite side of the carriage, who gave a nod of approval at the effect she'd had on the lads.

Kelly returned her look with a smile. 'Good day?'

'Better now it's over,' the woman said. 'Roll on the weekend, eh?'

'I'm working. Not off till Tuesday.' And even then only one day off before another six on the trot, she thought, inwardly groaning at the thought. The woman looked aghast. Kelly shrugged. 'Someone's got to, right?'

'I guess so.' As the train slowed down for Oxford Circus, the woman began moving towards the doors. 'I hope it's a quiet one for you.'

That's jinxed it, Kelly thought. She glanced at her watch. Nine stops to Stratford: ditch her stuff, then head back. Home by eight, maybe eight thirty. In again for 7 a.m. She yawned hard, not bothering to cover her mouth, and wondered if there was any food at home. She shared a house near Elephant and Castle with three others, whose full names she knew only from the rent cheques pinned neatly to the board in the hall, ready for collection each month. The sitting room had been converted to a bedroom by a landlord keen to maximise his income, leaving the small kitchen the one communal area. There was only room for two chairs, but her housemates' shift patterns and erratic hours meant Kelly could go days without seeing anyone at all. The woman in the biggest bedroom, Dawn, was a nurse. Younger than Kelly, but far more domesticated, Dawn occasionally left a portion for Kelly on the side by the micro-wave, with one of her bright pink Post-It notes telling Kelly to help yourself! Her stomach rumbled at the thought of food, and she glanced at her watch. The afternoon had been busier than she'd thought; she was going to have to put in some extra hours next week, or she'd never get through it all.

A handful of businessmen got on at Holborn and Kelly cast a practised eye over them. At first glance they looked identical, with their short hair, dark suits and briefcases. The devil was in the detail, Kelly thought. She searched out the faint pinstripe; the title of a book pushed carelessly into a bag; wire-framed glasses with a kink in one arm; a brown leather watch strap beneath a white cotton shirtsleeve. The idiosyncrasies and

384

appearance tics that made them stand out in a line-up of near-identical men. Kelly watched them openly, dispassionately. She was just practising, she told herself, not caring when one of them looked up and found her cool gaze on him. She thought he might look away, but instead he winked, his mouth moving into a confident smile. Kelly's eyes flicked to his left hand. Married. White, well-built, around six foot tall, with a shadow around his jaw that probably wasn't there a few hours ago. The yellow flash of a forgotten dry-cleaning tag on the inside of his overcoat. Standing so straight she'd put money on ex-military. Nondescript in appearance, but Kelly would know him if they met again.

Satisfied, she turned her attention to the latest influx of passengers, getting on at Bank and filtering through the carriage to find the remaining few seats. Almost everyone had a phone in their hand; playing games, listening to music, or simply clutching it as though grafted to their palm. At the other end of the carriage someone lifted their phone in front of them and Kelly instinctively turned away. Tourists, getting an iconic shot of the London Underground to show back home, but she found the idea of being background scenery in someone's holiday snaps too weird to contemplate.

Her shoulder ached where she'd slammed into a wall, taking the corner too tight as she ran down the escalators and on to the platform at Marble Arch. She'd been seconds too late, and it annoyed her that the blooming bruise on her upper arm was in vain. She'd be quicker next time.

The train pulled in to Liverpool Street; a throng of people waiting on the platform, impatient for the doors to open.

Kelly's pulse quickened.

There, in the centre of the crowd, half-hidden beneath over-sized jeans, a hooded top and a baseball cap, was Carl. Instantly recognisable and – desperate though Kelly was to get home – impossible to walk away from. It was clear from the way he melted into the crowd that Carl had seen Kelly a split second before she had seen him, and was equally unenthusiastic about the encounter. She was going to have to move fast.

Kelly jumped off the train just as the doors hissed behind her. She thought at first she'd lost him, then she caught sight of a baseball cap ten or so yards ahead; not running, but weaving swiftly through the throng of passengers leaving the platform.

If Kelly had learned one thing over the last ten years on the Underground, it was that politeness got you nowhere.

'Mind your backs!' she yelled, breaking into a run and shoving her way between two elderly tourists dragging suitcases. 'Coming through!' She might have lost him that morning, and copped a bruised shoulder as a result, but she wasn't about to let him get away again. She thought fleetingly of the supper she had hoped would be waiting for her at home, and calculated this was going to add at least two hours on to her day. But needs must. She could always grab a kebab on the way home.

Carl was legging it up the escalator. Rookie error, Kelly knew, taking the steps instead. Fewer tourists to negotiate and easier on the thighs than the jerky, uneven motion of a moving stairway. Even so Kelly's muscles were burning as she drew parallel with Carl. He threw a quick look over his left shoulder as they reached the top, then swerved right. For fuck's sake, Carl, she thought. I should be booking off now.

With a final burst of speed she caught up with him as he was preparing to vault the ticket barrier, grabbing a handful of jacket with her left hand and twisting one arm up behind his back with her right. Carl made a half-hearted attempt to pull away, knocking her off balance and causing her hat to fall to the ground. Kelly was aware of someone picking it up and hoped they weren't going to run off with it. She was already in the dog house with Stores for losing her baton in a scrap the other week – she could do without another telling off.

'Warrants have got a Fail to Appear with your name on it,

mate,' Kelly said, her words punctuated with breaths that were hard to take within the confines of a stab vest. She reached for her belt and unclipped her cuffs, snapping them deftly on to Carl's wrists and checking for tightness. 'You're nicked.'